M000278170

'This is ace. Very, very acute on class, aspiration, women and status and all those agonising negotiations and anxieties.'
SARAH PERRY

'Delicious, a slow-burn thriller that carefully draws the reader in, catches fire in the middle and burns with an intensity until the end.'
FIONA CUMMINS

'A totally twisted look at the lengths some people will go to to project a perfect life.'
ERIN KELLY

'A deliciously dark debut which had me reading into the early hours.'
VICTORIA SELMAN

'Fabulously twisted, disturbing slow burn of a thriller that explores the relationship between a life coach and her protégée where nothing is as it first seems. I loved it.'
NIKKI SMITH

'Outstanding. An electrifying debut.'
ROBIN MORGAN-BENTLEY

'Creepy and disturbing. Kate's descent into Della's Stepford-like world is believable and chilling.'
ROZ WATKINS

'Unsettling – I read this with a growing sense of unease.'
LOUISE JENSEN

'Complex and gripping, the darkest revenge-noir I've read since *Gone Girl*.'
POLLY SAMSON

'A dark and addictive psychological thriller with compelling characters and an original story exploring motherhood, obsession and lies.'
JENNY QUINTANA

THE HOUSE GUEST

Charlotte Northedge is Head of Books for the *Guardian*. Charlotte has previously written for a range of newspapers and magazines, including the *Guardian*, *Psychologies* and *Cosmopolitan*. She has an MA in Modern and Contemporary Literature from Birkbeck and is an alumna of the Curtis Brown Creative writing course.

🐦 @charnorth

The House Guest

CHARLOTTE NORTHEDGE

HarperCollins*Publishers*

HarperCollins*Publishers*
1 London Bridge Street
London SE1 9GF

www.harpercollins.co.uk

HarperCollins*Publishers*
1st Floor, Watermarque Building, Ringsend Road
Dublin 4, Ireland

First published by HarperCollins*Publishers* 2021
1

Copyright © Charlotte Northedge 2021

Charlotte Northedge asserts the moral right to
be identified as the author of this work

A catalogue record for this book is available from the British Library

ISBN: 978-0-00-840253-2 (HB)

This novel is entirely a work of fiction.
The names, characters and incidents portrayed in it are
the work of the author's imagination. Any resemblance to
actual persons, living or dead, events or localities is
entirely coincidental.

Set in Sabon LT Std by Palimpsest Book Production Limited,
Falkirk, Stirlingshire

Printed and bound in the UK by
CPI Group (UK) Ltd, Croydon CR0 4YY

All rights reserved. No part of this publication may be
reproduced, stored in a retrieval system, or transmitted,
in any form or by any means, electronic, mechanical,
photocopying, recording or otherwise, without the prior
permission of the publishers.

MIX
Paper from
responsible sources
FSC™ C007454

This book is produced from independently certified FSC™ paper
to ensure responsible forest management.

For more information visit: www.harpercollins.co.uk/green

For Nigel, Sammy and Matilda

Prologue

It's a strong word, kidnap. It's the one they use on the front of the newspapers and websites, of course. It rolls along the ticker at the bottom of the screen as she sits, his sandy hair in her lap, long eyelashes resting on pale cheeks in the blue light. For a few days, the word seems to be everywhere she looks. And then, nothing.

She waits, keeping him close to begin with. He sleeps in her bed, his warm knees nestled into her back, the only time he truly relaxes in her presence. Heavy sighs wake her at odd times of night, a flailing hand startling her out of fitful sleep. Until, gradually, she dares to stop holding her breath.

She makes up the small sofa bed across the room. Watches him late into the night, waiting for a twitch, a sign of life.

Is it normal to lie so still? Do children always go so deathly pale when they are asleep? They're the kind of questions that would have been answered in a parenting class. Where she could have chuckled along with the other mothers, rolling their eyes at their own neuroses, laughing in the face of their naked fear.

Instead, she is alone. Or rather, alone-but-not. Always in

the presence of this silent two-year-old, who hasn't spoken once since they arrived, the shock of his sudden departure rendering him mute. He cries, often. But he never speaks.

As the news stories dwindle, they venture out of their top-floor studio, escaping for a short while the incessant beat of their downstairs neighbour's heavy bass, and the smell of frying food that fills the air at odd times of day. She tries to raise a smile from him at the small playground on the corner, pushing the swing back and forth, back and forth, but the trips are fraught with anxiety on both their parts. She can't help searching every passing face for a flicker of recognition, while he keeps his eyes downcast, occasionally throwing her a questioning look. What am I doing here?

How long can this go on, she wonders. How long before someone recognises them? She almost wills it to happen, unsure of her next move, unable to plan beyond the end of each day. But still they continue their short trips out, to the supermarket, the park, even to the library once, though the presence of so many computers unnerves her. Surely someone flicking through news sites will look up, make the connection. But nobody does.

To all around them, she comes to realise, they look just like any other mother and son.

PART ONE

London, 2015

Chapter One

It was hard to say what was odd about the group. They were women my age, of a type I recognised: unattached, unfulfilled at work, not yet defined by anything or anyone. They were extremely familiar, in fact. Perhaps that was it. I could see myself in each of them, more than I wanted to admit.

But there was something else, too. Their uniformity: fair or light brown hair, jeans and Converse, or smart work boots, a patterned scarf or big earrings adding a touch of individuality. I was blonde too then, though my hair had frizzed on the way over, and I tugged off the bluebird scarf I'd put on at the last minute, scrunching it in my hand. Was I really so predictable?

I looked around the room full of strangers with a tight feeling taking hold, as though something was tugging at my stomach from the inside. I needed to leave. Perhaps I could go to the toilet, and slip out. But then the only door to the room was pushed shut with a small click, and it was too late.

The first woman to speak was called Jane. Later, Liam and I would call them all 'the Janes': Jane One, Jane Two, Jane Three, Jane Four. Later still, I would struggle to picture their individual faces, blurred into one in my memory, as I tried to understand what it was that had made me stand out, why I had been the one who was chosen. But for now I listened warily to Jane One, translucent-skinned and high-pitched, as she recapped her week's 'progress', her silver hoops bouncing as she spoke.

'It's been quite a hard one, to be honest.' Wisps of fair hair fell forward as Jane looked at her hands. She was picking her nails, bitten short with frayed cuticles, but her tone was clear, a hint of North London rounding her vowels. She might have problems, but she belonged: she owned the space she sat in, her oversized cardigan draped around raised knees. 'I've had to face up to the fact that I'm not really moving forward with Rob, and . . . it was all down to the motivational mantras, really.'

I looked at the other women. They were nodding, but their eyes darted towards Della, her face still and expectant. They were waiting to gauge her response.

'The thing was, every time I said them, he took the piss. And I just thought, well, if you really don't care enough to come with me on my journey, then I can't do this any more.'

The women murmured, there were more nods, but Della's smile was tight, her eyes narrowed at the corners. This clearly wasn't the kind of inner transformation she wanted to hear about.

'Thanks for sharing that, Jane,' Della said. 'And do you think the mantras made a difference to how *decisive* you felt in that moment?'

'Oh yes, definitely.' Jane was as quick as the others to pick up on Della's cues. 'I don't think I'd ever have had the courage to end it if it wasn't for you . . . I mean, for the group. I feel like I'm making so much progress.'

'That's wonderful.' The straight lines of Della's face transformed into curves, and Jane's pale cheeks pinkened. I felt a
shiver run through me. I should never have come.

I'd known it as soon as I'd arrived. Something about the
imposing, three-storey Victorian terrace had made me take a
step back. I should have walked away then, forgotten all about
the group – life-coaching, the flyer said. How many times
have I gone over that moment, wishing I had? Instead I stood
there rocking on the outside edges of my Converse, fiddling
with my phone in my pocket, rooted to the spot.

I'd been expecting a hall or a meeting space of some kind,
not this: an enormous family home – front garden full of pink
and white roses, surrounded by chips of slate, a red and black
tiled pathway leading up to a wide bottle-green door with
stained-glass panels.

I don't know how long I'd been standing there when the
door disappeared, and suddenly in its place stood Della, blond
hair swept up in a messy chignon. She was wearing the same
expensive skinny jeans she'd had on the first time we met, or
an identical pair. Another crisp, oversized shirt, buttoned low
– this one pale blue like her eyes and tucked in at one side,
as though she was far too busy to check her reflection; her
style was natural, effortless. Her feet were bare, her brown
bony toes and pearly nails curled against the March air.

'Kate, you came,' she said, her voice rich and gravelly, her
smile lifting her eyes in what looked like genuine pleasure.
'Come in.' She extended a long arm into the high-ceilinged
hallway, as if it was entirely natural to be welcomed into this
grand house by a woman I'd met only days before.

Once inside, there was no space to think at all. Only to
process my surroundings. The kitchen, overwhelmingly white,
flashes of yellow here and there: an Eames-style armchair, a

vase of primroses, a golden head bent over a colouring book, warm evening sun framed in the wide folding doors. I perched on a stool at the marble-top island and tried not to look out of place but, catching my reflection in the shiny cooker hood, I could see I'd failed. I'd taken extra care with my appearance in the café toilets, taming the frizz of my hair, adding eyeliner, smoothing out my green New Look top, but the girl staring back at me looked cheaply dressed and startled.

Did people really live like this? I walked past houses like these every day on my way to work, imagining the family scenes playing out behind the white shutters and well-kept window boxes. I took a strange comfort in those fantasies, like I had on the nicer streets near school in Cambridge. As if by living close to these people I could somehow absorb some of whatever it was that made their lives so much better than mine. I didn't realise then how much more complicated life could get. I didn't appreciate the value of simple comforts, familiarity, innocence.

The space Della led me into wasn't a room so much as an entire floor: open plan, white designer kitchen leading into a white-walled living room, panelled partition doors revealing large cream sofas, a shiny chrome standing lamp and a reading nook in one corner, where a straight-backed green armchair nestled next to tall bookshelves. Both rooms had high ceilings and ornate coving, the line between them marked by the transition from deep cream carpet to oak parquet floor. A row of three matching pendant lights hung above the huge central island where I sat at the breakfast bar, in front of me a double sink, arched shiny mixer taps and a hot tap, like the one they had in the café. I'd never seen one in a house before.

I watched Della sweep around the room, picking up scraps of paper and shuffling them into a pile, which she hid away in a vast neatly organised cupboard of art supplies. On the walls of the kitchen were one or two splotchy children's paintings, sympathetically framed, alongside a row of four artfully-shot canvas prints of tree-lined hills and grass-edged sandy beaches, the greens echoing the flash of lawn visible through the bifold doors.

'I'm so pleased you got here first,' Della said as she ushered a small child from the long oak table towards the door. He looked about two or three, with a mop of white-blond hair, and he scuttled off obediently, flashing me an eager smile as he disappeared. 'That's Jasper,' Della said in a stage whisper, 'pretend you didn't see him!' I laughed with her, though I wasn't sure why.

'He's very sweet.' My voice sounded smaller than usual. 'Am I early?'

'Not at all. Mark should have taken them both upstairs by now. Mark!'

He appeared almost immediately, tall, broad-shouldered, his shirt sleeves rolled up and curly light brown hair ruffled, as though he had been grappling with another child elsewhere. He received his orders regarding the putting to bed of the two children and gave Della a mock salute, catching my eye with a grin as he left. I felt my cheeks grow warm and turned away, but when I looked back, Della's smile was amused, indulgent even. She was clearly used to people admiring her husband, her house, her life.

The rest of the group arrived one by one, eyeing me warily as we settled on the two large sofas, the kind you sink so far into you don't know where to put your feet. Of course we had shed our trainers at the door, this was unmistakably a shoes-off house, and the others seemed to find a comfortable position, tucking feet under or hugging their knees. One woman arranged herself on a herringbone rug by the fireplace, legs entwined self-consciously in what looked like a complicated yoga pose.

Large abstract paintings hung behind each of the sofas,

splashes of yellow and gold picking up on the cushions and assorted objects on the shelves either side of the marble mantel-piece – copper vase, shiny bowl, gold-framed photographs and pictures. I sat stiffly at one end of the sofa nearest to Della. She was set apart in the corner armchair, the tall lamp glowing white against her hair, a pink Smythson diary resting on her crossed legs. She listened intently, making notes as each of the women spoke in turn, introducing themselves to me and recapping on their 'homework' assignments.

They all looked younger than Della. None of them over thirty. None appeared to have children, or mapped-out career paths, or the kind of home life they found themselves at the heart of here. Some, it seemed, had been coming for months, though it was hard to work out exactly why.

There was Helen, a bottle-blonde whose large, glassy eyes watered and round cheeks flushed when she spoke, and who seemed preoccupied with finding 'the one' at any cost. She looked uncomfortable, in tight jeans and a striped jumper she tugged at, a tide of red creeping up her neck. Next to her was Eva, an events organiser who had moved to London from Poland ten years ago. She was slightly older, thirty even, with fine lines beginning to appear around her dark eyes. She wanted to get into the fashion industry, with her pixie crop and black asymmetric top exposing one bony shoulder. Everything she said came back to her frustration with her hapless musician boyfriend, and I started to feel some sympathy towards Jack, and his desire for freedom.

Jane looked much more ordinary, in an oatmeal cardigan and skinny jeans, but she was desperate to find her feet as an actress, flicking her hair dramatically and weighing each word she uttered for maximum impact. And then there was Jasmine, the hardest to read, tall and very slim with long loose curls, her body seeming to fold over itself where she sat on the floor, floral skirt gathered around her ankles. She was a frustrated writer with 'creativity issues', and seemed keen to avoid my eye at all costs.

These women all had a quality I lacked. I hadn't even been aware of its absence until I sat in that room, surrounded by it like a low hum. It wasn't confidence exactly – far from it in some cases – it was more like certainty. They seemed to occupy their place in the world, they felt entitled to their neuroses. They didn't question, as I did, the very notion of having problems. As though even that was an imposition. Here they all were, laying out their weaknesses to be picked over. It was liberating, somehow. And also terrifying.

At the centre of it all was Della. She didn't disclose – that clearly wasn't her role, she was there to listen. Like a weather-vane, she turned towards the most interesting person in the room at any given moment, their petals unfurling under her gaze. Once it passed, they retracted, their energy sapped.

Della had an immediate, energising quality I'd never come across before. A beam of warmth and attention that fell like a spotlight, with all the glare and adrenaline and excitement that brought, and a corresponding flatness afterwards. Later, when I tried to understand how I got swept so quickly into her orbit, I would picture her as a bright star in the darkness of my twenties. A point of light that illuminated both the significant moments and the shadows.

At the time, the effect of it all – the energy, the honesty, the eager women jostling for position – was almost too much to bear. I had turned to pick at the hole in the knee of my jeans when the room fell silent. I realised it was my turn to speak.

I had been going over what I might say, but now the moment came it added up to so much less than I'd hoped. I certainly wasn't going to tell them why I was really here.

'Right now I'm just a waitress in a café down . . .' I became aware of Della shaking her head and faltered.

'We never share addresses, or surnames, do we?' Della looked around. 'There's no contact outside of the group,' she said, turning back to me. 'We can only be fully honest and true to ourselves within our safe space if we know there are no consequences. Nothing we say in these four walls can be connected to the people we are outside. Does that make sense?'

I nodded, but of course it didn't make sense. Here I was – lonely, new to London – and here were other women my age, opening up in a way I'd struggled to my whole life. And now she was telling me that even if I did let them in, they were off limits anyway. We could never be friends. It didn't make sense at all.

'Remember Claire?' Jasmine said, looking around before her eyes finally landed on me. 'She tried to arrange a drink after one of the meetings . . . That was the last we saw of—'

'That's enough, Jasmine,' Della said, the coldness of her tone making us all sit up a little. I felt a shiver run through me. Della stood and moved towards the fireplace, bending forward, straight-backed. For a moment it looked as though she was going to lower herself into a yoga pose – she knew how to hold her audience, I found that out later – but then she picked up a large candle and lit it, placing it carefully back at the centre of the hearth. She took a deep breath and turned around, settling in her chair with a feline elegance, legs curled under her and chin resting on one hand.

'Let's not dwell on the past,' she said, as the flame took hold, throwing a softer light across the upward flick of her eyes. 'This group is all about the future, about moving forward. Anyway, Kate has the floor now, let's make her feel heard.'

Everyone turned to face me. I felt hot, unsettled. The mood had shifted so quickly, I was hoping I'd somehow been forgotten.

'I, um, I grew up in Cambridge, and I've been living there, well, until now, more or less. I've been in London three months. And . . . it's great – so far.' I knew how unconvincing I sounded, and the smiles looked sympathetic. Perhaps the others were remembering the shock of arriving in London, the disorientation of their first months in this sprawling city.

'And how about in five years' time?' Della asked. 'What do you picture your life looking like then?'

The question caught me by surprise. No one ever bothered to ask me what I wanted to do with my life. That had been decided for me years ago. And now that I'd left that life behind, finally made it to London, I was finding it hard to imagine five weeks into the future.

'I really don't know.' How could I possibly give voice to my ridiculous fantasies? But I could almost see the disappointment pass across Della's face like a cloud, as though the sun had gone in, leaving me in the cold.

'Well, that's why you're here, isn't it?' she said suddenly, smiling again. 'This group is all about finding your path, Kate. Understanding your true purpose. Now,' she turned to the others, 'this week we're going to be speaking in our inner voices.' I must have looked horrified, because Della added, 'You can sit this one out, Kate, since it's your first meeting. For the rest of you, I want you to really let go. Listen to that person who tells you you're not good enough.' She held contact with each pair of eyes in turn, for that one beat too long, so the other person had to look away. '*Mimic* her. *Impersonate* her. Really show her who's boss.'

I wanted to disappear. Was this the kind of thing that went on in these parts of London, behind all the vintage green and grey doors?

But Helen, face flushed, half-raised her hand and began, in a shrill tone, to berate herself for a series of failed internet dates. 'You were too keen! How could anyone ever fancy someone so desperate?'

11

'That's it,' said Della. 'Wonderful work.' She turned her full beam on Helen and immediately I saw the other three women gathering their courage, eager to take their turn in the spotlight.

By the end of the session, the women looked exhausted, their private thoughts and fears exposed so fully I could barely hide my embarrassment. 'You should all be proud of yourselves,' Della was saying as they sank into the expensive sofas, though they didn't look it, and I imagined with dread having to take part in one of these exercises myself. Like the excruciating improv sessions for Drama GCSE, only worse.

But despite it all, there was something bewitching about that evening that stays with me, even now, after everything that's happened – the sense of secrets shared, confessions absolved, our spotless, minimalist surroundings. I can still picture myself, that uncertain suburban girl, taking one last look around this sophisticated North London home. It was dark outside, and the room had taken on a warm glow, thanks to the vanilla candles that gave off a sweet, almost sickly scent. I knew that the house I shared with Liam and Gina would look even smaller and gloomier when I got back that evening, and I had a pang of something that could have been envy but felt more like ambition. Here was a life I had not believed existed. But perhaps it could be mine, too, one day. Anything seemed possible in that moment.

I turned to leave with the others, but Della pulled my arm, motioning for me to wait while they put on their coats and said their goodbyes. It was only when we were standing on the doorstep, alone in the cool evening air, that the sense of familiarity hit me fully. I'd felt it when we first met, and I felt it then, that dizzying rush of memory. Where did I know her from?

'You will come again, won't you?' she was saying, squeezing my arm.

'I'll try to . . .' I shifted away slightly. Was it her eyes? The steady gaze. That confidence.

'I was like you once, you know,' she said, after a pause.

I turned to look at her, the old paranoia kicking in immediately.

'Always searching. Never able to rest,' she continued. My heart rate picked up. There she was, talking as though she knew all about Scarlett. Knew what we'd been through. But she couldn't, could she?

'I'm just . . . I'm really busy. And it's—'

'I know,' Della interrupted, laying a hand on my arm. 'You feel lost. But eventually you realise that what you're looking for is inside *you*. And it takes work – that's where I come in. I can help you find yourself.'

I exhaled, my breathing slowing. Of course she didn't know. It was more of that therapy talk. But I couldn't deny that I needed to move on. Perhaps I might even learn something about myself, at least until the free sessions ran out.

'I'll see you next week,' I said uncertainly, taking a step back. Della smiled, her eyes seeming almost to tear up in the light from the street lamp.

'I'm so pleased,' she said, and I felt my body expand as I drank in her approval.

I was like a wilting plant then. Like any young woman, thirsty for recognition, reassurance, comfort. It could have been anyone who came across me, nurtured me, watched me grow. But it was her. It was our lives that became twisted together like vines, impossible to untangle.

'You won't regret it,' she said, almost under her breath, as I walked down the path into the darkness of the street.

Sometimes when I wake in the night, I can still hear those words.

Chapter Two

The sun streams through the small high window, casting a shadow that draws a line diagonally across the bare, greying wall. I follow it with my eyes until it reaches the corner of the room, a spider scuttling into the darkness. I let my head fall back on the bed, listening for the creak of the spring, the one that reminds me where I am, even in the early hours, when I wake shivering and damp from the cooling sweat.

I reach my arm out and touch the cold Formica side table, feeling for my plastic cup. Glass could break and create a weapon, or worse. I hear shouts, followed by silence – enforced or cajoled? It's hard to tell.

Why am I going over all this again? What could possibly be gained from reliving those months in London, the girl I was then? Still, I can't help it. Scenes run through my mind over and over, memories projected like film reel. I lie awake late into the night, sifting through each encounter for clues, replaying conversations, listening out for giveaway words, a sign, anything that could have served as a warning.

What else is there to do in here, anyway? At least this way I can fill the tiny, bare room with people, noises, light. I can

14

create a world for myself inside my head, like I've always done, one way or another. Maybe, somehow, I'll be able to work out how I ended up here. This hollow shell, the emptiness inside the biggest part of me.

I swallow, that bitter taste. The anger rises in my chest. My shoulders tense. That's why I'm doing this, really: I need to piece it all together. To understand how I came to give up everything I had. Or to have it taken away.

But why start there – with the Janes? Why not start with Della? With the day she turned up at the café, changing the temperature of the room, the energy around us, the sense of possibility almost tangible. Changing everything.

She was watching me, I could feel it. The blonde woman in the corner. I'd been trying to clear tables, but I felt hot, the left side of my face prickling as if I'd fallen asleep in the sun. I let my hair fall forward – the steam from the coffee machine had made it into strings, and I peered through them, over my shoulder. But she'd looked away; she was reading her book, pen in hand. Perhaps I'd been imagining it. Anything to distract myself from the squawking babies and the relentless drone of the grinder.

It was mid-shift on a Wednesday. I'd already gone to that place I went in my mind, when it all got too much. I didn't even see the kid's smoothie as I swept my cloth across the table. And then it was too late.

'That's an iPhone, you know,' a woman hissed, her face pink against an auburn bob, pointing her phone at me, its screen blank. A copper-haired boy of three or four was standing next to her, red juice dripping down his beige dungarees.

'I'm sorry, I . . .'

'It's going to need fixing. That's if it can be fixed. I'm going

15

to have to talk to the manager. We'll need some kind of reimbursement . . .'

'What?' I could barely hear above the blood pounding in my ears. What would that be: two weeks' wages? A month's rent? And for her – probably an afternoon's spending money.

Pete must have seen the way I was staring because he swooped in and took over.

'I'm really sorry about all this. I'm the manager, can I offer you some free drinks? A pastry?'

I turned away, grateful, though I knew I'd be for it later. I busied myself with the tables by the door, as far away as possible from the bowing and scraping going on at the till. Pete was using his soothing voice, the rueful smile he saved for the more attractive customers; the one that said he could be running somewhere much more impressive than this small organic café on Crouch Hill, with its bleached pine and signs exhorting customers to *Keep Calm And Drink Coffee*. The scene was quieter now, the phone restarted, the mishap smoothed over. But the hum in my head hadn't died down. The blonde woman had to touch my arm twice before I even registered.

'Are you OK?' she asked. I was slow to turn around. She was another one of those Crouch End mums, after all – the ones who usually ignored me, unless I'd recently ruined their top-of-the-range smartphone. But when I looked up, the concern in her eyes seemed genuine. She'd put her book to one side.

'Fine, thanks.' I brushed away the tears that were gathering.

'It's just, you seem a bit . . .' The woman trailed off. 'Here, sit down a minute, have a drink of something.' She pulled out a chair, but I shook my head, glancing over at Pete.

'Thanks, that's really kind, but I'd better not. Not after all that.' I motioned towards the till and she raised an eyebrow with a smile. Perhaps she wasn't one of them after all.

'Can I get you a refill?' I asked, looking at her empty cup.

'Well, if you're sure you don't want anything . . . I'll have a black Americano.'

'Good choice.' I nodded. Not like most of the customers around here, with their skinny lattes and cappuccinos.

'I like to taste my coffee, rather than turning it into a . . .'

'Milkshake?' We both smiled, and then I looked away, my eye resting on her book. *The Power of Now*. Self-help. I don't know why I felt disappointed. It was so rare to see a customer reading a book instead of a phone, I suppose, and I'd hoped it might be one I'd read, so we could have a proper conversation for once. One of the classics I'd gone through in those years at the library; maybe even a mystery, though she didn't look the type.

'Eckhart Tolle,' she said as I brought over her coffee. 'The book, I mean. Very inspiring. Though maybe not your thing?' She put the paperback into her large, expensive-looking leather handbag and a look passed between us. An understanding – between me and this glamorous older woman, who seemed to care what some young waitress thought of her reading material. What would she say if she could see the stash of children's books I kept hidden under my bed, for the nights when I woke panting after running down empty streets, shouting in a voice that wouldn't come? *Anne of Green Gables*. *Little Women*. The ones that made me feel safe, like they had all those years ago.

After a moment's pause, the woman reached into her bag and pulled out a piece of pink paper.

'I hope you don't think I'm being too forward, but I wondered if you might like to . . .' she held out a flyer, with the letters AIM written in block capitals. 'I'm holding a group session next week. It might be exactly what you need.'

I must have looked confused, because she added, 'My name's

17

Della Hunter. I'm a life coach. You might have seen me on television?'

I looked at her more closely. For a moment I had that stomach-sinking feeling, when a face from the past appears in the wrong place. Blond hair tied loosely, light eyes, confident, as though she was daring me to recognise her. Perhaps I had seen her on TV, but those eyes, so pale blue they looked almost unreal, the way they seemed to cut right through you – she was almost more familiar than that. Closer to home. Anyway, I didn't have much time for telly, what with my shifts and the search. I felt a memory pulling at me and I concentrated on trying to bring it into focus, but it was no good.

'Sorry, I . . . yes, I think I have seen you on TV,' I said, and she gave the kind of self-assured smile I was used to seeing in that setting. Perhaps that's all it was: she looked like all the other women in Crouch End. The same expensively casual style – a crisp white shirt, gold chain, designer jeans. None of them had stains at the sleeves where they'd accidentally mopped up spills. They didn't wear comfortable shoes because they were on their feet all day.

I looked at the flyer, trying to ignore the niggling feeling that there was a face that matched hers, somewhere in my memory bank. There was a tiny nick in her skin, just under her right eye, and my mind snagged on that. Where had I seen it before?

I heard a small sigh and tried to focus on what I was reading. AIM: Accessing Inner Motivation. What was all this?

'Thanks,' I said. 'I might come along.' I was sure I wouldn't.

'I hope you do,' Della said and then, resting her hand on my arm, she held my eye, lowering her voice. 'You will find what you've lost, Kate. Don't give up.'

My stomach lurched. What did she know? But she'd already

switched back into a breezy sales patter. 'The first three sessions are free, while you see whether my style of coaching is for you . . . People always stay.' She smiled. 'All the details are on the flyer.' And then from nowhere, with what must have been a surge of sympathy for a waitress down on her luck, she hugged me.

'Don't worry,' she said, into my ear, 'everything will get better, you'll see.'

She held me at arm's length, studying my face, and I felt my eyes fill with tears again, though not the frustrated kind this time. It was more like relief, a sense of acceptance.

And then, without warning she was gone, the door slamming shut behind her.

'Who was that?' Pete asked. He was looking at me as though I'd grown a new head – his awkward waitress, not long arrived in London, hugging some beautiful customer out of nowhere. But I just shrugged.

'I don't know. Isn't she a regular?' I could still feel the weight of her hands resting on my shoulders. Had she been able to tell in those few moments how much I'd been struggling since I got to London? Or even, somehow, why I was here?

'Never seen her before,' Pete said, shaking his head, and we both watched the door as though she might walk back in at any minute – this stranger, so familiar, who had turned up at the right moment and made me feel, fleetingly, so understood; so at home.

'We're having a house meeting.'

It was the last thing I wanted to hear as I closed the front door. I was desperate to get upstairs and google 'Della Hunter'; work out where I knew her from. The café Wi-Fi had been patchy all day, and I'd run out of data. But Liam was standing

19

in the doorway to the living room, his dark eyes glinting, and beyond him Gina was slumped on the threadbare sofa, looking like she was waiting for a detention.

'The rent's going up,' Liam said, before I'd even got my coat off. I looked at him in shock. I was barely making it through the month as it was.

But Liam was caught up in the drama of it all – any opportunity to bring his reluctant housemates together. 'Joanne's well aware of the upturn in the housing market and she wants to cash in,' he said, sitting down next to Gina and scooping up the pile of papers lying on the grubby glass coffee table. 'Don't worry, though. We're not giving in without a fight. This place is a dump.'

I sat down and tried to catch Gina's eye, but she was too busy picking her nails to notice – they were painted bright pink today, to match her workout leggings.

Liam was right, of course. The house smelled of rotting carpets, and there had been almost constant infestations in the three months I'd lived there – rats, then mice, then flies. The fabrics Gina bought visiting her gran in Nigeria hadn't done much to cover up the tatty sofas, and the crimson velvet curtains created a gloom even on sunny days, though they did at least shield us from next door's drug deals, and the almost constant traffic crossing our section of the Harringay ladder and onto Green Lanes. But what could you expect for what we were paying? If Liam started making a fuss, we might get thrown out. Where could I possibly find to live in London that was cheaper than this?

'Seriously, look at this place though,' Gina said, fiddling with her braids. 'That woman's taking the piss.'

'Well, you're always at your mum's or in Dalston.' Liam shot Gina a look. We clearly weren't the sitcom house-share he'd had in mind.

'God, what do you care?' Gina rolled her eyes at me and stretched up from the sofa. 'Anyway, I've got hot yoga, and then I'm staying at Nate's. Later.' She shut the living-room door behind her.

'Give her a break,' I said to Liam. 'She doesn't owe you anything.'

I didn't understand what Liam was doing there, really. He'd moved from Dublin six years earlier and worked in computers for a media company – something called front-end development. He must have earned a decent amount, more than Gina or me on our zero-hours contracts, but he chose to live in this dump, watching his flatmates come and go every six months or so, trying to create some kind of weird, forced friendship dynamic. He was older, too. Only by three years, but I sure as hell hoped I wasn't living somewhere like this by the time I was twenty-eight.

Liam was always on the verge of launching the next website or app that was going to make his fortune, and he told me about his latest as I heated up some leftovers.

'It's called "online reputation management",' he was saying, sitting down opposite me as I finished off the rest of last night's pasta pesto. 'Everyone wants to clean up their Google search, don't they?'

'Do they?'

'Course they do. I can make sure only good things come up when someone searches for you online.' He was watching each forkful as it left my plate, and I sped up a little, keen to get upstairs. 'Imagine you're looking for a job, or you're a business. Or you said the wrong thing once on Facebook. I can make that go away.'

I paused, my fork mid-air. 'So, you can make people disappear . . . But can you find them?'

'No problem. Who are you looking for?'

'No one in particular. Just wondering.' I didn't know if I could trust him with that information yet.

I watched him push his dark hair from his face as he went on about personal brands and unique selling points. He wasn't bad looking, with sharp-angled features and thick brows, and he was sweet, bringing home crosswords from the newspapers at work ever since he'd heard me discussing clues with Dad on the phone one Sunday. But Liam wasn't such a wordsmith, and sitting bent over the kitchen table together, I couldn't help feeling like we were playing parts – the long-married couple, rather than two relative strangers who'd found themselves in the same dingy London terrace. Besides, I didn't have time to get distracted by any kind of house-share romance.

'Kate? I've lost you, haven't I? Sorry.' He looked hurt, or maybe embarrassed. 'What have you been up to? We've barely seen you the last few days.'

I considered telling him about the woman who'd come into the café that afternoon and the flyer she'd given me. But I already knew it would come out all wrong – she'd end up sounding odd, or I would. I hadn't had a chance to make sense of it all yet. So instead I grabbed my bag and dumped my plate in the sink.

'Nothing much. Just working, you know. Trying to get extra shifts so I can make the rent. Thanks for talking to the land-lady.' I smiled and Liam looked all pleased. 'You give her hell.'

I closed my bedroom door behind me, appreciating for a moment the feeling of shutting myself away in the one small space I'd carved out for myself. Even if it was a featureless box, one grimy window, tatty desk, Ikea bookshelf. It was mine. I flopped onto my single bed and opened up my laptop.

Della Hunter: *Be Your Own Life Coach*. That was her latest book, though she'd published a few and been on most of the daytime TV shows by the looks of it. I couldn't find anything about her group though, this AIM business, so I read up a bit on life-coaching and what it involved – personal goals, achievement targets. And then I skimmed the missing persons forums, as I did every night, to see if there were any new developments, any sightings, any leads.

By the time I got through it all, it was gone eleven. I needed to get some sleep before my early shift, but I found myself looping back to her web page: 'Della Dares, Do You?' A headshot took up most of the home screen, a close-up of that broad smile, pale eyes animated, white collar crisp and hair twisted up, with wisps arranged prettily around her face.

She must have been at least ten years older than me, maybe more, but in this picture her face was entirely without lines. Perhaps there was a filter on it . . . but there was that little dip, under her eye. That tiny imperfection.

I felt a nagging again in the pit of my stomach. I closed my eyes and tried to give shape to a memory that wanted to break through, but I got lost in the haze. Ragged cartwheels on a small patch of lawn. Whispers from bed to bed. The fragments, before everything went dim.

Della's face faded into all the others over the years. It was no use. I lay on my bed and tried to clear my mind. I pictured the blue sea, the waves stretching out. I listened for the birds, the long grass swishing in the wind.

As I drifted off, I replayed the words Della had said to me in the café, so kind and reassuring, so perceptive. 'You will find what you've lost, Kate.' I was just sinking under, giving in to the pull, when my eyes shot open. I sat up in bed, my heart racing.

How had she known my name?

Chapter Three

The market was quiet. It was early April, a couple of days after the first meeting at Della's house. I was still deciding whether I should go again. The meeting itself had left me on edge, as our encounter at the café had. Della must have heard Pete address me during the smoothie fallout, there was no other rational explanation. But that still didn't account for the sense of recognition I'd had, the feeling we'd met somewhere before.

That was why I wanted to see her, I suppose. To work out where I knew her from. And to get another fix of her attention. Already, I felt more like my old self, more alive, more confident. Anyway, I'd said I would go, and it wasn't like I had any other pressing engagements after work on a Tuesday. There were only so many hours I could spend at the market.

I usually got there earlier, when it was in full swing and the tourists were everywhere. But today I'd caught the 29 to Camden straight after work, hoping to catch a different crowd.

It was still busy; everywhere I looked a blur of eyes, mouths, phones pressed to cheeks, heads turning away from the low sun's glare. I walked along the canalside searching the faces.

Every stall I went past, I was sure would be the one. At every turn, I was ready to see Scarlett's eyes – knowing, mocking. The tangle of curls. The upright back. The way she always held herself, defiant.

I studied the lines on the faces, the crinkles of foreheads, the piercings, the tattoos, the dye-jobs, the dreadlocks. The stallholders were a more alternative bunch than their customers on the whole, though you did see the odd punk browsing the stands, left behind from another century. Mostly it was school groups, tours, visitors on a pilgrimage to a once trendy part of London. And, at this time in the evening, the late workers and early drinkers, heading towards pubs, a day done and an evening yet to come.

It was the locals I was interested in, though. The ones who seemed to have made a life for themselves here, standing by as their market got polished up, re-paved, sanitised. I watched them as they stood by their over-priced puppets and vintage beer mats, sharing knowing looks across the heads of tourists. They lit joss sticks and cradled cups of chai from the stall by the lock. And occasionally they caught my eye. Some of them had started to notice me, I think – loitering in the corners, haunting the market, watching.

I'd always had an eye for faces. Nosy, Mum called it. Stop staring. Even as a baby I'd just looked at her, silently, she said. Slow to talk. Disconcerting. But it had come in useful in recent months. Perhaps I'd been preparing the skill my whole life, without even knowing it. Sometimes I wondered about that – how much life shaped you, and how far you made your own fate. Had I known what was coming? My eyes and brain perfecting the flicker and scan, flicker and scan.

Today was one of the good days, when I felt hopeful. I enjoyed getting caught up in the forward motion, swept along, able to disappear. Surrounded by so many others, I didn't have to worry about what anyone thought of me. Whether they were looking at me. Whether I was being judged.

It was only when the crowd thinned out, as I got further along the canal, that the loneliness hit. I stopped in the patchy sunlight on a bench by the towpath, watching the students and suits go by, earphones in, silently marching to the same beat. Furtively, though barely anyone glanced in my direction, I checked the map on my phone, tracing my finger over the spread of the market either side of Camden High Street, reminding myself of its contours.

It was much bigger than I'd remembered from my few visits as a teenager. When I first got to London, I'd imagined my task would be fairly easy. Scarlett worked here somewhere, it was just a case of finding her. That was before I discovered it was made up of different sections, with different names. Some of the stalls would rotate. Others were on different floors, up steep staircases and through narrow corridors.

Three months of coming here two or three times a week, and I still hadn't caught a glimpse. To begin with I'd walked around with a picture, showing it to anyone who'd take the time to look. But no one recognised her, or would admit to it, and so I'd resorted to circling the market over and over, hoping for a moment of connection.

Sometimes it would come, that jolt of recognition. Working my way through the stalls, I spotted a woman I hadn't seen before, talking to a man selling mirrored pots. She was heavier, with dyed black hair and a piercing through one nostril. But there was something familiar about the way she tilted her head as she laughed.

I stood, frozen to the spot, holding my breath. It had been fifteen years. Who knew how she might have changed?

The woman handed over a tray of noodles, bent over to

look more closely at something on the stall, straightened up. I remembered to breathe. I held my body still as she turned towards me. And then I felt my chest deflate, my shoulders sag. Of course it wasn't my sister. The mouth was all wrong. She was much older. What had I been thinking?

The sun was setting over the canal as I walked slowly to the bus stop, the shafts of light illuminating a rotting kebab abandoned by the water's edge and green scum floating on its surface. I felt weak, defeated. I caught the 29 and slumped in my seat, closing my eyes as if to mark the end of their shift. It was ridiculous. What did I expect? That I'd suddenly bump into her after all these years?

I rested my head against the window and pictured the pure light of Della's white living room, the calm I had felt in her home. That sense of being a part of something in the group, however strange.

When I opened my eyes, we were crawling past Manor House. I remembered the grotty kitchen I'd be returning to that evening and counted the hours until I'd have to be back at the café in the morning. It was nearly eight. By the time I got home and heated up some soup it would be nine. Then I'd have to do another job search and look on the missing persons forums before I fell into bed. And speak to my parents. It was a Thursday, and they always called the landline even though I told them to use my mobile – they knew Liam would pick up and I wouldn't be able to avoid them.

I had all that to come when I got home, and it felt relentless. Impossible. To hold down a job so that I could afford to live in London and, at the same time, look for something better paid, all the while continuing my search. To hold all the responsibility for my family's happiness. I resented them for it. I couldn't help it.

* * *

27

'They do what? They sit around and chant mantras? You're making it up!'

Liam had found me in the kitchen stirring my tomato soup and wanted to know where I'd been. I hadn't told him about my search, so I found it hard to account for all the hours I spent out of the house. Usually I'd make up lies about extra shifts or friends from work, but this evening I was distracting him with tales of Tuesday's meeting. Only I was already regretting having said anything.

'Can I come next time?' he asked, laughing.

'No, you can't. It's all women. And anyway, it's top secret.' I smiled. I was trying to make light of it, but actually I probably was breaking the rules by mentioning it at all. I sat down at the table with my bowl and a plate of toast and tried to change the subject.

'So what's happening with your deleting stuff app?'

'Oh, nothing much. I'm more interested in this secret meeting of yours. So who goes then? Why's it all women? Sounds a bit sexist.'

'No, it's not.'

'Well you would say that, wouldn't you? It's not only women who are oppressed, you know.' Liam grinned at me. He'd taken to teasing me since he found me reading *We Should All Be Feminists* one evening in the living room. I'd picked it up at the library because I'd loved *Americanah*, by the same author, and it had clearly been instrumental in shaping Liam's opinion of me. Sometimes I went along with it, allowed myself to be baited. But tonight I wasn't in the mood.

'It's all women who are sort of in the same boat, you know?' I was spooning up my soup furiously. 'We're all about the same age. All trying to find our feet a bit.' I shrugged, casting around for details I could pass on that wouldn't give anything away.

'There's this one girl, Jane. She's recently gone through a break-up. She's quite small and blonde . . . They all are, really. Fair hair, twenty-something . . .' I saw Liam's eyes dart towards me with interest and realised I'd said too much. 'Anyway, I'd better get on. I've got stuff to do before bed.'

'Oh yeah, your mum called. Again,' Liam said as I dumped my dishes on the pile in the sink.

'Thanks. Sorry she always rings the landline, I'll have another word about that,' I said, but I could see Liam wasn't listening. He was deep in thought.

I was heading towards the door with a glass of water in my hand when he looked up. The strip lighting threw an odd glow on his glasses, casting a shadow, so I couldn't see his eyes.

'They sound like a cult. The Janes,' he said, and I forced a laugh.

At the time, I didn't want to hear it.

Chapter Four

'This week we'll be discussing families and children – hopes and dreams for the future.' We were sitting in Della's high-ceilinged living room, the sky outside heavy with dark clouds, ready to burst. Inside, too, there was a sense of anticipation – as though we had taken a collective deep breath. Helen and Eva leaned forward as if preparing to take notes, elbows on knees. Jane was fiddling with her necklace, looking up through strands of hair. Jasmine, sitting on the floor with long legs stretched out and her back resting on the sofa, twisted a ring around her bony finger. I was hit again by the disorienting weirdness of them all: sunflowers lined in a row – fair heads turned towards the brightest point in the room.

I was the only one sitting back, distracted by the framed photographs on the mantelpiece. Mark on a boat with six-year-old Tabitha, white-blonde and doll-like on his knee. Della, holding their chubby two-year-old, Jasper, next to an enormous Christmas tree. At the centre, a recent portrait of the four of them, posed neatly in a white studio, the coordinated blues and whites of their trousers and crisp shirts, shorts and patterned dresses picking up the colour of their eyes. Next to it, in a holiday snap, they sat around a long table in the sunshine, laughing, with another couple of a similar age and a younger woman in sunglasses. All were turned in the direction of a glistening swimming pool where an older child was pushing in a younger one. It was like a scene from a film, the large stone house in the background, the blue of the pool, dappled sunlight on the tablecloth. Mark, caught off guard, resting one arm across Della's shoulder, the other cradling a baby Jasper on his chest. Della the only one not laughing, whispering something in Tabitha's ear. It was the kind of holiday I'd heard girls at school talking about: where people drifted in and out, lunches lasted hours, the pool was just for you. No screaming kids from nearby tents, no persistent south-coast drizzle.

It was my third meeting, and already I'd set myself apart from the group, somehow. I listened as they took turns to confess their dreams of having children, their fears that they might not be able to, or wouldn't meet the right person in time.

'I don't want to settle – but I've been single for so long. When's it going to happen for me?'

'I feel like time's running out. How can I make it as an actress *and* have a family?'

'Writing doesn't pay the bills as it is, let alone buy a flat. How will I ever afford to have kids?'

'What if Jack isn't the father I want my children to have? He won't come home most evenings as it is. I don't want to bring them up on my own.'

Della nodded in understanding, though she kept glancing at the photographs too, as if to reassure herself that the fate of these women was not her own. She had curled up in her chair, her pleated satin skirt gathered around her knees, and was pulling the sleeves of her soft grey jumper over her hands

31

as she listened. It looked like cashmere, or something equally expensive. I imagined how the fabric would feel against her fingertips – luxurious, comforting. My own cardigan was faded and stiff from where I'd dried it on the radiator. I tugged it around me and caught her eye. I sensed she was waiting – ready for me to reveal to the room how much I wanted what she had, too – and I felt a small thrill at the prospect of surprising her; revealing hidden depths even she hadn't picked up on.

'I don't think I do want children,' I said, when it was my turn. 'I babysat a bit when I was younger. I like being around kids. But I don't know if I want to be a mum, really. I'd quite like to be a dad,' I continued, with a little laugh. Why did I always feel the need to apologise? 'I mean, like, be around sometimes, there for the fun bits, not full time. You know?' I looked up, but the faces around me were blank. Only Della nodded.

'Yes, Kate, yes. I think we're making real progress here. Go on.'

'Well, that's it, really. I know I'm only twenty-five, but I can't see myself being a mum. I'd probably be more like the fun aunt—' As soon as the word came out of my mouth, I stopped.

'Do you have a brother or sister?' Della asked. Her eyes searched my face, she wanted more, but I just nodded. There was no way I was getting into all that.

'So that might be on the cards for you then,' Della said. 'And if not, I'm sure there will be other ways of having children in your life.' She turned to the group. 'I think it's very brave, what Kate has shared. I'm sure you have your reasons for not wanting children, Kate, and perhaps we'll touch on those another time. But it takes a strong mind to know yourself so well, at such a young age.'

I felt my cheeks grow warm. I had the feeling I'd passed a

test of some kind. The others had sensed my advantage, and were quick to chip in with their own misgivings about motherhood – the emotional toll, the drudgery, the loss of freedom. But they didn't really mean it, and I could see Della wasn't convinced. She was watching me, long after the conversation had moved on. I met her eyes and looked quickly away. These other women didn't get it, but she did.

As the session wound up and we headed into the large black-and-white tiled hallway to put our shoes on, Helen fell into step with me.

'That was so brave,' she said quietly. 'Do you really think you never want kids?'

I shrugged. I couldn't see why it was such a big deal. And anyway, I wanted to join in with Della's conversation. She gave herself to us in these moments, at the end of the session – flashes of the woman who mingled with TV presenters and went to intimate book launches. I watched Jane and Jasmine, standing by the coat rack next to Della, adopting her animated expressions and gestures, as though trying on a dress they could never afford.

'It doesn't feel like it's on the cards for me, I suppose,' I said to Helen, turning to try and catch Della's eye.

'Let's just say, he's not the only one who needs a confidentiality clause . . .' Della was saying, to more laughter. She pushed her loose hair behind her ears, her eyes glinting in that inviting way, as though she was turning over an amusing story in her mind, wondering whether to share it or keep it for herself. I desperately wanted to know who they were talking about.

'I wish I felt so certain about *any*thing,' Helen said stooping to tie her laces, and I looked down at her, surprised. At the unlikely idea that I might be the one who seemed sure of myself.

33

'Kate, have you got a moment?' Della was suddenly behind us, and I felt a jolt of energy. I had been called on. The others melted away, huddling at the front door.

'Cheerio, ladies,' Della called out, as if dismissing the class, and then she lowered her voice and turned to me. 'I wanted to touch base,' she said, as the door slammed. 'To make sure you're OK. I get the sense there's something holding you back.' She rested an arm against the large glossy bannister that dominated the hallway, her eyes searching my face.

'It's just . . . I don't think I can afford to keep coming,' I said, aware that I was avoiding the larger truth she was driving at. 'Next week I'll need to start paying, and it's really too much for me to stretch to, so . . .' I shrugged. I was being honest. I couldn't afford it.

'I really think we're on the verge of a breakthrough. I think you should stick with this.' Della held my eye. 'If you've had any kind of mental health problems in the past, it's important to keep an eye out for signs of a relapse, however slight. This coaching can help you stay on track with your recovery, keep you focused on the path ahead.'

I bent down, pushing my feet into my Converse, trying to hide my alarm. There was no way she could know, was there? She couldn't have been looking into my background. Maybe it was evident from the way I spoke, the way I held myself. That was always my fear. Could everybody tell – or did Della have a special sense for these things?

'I know. It's just I . . .' I stood up. I needed to get outside, get some fresh air. I reached up for my coat, but Della caught my arm.

'Look, I know how it is,' Della said. 'I felt the same way you do, once, and I . . .' She looked down. Her feet were bare on the tiled floor and she seemed suddenly smaller, more vulnerable than I had seen before. 'I'd like to extend your free ssessions for a little while.' I turned to her, surprised. 'I don't want to give up on you yet,' she said, smiling now and loosening her grip. It was only after she stopped making physical contact with me, after that phase of our relationship was over, that I realised how often she used touch to get her point across. To establish connection.

'Are you sure?' It seemed like too much. She couldn't afford to give free coaching to anyone she happened to feel a bit sorry for, could she?

'Absolutely.' Della lifted the coat I'd been trying to get and helped me into it, making me feel like a nursery child who hadn't been able to reach her peg. 'This is nice,' she said, running a thumb along the lapel of my old blue jacket. 'I've been eyeing up a peacoat. Is it Gap?' I smiled non-committally, too embarrassed to say the word Primark in Della's presence.

'Listen, Kate, you've got huge potential, but you need to reconnect with yourself. And I'm here to help you with that.'

'Thank you.' I tried to smile as she opened the door. 'I guess I could come along for a few more sessions. Until I find out what it is that I really want—'

'What you *really, really want*?' Della half-sang from the doorway, and I turned to see those pale eyes glinting as she mimicked the Spice Girls song from my youth. The laugh I tried to rouse died in my throat. It wasn't just the shift in register – that song held painful memories. Della couldn't possibly have known, but it had been Scarlett's favourite.

As I walked home through the darkened, silent streets that led from Della's house to mine, each road scruffier than the last, I thought about how determined Della seemed to share her good fortune. All the popular girls at school – the ones who had looked like teenagers, and then women, before the rest of us – had always been horrible with it. They wanted to rub your inadequacy in your face. But Della was different.

35

She knew she was lucky, and she'd chosen a group of younger women to nurture and encourage.

Did she remind me of those girls? The thought sent blood rushing past my ears. Is that where I remembered Della from, was it school? A few years above, perhaps? But no, she'd have told me if she came from Cambridge. And besides, there was too much of an age difference between us.

I talked myself down as I shut the front door behind me, Liam and Gina in their rooms already, or out. It was my mind playing tricks on me again. My brain looking for connections where there were none to be made. It was rest I needed. Everything would seem clearer in the morning.

I got ready for bed, sank into the sheets feeling exhausted after all the emotion of the evening. In the half-lucid moments before sleep took hold, my memory jolted. A picture swam to the surface. A group of people, a girl on the edge. But too quickly it flickered and flashed away. I had missed the moment. I was sure it would come back to me.

'How are the Janes?' I had managed to avoid Liam's awkward questions for a couple of days but this morning he was impossible to get past, scooping up cornflakes at the kitchen table while I made my toast.

'Still crazy,' I said, trying to keep up the joke – easier than telling the truth.

'So why d'you keep going then? Do you have deep dark secrets we can only imagine?' Liam grinned as he drank the last of the milk from his bowl. I looked away, packing my bag for work.

'Of course not. It's life-coaching, not therapy. She's helping me fulfil my potential. You know, like why am I working in a café? Why am I living in this grotty house-share?' My laugh sounded flat, even to me.

I grabbed my toast and bag, ready to go as the door slammed. Gina, leaving without a word to either of us, as usual.

'Nice.' Liam raised an eyebrow. 'Well at least I get a goodbye from you.' He smiled, and our eyes met. Then I turned, feeling almost breathless, stifled by the enforced domesticity of it all. Next thing I knew he'd be wanting a peck on the cheek and a lunch bag. I ducked away, enjoying the sense of freedom as I shut the door behind me. Did everyone feel an urge to run the minute anyone got too close, or was it just me? My insecurities.

The walk to the café was sunlit and fresh, with birds hopping between clouds of blossom and a vibrant blue sky stretching all the way to Alexandra Palace in the distance, so I took the longer route, climbing up beyond the train station, passing through clusters of commuters heading in the other direction.

Even on a morning like this, I found myself looking, focusing on every face I went past. What would it be like, to walk around without feeling compelled to find someone? To have the time to look at men for once, and not just women. To go on the odd date, like in the early days with Dan. Even to give Liam a chance.

Rachel, Zoe, Meena – all my Nottingham friends had boyfriends now, their single, student days behind them. They'd mostly stayed up there, sending the occasional message whenever there was news. Even Layla had a boyfriend now, or so it seemed from her status updates.

I'd barely seen anyone in person since things had gone so wrong after university – just dropped in every once in a while with a group chat. I'd told them all when Dan and I split up, of course – got some sympathetic messages, a phone call from Rach – but what I didn't tell them, couldn't express in a message, was how excited I felt some days, full to bursting with this sense of possibility, especially since I'd met Della.

How it seemed as if I was on the brink of some momentous change, one that hadn't seemed even vaguely within reach back in Cambridge. Then there were the other days, when the air escaped and I felt flat. As though life pulled me down further with each hour that passed. I was entirely alone in this new city and nobody would notice if I never got out of bed again. The highs and lows of independent life were higher and lower. The middle ground seemed to have fallen away.

I was so caught up in my thoughts, I barely noticed my feet retracing the steps. Not until I was at the foot of the road did I realise I'd continued climbing, instead of taking a right turn down Crouch Hill like I usually did.

And then, there it was. Della's house. Tall and grand, the upstairs curtains flung apart, the downstairs shutters pushed back, revealing the light-filled living room and designer kitchen beyond. It was so alien to me, this idea of having your whole interior on show. I'd grown up in a world of heavy net curtains and small windows and frosted glass. Here they seemed to be putting on a performance, inviting passers-by to look in, and I stopped behind a tree across the road, with a clear view through the downstairs.

Mark was setting the long kitchen table with the two children. Tabitha was dressed for school and Mark was in shorts and a T-shirt, as though he was off to the gym, or had just been, reaching a fresh loaf out of the bread-maker – so golden I could almost smell it. The children were putting out jam and butter and laughing about something. Jasper ran to fetch a piece of paper and they all bent over it, Mark's brown hair and their fair curls mingling as they examined whatever it was. A note perhaps. Or, more likely, a drawing, since Mark pinned it to the tall double fridge with a magnet while Jasper looked on. I smiled as I saw him lean in closer to examine it, tracing over it with his fingers proudly.

38

Watching them, I felt suddenly hungry; hollow to the pit of my stomach. I thought about the last meeting. How casually I'd announced to the room that I didn't want any of this. Family life. So why was I feeling tearful, almost homesick?

For a moment, I let myself picture the scene – walking into the kitchen, caught around the waist by Mark, a kiss on the neck, the children pulling me by the hands to join them at the table. It was a life I'd never even been able to imagine before and, seeing it play out in front of me, the whole set-up felt almost within reach.

I steadied myself on the tree, pushing my hand against the bark so that its jagged edges punctured my skin. The pain brought me back to myself. No, it wasn't that I wanted to *have* children like these. I wanted to have had their childhood – happy, loving, entitled. No apologies, no misery, no absence.

I pushed harder, watching a small trickle of blood snake down my finger. Bending down to lick it, I sensed a movement, a twitch of the curtain falling back into place in the upstairs window. Or perhaps just fluttering in the breeze.

Either way, it was enough to spook me. I retreated a few paces. What if Della had seen me, standing outside her house, watching her family? What would she think – that I was obsessed with them? I looked up again, but the curtain was still. In the kitchen, Mark had turned towards the door, shouting something upstairs. She would be coming down. I knew I needed to get away before she saw me, and yet something rooted me to the spot.

The kitchen door swung open and the children sat at the table immediately while Della swept in, a vision in head-to-toe white: shirt, slim-fitting jeans, box-fresh trainers. Who was I trying to kid? I could never even dream of measuring up. For a minute, I thought Mark was going to embrace her, just as I'd imagined him doing to me, and I got ready to turn my head, though I knew I wouldn't be able to drag my eyes away. But instead, Della held up her phone screen and pointed to it, gesticulating, while the children sat still, eyes on the plates in front of them.

It could have been over anything, their argument, but for some reason I felt implicated, caught up in it all, though I couldn't possibly be. And then Della looked up, seeming to stare directly at me. I froze, hardly daring to breathe until she turned back to her screen.

Had she seen me? I couldn't be sure. But while she was occupied, I fled down the road, wondering what on earth I could say to explain myself. 'Oh sorry, Della. I somehow found myself here. I'm watching your family. You don't mind, do you?'

What had come over me? I quickened my pace to get to work, aware that my detour had already cost me precious minutes. My heart was fluttering, my head was pounding. But there was also excitement, exhilaration. I had secret knowledge, insider information. I'd had a glimpse behind the scenes of Della's grand performance. I'd seen something she didn't want me to see.

Chapter Five

I arrived early for the next meeting. If there was going to be any awkwardness about the incident outside the house, I wanted to get it out of the way before everyone arrived. I was all ready with an excuse: I thought I'd dropped something coming out of the previous meeting. A favourite earring. I'd been looking for it. I was only sorry I hadn't popped in to say hello.

But this time it was Mark who answered the door, straightening his T-shirt over his jeans, a tang in the air as though he had recently played sport. I felt a jolt in my stomach, pulling myself up a little taller and smoothing down my hair as he stooped to pick up a pair of shoes.

'Oh, hello,' he said. 'Della's just getting everything set up.' Mark seemed to fill the hallway in a way that Della didn't, and it wasn't only his height. There was something about his presence that took up space, his confidence, his good looks, his ease.

'Sorry. I'm early, aren't I?'

'It's fine, come on through. The kids are finishing their tea.'

Mark smiled, though he seemed preoccupied, and I wasn't sure where to put myself. I edged into the living room and perched on a sofa, wondering as I did whether he knew my

41

little secret ('Della, your stalker's here!'). But he was caught up in the family scene and I sat awkwardly, watching through the partition doors as he marched toast soldiers up spoons and scooped up runny egg. The children laughed delightedly, looking across at me every now and then with interest.

'Why is that lady staring at us, Daddy?' asked the little girl, Tabitha.

I sprang back, pretending to search for something in my bag, but Mark looked up and caught my eye, smiling.

'She's not staring, Tabby. Kate, why don't you join us? Cup of tea?'

Before I could answer, Della walked in, barefoot and elegant in a navy silk jumpsuit, her back to me. She was pulling strands of hair from a high bun and arranging them around her face.

'Mark, for God's sake. What are you doing mucking around? They're going to be here in a minute. And I asked you to tidy the—'

'They're already here,' Mark interrupted, nodding over Della's shoulder and she spun around, glancing at the clock.

'Kate, how wonderful . . . Please excuse us, we're in a bit of disarray here. Mark was just taking the children upstairs.' As Della closed the partition doors, I got one last glimpse of Mark, sweeping dishes into the sink. He caught my eye and smiled, with a little shrug. I risked a smile in return, though my attention was really on Della.

'Sorry I'm early,' I said, turning to her, my shoulders still stiff with anxiety.

'Not at all. I'm so pleased you came. I wasn't sure you would after . . .'

'The other day?' I offered, about to blurt out my excuses.

'Well, yes. You were so honest in the meeting, and I felt the others weren't as accepting as they could have been. They

42

weren't as prepared to open themselves up and really examine
their motivations. I think they could all learn from you.' Della
smiled, and I sat down quickly, the relief making me light-
headed. She hadn't seen me.

'Oh, it was fine. It's just . . . I do find the exercises a bit
tricky at the moment. I find I'm—'

'Look, it's no problem.' Della sat down next to me, tucking
one long leg under her and putting a hand on my arm. 'Why
don't you sit out the exercises tonight? Then, after that, you
can join in when you feel like it. Whatever makes you comfortable. In fact, I was—' There was a knock at the door. 'I'd
better get that.'

I settled into the sofa, smoothing down the pleated skirt
I'd picked up at the market, hoping Della hadn't spotted it
as a cheap rip-off of the one she'd worn. I could hear chatter
in the hallway, but not a sound from upstairs. Della's children
were so quiet. So well behaved. And Mark was just as discreet
– to my barely acknowledged disappointment. Who could
blame him for keeping out of the way, though? I wouldn't
want a troupe of strangers invading my house once a week.
Especially not if it looked like this.

At the time I thought Della invited us into her home so she
could help us. It never occurred to me that perhaps what she
really wanted was witnesses. Younger women who could validate
the successful life she had curated for herself – who would envy
it, yearn for it, secretly put themselves at the heart of it. Now
I wonder if she *had* seen me outside her house. If so, it would
only have reinforced how much I wanted her life. And I did. I
couldn't deny it. If I had a house, a husband and children like
Della's, I remember thinking, I wouldn't let anyone else in.

The focus that evening was on career paths. As usual, we began
by reporting on our personal 'homework' assignments, before

engaging in an 'exercise' and finally 'mind-mapping' our next steps. Our homework had been to come up with a five-year career plan. Mine involved finding a well-paid admin job, earning as much as I possibly could, while writing in my free time – in an alternative universe where those jobs were available and I didn't spend every spare moment I had searching. But when it came to my turn, Della gave me just the slightest nod and passed on to Eva on my right. Della had said I didn't have to join in with the exercises, but I hadn't expected it to be so obvious. Jasmine looked at me sharply, and then at Della, her mouth opened as if to object, before thinking better of it.

When it came to mind-mapping our longer term goals, I'd only managed to scribble the words 'new job', 'creative writing' and 'find purpose' before Della crouched beside me, arms resting on my knees, to murmur her encouragement.

'Excellent, Kate. I wonder whether you could expand on that last point,' she said softly, circling the word purpose, 'break it down, really explore how you might achieve that aim. I'd be interested to hear more about your writing, too,' she added, as she straightened herself up. I saw Jasmine's head jerk towards me, her knees rising as she tried to shield her list, as though I might be trying to copy from it.

Jasmine was wearing a pleated skirt, too. Surely no coincidence, though I could hardly judge her for copying Della when I'd done the same. She looked up eagerly as Della knelt beside her. She was speaking softly, but I made out the words 'agent' and 'publisher' before Della stood up abruptly. She addressed the group as she sat back in her chair.

'The focus here is on ambition and direction. We're not having a how-to session for any particular industry, tempting though it may be.' There was a coldness to her tone that made me feel almost sorry for Jasmine, if she hadn't been shooting furious looks in my direction.

'That's the problem though, isn't it?' Eva tried to interject. 'We *need* mentors and support these days. I know with fashion, it's totally impossible to break in unless you know the right people, or you've got rich parents to support you while you skivvy around for free. It's different to when *you* were starting out. Things are harder now.' Eva tried to catch Jasmine's eye for support, but she was studying her nails.

'It's interesting to hear your thoughts, Eva, but I'm not sure your generation has it harder than any others.' Della's voice had an edge. 'And from what I remember you were making pretty good money as a model when we first met. I'm sure if you'd been focused enough, you could have used your connections there, rather than getting sidetracked into events.'

'Well, I . . . I never made that much money. I was always doing events work on the side. And anyway, I thought you were the one with contacts in the industry, that's what you said when—'

'It's always been a struggle starting out in a *creative* industry,' Della interrupted. 'That's why you need these techniques of self-esteem and self-inquiry in your toolkit – as well as integrity. If you're looking for a leg-up, I'm afraid you're in the wrong place.'

The room fell silent and Eva looked down at her notebook. I shifted uncomfortably in my seat. How had they met? And what had Della said to entice Eva along to these sessions? I was desperate to know how long the others had been coming and why, but I couldn't see how I was ever going to find out.

'What's your advice though, Della,' Helen asked, 'as someone who's got to where she wants to be? There must be some wisdom you can pass on to us . . .' Helen's smile wrinkled her nose and broke through the atmosphere a little.

'That's assuming I *am* where I want to be,' Della said, and a ripple of polite laughter passed around the room. Where else could she possibly want to be? 'But it's *you* who need to find those answers within yourselves. I can only be your guide.'

'What about your book?' Jane tried. 'I know *I* found that a real insight into how to get the best out of myself in auditions.' At this, Della's face softened, and she turned to a shelf beside her holding a small row of books in bright pink jackets, the same black lettering down each spine: *Be Your Own Life Coach*. I thought she might be about to hand them out. I'd considered buying one, but at £16 it was out of my price range.

'I'm so pleased to hear you say that, Jane.' Della held up a copy before resting it gently on the coffee table beside her. 'If you haven't already, I can certainly recommend reading the chapter on careers.' She turned to Eva. 'But ultimately, you have to be prepared to take risks, to take a leap into the unknown. You can't give yourself excuses about having it harder. *Nothing* is more important than achieving your dreams, but it takes a lot of work and, crucially, it takes self-knowledge.' She smiled approvingly in my direction and, without thinking, I smiled back.

It was noted by the others. I could tell by the way they clustered as soon as the session wound up, speaking in hushed voices. I saw Jasmine and Eva look over their shoulders at me as they gathered their bags and coats. I didn't even agree with Della. We did have it harder – we'd graduated into a recession. The only jobs around were temporary, and menial. But it was too late to say that now. Besides, Della had asked me to stay behind again. I watched helplessly as the four of them were ushered out, feeling more distant than ever.

I wasn't used to being envied. At school, Layla and I had stayed under the radar, out of the orbit of the kind of girls whose cliques made school headlines. Now here I was creating rifts, through no fault of my own.

'I wanted to talk to you,' Della said as she came into the living room, pulling the shutters across the bay window and straightening the yellow cushions that adorned both sofas, the only points of colour in a sea of creams and whites. 'You're making such wonderful progress, but I wonder whether you might do better with a solo session?'

'What do you mean?' I was still wondering how I might establish a bond with Helen and the others, find out more about the group, but I couldn't deny the glow of being singled out. The chosen one.

'You should keep coming to the group, of course,' Della said. 'And please don't mention this to anyone. But I think we should try some one-on-one meetings, to talk through anything you can't raise in front of the others.'

'Oh, I see . . .' I watched Della blow out the candles in turn with a sharp breath, smoke rising from each like a tiny signal. Were my problems clearly so much worse than anyone else's? Or was it that she saw more potential in me?

'You shut people out, I can see that.' Della sat opposite me, leaning forward. 'Maybe you've struggled to find someone to confide in – you've had to be strong for the people close to you? And now you don't want to show your weakness . . . even though you've been through so much. But you can't do this on your own. You need to let someone in.'

I looked at her, my eyes filling with tears, but Della seemed oblivious to the effect of her words. As so often, she had already switched into another mode – smoothing cushions down as she explained the practicalities of a solo session, the closer focus, the tailored targets – leaving me to catch up with the emotional impact of what she had just said.

'But, I really can't afford it,' I said, realising as I did that it was true. Della had already waived the group fees. Two free sessions a week would be too much to ask.

'Listen, you've done babysitting before, haven't you?' I nodded. 'Why don't you come round for an hour's coaching session at six on a Thursday, and afterwards you can look after the kids for the evening while Mark and I go out. You'd be doing us all a favour, really.'

'Well, I . . . Are you sure?' I couldn't deny the appeal of spending more time with Della, more time at their house, even if she and Mark weren't there. I'd barely even met the children, but they'd be in bed. And anyway, Della was already squeezing my shoulders as if it had all been arranged. I found myself guided out of the house, my coat and bag in my arms, with a firm plan for the following week.

'See you on Thursday then!' Della called, and I nodded, smiling into the warm evening air as I turned down the street. It all seemed so simple to Della, her enthusiasm was impossible to resist. And in any case, I had nothing to lose. Or so I thought then.

Chapter Six

It took just twenty minutes of our first one-to-one session for Della to get to the truth. We were enjoying the last of the spring sunshine in her neat city garden. Rows of crocuses and tulips framed a lawn so vibrant green it could almost have been fake, except that didn't seem Della's style. Mark and the kids were nowhere to be seen. I was sipping an elderflower cordial and wondering what my babysitting duties could possibly involve with such well-drilled children.

'I want you to feel you can confide in me,' Della was saying, leaning forward. She was softer with no one around. Less of a performer and more of a person.

I'd been watching some of her TV appearances online, on those breakfast shows where experts are needed to demystify the behaviour of minor celebrities. She was good on TV. Her extreme expressiveness found its natural home. It was impossible not to watch her face. I looked at her now, her pale hair loose and silky, while mine hung limp and flat. I had braved my first summer dress of the year, and my bare legs gleamed beneath the wrought-iron table. Della, by contrast, was tanned and moisturised, casually chic in cropped chinos and a plain white T-shirt. She sat with her elbows on the table and shoulders held back, as if to say: this is what I've got. Next to her I felt like a walking apology: this is all I've got.

'You can talk to me, even if you don't want to do it in front of the group,' she went on. I gave a little nod and looked down at my hands. I didn't want to cry. I've never dealt well with sympathy.

'My sister disappeared when I was ten,' I began, and then stopped. Mark had come into the garden and was standing by the bifold door, trying to get Della's attention.

'What is it?' Della said, the impatience clear in her voice.

'Sorry. The kids want to say goodnight.'

Della stood up with a sigh and disappeared into the house, leaving me alone in the dusk, feeling exposed. I was struck suddenly by the strangeness of the situation – sitting in this manicured garden, about to unburden myself to a glamorous older woman who would rather help me, a relative stranger, than put her own children to bed.

I was just beginning to give in to my doubt about the whole set-up when Della reappeared with a smile so full of warmth I was plunged back into the moment. It was flattering, to have her full attention, when she clearly had so many other demands. And I felt I owed her something: an explanation, a reason for being there. I needed to keep up my side of the bargain.

'I'm so sorry about that,' she said. 'Where were we?' She sat down. We were both waiting for me to begin.

I closed my eyes. I really didn't know if I could go through it all again.

'It was summer, in Eype.' I looked up at Della to see whether I needed to explain. Sometimes I felt Della already knew me so well I didn't need to bother her with the details, but why would she know the village we'd gone to every summer? 'In

Dorset. My parents worked at Cambridge University, so they got the summer off. We'd go for weeks and weeks.'

'Were they academics?' The question surprised me. I was expecting Della to be focused on the disappearance, but she clearly wanted to establish the background first.

'No,' I said, experiencing the usual twinge of shame. And then shame for the shame. 'Mum worked in the library, and Dad was a lab technician. They're retired now. Most of the other girls at school had parents who were lecturers, or professors, but . . .' I trailed off. I didn't want to remember that time. The jokes about Mum and Dad. About our house, on a sixties estate, rather than one of the tall terraces that line the nicer streets in Cambridge. About Scarlett, who hung around the gates of the boys' school, skirt hitched up and tie abandoned. No one ever laughed in front of Scarlett though. They wouldn't dare.

The static caravan in Dorset was part of the joke, the other girls giggling amongst themselves as they set off for their holidays in Greece and the South of France. They probably imagined some rusting old box on a grim caravan site. They couldn't possibly have known how beautiful it was. Not the caravan itself, which was rickety and seemed to lean to one side, so that Scarlett and I were forever rolling into each other in our too-small bed. But the endless skies, the waves washing over the pebbles below the clifftops, the long grass swaying in the bracing wind.

'Were you all there that summer?' Della prompted, making me aware that I'd fallen into silence.

'No, Scarlett didn't come that year. She was older,' I added, by way of explanation. 'Seventeen. She wanted to stay behind with her boyfriend.'

'Seven years. That's a big gap.'

'It became more obvious the older we got. Especially that

year.' Since she'd started sixth form college, Scarlett had lost interest in whether it was Jessie or Lucy who was my best friend that week. She stopped telling me what had happened at last night's party, or where her boyfriend Luke had taken her. I'd been longing for the summer, when I'd have her to myself – and we'd sit up, like the summer before, long after our parents had gone to bed, whispering while Scarlett smoked illicit cigarettes and sneaked swigs from their half-empty wine bottles.

'Did you feel betrayed by her, for not coming?' Della asked and I nodded, looking away. This wasn't what I'd thought life-coaching would involve. From what I'd read online, it was usually focused on the future – the kind of stuff we did in the group sessions. This felt more like therapy. But then, what did I know? Della was the one with training, qualifications. And I'd never met anyone so easy to talk to.

I didn't stop to wonder for a moment why she was so interested.

'Yeah, I suppose I did. My parents certainly weren't happy about it.' The shouting had gone on late into the night, while I hid under my Snoopy duvet, straining to make out what was being said. My parents had insisted they weren't going to leave their seventeen-year-old daughter at home alone with that druggie boyfriend. Dad had stormed up to bed, but Mum and Scarlett were still deep in discussion when I fell asleep. And when I woke up in the morning, it had been decided. Scarlett was allowed to stay. 'I did feel abandoned, I guess. We all tried to get on with the holiday, but it wasn't the same. And my parents got more and more worried as the days went by.'

They couldn't get through to Scarlett on the home phone. They'd heard from the neighbours about parties and a fight at the house. 'There was something going on with her boyfriend, Luke, but we didn't know what. We'd been there about two weeks, and my parents had gone up to the reception at the caravan park to try calling Scarlett . . .'

They'd left me, sitting at the folding table, distracting myself with an Enchanted Elsie picture. I'd written stories since I was little, about a young girl who discovers a magical fairyland in the lush green Dorset countryside, and I always illustrated them with a bright blue sea on the horizon.

When I think about that early evening, it's the particular quality of light I remember. Sometimes the sun will slant at an angle that takes me back, in an instant, to my ten-year-old self, sitting outside the caravan, feeling more alone than I ever had in my life, felt pen poised over my drawing pad as I watched my parents return and pack up the remnants of our summer, my childhood.

'They got through to one of the neighbours, heard there'd been no sign of her for days. So it was decided. We were going home.' I'd had a premonition as we drove away that evening, and I had been right. We never returned to Eype.

'What had happened to Scarlett?' Della had dropped her detached coaching pose and was leaning forward, chin in her hands. 'Did you ever find out?'

I shook my head. 'She'd just gone. When we got home, we found clothes and money missing, but no note. Luke said they'd had a fight. He hadn't seen her for days.' I could still remember the shouting, Dad's voice tight and high; Luke staring at his feet. He'd been twenty then, not that much older than Scarlett, though he seemed it at the time.

'All Mum did was cry. Sometimes she'd drink too much and stay up late, raging at Dad. They'd go off at weekends, looking for Scarlett, leaving me with my Aunt Christine. And then, after a while, they seemed to give up. They stopped talking about her at all.'

53

I rubbed my throat, self-conscious. 'I stopped speaking, too, I suppose. My big sister left us and so I left too, in my own way. I missed her so much. I still do.' I didn't feel I'd ever returned to full volume, really.

'So, Scarlett never came back?'

'No – and no one knew anything, or would admit to it. We found out the drugs had been worse than we thought, there was debt, she'd fallen out with friends, she wasn't doing well at school. But it was all stuff that could have been dealt with, if only we'd known where to find her.' I stopped. I didn't want to give voice to our darkest fears, the ones we didn't even dare say to each other. That the drugs had won out. That Scarlett might not be out there to find any more. 'The police gave up pretty quickly. She was seventeen, so she was legally allowed to leave home. But my parents couldn't move on. And they made sure I didn't either.' My smile felt tight, twisted. I was trying not to let the bitterness show. But Della just nodded, no sign of judgement in her steady gaze.

'Go on,' she said.

'Well, you know . . . Scarlett was always the pretty one, the popular one, the one who sailed through her exams, even though she didn't try. After she left, I felt like I had to make my parents proud enough for both of us.' I looked away, blinking, trying to speak past the lump in my throat. 'But whatever I did, it was never enough. They made it clear they'd find Scarlett one day, or she'd find them. And in the meantime, I wasn't going anywhere. I'd stay at home day and night. Proof that it's possible to know where at least one of your children is at all times.'

Della squeezed my hand. She didn't offer any of the usual responses – *I don't know how you've coped*, or *I can't imagine* – with their unspoken subtext: *It would never happen to me. I don't have that kind of family*. She just allowed me

54

to talk, nudging me on with a tilt of the head, an understanding nod.

'I did get away, for a while, to university in Nottingham. I
got the English degree we all knew Scarlett would have breezed
through . . . But afterwards it was straight back home to a
job in the university library, with Mum. No hanging about
in Nottingham, working behind bars with my mates. No
heading to London to do unpaid internships like the other
girls from school. Never mind that I'd always wanted to write
. . .' I broke off. Even after everything I'd revealed already,
that felt like one confidence too many. The hours spent in my
room, scribbling across page after page of those green note-
books Dad bought me. And then later, typing into the night,
stories that I'd send off to magazines, competitions. The
humiliation and shame at all that wasted time.

Even once I gave up submitting stories and instead began
applying for work placements, it was a little more obvious,
with each rejection letter, how ridiculously naive I'd been.
And when it became clear that Dad would need to retire early,
that it was money we needed, I resigned myself to working
my way up at the library.

'I ended up scanning and stapling, living at home, going
out with Dan from Dad's department.' My voice was barely
a whisper now, thinking back to those days. 'And that's when
I heard about the sighting.'

'What sighting? Of Scarlett do you mean?' Della sat up,
looking almost excited.

'Yes, someone I used to know got in touch to say she
thought she'd seen her, working behind a stall in Camden. So
obviously, I had to look. I came up a few times, but there
was no sign of her . . .'

'So now you've moved here to find her?'

'Yes. I didn't tell my parents though. I couldn't get their

hopes up like that. They think I'm here to earn more money – and I am here for that, too. But I think it was the jolt I needed, really. I'd been coasting along at home, at work, with Dan . . . Suddenly I realised there was a whole other world out there. And that Scarlett might be in it.'

'So if you find her, what will you do?'

'If I find her . . . then I'll finally be free.' I knew it sounded a bit much, but it was how I felt. 'My parents would be so happy, so relieved, they'd barely have time to think about me. I could be the one to leave. Not for good – but I'd be able to live my own life at last.'

Della squeezed my hand across the table. 'You poor thing. No wonder you've been keeping quiet in front of everyone.' She glanced away, tucking a strand of hair behind her ear, lost in thought, and then she seemed to gather herself.

'Now, you know this already, but it's time to make a plan for the future. To put yourself first. Make your own decisions. Tell your parents how you really feel.'

I nodded, believing in that moment that I did already know it, and that it might all be possible. It was part of Della's gift, I see now, to convince you that her suggestion had been your idea all along. And to reflect a part of herself back on you, so that I felt a little more confident every time I was in her presence. I saw myself, through her eyes, as someone with agency, potential, a future.

Della was the only person in London who knew why I was really there. At the time it felt like a relief, to have unburdened myself. I didn't stop to think about the power I'd handed to her.

Chapter Seven

Mum and Dad both met me at the bus station, meaning I had to sit in the back of their Fiat like a child being collected from a school trip. The small talk they struck up almost immediately – London transport, extortionate rents – only reinforced that impression. In their minds, I was just having a few months away, and then everything would return to normal.

'Good to get it out of your system,' Mum said in that strained voice as she craned her neck to where I was sitting, strapped in the seat behind Dad, like I had been my whole life. Scarlett always sat behind Mum; more room for her longer legs. Even after she'd gone, we'd stayed in our positions.

'I've always said, London's a great place for a little bit of fun, let your hair down, but you wouldn't want to live there forever, would you?' Dad said, while Mum gave her head a vigorous shake and I tried to picture him letting what was left of his hair down, anywhere.

'It's actually a lot friendlier than I was expecting,' I said, watching the familiar scenes of my childhood speed by the window – the McDonald's where Layla and I hung out on Saturdays as teenagers, the riverbank where we'd cycled as kids. It wasn't true. London felt no more like home than it had when I'd arrived four months earlier. But for the first time in my life, this didn't feel like home, either. I was trapped between two places that felt alien. Or I was the alien. I'd floated free, and I was looking down on the world I used to inhabit.

'I shouldn't think you've had much time for making friends though, have you?' Dad asked. 'What with work and everything.' I felt a pang of guilt about the secret I was keeping from them, all the hours spent searching, the spectre of Scarlett hanging over us like it always did.

'Well, I've made a few – girls, mostly my age, we get together once a week . . .' I said, and then added, 'or so.' I didn't want it to sound weird.

That seemed to be enough for them, and Dad moved on to the crossword clues he'd got stuck on that morning. As we waited at the traffic lights, he turned with an arched eyebrow to tell me that Mum's latest jigsaw was the Battle of the Somme. Her obsession with epic puzzles was a running joke between us. Something for her to focus on, a small controllable world that no one else ever dared interfere with. But I could barely raise a smile after the long coach journey, the waiting around, the crawling forward in Saturday traffic. It was my first visit home since the move, to celebrate Dad's birthday, and I knew I should be making an effort. But I felt suddenly exhausted. We fell into silence, Mum patting down her grey bob, smoothing the loose hairs the way I know I do when I'm anxious. The top of her head only just reached over the headrest, and I watched as she sank lower still.

'So when are you planning on coming home?' Mum asked, as if my departure was only temporary.

'I don't know, Mum. Can we talk about it later?'

'We want to make sure you're OK,' Dad was saying, as we pulled into the small driveway in front of their bungalow. 'You never say much . . . when we call.' They knew how much I hated talking to them on speakerphone, but they insisted on it. I couldn't remember if it had always been that way, but since Scarlett left, they couldn't even have a phone conversation separately.

Dad extended his tall frame out of the car, his tremor more obvious as he fumbled for his keys. His earlobes seemed to hang forward in a way I didn't remember, the folds of his face falling with them. He was turning sixty-five. When had he got so old?

'Let's get in, get the kettle on. We can work it all out later,' Mum said, finding her own set and opening the door, that old smell hitting me, of pine furniture polish and stale Digestives and something stewing on the hob. 'I've put clean towels and sheets in your room. There's a lasagne in the oven.'

I swallowed hard and dug my nails into my palms. Mum didn't respond well to outbreaks of emotion. But the thought of her hunting out that seventies cookbook, buying in the ingredients when she could hardly bring herself to boil an egg most days, was enough to break down my resolve. I was determined not to get sucked back into this house – and yet, the familiar net-curtained darkness, the small picture window, the Scottish landscape watercolours, all conspired to make me feel weak with homesickness.

'Thanks, Mum, I can't wait,' I said, even though lasagne hadn't been my favourite since I was ten years old.

I spent a few moments in my room, gathering myself, taking in the faded origami birds Scarlett and I had made all those years ago and strung from the ceiling, the chipped paint I

59

chose at fourteen, the Snoopy pillowcase Mum still put on my bed. I'd spent so much more time living there than anywhere else, most of my life, in fact. Yet already it seemed smaller, the ceilings lower, the textured walls coming in on me.

I poked my head around the door of Scarlett's room. It was just as it had been the last time I was home. No one went in there now, except Mum, to dust. The ancient boyband posters, heart-shaped mirror, rows of picture frames, all exactly where they had been. Mum had moved all the photos we had of Scarlett into this room in the early days after her disappearance. She couldn't bear to look at them every day, she'd said. So here were all our family memories, lined up behind a closed door on Scarlett's old writing desk – the caravan in Eype, a dark, out-of-focus shot of the Christmas table, Mum's birthday meal in that cheap Chinese down the road.

I didn't go in. I never did. It was as though it might break something within me, to find myself so close to her. Instead I looked at the pictures from a distance, the fixed smiles, the arms on shoulders, the closest our family ever got to affection.

It was only as I was turning to leave that I noticed on Scarlett's desk a book I was sure I recognised. Inching a little closer, I saw that I was right. The same pink spine and black lettering. *Be Your Own Life Coach*. It was Della's book.

I felt a jolt in my stomach. Everything around me swam in and out of focus. What was that doing here? This object from my new life invading my old. It didn't make any sense. I hadn't even mentioned Della to Mum. Had she happened to pick it up from the library? Or seen it in the supermarket and been intrigued? That was too much of a coincidence, surely. And if she had bought it to read, why had she left it in here?

I backed out of the room without touching the book, as

60

though by leaving it undisturbed I might be able to ignore it. I almost didn't want to ask Mum where she'd got it. What if she'd been spying on me? And if it was just a random purchase, which was the most likely explanation, then I couldn't start throwing accusations around. Mum was desperate for an excuse to get me back home. Any slightly odd behaviour on my part would put her on high alert.

'Kate?' I walked slowly into the living room, still thinking about how to broach the subject. 'Have a cup of tea.' Mum was sitting next to Dad on the leather sofa, a small shop-bought carrot cake on the coffee table in front of them with a single candle in it. I couldn't bring up the book now.

I sat on the armchair next to them, Mum and I singing a half-hearted rendition of 'Happy Birthday' while Dad attempted to blow out his candle. Since Scarlett had gone, celebrations had become something to be endured. Day-to-day we could carry on almost as normal after all this time, but gathered awkwardly together, her absence seemed to take on a solid dimension. I could almost picture her between us, as she was, singing in that high-pitched tone, swiping the icing carrot from the top of the cake, making us all laugh.

I watched Mum pour the tea, carefully. Though her face was drawn and hair a wispy silver, she hardly looked any different to how I remembered her in my childhood – the same bob and sensible trousers. It was Dad who had changed. His white hair grew in tufts now, and his face looked tired, lined. I listened as his cup rattled in his saucer. Why didn't Mum use mugs now that he was getting so much worse? Watching him struggle to still his hand made me want to hurl the cup across the room and throw my arms around him.

'By the way, Dan's going to pop round in a bit.' Mum was trying to sound casual, but I heard her voice catch.

'What?' I put my plate down and stood up. 'Why is Dan coming *here*? How does he even know I'm back?'

'Dan knew it was my birthday, he asked if you were coming. What did you expect me to say?' Dad asked, his slur more obvious in his anxiety.

'He still calls sometimes,' Mum said, 'to see how your dad's doing.'

I paced to the conservatory doors and looked out. At one time I would have gone along with it, talked to Dan for their sake. But I thought about what Della had said. It was time to put myself first. 'You'll have to call him and tell him not to come,' I said in a low voice. 'I don't want to see him.'

'But he misses you,' Mum said. 'He's got some things to return to you. It all happened so quickly . . . I mean, Dan was good for you. He helped you through everything, when we were so worried about you. You'd barely recovered. And even if you wanted to go to London, it didn't mean you had to end everything with him.' I listened as her voice rose, pleading on Dan's behalf, and in my fury, an image came to my mind of his thick arms resting on my chair, his dark head bent, talking to my parents about how he could win me back. The three of them plotting over how to lure me to Cambridge, to the life they had determined for me.

'I went to London to get a better-paid job, you know that,' I snapped at Mum. 'To help you both, for when Dad needs more care—'

'We told you, you don't need to take all that on your shoulders,' Dad interrupted. But we all knew Mum wasn't going to be able to pay for extra help with his Parkinson's on her library salary. The well-paid admin jobs were in London.

'And anyway, that hasn't exactly worked, has it?' Mum said. 'Why don't you come home? I'm sure the library would take you back. I could put in a good word.'

'The café's a stopgap, while I find something else,' I said. And find your other daughter, I wanted to say, but I stopped myself throwing that at them. 'Look, I didn't realise that's what this was.' I headed for the door. 'I thought I was coming here to see you. A visit. I didn't know you were going to stage some kind of intervention.'

I slammed my bedroom door, breathless, as though re-enacting a scene from my teenage years. Except that this time I'd spoken up for myself for once. I'd seen the shock on my parents' faces. Saw Mum head for the landline to call Dan and warn him away. I'd changed since I'd moved to London. I'd entered another world, full of ambition, success, freedom. I wasn't the girl they could keep in her place any more.

As I lay on my childhood bed my phone pinged. It was a text, from Della: *Could you possibly watch the kids tomorrow evening, from 6pm? Something's come up at the last minute and we're in a fix. I can pay! Let me know. Dx*

My heart rate picked up. It would mean leaving early, my parents would be disappointed. But it was almost as though Della had sensed I needed rescuing. She must have forgotten I was at home this weekend, though I'd mentioned it when we'd talked a few days earlier. And now she had offered me an escape – from these dark rooms, the creeping despair. And I'd done my bit, hadn't I? My parents had seen I was OK. Suddenly I couldn't wait to get back to Della's house, so full of light and life.

I heard the click of the kettle in the kitchen and considered going in, asking Mum about Della's book and where it had come from. But I didn't want a confrontation, especially when I'd have to tell them I was getting an earlier coach to London. I made a mental note to bring it up with her another time, when things were less fraught. I couldn't have known that by then it would be too late.

Chapter Eight

'Are you our new nanny?' Tabitha broke me off halfway through the Enchanted Elsie story I was telling them, complete with hand puppets and musical accompaniment from Jasper on the tambourine. 'We do need a new nanny, you know.'

I couldn't help but laugh, faced with her furrowed brow. Tabitha was six going on sixteen, or maybe even twenty-six. She seemed to carry the weight of responsibility for herself and Jasper very heavily.

'Why are you laughing? I mean it.' She pouted, shuffling away from where we were all sitting, cross-legged on the deep cream carpet of Della's house, surrounded by strings of pink and blue bunting and fairy lights. Even the children's bedroom was tastefully done, with its pale pastels and neatly arranged boxes of toys. I moved to crouch beside her, smoothing her white-blond hair.

'I'm not your nanny, no,' I said, gently. It was only the second time I'd looked after the children, and from what I could gather, Della had given them no indication of how long I might be around, not that Jasper seemed to mind. He was shaking a maraca around his head now with a gleeful abandon I hadn't yet witnessed in Della's presence.

'Our last nanny left us. They're always leaving us,' Tabitha said, sleepy now, allowing me to guide her towards her bed.

'Well, I'm sure you'll find another one very soon. It's time for bed. Come on, Jasper, jump in.' I lifted the pirate duvet and he took a running leap between the covers with a joyful shout. 'Aarrgh, me hearties!'

'I didn't mean actually *jump*,' I said, laughing as Tabitha giggled from the other bed. I hadn't expected the children to be such good company. Tucking them in and smoothing down their covers I felt strangely maternal, acting out a scene I couldn't really remember from my own childhood. Perhaps I wouldn't make a bad mum after all. Maybe it was just that my own mum hadn't shown me how to be natural around children. She'd barely even responded when I'd announced I was leaving early for London. Dad's disappointment had been clear in the downturned corners of his mouth, the feeble hug he'd enveloped me in, that had almost changed my mind. But Mum only nodded, her lips tight, giving me a brief pat on the shoulder as I tried to embrace her. She'd locked down her emotions all those years ago.

So much of my early life had been shaped by Scarlett's disappearance, it was only now that I was learning how to be child-like again. Spending time with Tabitha and Jasper was like dusting off a part of me that had been packed away years ago, discovering that it had been hiding there all along – my capacity for fun, helpless laughter, silliness. I hadn't thought about my Enchanted Elsie stories for years, not since Scarlett and I stopped telling them to each other, when she grew out of it, but it turned out they were still there, under the surface, just waiting for the right audience.

'I hope you are our new nanny,' Tabitha said, looking up at me from under her fairy print duvet, hair splayed across the pillow. 'You could come and live with us. They sometimes do.' She looked towards the door across the hall from theirs, at the room Della had gestured to earlier, before they'd gone out. 'If we're home late, you could always crash in the guest room,' Della had said, with a conspiratorial smile, as though we both knew that would be my preferred option. 'The bed's made up, it'd be no trouble.' I'd brushed it off then, said I was sure I could get myself home. Mark and Della were only going for an 'impromptu kitchen supper' locally, casual in chinos and a shirt dress, like a couple from a holiday advert. I had watched them from the top of the stairs as they let themselves out of the wide stained-glass door and walked down the brick pathway hand-in-hand, feeling a sharp pang. Jealousy maybe, or regret.

Now, tiptoeing out of the children's room, their eyes half-closing as a lullaby played on Jasper's monitor, I poked my head around the door of the guest bedroom. It was a neat room, facing the street, as Tabitha and Jasper's did. Neutrally decorated in pale green with a mahogany desk, antique rocking chair and a large double bed, topped with a white, fluffy duvet. I imagined sinking into it, spreading out as I never could on my single mattress. No clanking pipes or revving cars outside. No lingering smell of mould – only fresh laundry and, in the morning, coffee and home-baked bread. I thought of the breakfast scene I had witnessed so longingly from the outside just a few weeks earlier. Now I had been invited in. So what had made me hesitate? I couldn't quite identify it. An anxiety, perhaps, still hovering out of reach.

Who were these other nannies, I wondered as I crept downstairs and made a cup of tea, sitting awkwardly on the sofa as though being watched, even though the house was empty, quiet. I switched the large flat-screen TV on low. Had Della invited members of the group to babysit before? Had they stayed over – even moved in? Was that how she found her help?

It seemed unlikely. Surely there were agencies for that kind of thing. And you'd need references, training. Not that I wanted to be a nanny. I was only helping Della and Mark, in return for all the guidance and support Della had been giving me, the many hours she was dedicating to talking about my past, my family, where I'd come from. She even wanted to know about my parents, when they'd met, whether they'd been married before, had other children. It all seemed to feed into the picture she was building, to explain what had made me the way I am.

I flicked through channels aimlessly, my eyes drawn towards the photographs on the mantelpiece, and the tall bookcases built into the alcoves either side, always slightly too far away during group sessions to make out the titles. What exactly were Della's qualifications?

I stood up and moved over to the shelves, looking for any signs of her training, her professional background. There were rows of self-help books and some psychology titles I recognised from the library in Cambridge: *How to Make Friends and Influence People, Feel the Fear and Do It Anyway*. There was a shelf below which seemed likely to be Mark's, holding the only fiction – Thomas Pynchon, Saul Bellow, Faulkner – and various books on finance. There were pink and white photo albums, *My First Baby* books, CDs of chill-out tunes and mindfulness meditations.

A car door slammed outside and I sprang back. What if Della and Mark came home early and found me rifling through their things? I stood still, listening as two voices got louder, and then quieter. The heels clacked past and down the street. It wasn't them.

I moved towards the sofa and picked up the remote control.

I was about to change channels again when I spotted on the lower shelves, behind the armchair, a book I recognised instantly, intimately, the sight of it making my stomach turn over.

It was *The Little Prince*. Scarlett's childhood favourite. And going over to the shelf, pushing aside the chair, sinking to my knees on the carpet, I saw that this copy was equally dogeared. Scarlett had never read much, beyond magazines and Sweet Valley Highs, not like me. But this had been one book that had seen her through her childhood – read to us by Dad, at her request, though I had been too young to understand it really – and then her teenage years. She kept it on the shelf by her bed, in the days when we'd shared a room, and I could still remember falling asleep to the rustle of its pages, waking in the morning to see the familiar picture lying on the floor, discarded, the line drawing of a little boy surrounded by stars, alone in the sky.

She'd stopped reading it as we got older, but seeing it now returned me to those warm nights of early childhood, the comfort of knowing my older sister was awake by my side as I drifted off. I'd looked for it once, after Scarlett had gone, hoping to find reassurance, maybe even understanding. It wasn't a book I'd ever been drawn to. I preferred long sagas of girlhood – Alice, Anne, Katy, Jo and Beth – and later, the classics, or mysteries. But I hadn't been able to find it anywhere. She must have taken it with her. Now here was another copy, just as well loved, hidden away on a low shelf in Della's house.

I shuffled closer on my knees and tried to pull it out, but it was wedged in and as I released it, another book fell with it. It was of a similar type to the self-help Della published, though it looked more dated, less designed. On the back was a picture of a woman. Younger, darker, but very clearly Della.

68

I picked it up and read the front cover. *You, But Better* by Adele Walker. I flipped to the picture. She was less obviously groomed, posing awkwardly with her hands on her hips. If anything, she was more familiar, with brown hair. Her clothes looked cheaper – a garish orange blouse and pink jacket, almost neon. It made me warm to her even more, seeing this vulnerable early incarnation.

Inside the book were chapter headings like 'The Man You Need', 'The Family Plan', 'Your Career Your Way'. I scanned the author's note. This Adele Walker was a journalist for women's magazines. She grew up in Somerset and lived alone in North London. This must have been before Mark and the kids, though it had only been published eight years earlier. No mention of therapy or life-coaching qualifications, but perhaps all that had come after, too. She must have married Mark, retrained and rebranded herself under a shorter version of her name. And she'd managed to have two children along the way. Della had clearly taken her own advice, and fast.

I heard a bang. Upstairs, or next door? Hard to tell. I stood quietly, listening, the book in my hand. I was desperate to read more about this other side of Della, to study the photos. I'd always assumed, with her clear tone and casual confidence, that Della came from money – some country pile in Sussex, or a Thames-view London mansion. Not the West Country. She didn't have a trace of an accent, and she'd never once mentioned her family. But then, she didn't talk about herself much, beyond her work. It was only coming away from an encounter with Della that you realised how much you'd given away, without receiving a single confidence in return.

My fingers itched to open the book, but how would I explain myself if one of the children appeared at the door? I waited a while longer and then, when I was satisfied there was no more movement in the house, I sank to my knees and began flicking through the pages, quickly, intently – as if looking for clues. It was straight-forward self-help, though. Nothing personal, no anecdotes. No mention of a professional background. No more hints about Della's past.

I was there on the floor, scanning a section on personal branding, when a key turned in the front door. There had been no warning: no creak of the gate, no footsteps approaching the house.

I fumbled with the book, dropping it in my panic. The door banged open. 'Hello?' It was Mark. I pushed both books quickly back onto the shelf, but I was still on my knees by the armchair when he walked in.

'Hello. What are you doing down there?' He smiled, but his eyes scanned the room in confusion.

'Oh, I'm sorry.' I rubbed the carpet with my sleeve, my heart pounding. 'I spilled some tea. I was trying to clean it up before you saw it.'

'Or Della, more like.' Mark laughed, and walked over to where I was crouched. 'I can't see anything. I'm sure the cleaner will get it up. Don't worry about it.' He put out an arm and helped me up. As I stood, I glanced at the shelf, making sure everything was in place.

'I'm really sorry,' I said again, trying to calm myself, adjusting my denim skirt.

'Honestly, it's nothing. Anyway, we both have a secret now.' I watched, unsettled, as Mark walked over to a tall cabinet in the corner and poured whisky into two glasses. 'Drink?' He handed one to me and I sipped it obediently, not even thinking. The spirit burned my throat.

'That dinner was excruciating. I couldn't stand another minute. So I pretended I'd missed a call from you, saying Jasper was upset and I had to come home.' He grinned. 'You don't mind, do you?'

I didn't know what to say. I laughed, feeling uncomfortable, complicit somehow. I put my glass down on the table, next to the mug. 'Really? Couldn't you have told them you'd had enough?'

'Oh come on. Surely you know Della better than that by now?' Mark was swaying slightly. 'So, if she asks, just say Jasper was crying. OK? He'd never remember.'

I nodded as Mark sank his whisky. The ease of his deception put me on edge. Then again, I could talk. What had I been trying to cover up as he walked in?

'Another one?'

I watched as Mark refilled his glass. I'd never seen him without the children around. He was an entirely different presence off duty – relaxed, flirtatious even. But there was an edge to him. Why had he lied?

I shook my head. 'No thanks, I'd better be heading off,' I said, remembering too late about Della's offer of a bed. It was tempting, the thought of slipping between those clean sheets, a few metres from where Della and Mark were sleeping. Taking on the status of overnight guest, rather than just a babysitter. But I didn't want Della to come home and find me here, drinking with Mark. What would she think?

I stood up and moved quickly over to the shelf, pushing the books into alignment. Mark turned around and looked at me with a glint in his eye.

'What are you up to?' he asked, as if ready to be let in on the joke.

'My tea.' I picked up the mug along with my barely touched whisky. I didn't want Della to find that. 'I'll put these in the sink on my way out.'

I could feel Mark's eyes on me as I returned from the kitchen. 'Thanks, Kate,' he said, quietly.

'Oh it's fine. The kids are no bother.' Why was I blushing?

71

'No, I mean thanks, for everything.' Mark was standing by the mantelpiece, next to the portraits. He was recognisable as the handsome, family man, his hands placed protectively on Della's shoulders. But there was something different in his manner tonight – unruly almost. He held my eye, as though daring me to look away first.

'It means a lot to Della, you coming round. She's happier than I've seen her in a while. She needs a project. It helps her, what with all the, you know . . .' Mark tailed off. I didn't know. But I wasn't sure how to ask, and Mark was already moving towards the door. 'We all like having you around,' he said, his hand on my lower back as he saw me out. He'd taken off his shoes and there was something endearing about his bare feet, shirt unbuttoned, sleeves rolled up. He seemed more approachable, almost within reach, and it was hard to ignore the pull I felt towards him, towards staying in his company. But I couldn't risk Della finding us together.

'Look after yourself, Kate,' he said softly as I left and I thought I heard a note of something in his voice – regret, or maybe concern. I couldn't make out his expression in the darkness.

After the door closed I lingered on the path, watching his tall frame silhouetted behind the half-closed shutters as he crossed the room and downed another drink. And then I turned, pulling my jacket around me with a shiver and walking down the road, feeling as though I'd cleared a level in a game I didn't even know I was playing.

Chapter Nine

'Don't you think it's weird, though?' Helen tore apart a piece of pitta. We had arranged to meet in a Greek restaurant in Hampstead village, near where she lived with her family, and well away from Della's stomping ground.

'Weird how?' I had to raise my voice to be heard over the folk music and high-pitched chatter. We were sharing a mixed meze and a bottle of house white, and Helen topped me up, even though I was trying to slow down, unsure how I was going to pay my share of the bill when it came.

'You know, that Della's got this group together and she holds court, in her own house. And we're not even allowed to talk to each other.' She looked at me, eyebrows raised, waiting for my response. But I was already regretting having given Helen my number, let alone agreeing to an illicit meeting. I was only here because I had questions I wanted answers to.

'Then why do you come?' I asked. 'Surely it's not to find out how to meet men? Wouldn't you be better off going on Tinder or something?'

'Oh, I know. I do that too. It's not that I can't meet men, it's just that I don't meet the right ones.' Helen looked around,

73

as though the right one might be lurking at the other end of the bar. She'd certainly dressed for that eventuality, in a tight sparkly top and heavy eye make-up. I'd been relieved when we were seated in a dark corner, surrounded by wall-hangings and ornate pots – at least no one could make out how under-dressed I was by comparison, in my frayed jeans and striped T-shirt. 'Anyway, that's not the only reason I come,' Helen said, reaching for the hummus. 'I'm like you, I suppose, I want more confidence, some direction. I want a bit of Della to rub off on me. Don't we all?'

I smiled, though I didn't like the suggestion that my motivations were so easy to read. And I didn't particularly want to be lumped in with all the others. My relationship with Della was already so different to theirs, surely Helen could see that.

'How long have you been having the coaching?' I asked, trying another tack.

'Oh, six months or something. Not that long. I wasn't really sure when Della first invited me. It all sounded a bit woo-woo. But she's pretty persuasive, isn't she?' She smiled indulgently, like we were both in on a secret, though I didn't know what it was.

'You were invited?' For some reason I'd assumed the others had found the group themselves. That I'd been one of the few, perhaps the only one, to have been picked out from the crowd.

'Yeah, she's a friend of my mum's. An associate, really. Mum works in TV. She books Della on her show sometimes. They got chatting and Della convinced Mum that a few sessions might be good for me. How did you find out about it then?'

'Well I . . . bumped into Della, really.'

'What, out of the blue?' I nodded and Helen studied my face for a moment. 'Yeah, well, I guess we've all got our reasons. Della must be able to tell somehow, you know, that we need encouragement, or motivation.'

74

'Were the others invited too, then?'

Helen shrugged. 'I think Eva knew someone who knew Della. Maybe Jane, too, through her acting. And Jasmine went to a talk Della gave – that's how she met her. She's been at the group the longest I think.' She didn't look particularly interested as she recounted this, but I was hanging on her every word.

'But wouldn't it be easier to advertise, to wait for people to come to you?' I asked, thinking aloud.

'I suppose it's more *bespoke* than that. She can't have any old person wandering into her house, can she?' Helen waved at the waiter for more wine.

'I guess so, but it's not like she *knew* any of us. I don't think I'd let a lot of strangers come and sit in my living room once a week.' I was still trying to piece it together. 'And does she sometimes invite people to stay, you know, as like a nanny or something?' I'd barely eaten since I'd been swimming earlier. I needed to stop drinking or I'd give myself away.

Helen shrugged. 'Dunno,' she said. 'It's all a bit odd though, isn't it. I mean, there we all are pouring out our woes, and she's getting a nice fat pay cheque. There's the three-storey mansion in Crouch End, plus have you seen that house she's got in France?'

I shook my head. 'What house?'

'You know, in that picture in her living room. They call it "The Pines" or something. They go out there for the whole summer every year. Sounds amazing. Anyway, she's got all this stuff, and all this money, and what are we getting out of it, really?'

'She's making us believe in ourselves, helping us move on with our lives . . .' I thought about the pictures. The people on the lawn. The swimming pool. So Della owned that house? 'And Mark's a banker. It's not all paid for by the money we give her.'

'Hmm. I just don't know how much I trust her. Mum says nobody at work knows where she came from.' Helen paused dramatically. I put down my wine glass to steady my hand. 'Apparently she arrived at the studio one day and no one could remember who'd booked her, or knew what her qualifications were. But she was good on TV, so they kept getting her in. And she is charming when she wants to be. But she's got us hanging off her every word. And sometimes I wonder what we're all doing there. Don't you?'

'No,' I said, draining my glass. I didn't want to hear any more. 'I was a bit of a mess when I met her, to be honest. And I already feel better, more sure of myself.'

'I guess so.' Helen looked unconvinced. 'Oh well, Mum's paying. I couldn't afford it with what I earn as a receptionist. And she covers my cab fare – she says it's worth it for the confidence I'm gaining.'

I nodded, as though I was perfectly used to mums who concerned themselves with their daughters' confidence levels, who splashed out on expensive coaching and unnecessary cabs. It was such an unfamiliar world to me, this affluent existence on the edges of London. The security, the certainty it bred.

'But how can *you* afford it, you don't even live at home, do you?' Helen asked. I shrugged, trying to push aside the question of my finances. I didn't want her to know I wasn't paying.

'Oh I don't know. But it seems worth it. It's only since I started coming that I've realised how lost I felt before, you know?' I looked at Helen, to see whether she might be someone I could confide in, but I could see she wasn't interested. She was only in it for the gossip.

'What about Jasmine? Why's she taken against you? And Eva the other day – what was that all about? Do you think they get together outside meetings?' I watched Helen pause for a gulp of wine and thought of all the questions I'd been longing to ask – about Della's qualifications, the other nannies. I couldn't trust her, I could see that now. It was time to call it a night.

'No idea,' I said, looking around for the waiter. Della was much more important to me than Helen or Jasmine or any of them. What was I doing stirring things up, when she'd been so kind, so trusting? When she'd invited me into her home?

I searched in my bag and pulled out my last twenty. It was all I had until payday, but Helen took it without pause and added one from the stash in her wallet. 'I don't know how long I'll keep coming to the group,' she said, after the waiter had taken our money. 'There's something off about it that I can't put my finger on. What was it Jasmine said about that girl, the one who stopped coming suddenly? Claire, wasn't it – I mean, what happened to her? And we're not even meant to be meeting up . . . I just think we should be careful, Kate.' Helen held my eye, but I looked away, fumbling for my Oyster card.

On the bus home, I thought about what Helen had said. Of course I was going to be careful. I didn't want to risk Della finding out that we'd met up in secret any more than she did. I deleted Helen's number from my phone and then sat back, watching the tower blocks and tatty shop fronts roll slowly by. Helen was right: no more meetings outside the group.

It wasn't until much later I realised that wasn't what she'd meant at all. She was trying to warn me about something else altogether. But by the time I figured that out, and tried to track down the Janes, every single one of them had disappeared.

Chapter Ten

'After university, when you got back to Cambridge, something happened, didn't it?' Della was sitting forward, her elbows resting on the wrought-iron garden table, a pale scarf draped around her bare shoulders. Her approach was more direct this evening, as though she was trying to get something out of me. And I was twitchy, defensive – sure she could read on my face exactly how I'd betrayed her with Helen.

'Well I . . . I think it all caught up with me. Scarlett's disappearance, the reality that she wasn't coming home . . .'

'A lot of people have a rough patch after university.'

'Yes, but it was more than that.' I paused, trying to return myself to that desperate moment, a shudder going through me involuntarily. 'I think, I'd been so focused on getting away, getting a degree, doing what Scarlett would have done . . . And then after that, I didn't know what came next. I thought she'd come back.' My voice broke and I wiped a tear away, feeling angry with myself. But Della stilled my hand with hers and nodded me on. 'And when she didn't, I didn't know what to do. Scarlett had always encouraged my writing, even helped me with my stories, but without her I didn't have any confidence. And then I got all these rejections. It got too much.'

'And your parents?'

'They wanted me to stay at home, get a job, get on with life. Even though they were barely living themselves. How could they really, when we didn't know what had happened to Scarlett, whether she was even . . .' I couldn't say it out loud. 'And then everything began to unravel. I couldn't hold it all together any more. And Mum and Dad couldn't cope so I went to . . . had a short stay . . .'

'Hospital?' Della asked gently. 'You had a breakdown.'

I nodded. Trying to focus on that time was like looking through a fogged-up window. I could make out shapes, atmospheres, but nothing distinct. 'I felt so lost, so abandoned. I thought, surely, if she was still alive, if she hadn't wrecked her life through drugs, she'd come back for me . . .' I held my breath. If I started crying, I didn't know whether I could stop.

'And now that you've come to London, now you feel you've actually got a chance of finding her, that's stirred it all up again, hasn't it?' I nodded. How could Della tell? At every turn, she seemed to know what I was going to say before I could put it into words.

'Yes, and also I'm under so much pressure. I need to earn more money. To help my parents.'

'And you're going to be able to do that at the café?'

'Well, no, that's to pay my rent. That friend from school, Amy, the one who saw Scarlett in Camden – she sent me the link to the job in the café. And then I found the house-share. The idea was that, once I was here, I'd be able to apply for better-paid jobs – receptionist, personal assistant, something like that. And look for Scarlett, of course. But it hasn't really worked out that way, yet . . .' I thought of all the applications I'd sent off so far, without a single positive response.

'Didn't you go to the police, when you heard about Scarlett?'

'No. I hadn't seen Amy for years. I could hardly remember her really. She'd left Cambridge when we were at primary school, and I couldn't be sure she'd remember what Scarlett looked like . . . She didn't even know she'd gone missing.'

'So why . . .'

'Did she get in touch with me? It was a friendly message on Facebook, catching up. And then she mentioned seeing Scarlett in Camden.' Amy had been a bit taken aback when I'd pounced on the information so eagerly, demanding to know where exactly, what she'd looked like, what she was doing. She hadn't meant to stir things up, she said. She just recognised Scarlett from school, serving behind a stall at the market. She didn't know it was significant. She hadn't even got that close, but it had made her think of me, of getting in touch.

'So did Amy take you to the stall where she'd seen her?'

'No, that was the annoying part. She was never free when I came down to look. She worked weekends in a shop in Carnaby Street. She described the stall to me, but I was never sure I'd found exactly the right one. And I never saw anyone who looked like Scarlett.'

'But now you're here you can go looking together?'

'That's the thing. We never actually met up in person. We agreed to, once I'd moved down here, but then she left Facebook. Loads of my friends have. It's the privacy stuff, you know?' Della nodded quickly. 'And stupidly we hadn't exchanged emails or phone numbers or anything, so I've got no way of getting hold of her. I've tried looking in Carnaby Street a few times, but I don't really know what she looks like now. She had one of those arty profile pictures, where you couldn't really see her face.'

Della looked away, rolling her shoulders and taking a deep

breath. Then she turned to me. 'Does it ever occur to you how much of your time you spend looking for people, watching people?'

I nodded, my eyes cast down. At school I'd always been on the outside, silently observing the louder, more confident girls. It had been the same at university, and at work.

'What is it about these people that makes them seem like the answer to you? Like they might hold some magic key to all your problems?'

'I . . . I don't know.' I'd never been someone who could content myself with the one or two unassuming friends I picked up along the way. I was always drawn to the most dynamic person in the room, even though I knew I couldn't possibly measure up. That was how it had been with Layla, as teenagers. And Rachel at university.

'It all comes back to Scarlett, doesn't it?' Della prodded my silence. 'You've become locked in this pattern.'

My stomach tightened. Had my search for Scarlett turned me into a stalker all round? The afternoons I'd spent looking for Amy. My detour down Della's street, watching her family, longing to be let in . . . My face grew hot just thinking about it.

'I . . .' My voice sounded hoarse, barely a whisper. 'I'm drawn to people. I imagine their stories. Maybe that's why I like to write.' I felt exposed, as though Della could somehow read my thoughts.

She paused, plucking a piece of honeysuckle from the vine and twirling it slowly in her fingers. It was nearly summer; the sweet scent was hanging heavy in the air. 'Maybe it's time you put the search on hold. Have you ever considered getting away from your family for a while? From everything?'

I looked up, surprised. Did she want to end our sessions already? Had I done something wrong?

81

'Not really. I guess I'm still finding my feet in London, and I'd miss . . . I think this is really helping.' I didn't want to let on how important our weekly conversations had become. But Della was deep in thought.

'It might be exactly what you need, for your writing, your creativity, your development . . .' I nodded, trying not to show my hurt at the sense of being pushed away. But Della was already looking towards the house, her signal that the session was over.

Standing up, she turned and addressed me, casually, as if what she was saying was no big deal. 'Why don't you show me some of your stories?'

'Are you sure? I . . .' I hadn't let anyone read them in years.

'Yes, print them off. I'll have a read. I've got an agent friend I could show them to.'

And then Della walked down the garden and through the bifold doors into the kitchen, hardly aware of the state she had left me in – the mixture of panic and possibility that had fixed me to my seat.

At the beginning of the next group meeting, I handed Della an unmarked A4 envelope. In it were four stories: the ones I felt least sick and desperate on re-reading. I wanted to do it quickly, before I lost my nerve, and Della took them with a discreet nod, slotting the envelope onto a shelf in the hallway as she looked over her shoulder to where Jasmine stood at the bottom of the stairs, hanging up her coat and watching us intently.

There was something in the look that passed between them that sent a jolt through my body. Had Jasmine been Della's favourite in the past? Is that why she resented me so much? As we took our seats on the sofas, I avoided Jasmine's eye; and Helen's, too. It was the first time we'd seen each other

82

since our meeting in Hampstead, and the guilt was still a low hum at the back of my brain. I was so caught up with all the unspoken alliances and rivalries within the group, I barely stopped to consider the real source of all the secrecy and distrust – the person who had brought us all together and who inspired such unquestioning loyalty.

But Della knew how to make an entrance, and we all sat up as she wafted past us in a long floral skirt, similar to the kind Jasmine wore, though I was sure Della had got there first. I couldn't help noticing that Eva was wearing a jumpsuit like the one Della had on the previous week. And all around the room were flashes of hot pink, on laps or on top of note-books to one side. Everyone had gone out and bought Della's book, or at least brought in the copy they already had. Everyone except me.

'I see you've all been doing your homework.' Della smiled broadly, and I felt a twinge of shame. Had they made a silent agreement to show me up? After our difficult solo session, I'd been determined to please Della this week, but I was already on the back foot. What if she decided she'd had enough of me; that it was someone else's turn? 'As you know, we're talking this week about how to "future-proof" our lives – long-term planning to ensure we make the most of every opportunity. So who wants to report first?'

I was about to put up my hand when Eva cleared her throat. 'I've made some real progress this week, after . . . well, after what you said before. And re-reading your book.' She looked to Della for the nod of approval she knew would follow. 'And I've quit my job!'

There were gasps. Even Della looked taken aback, recoiling slightly in her armchair.

'Gosh, Eva. That's big news. Have you actually handed in your notice?'

'Yep.' Eva grinned. 'It was after everything you said about following your dream and taking a leap, and I thought, what am I waiting for? I don't want to work in events forever. I'm not getting any younger. If I want to break into fashion, I've got to do it now.'

'And do you have any plans for how you're going to do that? Would that have been something worth exploring before you walked away from a regular salary? We could have mind-mapped it together if you'd only have talked to us about this first . . .' Eva's smile faded. She looked around at all the concerned faces.

'But you said we should take risks and be true to ourselves . . . I thought . . .'

'Yes, Eva, within reason. But I didn't say to behave impulsively. Or put yourself in a difficult position, financially. You can't expect me to take responsibility for this decision *you've* made.'

Eva stood up, looking close to tears. 'I'm not asking you to take responsibility. I'm telling you what I've done. I thought you'd be pleased.'

'Eva, please sit down,' Della said quietly. 'You're intimidating the group.' She always grew calmer the more agitated a situation became, I discovered that later. 'This isn't about *me*. You shouldn't be making any decisions with me in mind. This is about *you*.'

A tear rolled down Eva's cheek. 'But I thought this would be a step in the right direction. I thought that's what you meant when you said . . .'

'Can we agree that I didn't mean for you to quit your job, Eva? Now, shall we move on while you go and get yourself a tissue?' Della sighed and we all turned to find a fresh page in our notebooks. But I felt rattled. Eva had taken a huge step, in the hope of gaining Della's approval, and she didn't even get a 'well done'. Then again, who gave up a good job just to score a few points?

As Eva left the room, I was about to take my turn when Della moved on to Jane on my left. This time it was Jasmine who got to her feet.

'Hang on, shouldn't we hear from Kate first,' she said, standing by the fireplace, her arms crossed. 'She barely said a word last week, and now she's getting passed over again?'

'That's enough, Jasmine,' Della said. 'This is a safe space, not somewhere to single people out.'

'But no one else gets to sit out,' Jasmine complained. 'Here's Eva, changing her *life* for this group, and all Kate does is sit there silently, *staring* at us every week. What's she even doing here, if she's not going to join in?' She glared at me with such hostility I shrank back.

'*Enough*, Jasmine,' Della said, raising her voice this time. 'There are confidentiality rules in these meetings for good reason. We need to protect people who have had mental health problems, or have other reasons why their personal details can't be shared, don't we?' They all looked at me as blood pounded in my ears. Why had Della brought that up in front of everyone? 'Anyway, you've barely been coming to these meetings more than a year, you couldn't possibly understand how it all works. I've actually been starting to wonder whether you're getting enough out of these sessions . . .'

'I'm sorry, Della.' Jasmine was visibly shaking as she took a seat on the sofa. 'I didn't mean to . . . I *don't* know how it all works. But, I won't . . . I'm sorry.' She turned her head downward and in the silence that followed I dared to look around. Eva walked silently to her seat. Everyone sat perfectly still, waiting.

Della pulled herself up in her high-backed armchair and composed herself, breathing deeply before speaking. 'Jasmine, let's forget this happened. Let's move on,' she said, looking around. 'Does everyone feel that the group can move beyond this?'

We all nodded, though I could feel my hands trembling. I hadn't witnessed a telling-off like this since school. Certainly never of an adult. I should have been gratified that Della had defended me, but I felt sorry for Jasmine. And Eva. They so desperately wanted Della's approval, and yet for some reason she had chosen me.

At the time, I thought I was the lucky one. It took me too long to realise that, in fact, the opposite was true.

Chapter Eleven

The invitation, when it came, marked both an end and a beginning. I can see that now. I was no longer just another member of the group. Neither Della nor I could pretend that was the case any more. I became something else. I crossed a threshold. And there was no going back.

It had started as a normal coaching session, only Della was distracted, on edge. The activity in the background was throwing us both off course.

This time, it was Della and Mark's turn to host the kitchen supper, and behind where we sat on the sofas, two caterers were whirling around the room, clattering, whisking and conversing in a language I didn't recognise.

'I'm going to have to cut this short tonight. I'm sure you understand,' Della was saying, looking over her shoulder. 'There are quite a few people coming, and I need to get myself ready.'

'Of course,' I said with a glance at her floor-length Chinese print dress. How much readier did she need to be? I wondered what I'd be doing with myself while the dinner party was going on. Would I be expected to sit upstairs, outside the children's room? Perhaps I'd be excused for the evening.

'We'll need you to get the kids into bed and—' Della was cut short by the chime of her mobile phone. She paused, picked it up, poking and frowning at the screen.

'God, I knew she'd do that.'

She looked up with that blank face she sometimes had, as though she hadn't yet decided which expression to arrange. And then she seemed to focus on me, and she smiled.

'Would you like to join us?' she asked. 'For supper?'

'Really?' I felt flattered, and immediately on edge. What would I say? What would I wear? I caught sight of myself in the glass of the bifold doors: old denim skirt, white T-shirt, limp hair.

'I'm sure I can find you something of mine to wear,' Della added.

'Well, if you're sure . . .' I found myself following her up the grand staircase, wondering at this sudden turn of events. I had gone from babysitter to guest in a matter of moments, and I wasn't sure why.

I'd never seen inside Della's bedroom before, and it was a disorienting experience – wall-to-wall mirrored wardrobes and yet more white: curtains, bedspread, thick springy carpets and shaggy rugs.

'How about this?' Della suggested, holding up a tailored black dress. I looked at it doubtfully. I was at least a size bigger than Della.

'No, I think we need something less fitted . . . Hmm, let's see. This!' She held up an expensive-looking light-grey bias-cut chiffon dress. 'Not with that old necklace though.' Della waved a hand towards my silver chain with its small origami bird pendant, the one Scarlett had left under my pillow before she disappeared. 'This should go well.' She held out a fine gold chain with a tiny, ornate flower on the end. It had the feathery weight of a precious gift.

'Are you sure?' I asked, uneasy, but Della seemed unaware of any oddness in inviting me to dress up in her clothes. Perhaps she'd never realised how much I'd admired them, coveted them. How many times I'd mentally tried on her life for size.

Della left me alone in the bedroom while she went downstairs to check on the caterers.

'I don't do cooking on this scale,' she'd laughed, over her shoulder and I smiled as though I knew what she meant, though I couldn't imagine ever hiring strangers to come and cook a meal in my house. 'Mark's busy with the children at the moment. You can go and see them when you're ready, if you like, but don't let them touch that dress.'

I got changed, feeling self-conscious around so many mirrors. I tried to tidy up my hair and face, borrowing a bit of Della's make-up and a spray of her Rive Gauche. It was only as I left the room that I felt the strangeness of it, of smelling like Della.

'Kate, is that you?' Mark called out as I tried to creep past the children's bedroom. 'Come in and say goodnight to the kids. They're a bit disappointed we're staying in tonight, to cramp your style!' He laughed and, as I walked in, added, 'You look nice,' his eyes on me in a way that made me flush.

'Thanks.' Mark was wearing a crisp shirt, his hair slicked back as though he had just showered. Standing next to him, I allowed myself to imagine that the two of us were the parents, kissing our children goodnight before an evening concert or dinner.

'Wow, Kate, you look so pretty!' Tabitha cried. 'That's a lovely dress. And you smell like Mummy . . .' I was bending over to kiss her, but I stood up quickly, my face warm.

'OK, I'll leave you to it,' Mark said, hugging Jasper as he left. I watched the door for a moment and then turned to find both the children looking at me, shyly, confused by the sight of their babysitter in their mother's clothing. I was sitting down to read them a story when I was summoned by a shriek.

'Kate! Kate, I need you.'

'Sorry,' I said to the children, 'another night.' I could see they were disappointed, but they didn't make a murmur. Not when their mother was in the house.

As I came downstairs, Della greeted me with a pile of plates and cutlery.

'Sorry, darling, do you mind helping out? It's all a bit chaotic.' I hadn't seen her like this before – on edge, nervous even. 'Honestly, ladies, you need to get a move on,' she was saying to the caterers. 'Everyone's going to be here in forty minutes, so I need every trace of you gone in twenty.'

I understood then that Della would be passing the evening's meal off as her own, and I caught Mark smile as he watched the realisation dawn. It was hard to believe, really, but then, she was so busy, with her work, the children, giving so much of her time to me. At the time it didn't seem so surprising that she needed a bit of outside help. Mark was hard at work, too, coordinating drinks and glasses, arranging cushions that were then rearranged by Della. I noticed that the children's drawings had been taken off the fridge, and a copy of Della's book placed casually on the coffee table, along with some *Elle Decorations* and the latest *Vogue*.

The caterers were indeed gone in twenty, and I'd laid the table for eight, put out two large vases of lilies and was opening Prosecco when the doorbell rang. There hadn't been time for Della to tell me anything about the guests or how I was to be presented. I'd have to play it by ear.

I had never witnessed such a transformation as the one that overcame the house as Della opened the door. A jazz orchestra struck up, courtesy of Mark in the living room, the lights were dimmed and Della's voice dropped about ten pitches as she threw her arms around two guests, who had arrived together.

'Jonathan, Dee, how lovely,' she said, showing them into the kitchen where I was hovering, unsure where to put myself. 'This is Kate, a family friend. She's staying in London for a while.'

I smiled and kissed both the guests, who thrust two bottles of wine and some artisan chocolates in my direction. They didn't remark on my presence, and I wondered how many more of these 'family friends' had hung around over the years. The word 'staying' lingered in my mind as I put away the gifts. It seemed like an unnecessary lie. Why was Della giving the impression that I was only in London temporarily?

'Jonathan, now tell me, how is the play going?' Della asked, turning to me. 'Jonathan's starring in a *wonderful* production at the Donmar.'

'Well, it's hardly a starring role. And you haven't actually seen it yet, darling.' Jonathan smiled. He looked a fair bit older than Della and Mark, with a receding hairline and a mischievous glint in his eyes.

'No, I know, but I've read the reviews. Shakespeare, isn't it?'

'Marlowe,' Jonathan corrected.

'Absolutely. Even better!' Della laughed. As she handed me the sparkling wine, I caught a smile pass between Jonathan and Dee.

'How's your *thing* going, Dee?' Della asked. I poured Prosecco in Dee's glass and watched a flicker of irritation pass across her face. She was quite a bit younger than Jonathan, probably around my age, with a strong Australian accent, dark hair, startlingly white teeth and a glow that made her look as though she might have jogged to Crouch End across

Hampstead Heath – where, as Della informed me, they lived together in Jonathan's penthouse.

'My wellbeing blog? It's going well, thanks,' Dee said, in a voice that made it clear this wasn't the first time she'd had to remind Della. 'I write blogs and make videos about health and beauty regimes,' she added, for my benefit. 'Lots of people watch them online.'

'Oh, right,' I said, handing a glass to Jonathan, 'so you're an influencer?'

'I prefer the term "wellness entrepreneur",' Dee said the words carefully, and Della rolled her eyes in my direction.

'Dee gets millions of hits,' Jonathan said. 'They want to make a book out of her lifestyle plan.'

'Really?' Della raised her eyebrows. 'And who's going to publish that, Dee?'

'We're not sure yet.' Dee smiled at Jonathan. 'It's early days.'

'Well, let me know if you have any trouble and I'll put a word in with my publisher,' Della said. 'I know what it's like when you're starting out. It can really help to have connections.' She looked from Dee to Jonathan. 'And of course, Twitter is key. It does wonders for the book sales.'

'Thanks, Della,' Dee said, with effort. 'I'm already on Twitter, but younger audiences are more into Insta, Snapchat, that kind of thing . . .'

I smiled at Dee, hoping to convey solidarity, as the two youngest people in the room by a good decade, but she had already moved on, retaliating by offering Della advice on the life-coaching blog she hoped to set up, the two of them locked in a competitive conversation about followers and hits and attention time. Though Mark smiled and laughed in all the right places, he barely said a word. Neither did I. It didn't seem necessary, or expected.

The next guests arrived soon after, a couple called Amisha

and Suzanne, and we all moved into the living room to eat the fiddly quail's egg canapés I'd helped put together.

'That's a gorgeous dress,' Amisha said, looking me slowly up and down. 'Isn't that one of yours, Della?'

'Oh, that? Yes, I hardly wear it now. It looks better on Kate, really. I don't have the curves for it – you know me, straight up and down.'

We all turned to admire Della's taut figure, and I smoothed my hands self-consciously over the silky fabric that clung to my hips. 'Oh Della, you'd look gorgeous in a plastic bag. She's so generous though, isn't she?' Amisha turned to me. 'With her clothes, her time, her house . . . everything. You and these girls, Della. It's a wonder you've got time for anything else!' She laughed and I turned away to hand around a plate of canapés, wondering what she was getting at.

Amisha was a model, tall and angular, with long glossy black hair and bright red lipstick. She lived locally and had, it transpired, worked with Della on various coaching videos.

'How's Eva getting on, by the way?' she asked, as Della handed me a bottle of Prosecco to top everyone up. 'Any further on with that design career?'

'Hmm, she's in something of a transition period.' Della raised an eyebrow. 'I'll fill you in on it later.' A look of amusement passed between them that made me feel uncomfortable. Wasn't what went on in our sessions confidential?

As I watched Della circulate, I started piecing it together. So it must have been Amisha who introduced Eva to the group. And perhaps it was Jonathan who knew Jane, through acting. I thought of all the Janes, and what they'd say if they could see me here, mingling in Della's world. Surely Della wouldn't talk about them in front of me unless she saw me in a different league somehow. I'd been let in on the joke now. I only hoped I wasn't part of it.

I bent to refill a glass for Suzanne, a psychotherapist who must have been in her late forties, elegant, with short grey hair and a chunky orange necklace.

'Don't you have any celery salt, Della?' she asked, over my head. 'It really is better with quail eggs.'

'I'm afraid we don't.' Della smiled. 'We try not to have too much sodium in the house.'

'Never mind, next time.' Suzanne picked at a canapé. 'How's business?'

'Never been busier. How's yours?'

Suzanne snorted. 'It's not really a business, Della. It's a life's work. But it's going very well, thank you. Sadly, people will always have problems that need the attention of a serious therapist, that can't be magicked away with positive thinking.'

'Oh Suzanne, we really must agree to disagree on this one,' Della said, laughing as she motioned to me to join her in the kitchen.

'That woman is *such* a cow,' she whispered, as we gathered the starters the caterers had plated up and left in the fridge. 'I so wanted to see Amisha, and I planned the entire thing so Suzanne couldn't make it tonight. She normally has clients on a Thursday, so we had even numbers. But she cancelled them at the last minute, and threw out the whole balance of the evening.'

So that was why I'd been invited. Della had asked me at the last minute because they had an odd number of guests. I tried to ignore my disappointment. After all, what could I expect? She was hardly going to hold a dinner party in my honour.

'And now Alan's running late as usual, and we're going to have to start without him.'

As she spoke, the doorbell rang. 'He's here,' Della said, looking relieved and a little excited. 'I'll show him in. He's

94

the *literary agent*,' she hissed. 'Keep an eye on Suzanne, will you. If anyone can keep her at bay, you can.'

I watched Della take a deep breath and leave the kitchen, smiling to myself. I thought of Dan. He'd never believe I was about to have dinner with someone important in publishing. Someone who might possibly be interested in reading my stories. I felt I'd been let into another world, behind the scenes. Della had never spoken to me so conspiratorially before. And she thought *I* of all people could manage Suzanne. Why, I had not a clue, but I liked the idea of myself as a peacemaker, a reassuring presence.

Suzanne did seem to take a special interest in me over dinner. We'd been seated opposite each other at one end, with Della and Alan at the other. Alan was older, too. Late forties, maybe, with silvering hair and thick-framed glasses. He seemed to have come straight from the office, or client drinks, in his dark blue suit and tie, and he spoke authoritatively, as though used to holding an audience.

Next to him, Mark looked boyishly handsome, casual in his open-necked shirt, yet Della had her back turned, attention focused entirely in the other direction. 'He won't admit it, but he's blocked,' Alan was saying. Mark rolled his eyes at me, a smile passing between us before I noticed Suzanne watching us.

'So you're staying in London, are you?' Suzanne asked, looking from me to Mark and back again.

'Yes,' I said, uncertain what to add. 'I, um, I'm working locally.'

'Where are you from?'

'Cambridge. I've lived there most of my life, on and off.'

'And how do you know Della and Mark?' Suzanne looked at Mark, who was talking to Amisha now.

'Well, I . . .' Della must have had one ear on our conversation because she quickly joined in.

'Our families go way back,' she announced across the table. 'Kate's been having a hard time recently, so we've stepped in to help.' I felt my stomach lurch. Why would Della lie like that? And why draw attention to my problems? I thought I was meant to be impressing Alan, not going for his sympathy.

'So, are you staying here?' Suzanne persisted. 'Della's always one for a house guest.' There was something in her tone that made me fall silent. What was she getting at? But Della was quick to take over.

'No, Kate's staying with friends nearby. But she's around here a lot, aren't you, Kate?' She smiled at the others. 'Kate's a writer,' she announced. 'Wonderful stories. You must read them, Alan. And the kids love her, she's like part of the family.'

Mark caught my eye and I murmured something about the children being very sweet.

'You'll have to come to France then, won't she Della?' Jonathan boomed, slapping his hand on the table. 'You'd absolutely love The Pines,' he added, turning to me. 'Beautiful spot.'

'Yes, such a gorgeous house – the views, the trees, the pool,' Amisha said. 'Have you been to Montpellier?' Distracted by the way Suzanne was frowning, I realised a beat too late that Amisha was addressing me.

'I've actually . . . well, I've never been to France.'

'What, not even on an exchange?' Alan had taken notice of me now, but for the wrong reason. 'But it's so close . . .'

'I've always wanted to,' I said, 'but we had our holidays in Dorset. We weren't big travellers.' My cheeks were hot with humiliation.

'Wonderful county,' Jonathan said approvingly. 'And a wonderful meal, Della,' he added, moving the conversation on, as Della accepted compliments on the lamb tagine and Mark excused himself to select a new jazz compilation.

I retreated to the kitchen to gather myself, running water in the sink and rinsing the dishes. What was I doing here? Had I been invited so they all had someone to laugh at? Was I here to wait on them? Of course they were never going to take me to France. I'd probably never be invited to another dinner party. Why wouldn't Della just be honest about who I was?

'I'm so sorry about all that. I didn't know *what* to say!' Della walked in with a pile of plates and dumped them by the sink, beckoning me to the fridge where the caterers had left the desserts, already plated up. 'It's not done to socialise with one's clients, so I didn't want to let on . . . especially in front of Suzanne.'

'I suppose I wasn't expecting you to bring up the . . . difficulties I've been having.' I looked away.

'Oh, Kate. I didn't mean *that*. I'm so sorry, it didn't even occur to me that's what you'd think.' Della looked up from where she was sprinkling lavender across the chocolate puddings. 'I just meant money troubles, you know, the usual millennial stuff. Besides, everyone knows writers are tortured – Alan's very interested in seeing what you've written, you know.'

'Really?' I joined her, dusting the icing sugar. 'I didn't realise you'd already read the stories. Thanks so much for saying you'd give them to him . . .'

Della smiled. 'Well, I haven't had time to read them yet. But I'm sure they *are* wonderful. And once I've read them, I'll be sure to pass them on.' She looked at me, pushing a wisp of loose hair behind my ear. 'I want to help you. You can do anything you put your mind to. You remind me so much of myself when I was—'

'What's going on in here then?' Mark walked in and put an arm around each of us. I could see he'd been knocking back the wine faster than the rest of the group. 'How are you two lovely ladies doing?'

'Oh Mark, for God's sake, hold it together.' Della pushed him away and rolled her eyes at me. 'Honestly, he's a liability. Keep an eye on him, will you.'

I laughed, feeling the weight of Mark's arm still around my shoulder, and the warmth of Della's words, the intimacy of her gesture. The sense of belonging I had in that moment was stronger than anything I'd experienced for a long time before, or since. It's a memory I return to often – the glow of the kitchen, the clatter and voices next door, the feeling of being part of an inner circle, accepted among the kind of people I'd thought were so far beyond my reach. It reminds me why I went on to do what I did.

The rest of the evening passed by too quickly. There was no more mention of France and, stuck at our opposite ends of the table, I didn't get my chance to talk to Alan. There would be other times, I told myself. In fact, I barely spoke through dessert or during the long, drawn-out goodbyes. But I was the last to leave. I half wondered whether Della would invite me to stay in the guest room. This time I had decided to say yes. I was practically family, after all. Della had said as much, and I felt it then, almost believing myself in the story we'd told everyone.

But there was no mention of staying, and when it was time to go, I came out of the bathroom in my own clothes, handing Della the dress, neatly folded, with the necklace resting on top. Della took the dress, but put the necklace in my hand and pressed my fingers down over it.

'You keep it,' she said. 'To say thank you for all your help tonight.'

'Are you sure?' It felt like too much. 'It's me who should be saying thank you – for this evening, for the stories, for everything.'

'Don't mention it. Anyway, it means you can stop wearing that rusty old bird.' Della smiled. 'The lotus is the flower of life, you know. It signifies new beginnings. Out with the old, in with the new.'

Later, sitting on my single bed, I ran my fingers over the bird pendant, worn with age. I had found it hidden under my pillow when we'd got back from Eype, and known straight away that Scarlett had left it for me. I also knew not to mention it to my parents. Only to wear it, every day, the secret message that Scarlett had left behind.

We'd spent weeks making origami birds once. It was one of those rare activities we could both enjoy – me around seven, Scarlett fourteen. I'd come home from school with a book of designs, and Scarlett had bought some brightly coloured paper and string. We'd made dozens of cranes – intricate, slightly crooked, fragile – and strung them from the walls and ceiling of our bedroom, as though we slept in an aviary, and these small birds watched over us in the night. I kept them up long after Scarlett disappeared, until they discoloured and began to fall to the ground.

Now I dropped the small crane into my jewellery box. Next to Della's gift, the charm looked dull, childish. Della was right: that was the past. It was time to look to the future.

Chapter Twelve

'That woman has been staring at you for *hours*.' Marco nudged me. He was one of the friendlier baristas, and I watched him bustle over to the pale woman by the door, who had been nursing a dead coffee for at least half an hour. As he cleared her cup, she shot me another look before motioning for the bill. It looked as though she was actually going to come over on her way out.

'I'm sorry to bother you,' the woman said, her face set in an anxious frown, 'but do you think we could have a quick chat – outside?'

I looked around. Pete was nowhere to be seen and Marco was smirking behind the counter. What on earth did this woman want?

'OK,' I said. 'I can only be a minute, though.' I followed her outside. She was smaller than me, with bobbed hair and wide-set, nervous eyes. Although we were probably around the same age, her forehead was creased with worry lines.

'What's this about?' I asked as I closed the café door behind us. 'I really can't be caught taking a break in the middle of my shift.'

'I know. I'm sorry,' the woman said, folding her arms defensively across her chest. 'This must look so weird to you. I didn't mean to freak you out, but I could see that you'd spotted me. I don't know if you saw me in here last week?' I shook my head. 'I think we have someone in common.' My stomach began to contract. Scarlett. Was this going to be the moment?

'Do you know a woman called Della Hunter?'

'Yes, why? What's it to you?' My voice sounded harsher than I meant it to. It was the disappointment.

'Well, last summer I was working for Della. I was a . . . sort of a nanny. But it all got a bit too much, and I ended up leaving. I haven't seen her since. But when Jasmine told me—'

'You know Jasmine?' I looked at her more closely now. 'Has Jasmine been talking about me? How does she know I work here?'

'Look, all I wanted to say is, you need to be careful with Della.' She had lowered her voice and her eyes were shooting from side to side, as though someone might be watching us – two ordinary-looking women having a conversation in the street.

'What do you mean?' I felt instinctively protective, but I couldn't ignore the anxiety that had been floating out of reach for weeks and now came to the surface once again.

'Just don't get too caught up in it all. Della's not what she seems . . .'

'Is that it? Are you talking about her past, how she's changed herself?'

'It's Della, Mark, the whole family – there's something weird going on there. I got caught up in it all for a while, and I didn't like the way it was going. Has she invited you—'

'Kate?' Pete had opened the door and was standing behind me. 'Is this something you could continue after your shift?' Pete was usually pretty casual. A New Zealander with a hipster beard and a pierced ear, he saw himself as the kind of cool boss who didn't pull rank, so I knew I'd overstepped the mark.

'I'm so sorry, I was . . . I'll be in now,' I said, flustered. 'Has she invited me to what? What are you talking about?'

'It's nothing. Forget it.' The woman looked at Pete looming behind us and turned to leave. 'But Della can't know I've been here. OK?' Her eyes darted. She looked worried, scared even.

'Look, I can't talk now. Let me give you my number, or I can take yours. I don't even know your name.'

'It's Claire,' she said, already moving away. 'I shouldn't have come. Don't say anything. Please.'

'Wait, hang on . . .' I watched her walk quickly up the hill, her yellow cardigan disappearing into the crowd like a life jacket bobbing over the horizon. Was this the Claire who had left the group? What invitation did she mean? Was she talking about the dinner – had it been some kind of rite of passage?

My fingers reached up for the necklace Della had given me the week before. Why had Jasmine sent her now, when things were going so well? When I felt within arm's reach of a life I could actually imagine for myself; a future with interesting friends, a career, even a bit-part in Della's family life.

I considered whether to run and catch up with her. I wanted to reassure myself, really. She was probably bitter, or jealous – like Jasmine. But Pete was glaring at me from inside the café and I knew I couldn't risk it. My life was balanced too precariously. I couldn't afford to lose my job. My questions would have to wait.

I walked quickly to Della's house the following Tuesday. I planned to grab Jasmine before the session and confront her – to find out exactly what she'd been saying. But I'd been late leaving the café, and as I entered the living room, I saw that the session had already begun. Jasmine wasn't there.

'I'm afraid she won't be joining us this evening,' Della was saying. 'She feels she's gone as far as she can with the group for now. She's going to have a break – some time to process things.' It was clear who she was talking about. 'I know it can be unsettling, during these moments of transition. But if we all talk openly about how we're feeling, we'll pull through as a stronger unit. And who knows, perhaps another member will join us soon.'

I sat down heavily next to Eva. Why had Jasmine left so suddenly, just as Claire turned up in my life? And would a new member really come along to replace her so quickly? I was desperate to discuss it all, but Della had divided us so effectively, it was hard to imagine broaching the subject with any of the others now.

'As you all know, we'll be having our eight-week summer break in a few weeks' time,' Della continued. I suppose I must have known it was coming, with all the talk of the house in France, but it hit me harder than I'd expected. What was I going to do for the whole summer without Della, without her family? The weeks stretched out ahead of me, a series of café shifts, searching and more shifts.

'Right, enough admin, let's get down to business. Who wants to go first with their bucket list?'

I'd worked on mine the night before, but all I'd come up with was a series of countries I'd like to visit – each with some connection to Scarlett, a fact I knew I wouldn't mention. The others had thought of all manner of life-affirming experiences: 'Swimming with dolphins in Zanzibar,' was on Helen's list. Jane hoped to play Lady Macbeth at The Globe. Eva had been researching her family tree, so she was focused on visiting long-lost family members in Eastern Europe. I kept wondering what would have been on Jasmine's list, and what had happened to make her leave so abruptly.

103

I lingered by the coats at the end of the session, watching Jane and Helen let themselves out, waiting for Eva to finish her hushed conversation with Della. I planned to leave with her, ask her what had happened, how I could get hold of Jasmine.

But as soon as Della shut the door behind us, Eva put her phone to her ear and started talking fast in Polish, walking quickly away in the other direction. I watched her disappear out of view, helpless. If only I hadn't deleted Helen's number. I'd have to wait until my session on Thursday to get more information out of Della.

It was a warm evening, and we sat outside as usual, out of earshot of Mark and the children, who I knew by now would be in the bath at this time, ready for our reading marathon later. We had already discussed my week's progress, and my writing, as well as Della's continuing failure to read the stories I'd given her, when I plucked up the courage to raise the question that had been plaguing me.

'So, what happened with Jasmine?' I asked, trying to sound casual. 'Was it to do with that disagreement the other week?'

'Disagreement?' Della looked confused, and then she laughed lightly. 'Oh, that. No, of course not. She decided it was time to move on, that's all.' She smiled. 'It's really nothing to worry about. We all have to call it a day sometime, don't we? Besides, I never got the sense you were particularly close . . .'

'Well, it's hard to tell . . . I don't get to talk to anyone much. But no, Jasmine wasn't very welcoming, it's true.'

'There you go then. Let's put her out of our heads and get back to it, shall we? This week we were going to pick up on boundaries again.' A breeze ruffled the leaves that hung down over the table, and I felt a sudden chill. Della had nurtured and encouraged Jasmine for the best part of a year, and she seemed done with her, just like that.

'Yes, I was meant to be talking to my parents.' I looked at my hands.

'And have you? Have you told them that you're not going back to Cambridge? That it's time for you to move on with your life?'

I shook my head. 'I tried, I really did. I called them. But my dad answered, and he sounded so vulnerable. They really need me, even if Mum doesn't like to show it. So I was thinking maybe I could leave it a bit longer, until they realise I'm not coming back. Instead of making a big deal about it. And, if I can find Scarlett, then they'll forget about me coming—'

'Scarlett doesn't *want* to be found.'

'I know, I know. You keep saying that. But what if she does? I feel like I'm so close, after all this time. I can't give up now.'

'I thought we had agreed you were going to put the search for Scarlett to one side. Stop worrying about your family and put yourself first for once.'

I nodded, but I hadn't really agreed. I couldn't abandon my parents like that. Couldn't just forget about Scarlett. It wasn't like a switch I could turn off in my head.

'Kate, it's very hard to sit here with you every week having the same conversations when you're not prepared to act on them.'

'I'm sorry, but I have to pick my moment. I know you're going away – and you want all this . . . resolved. But I don't want to upset my parents. I'm all they've got.'

'I understand,' Della said, though her tone suggested the opposite. 'But you spend all your time worrying about other people and not what's best for *you*. It's a form of self-sabotage, you know. And here you are, putting me in the role of proxy parent – telling me one thing and doing another. You need to take responsibility for your own happiness. Be proactive.'

Della's words had a sting, and I thought again of Claire's

105

agitation at the café. The anxiety that had been dogging me ever since. OK then, I would be proactive.

'I met a friend of yours the other day, in the café,' I said, changing tack recklessly.

'Oh really,' Della said. 'And how did you make that connection? I thought we didn't discuss coaching matters outside of our meetings?'

'She approached me, actually. She asked if I knew you, said she'd spent some time with you last summer. Her name's Claire.' My heart rate had doubled. She'd asked me not to say anything, but I was speaking too fast to stop myself.

Della looked at me, her face blank. 'Claire? Oh yes, I do remember a girl called Claire. Funny little thing. Did some babysitting for us. What about her?'

'Did something happen with her? Did you invite her somewhere?'

'Invite her somewhere? No. Not that I remember. Nothing happened . . . she babysat, the children didn't like her, she left. That was it.'

Della stood up, pushing her chair aside. 'It's time to go in now. I want to get ready. And you don't want to keep the children waiting, do you?'

She walked towards the house and I was left alone in the semi-darkness, the words hanging over me like a threat. Don't let them grow tired of you, too.

After Della and Mark left for the evening, I tried a more direct approach with Tabitha.

'Do you know someone called Claire?' I asked as I put away the last Julia Donaldson of the evening.

'Yes.' Tabitha snuggled under her duvet.

'And when did you last see her?' I asked, feeling a tingle of anticipation.

106

'Yesterday, at school.' The tingle evaporated. 'Why? Do you know her?'

'No. Do you know any other Claires?'

'Claire Bear,' Jasper sang from the other bed. 'Claire, Claire, Claire Bear!'

'Who's Claire Bear?' I asked Tabitha.

'No one.' Tabitha giggled. 'Jasper's being silly.' And they both fell about laughing in that wild way they often had before bedtime. I could feel my impatience rising.

'So there was never a woman who came to look after you called Claire?'

'Oh, *that* Claire. Why didn't you say?' asked Tabitha, mid-laughing fit.

'Was she your nanny? Did she go somewhere with you?' Tabitha paused to consider the question, while Jasper continued his annoying song.

'Jasper, please. I'm trying to have a serious conversation here.' I never snapped at the children, and I could see that the wounded look on Jasper's face was about to turn into tears. I gave him a quick cuddle and began tucking them both in.

'I just wondered if you remembered Claire,' I tried again, 'and how long she looked after you for?'

'Not long,' said Tabitha, yawning. 'I'm tired now, can we go to sleep?'

'Of course. And was she nice, Claire? Did anything happen to make her leave?'

'Yes, she was nice,' said Tabitha, turning her back towards me to mark the end of the conversation. And then, as I was leaving the room, I heard her say softly, almost in her sleep, 'Mummy didn't like her . . . so she left. That's what always happens.'

Chapter Thirteen

Liam was not happy. I walked into the living room to find him standing, arms crossed, staring at the sofa. Following his gaze, I saw a pair of feet sticking out, blue toenails exposed in tatty flip-flops. A head emerged from behind a cushion. It was my school friend Layla, holding a bottle of my nail varnish, painting her toes in my living room.

'Layla, my God! What are you doing here?'

She sprang up, splattering varnish on the table as she put her arms around me.

'Kate, mate!' She held me at arm's length. 'It's so good to see you! You look like shit.'

I laughed. And then, seeing Liam's face, laughed again.

'As you can see, your *friend* has made herself at home,' Liam said. Layla had always been an acquired taste. I had been her best, and pretty much only, friend at secondary school. No one could understand what drew us together – me: quiet, studious, eager to please; Layla outspoken, wild, funny . . . and exactly what had been missing in my life since Scarlett left. But she clearly hadn't won Liam over yet.

'Liam tells me you've scored a permanent position in a

café.' Layla gave me an ironic high five as I sat down next to her.

'Well, what about you then, hotshot? Had your first solo show yet?' Layla had been an aspiring artist for as long as I'd known her. One who didn't produce a great deal of art.

Layla laughed. ''Course not. I've been travelling, haven't I.'

'So that's why I haven't heard from you. And what are you doing here? How long are you in London?'

'Is it OK if I stay a few nights?'

'Of course. Gina's practically moved in with her boyfriend, hasn't she? So it's all right if Layla stays?' Liam raised his eyebrows at me. 'She'll be in my room.'

Liam shrugged and walked towards the door. 'What bird is six letters and steals other birds' nests?' he asked, as if alluding to some shared code we'd established during our crossword sessions.

'Oh, come on, Liam,' I said as he shut the door behind him.

'God, what's his problem?' Layla asked. 'He wasn't even going to let me in the house. Said you weren't "expecting" me.' She did a bad impression of Liam's Dublin accent.

'I wasn't, to be fair.' I smiled, watching Layla roll up a joint and light it. Maybe that's what had got Liam's back up. 'Want some?'

I shook my head. 'Better not. Got to be up early for work in the morning. So what have you been up to?'

'Suit yourself.' Layla shrugged, ignoring my question. 'It's good stuff, though.' She threw her head back, inhaling deeply. Her hair was dark, above the blue tips, which matched her newly painted nails. Tattooed ivy climbed up her inner arm, a new addition since I'd last seen her.

'What's it been, two years? Three?' I asked. When Layla had left Cambridge, I hadn't been in a good way. And we'd never been great at long-distance communication.

'I was at the commune with Mum for a while, then India, Goa, South America . . .' Layla passed me the joint and I accepted this time.

'What's the deal with Liam?' she asked. 'Is there something going on with you two?'

'No,' I said quickly. 'He's very . . . friendly. But, not like that.'

'Good. He's not bad looking, but you don't want to get shacked up again after all that Dan shit.' Layla examined me. 'That's a cool necklace. Lotus, isn't it? Symbol of fertility.'

'Is it? A friend gave it to me, I don't know—'

'A male friend?' she raised her eyebrows, and I shook my head. 'Really, K. You need to get out there. Have some fun.'

Layla threw a bottle of purple nail varnish in my direction, and I painted my fingernails obediently. I had no intention of letting her make me over like she had when we were teenagers, though – on those rare nights when I escaped my parents' bungalow and stayed at Layla's mum's. She didn't care what we did. Sometimes I wondered why Layla had let me tag along with the older kids she hung out with outside school – drinking cider in the park or at someone's house. After a while I'd accepted it as good fortune and gone along for the ride. Now I could see that I'd played a crucial role in the performance: I was Layla's witness, I watched as she got drunk, took pills, dated older boys. I lent her my school notes to copy, and sometimes I'd confide in her about the troubles at home.

'How are your parents?' Layla asked, as if following my train of thought.

'Oh, you know.' I shrugged. 'You must have spoken to them. Isn't that how you found me here?'

'Yeah.' Layla took another deep drag. 'I've only been back in England a few months. Been down on the commune in Totnes.'

Layla's mum had sold up and moved to a 'shared living community'. Her dad was Algerian – he'd moved on years before. 'Don't know where he's living now,' she said a bit later on, as we laid on our backs on the adjoining sofas, my eyes half closed from the weed, listening to Layla talk about her travels, her mum's love life, the bounced emails to her dad's account.

It felt good to be in her company. To be with someone who knew my past, and didn't ask any questions, need any explanations. I felt closer to home, to the person I used to be. Before I'd become consumed by the search for Scarlett.

I'd been too young to join in, the first time around – when my parents were scouring the country, talking to her friends, the police, the papers, even hiring a private detective. And by the time I was old enough to get involved, they'd pretty much given up. But I'd never allowed myself to believe that Scarlett might not be somewhere in the world, continuing through life as we all were, with a large absence at the heart of everything she did. She must miss us, too. But whatever had happened to her was clearly too big to come back from. Or maybe, like Layla, she was off travelling the world, and one day she'd simply decide to come home. She'd arrive with a big rucksack, a dirty round-the-world tan, long-dreadlocks, but that same smile she'd always had, that wide, teasing . . .

'Kate? You've totally drifted off. Maybe it's time for bed?'

'Oh, sorry.' I stood up too quickly. It was past midnight already. 'I've got to be up in a few hours.'

'Hey, K,' Layla said as we headed upstairs. 'You know that café you work in – can I come there tomorrow, maybe get a coffee? I've not got much else on.'

'Yeah, 'course.' I smiled. 'It's really easy to find, right in the middle of Crouch End. Come whenever you like.'

* * *

Layla arrived as the lunchtime rush was subsiding, making exactly the kind of entrance I'd been dreading – flinging the door to one side, dressed in a tight black mini-dress with blue fishnets that matched her hair.

'Check her out.' Marco nudged Pete, who grinned.

'Hi, Layla.' I waved, and both men turned to look at me, not bothering to hide their surprise.

'Where have you been hiding her?' Marco asked, but I ignored him and went over to take Layla's order.

'Look at all these rich bitches,' Layla hissed. 'It's like a Boden catalogue in here.'

'Shhh, you'll get me into trouble,' I said as I headed off to make Layla's coffee, which Pete insisted on delivering to her table.

Within two hours though, the novelty was wearing off, with Layla still taking up the corner table, busy on her phone, and Pete shooting me impatient looks.

'Shall I meet you at home?' I said, clearing Layla's empty cup.

'I'll wait for you to finish, then we can walk home together.'

'Oh, right . . .' I'd been planning to go to Camden after work, and I was about to try another approach when I noticed Layla looking over my shoulder.

'Kate?' I turned around and found myself facing Jasmine, who was looking uncertainly from me to Layla and back again.

'Jasmine. What are you doing here?'

'Can I have a word?'

'Who's this?' Layla asked, looking Jasmine up and down. She was wearing a long, loose-fitting floral dress, hair in a ponytail, her face pale and sharp-edged.

'This is Jasmine, my . . . someone I know, from round here . . . Jasmine, this is Layla, she's an old friend.' This was not how I'd pictured confronting Jasmine. I'd been hoping to

112

bump into her on neutral ground, not with an audience. And especially not Layla.

'Kate, we need to talk,' Jasmine said.

'How did you find me?' I asked under my breath, and Layla looked up from her phone, her interest piqued.

'It wasn't hard. Look, can we go somewhere private?'

'Anything you've got to say to my friend, you can say in front of me.' Layla was so used to protecting me at school, she'd slipped straight into the role.

'Look, it's fine, Layla. Leave it,' I said. 'I need to talk to Jasmine.'

'We can't talk here,' Jasmine said, shooting Layla a hostile look.

'Listen, I don't know what you want, but I don't like the way you're talking to my friend.' Layla stood up and scraped her chair loudly. Jasmine sprang back, turning to leave.

'Layla, honestly, it's fine,' I said. 'Jasmine, don't go.'

'I'm not talking to you here.' Jasmine glared at Layla. She took out a pen and paper from her bag and wrote down a number. 'If you want to hear what I've got to say, meet me at the Broadway Café at midday next Saturday. Alone. If you can't make it, call me on this number.'

As we watched her leave, I tucked the piece of paper in the pocket of my jeans. Part of me wanted to go outside and ring it straight away, find out what was going on. But I could tell I wouldn't get anything out of Jasmine over the phone. I would just have to wait.

Chapter Fourteen

Rain lashed against the bifold doors as I sat alone on Della's sofa that Thursday. There had been an atmosphere ever since I'd arrived. I was trying hard to mask the disappointment that had settled over me the moment the email had arrived that morning. The one informing me that I didn't 'have the necessary experience required,' even for the administrative temping agency I'd been holding back as a last resort.

I needed to know whether Della had read my stories. I knew it was unrealistic to see an imaginary book deal as some kind of solution to my problems, but I didn't have much else to hope for. Della seemed impatient though, shooing the children into the kitchen and closing the partition doors, asking Mark to leave us in peace in the living room. She ignored the many empty seats and sat down right next to me on the sofa, our knees almost touching.

'I've got something to ask you,' she said, sounding excited, nervous even. 'Well, it's more of a proposition, really. How would you like to come to France with us?'

'On holiday? With you?' A few minutes earlier I'd been psyching myself up on the doorstep, preparing for my final session with Della, for my goodbyes with the children. I'd brought them little porcelain rabbits to remember me by. I had a sense that everything was coming to an end. Della and the family would be leaving for France, and I would be meeting Jasmine. I hadn't found Scarlett, hadn't got a proper job, and my money was running out. I didn't know if I'd even still be in London when they got back.

But now Della was inviting me away with them. 'To look after the children,' she continued. 'As a sort of live-in nanny. We'd need you for two months. Mark will be coming back and forth for work. And I've got some speaking engagements. But there will be plenty of time for you to enjoy yourself, swim, tap into your creativity . . .'

I listened, captivated, as Della mapped out our imaginary summer. My room at the top of their French farmhouse in the hills near Montpellier. Days spent supervising the children in the pool and accompanying them on trips to the beach. Evening meals shared with Della and Mark and their various guests. The chance to meet some of Della's publishing contacts. The odd afternoon off to write and think.

'We often have friends stopping by – Jonathan, Dee. Alan might even be coming,' Della said.

'But . . . what about my rent? My job . . .' I remembered. There was no way I could afford to give everything up.

'We'll pay you, of course, £600 a week. And you won't have any living expenses. That should be enough to cover your rent while you're away, shouldn't it?'

I looked at Della, barely able to process what she was saying. That was nearly double what I earned at the café. Even after my rent, I'd be able to save up for months of Dad's care.

'It's such a generous offer, thank you. But . . . they won't keep my job open if I disappear for two months. I'll have no way of making money when I get back.'

'Oh, you'll work something out. You need some creative time, a place to think. I'm sorry I haven't had a chance to read the stories yet, but I'll take them away with us and we can really workshop them. You've got so much potential, Kate. There's nothing keeping you here, except a few waitressing shifts and a house-share you don't even like.' I watched as Della waved away my entire existence with a flick of her wrist.

'But what about my parents, Scarlett—'

'I thought we'd agreed you were going to put the search on hold for a while. You were saying you needed to get away from it all, to find yourself, weren't you?'

I paused. It was Della who'd said all those things. But she did have a point. What *would* I be sticking around for? I thought about the rejection email that morning.

'But, I don't have any experience . . .' I pointed out.

'The children dote on you, that's enough for me, and Mark. And haven't you always wanted to go to France? The children would be so disappointed if you didn't come. And we would too.'

Della stood up, walking to the door to see me out. 'Take some time to think about it, Kate, but I do hope you'll say yes,' she said, squeezing my arm. 'You wouldn't just be our nanny, you'd be our guest of honour.'

The smile she gave me left me feeling flattered and uneasy at the same time.

'Let me get this straight. Some woman's going to *pay* you to go to France, for two months, and your problem is . . . ?' I'd walked in to find Layla and Liam sitting in the living room, sharing a joint. Layla seemed to have worked her charm, for now. 'I mean, I can see why you don't want to leave all this behind.' Layla ran her hand along the grubby wall.

'But what about your room?' Liam asked. 'Are you going to go off and leave us?'

'Look, if I do go, I'll cover the rent. It's only two months.'

'Since when did you get so loaded?' Liam looked at me suspiciously. 'And what do you actually know about this woman? Sounds a bit weird to me. Is it going to be some kind of spiritual retreat?' He and Layla shared a look, and I wondered what he'd been telling her about my new friend Della while I was out of the house.

'No! I know her pretty well by now. And she's going to pay me. I'll be their nanny. And . . . I haven't decided if I'm going or not yet.'

'Why wouldn't you? Seize the day, man.' Layla gave me a big, stoned smile.

'It does sound amazing, two months of sun, really good money – and there's a swimming pool, too,' I said, letting my excitement take over, before reality set in. 'What about work, though? They're not going to keep my job open. When I get back, I'll be stuck with no shifts, and no money to pay the rent. I know it's not much, that job, but I haven't been able to find anything else.'

'I'll take the shifts,' Layla said, looking pleased with herself. 'I'll cover you while you're away. And I can stay in your room – keep it cosy for you.'

'But you've only just got here.' I looked at Layla, who had made herself more at home than I'd felt in the five months I'd been here. 'We've barely had time to catch up.'

'There's plenty of time for all that,' Layla smiled, stretching out her toes. 'And you'd be doing me a favour really – I could do with the money.'

I could see Layla would rather have my shifts than my company, but Liam didn't seem so ready to give up.

'Who will I do the crossword with?' he asked looking up

at me, and for a moment, through the haze of Layla's smoke, I wondered whether the two of them might be enough to keep me here – a summer with my oldest friend and my newest one. After all, I hadn't really given Liam a chance yet. And now that he was getting on with Layla, who was to say where things might lead?

'You'll find someone, I'm sure,' I said, accepting the joint from Layla and sitting down next to Liam, aware of my leg brushing his. 'But, like I said, I don't know if I'm going.'

'No one else as good as you,' he said quietly, watching me as I inhaled, 'not another writer.' Liam had been very impressed by my stories – not that I'd let him read them, but the fact of them, that I had a 'creative outlet', as he put it. Everyone needed a passion, he'd said. He'd grown up in a big family, so much noise and drama and competition. For him, coding was an escape – growing up, he could spend hours alone in his room, bringing a program to life, making an object move around the screen, exploring its dimensions. I'd dismissed it as geeky when he'd first shown me but, thinking about it now, it was no less artistic than Layla's linocuts, or photomontage, or whatever she was working on these days.

'You can send me clues.' I smiled at Liam, passing him the joint. 'I'm sure I'll be able to pick up messages on my phone, or emails. We can keep in touch.'

Layla turned to look at us both, raising her eyebrows. 'If you're serious about your writing, this could be exactly what you need – inspiration, a fresh perspective, a break from reality . . .'

I knew she was right. I couldn't imagine regretting a summer away from the mould, the café, the search. And it was only two months. Liam and Layla would still be there when I got back. Could I really pass up on eight weeks of sunshine and writing, a generous salary, good food and company; of Della,

Mark and the children, maybe even the chance to talk to Alan about my stories?

And then I remembered Jasmine.

On our way to the café the next morning, Layla wouldn't let it go.

'Look, whoever that weirdo is, she's not going to come between you and your summer of *amour*.' She was already convinced I was going to meet some French barman and disappear off around Europe.

We were going to talk to Pete about the idea of Layla covering my shifts. It had been Layla's suggestion that she come along, but I could see the appeal: Layla would do all the talking and Pete would be powerless to resist. The whole arrangement seemed to have taken on a momentum of its own. All that remained was the question of what I was going to tell my parents. And what I would do about Jasmine.

'I can't just not turn up,' I said.

'Of course you can. Who *is* she anyway?'

'She's nobody . . .' I replied, giving up. I'd call Jasmine and arrange to meet her earlier. I needed to find out what she had to say before I made my decision.

As I suspected, Pete was almost too ready to accept Layla as a temporary substitute, and that evening she was full of the excitement of it all.

'It's gonna be so cool,' she enthused over a celebratory pizza, while Liam lurked in the background on his laptop, sulking. 'A real, proper job. You're such a good friend, Kate. You're really getting me back on my feet.'

I smiled, but I didn't feel like I'd had much to do with it.

'And you're gonna have such an amazing summer,' Layla continued, clinking chipped mugs of Cava. 'You'll come home all tanned and sophisticated, loads of cash in your pocket . . .'

My phone beeped. It was a text from Della. She wanted me to come round at eleven on Saturday to discuss arrangements. There was no suggestion in the message that I might be planning to decline her invitation. And there was also no chance I'd be able to get away to meet Jasmine.

I felt in my pocket for the number Jasmine had given me. I'd have to call and rearrange. But the piece of paper wasn't there. I must have been wearing my other jeans. Up in my room, I rummaged through my drawers.

'Has anyone seen my black jeans?' I shouted down the stairs. Layla appeared in the hallway, looking shifty.

'Oh, I borrowed them,' she said, bounding up the stairs to retrieve them from her room. 'But don't worry, I washed them. Here, look, they're all clean.'

She handed the jeans over, and I searched the pockets. When I pulled out my hand, it was covered in white fluff.

'Layla! That was Jasmine's number. Now I've got no way of getting hold of her.'

'Oh well.' Layla shrugged. 'That'll teach her.'

'No, that'll teach *me*. I wanted to see her. I wanted to know what she had to say. She might have given me a good reason not to go away. And now I'll never know . . .' I slammed the door behind me and threw the jeans on my bed. Had Layla done it on purpose? What was her problem with Jasmine?

I sat down and picked up my phone, scrolling through all the eager messages Della had sent since our last meeting – 'let us know and we'll book an extra seat on the plane', 'we'll sort your travel insurance', 'don't forget your bikini!!' I thought about Jonathan's description of the house, and Amisha's. The thrill I'd felt at being given a glimpse of another world, the seeming impossibility of ever truly being invited in.

And now I had been. I'd be working, of course, but I'd be

their guest of honour, that's what Della had said. I couldn't turn her down because of some strange conspiracy dreamt up by Jasmine and Claire, their bitterness and jealousy. I was at one of life's great turning points, leaving behind one life and embracing a whole new beginning. It was time to take the leap, as Della would say. *Della Dares, Do You?*

Now I can see she had got me exactly where she wanted. It was a turning point all right, but not of the kind I was expecting. Once I left for France with Della and her family, nothing would ever be the same again.

PART TWO

France, July

Chapter Fifteen

The sun warmed my face as I sat on the patio, listening to a lone bird cry in the treetops. It was a rare moment of peace, the children upstairs with Della while she picked outfits for them to wear for Jonathan and Dee's arrival. I held my water glass to my forehead, the ice clinking as I felt beads of condensation run down my face, my shorts and vest clinging to my skin. The sky was an arresting unbroken blue, the air still, the coconut smell of my sun cream mingling with the herbs planted in the small kitchen garden, rosemary, thyme, something lemon-scented. I stretched out my legs and became aware of that prickling sensation, as though I was being watched. Probably Della from the bedroom window, wondering when I would be coming in to take over.

I lifted my sunglasses and looked up at the stone farmhouse, but I couldn't make out any shapes at the small window. Through the patio doors, in the darkness of the kitchen, something shifted. Moments later, I heard a splash. I walked around the gardens at the side of the house to find Mark, muscled arms lifting rhythmically, making barely a ripple as he glided through the sparkling turquoise of the pool. I should

125

have gone upstairs then, to see whether Della needed my help. I thought he would reach the end and turn without lifting his head, as he usually did when the children were around, not wanting to be interrupted. But this time he stopped, raised himself out of the water and sat on the edge shaking drops from his hair. He held his hand up to shield the sun from his eyes and smiled straight at me. He knew I'd been watching.

It had only been two weeks, but already it was as though all time had been suspended, all the usual rules of behaviour forgotten. We lived here now, in this sultry, airless, lush landscape – the hot pinks and reds of the gardens, the low hum of insects; the farmhouse perched on a hilltop surrounded by woodlands, layer upon layer of vibrant green ebbing away from the house in a sea of trees. In the stifling, unrelenting heat, the old barriers had fallen away and new alliances formed. And there I was, caught in the middle, like one of the insects drawn to the citronella candles Della lit nightly as the three of us ate on the patio, trying to work out where I fitted in to this uneven family scene.

Now, Mark slipped back into the pool and I turned towards the house, reluctantly, wondering whether his hand gesture had in fact been a wave, inviting me in. But I could hear the children calling for me, and knew Della would be losing patience by now. I walked slowly through the French windows into the cavernous downstairs rooms, living room leading through into the kitchen, which opened out onto the front patio, the uneven stone walls of both rooms adorned with garish local pottery and abstract market scenes.

Upstairs were five bedrooms, some of which had been modernised, with en suite bathrooms boasting shiny chrome taps. Others, like mine, had been left untouched, old stone walls and splintered wooden floors, small-paned windows flanked by flaking shutters. 'Distressed,' Della had called it when we'd arrived, throwing open the windows and doors, letting out the musty smells that had lingered despite the best efforts of Manon, the cleaner who came in twice a week all year round to keep on top of the house and garden.

This morning Manon was whisking around the house, readying it for our first guests of the summer, and I found the children tucked away in their bedroom, playing quietly in their best clothes – a white dress for Tabitha, white shorts and a pale blue collared shirt for Jasper – no sign of their mother. I threw on a clean sundress and had begun telling them an Enchanted Elsie story about a wicked elf and a naughty prince when we heard the crunch of tyres on the stone driveway. After all this time with only their parents and me for company, the children were beside themselves. They tore through the house. It was all I could do to stop them running in front of the four-wheel drive as it pulled in.

Dee climbed out first, looking at the children with a half-smile and surprising me with a hug. Mark and Della were nowhere to be seen.

'You look great,' Dee said. 'The air out here obviously suits you.'

'It's true,' agreed Jonathan, joining us and clapping me on the back, 'you're positively glowing. It looks like this place has done you a world of good.'

I hadn't been aware of looking quite so in need of a holiday, but I was struck by how far away we all felt from the supper we'd shared in London. Here I was a fellow holiday-maker, a family guest, and one who looked the part, evidently – tanned and slim from all the swimming. I found myself chatting freely as I showed Dee and Jonathan to their room, the most recently done, with a breathtaking view across the treetops.

'We're miles from anywhere here, aren't we?' Dee peered out of the small window. She and Jonathan had driven across from his villa near Sète and, like me, Dee evidently hadn't been prepared for quite how remote the farmhouse would be, on the edge of a small group of villages, at least an hour from Montpellier.

'Isn't it beautiful, though?' I joined Dee at the window. 'About as far away from North London as you can get.' I smiled, breathing in the clear air and feeling, in that moment, entirely at home. I turned to find Dee watching me.

'Looks like you've settled right in,' Dee said, studying me.

'Come on,' Jonathan said. 'I'm dying for a swim. Wash off that drive.'

At the mention of the pool, my stomach lurched. The children. In all the excitement of the arrival, I'd left them on their own.

I ran from the room, indecisive in my panic. Should I look upstairs, where they sometimes played hide and seek in the wardrobes and behind the beds? Or downstairs, where we escaped the fierce heat of the midday sun? No, first the pool. That was the main source of anxiety, and the reason Jasper had to be watched at all times.

It had been made clear as soon as we arrived that this would be my responsibility, and I'd been vigilant every moment of every day. Until now.

Horrific scenes flashed through my mind as I bounded down the stairs and ran, panting, through the French windows. But outside, I stopped in the shadow of the house. There, sitting on loungers by the pool, were Tabitha and Jasper, with their parents, who had reappeared, freshly attired: Della in a white floor-length dress and Mark in chinos and a white shirt. Each had a child on their knee, and all four of them were giggling, eating raspberries off each other's fingertips.

My relief was mixed with disbelief. It was the first time I'd seen the family all together like this since we'd arrived in France – enjoying themselves, laughing. Most of the time, the children had been left to me, while Mark swam lengths or read reports and Della retreated under an umbrella with her laptop to catch up on social media. Sometimes Mark played with the children long enough for me to go to the toilet, grab a drink, do the washing up. But never this: the four of them, in a huddle, enjoying each other's company.

It made a striking tableau: the white of their clothes against the blue of the pool, blond heads leaning together. It was the scene that greeted Jonathan and Dee as they emerged from the house, and they stood together watching for a little while, a few feet away from me.

'Aren't they the most gorgeous family?' Dee came up by my side. 'They could be in a holiday brochure or something.' I murmured in agreement, half tempted to remark that this was probably the desired effect.

'Jonathan, Dee!' Della stood up, as though only now aware of their arrival. 'You should have told us you were standing there. Sit down, have some fruit – it's fresh from the market. And a drink? Wine? G&T? Something soft?' She hugged them both, as did Mark, before the hosts and their guests settled themselves down around the pool, taking up all the seats. I hovered by them, awkwardly.

'A G&T would be *divine*,' Jonathan said, to raised eyebrows from Dee.

'I'll have a juice,' she said to me, as I found myself in waitress mode.

'Three G&Ts and a juice then,' Della said, 'and get something for yourself and the children.'

I removed myself to the kitchen, my cheeks hot. I knew Della and Mark were paying me, but until now my only duty had been to look after the children. Della had prepared lunches and Mark barbecued in the evening. I hadn't been expected to wait on anyone.

But perhaps that *was* meant to be part of my duties. It had all been so unclear. And I'd been so over-friendly with Dee and Jonathan when they arrived. I'd shown them around the house as though I was a fellow guest, a host even – no wonder Dee had been taken aback.

As I carried the tray to the pool, I could see Della had had enough of the children. They were hanging off her arms excitedly, hoping for another glimmer of attention, but though she stroked Jasper's head absent-mindedly, she was in full swing with her guests.

'Thanks, Kate,' Mark said under his breath, meeting me halfway to relieve me of some of the glasses. 'Kate makes the best G&Ts,' he announced as I put the tray down. 'We've been having a grand old time, haven't we?' he added, with a smile. I knew it wasn't true; I'd only made G&Ts once so far, and they were far too strong – Della practically spat hers out. But I appreciated the gesture, and smiled back, feeling suddenly shy.

I'd got used to the sight of Mark lounging about in old swimming shorts and a T-shirt, but the white shirt he'd put on emphasised his tan and the stubble he'd grown since we'd been away. The difference in him was striking, and I became aware of having looked at him for too long.

'Yes. Thanks, Kate, that's really kind,' Dee said, looking from me to Mark, with a glint in her eye.

'Kate's a sweetheart, aren't you?' Della smiled, not at me, but at her guests. 'I think the children would really rather go inside and play now, darling. Do you mind?'

That evening, it was Mark who cooked, as usual, grilling steaks and fish on the patio barbecue, the sweet scent of charred meat filling the still air as we sat around the table in candlelight, the chirp of crickets our only soundtrack. I had been called upon to lay the long table, though not to serve the drinks this time. But I hung back in the conversation, listening as Della regaled her guests with tales of the local market and the characters they'd meet there the following day.

Eventually, with nothing to add, I got up and wandered over to where Mark stood. He was absent-mindedly flipping the food, but his eyes were fixed on the horizon, looking out across the treetops as the sun sank below them.

'Do you need any help?' I asked, and he turned to look at me, confused.

'Sorry, Kate, I was miles away. Isn't it stunning.' Mark looked out, the orange glow of the sun falling across his cheekbones.

'More beautiful than I could ever have imagined,' I said softly, enjoying this shared moment away from the others. Mark began transferring the meat and fish onto two plates, and he handed them to me, catching my eye.

'Thanks, Kate. I don't know what we'd do without you.'

I turned towards the table and saw that Dee had drifted off from what Della and Jonathan were saying. She seemed far more interested in me and Mark, and she watched me cross the patio without even thinking to get up and take one of the plates. The children and I had made a salad before they'd gone to bed, Tabitha taking great care to arrange the peppers and tomatoes according to colour and size, and as I laid it on the table, Dee stopped me in my tracks.

'Hold it there, that's right. With the light from the candle. Like that.' She pulled out her phone and took a series of photos from different angles. 'Perfect, that's the one.' She sat down and I watched her search her phone for the right filter, craft a caption and post it to Instagram, all while the rest of us began to eat, her dinner cooling on her plate.

'Well, that's dedication, I suppose,' Della said to Jonathan, over Dee's head. 'I really don't think I could be bothered.'

Dee looked up. 'You'll have to, if you want to make a success of your blog. That's how it's done these days.' She flashed Della a smile that looked like a challenge in the flickering candlelight.

'I know what you mean though,' I said. 'I'd rather live my life in the moment than keep stopping to record it. I sometimes wonder what it's going to do to our memories, to our lives, to be constantly framing and reframing, parcelling up every experience to be consumed by other people.'

Everyone looked at me. It was probably the most I'd said in their presence so far, but I meant it. I couldn't bear the idea that life might pass you by while you were scrolling through your phone. Especially not since Scarlett had left. I was living for the two of us.

'I wouldn't go that far.' Della smiled at Dee. 'I mean, you've got a very successful business to keep running. And I certainly wouldn't suggest you're not enjoying life at the same time.'

'No, that's not what I meant—' I tried to interject.

'It's OK. I completely get it,' Dee broke in. 'It's something I think about, too. You know, how far is the person I'm projecting the real me, the authentic me?'

'It's all changing so fast,' Della said, shrugging at Jonathan, who speared up a forkful of steak and muttered something about being too old for social media.

Only Mark didn't speak. I could feel his eyes on me as the discussion continued and I tried to concentrate on my salmon, wondering why Della had been so quick to dismiss me, when I was only defending her in the first place.

'This younger generation is so impressive,' I heard Mark say eventually, and I looked up. 'They seem so switched on, so wise beyond their years. I'm full of admiration.' Della smiled thinly as Mark raised a glass in my direction and I blushed, looking to Dee next to me, who was part of the compliment as well, after all.

But Dee turned to me and raised an eyebrow. 'There's a lot of admiration going on around here, that's for sure,' she said in a low voice. I looked around quickly, convinced the others had heard. But the conversation carried on around us and nothing more was aimed in my direction. Long into the evening I felt the warmth of Mark's words in my cheeks, the heat of his attention, the spark that Dee had noticed. I only hoped no one else could see.

Chapter Sixteen

I was floating on my back, eyes closed, ears submerged under-water. Everyone else had gone to the local town. It had been Dee's idea – she'd suggested taking the children and leaving me in peace for a few hours.

It hadn't even been a month since I'd left London, but the idea of two or three uninterrupted hours to myself in the middle of the day seemed like a distant memory. I hadn't had a single day off since we'd arrived. I was used to working long hours, but at least at the café the shifts were mine to choose – and my mind was my own. I didn't have to answer seven questions a minute, twelve hours a day. I felt as though my head had been invaded; colonised by a dictatorship of two.

Now that I was finally free to daydream, I allowed myself to pretend for a few moments that I was floating in my own pool, in my own French holiday house, perhaps even my home. Although Della was the designated food shopper – a task she relished as only someone with a regular Ocado delivery could – she occasionally let the children and me join her in a trip to the nearest small town, all tree-lined streets and sun-dappled squares. We'd visit the market, lingering over the stalls while Della conversed in broken French about the freshest cuts of meat and fish, the best olives and cheese.

I'd never tasted anything like it. Or eaten 'al fresco' every evening. Or witnessed good wine drunk in such quantities. It was hard now to imagine why anyone would live any other way. I couldn't speak a word of French, but that didn't stop me picturing the life I could build for myself, up here in the hills – swimming, writing, making new friends.

Layla certainly seemed convinced that's what was going to happen. I'd finally been able to check my emails in the past few days, thanks to Dee. The Wi-Fi on my phone was non-existent, and I hadn't wanted to waste my savings on an expensive data roaming package. I'd assumed I'd have the chance to use Della's laptop, or Mark's, but they hadn't offered. Dee had been more forthcoming though, and I'd found messages from Layla, and one from my parents, asking when I'd be back.

There had been a message from Liam, too – short but chatty, and ended with a kiss and a PS: *Got stuck on an anagram, twelve letters: demise yours.* I hadn't got it at the time but, lying in the pool, the letters rearranged themselves against my closed eyelids. You're missed. I smiled, feeling a gentle breeze blowing across the exposed parts of my body. Viewed from a distance, Liam seemed more appealing, his eagerness more touching. I allowed my mind to wander, to imagine what it would feel like to invite him here – and Layla. What would they make of it all? My eyelids felt heavy in the sunshine . . .

And then, suddenly, I was cold. A shadow fell across my face and upper body and I looked up, startled, my legs splashing below the surface. It took a few moments to make out the face silhouetted against the blazing sun.

'Dee! What are you doing here?' My heart was pounding. I'd thought I was alone.

135

'I decided to stay here,' Dee said, walking around the pool while I swam to the edge, feeling invaded all over again. 'I could do with a break from those kids. They're cute 'n' all, but . . .'

'I know.' I lifted myself out. 'They never stop. Maybe you get used to it?' I sat down, dripping, on the lounger next to Dee, drying myself off with a towel.

'Or maybe you get so bored of yourself, it's a relief to think about someone else,' Dee suggested, lying on her front and unclipping her bikini top, her dark skin smooth and glistening. 'I don't know, though, look at Della. She knows how to keep her distance. Maybe that's the answer – you outsource the kids to someone else and get on with your life. That's what they did in the olden days, isn't it. If they could afford it. Visit them at teatime, give them a pat on the head and a kiss before bed.'

We both considered this for a while, in silence.

'What do you make of her? Della, I mean.' Dee lifted her head and looked at me over her Ray-Bans.

I glanced at the Ruth Rendell novel I'd left face down by my lounger, wishing Dee had gone with the others so I could enjoy this rare free time in peace. 'What do you mean?'

'Oh, you know, she's so . . . perfect. Everything's just so. But she never relaxes, does she? It's as though her whole life is a performance. It's all for show.'

'But you're friends with her, aren't you? You must know there's more to her than that.'

Dee shrugged. 'Jonathan's friends with her. Though even he couldn't tell you exactly why. She attached herself to him, from the sounds of it. Started turning up at parties, holding court, even though no one really knew who'd invited her, or why she was there. But Jonathan's easily flattered . . . and Della's persistent. She certainly knows what she wants.'

I looked away, thinking about what Helen had said in the

136

restaurant. 'I don't know . . .' Dee carried on. 'I thought you of all people would see through the act – look at how she treats *you*. I mean, aren't you a friend of the family? And now she's got you running around her like some kind of maid. What's that all about?'

I bent down to rub sun cream into my legs, reminded of that dinner party in London, the oddness of the story Della had told. But that already felt so far away. Our relationship had shifted so much since then.

'Yeah, well . . . it's a long story. But, you know, I *am* the nanny. I'm paid to be here.' I could see how it looked. But Dee didn't know Della like I did. She didn't mean things to come out the way they sometimes did. That's why she needed someone like me around, who understood her, who could smooth things over.

'I know, but there's some weird power trip going on there. And then there's Mark. I mean, talk about a silent partner . . .'

'Mark's great,' I said quickly. 'He's brilliant with the kids, and he can be a good laugh, too.'

'I know all that.' Dee smiled at me in a way I didn't like. 'But what's he doing with *her*? She treats him like another one of her children. Like she does with you. Except *he* doesn't get paid. He must earn a packet – surely they're not being kept afloat by her "life-coaching" business?' She said the words with a sneer. 'So why stay with her?' She paused. 'I mean . . . we've all seen the way he is around you.'

I sat up and pulled my towel around me, my heart beating fast. I knew what Dee thought she'd seen, but I didn't expect her to say it out loud. I couldn't ignore the little thrill that ran through me, but almost as quickly, it was replaced by dread. What if Della had seen it, too?

'Look, I don't know what you're getting at, but they're really kind people. They're putting us both up, and—'

'You're an interesting one.' Dee gave me a sidelong glance, and I thought not for the first time how overrated all this antipodean honesty was. 'I mean, you're not the world's most natural nanny. And you're certainly not here for the nightlife. So what is it?'

I looked away, feeling annoyed by the suggestion that I hadn't bonded with the kids. What did Dee know? But she carried on, almost to herself, as though trying to piece it all together.

'What is it about a woman who wants to surround herself with these young girls . . . these mini-mes who hang on her every word?'

'The *girls* are her clients. I'm her nanny. There's nothing more to it than that.' I needed to get inside, out of the sun. I'd been trying hard not to think about it all: the Janes, what they were all doing now, why I'd been the one who was invited here. But the question that had been circling at the edges of my mind formed clearly now: what did Della and Mark want with me?

'There's something weird about it all.' Dee shuddered, flicking her hair. Then she stood up abruptly, throwing me into the shade. 'I'm getting out of here. Tomorrow. I want to go back to London. If you had any sense, you would too.'

None of us knew how the topic was broached, but we all heard the fallout. Jonathan's deep rumble and Dee's high-pitched response carrying on well into the evening, while I sat with Della and Mark on the terrace, trying to keep a conversation going as we watched our meal get cold. Eventually Jonathan emerged, alone, looking flustered.

'I'm sorry about this, but Dee's not going to be joining us for dinner,' he said, sitting down. 'She's not, er, feeling well. In fact, I think we're going to have to head off tomorrow.'

'What's going on? Is everything OK?' Della's concern was clearly for Jonathan, not Dee.

'Can we talk inside?' Jonathan threw Della a meaningful look and they retreated into the kitchen, leaving Mark and me alone on the terrace.

'I'd happily see the back of Dee *and* Jonathan,' Mark said, topping up our wine glasses and raising a toast. 'To peace and quiet, and the end of all drama.' We clinked glasses. 'What about you, Kate – are you enjoying yourself?'

'It's perfect.' I looked across the terrace at the sun lowering over the hilltop. The air was still and warm, the only sound the distant birds.

'I sometimes think we should sell up everything in London, give up work and move here,' Mark said. 'Life would be so much simpler, spending time with the kids, in the fresh air. Della would be able to relax, get back to herself . . .' He looked up, as though realising he was saying all this out loud. 'Stupid, really – it would never happen.'

'I was thinking that too, earlier. I can't imagine being in London now. I could happily live here for the rest of my life . . .' I looked at Mark, thinking how unfair it was – two people who wanted the same thing, but the wrong two people.

'Let's stay, then,' Mark said, with a smile. 'All of us. We could open a café . . . you could work behind the bar!' There was laughter in his voice, but the comment stung.

'Oh yes, my legendary G&Ts . . .' I could see Mark was trying to be generous, but he couldn't help putting me in that role: the hired help.

'No, I didn't mean it like that.' He looked uncomfortable now. 'I'm sorry about the other day. With Jonathan and Dee. The way Della spoke . . . She doesn't mean to.'

'I know. And I'm being paid to be here. I get it.'

'It's not like that, though.' Mark caught my eye. 'I'm really glad you came with us. We all are. I can't imagine the place without you now.'

'Rubbish, you'll be here next year with another nanny, saying exactly the same thing.' I laughed lightly and put down my wine glass, feeling self-conscious after what Dee had said by the pool.

'No, I mean it. Something about you just fits here.' Mark looked up at the sky, deep in thought, while I allowed myself to feel the glow of his words. 'Della says it's self-destructive, always wanting to be somewhere else. The idea of moving to France, starting a new life, my "plan B" – she calls it "self-sabotage".' He looked at me, smiling at my expression. 'Oh yes, she does it to me, too.'

'Isn't it more about not wanting to be where you are? Looking for an escape route anywhere you can.' I was picturing Green Lanes, the mice, the drug dealers. I wasn't expecting Mark to nod in agreement so eagerly.

'Yes, that's probably it,' he agreed. 'But is it really so impossible, to imagine another way of living?'

'It shouldn't be. I think it's too easy to get trapped in other people's ideas of what it means to live, what it means to succeed, to try to live up to some impossible standard . . .' I trailed off, thinking about Scarlett, my mum, Dan. But Mark was looking at me intently.

'How do you know so much, at your age? It's like you can see right through me.' He held my eye, until I looked away. Della might come outside at any minute. She could be watching from a window. But I couldn't get over how open Mark allowed himself to be. He might have been older than me, but he seemed so naive, so ready for every new experience, every conversation. It was freeing, somehow, to talk to him. He made me feel like I could say anything. For a moment, I was worried I might.

'I think I'd better call it a night,' I said, standing up. 'Those two will have me up early in the morning.'

'Night, Kate,' Mark said quietly, watching me from his chair as I walked to the kitchen, his long legs stretched out in front of him, utterly relaxed. 'Let's keep working on that plan B.'

I laughed lightly, but I didn't dare look back. Either he wasn't aware of the effect of his words, or he didn't mind. I couldn't decide which I wanted it to be.

Chapter Seventeen

Jonathan and Dee weren't the only ones to leave. On Sunday morning, I came downstairs to find Mark downing a coffee, his suitcase by the front door.

'What's going on?' I asked, quickly adjusting my dressing gown. I hadn't expected to find anyone else up so early in the morning. I'd even beaten the kids.

'Work,' Mark said with a grimace, looking up from his phone, where he was typing out a message. 'Got to go back to the office for a few days.'

'Oh. You didn't let on . . .' I tried not to let my disappointment show. But it felt so sudden. Della had gone to bed early the night before, after the excitement of the visitors, and Mark and I had sat up talking, about the children, the future, his frustration with his work. It seemed I was the first person he'd encountered in a long time who didn't think a high-powered job or a big salary was the true meaning of life. He'd always planned to give it up, he said, once he'd earned enough. 'But enough is never enough.' We'd talked for hours about consumerism, the climate crisis, the need for a simpler life. I'd voiced opinions to Mark I'd never said out loud before.

Things no one had bothered to ask me, or maybe I hadn't even really thought about. Talking to him was like going on a journey without knowing the destination. It was exciting, exhilarating. A few times during our conversation I'd almost let slip about Scarlett. I'd never really felt it before, but with Mark I wanted to be completely honest, transparent. I wanted him to know everything that had happened to me. Somehow it never seemed like quite the right moment to bring it up though.

Next time, I'd thought to myself as we headed to bed. When we'd said goodnight in the hallway, there had been something palpable in the air between us. I hadn't realised it was his imminent departure.

'I didn't want to mention it in front of the kids,' Mark said now. 'Didn't want a scene, you know. Just slip away. I'll be back before you know it.' He smiled helplessly and held out his hand. I took it and he stroked a thumb across my palm. As I watched him leave, I held the same hand to my cheek, a tear escaping before I was able to catch it.

Why hadn't he told me he was going? But then why would he, really? I was only the nanny. It was Della he discussed those things with, made plans with, whispered to after the lights were out. Sometimes I wondered what I would do, what I would give, to take her place. It seemed possible, somehow, out here. It was a fantasy I returned to at night, alone on the top floor. A dark one that made me uneasy, guilty. Perhaps it was for the best that Mark had gone. I needed to get over this infatuation, to focus on the children, and Della. She was the one who had invited me here in the first place, after all, and who had given so much of her time to me over the months.

That evening, Della and I sat in silence either side of the large terrace table, picking at the sea bass I'd attempted to grill in

Mark's absence. I'd been trying to relocate our common ground. When we'd first arrived in France, I'd been waiting for the workshops Della had mentioned, the chance to talk over my stories, once she'd actually read them. I'd even wondered whether we might find a way to continue our one-to-one sessions – after the children were in bed, perhaps. But soon, the hours we'd spent deep in conversation seemed so remote, I could hardly believe they had ever happened. I'd given up asking about my writing, since Della always changed the subject. There had been no mention of Alan visiting, and on the evenings when Della didn't retire early, I had begun making myself scarce, aware of the uncomfortable dynamic between the three of us.

'I really feel like I've been making some progress while we've been away,' I began tentatively, hoping to re-establish the bond we'd shared in London. Della looked at me for a moment and then, pushing her charred fish to one side and picking up her wine glass, she leaned forward.

'Have you? I've been giving you a bit of space. I think it's important after a period of intense work that you get a chance for it all to settle, in a new environment. That's why I thought it would be so good for you to come here.' Della smiled, and I felt reassured. Encouraged to go a little further.

'I've barely been thinking about my family at all since we got here, to be honest.' It was true, Scarlett had receded in my mind for the first time in months, maybe even years. I didn't know if that was a good thing or not. It was the longest I'd gone without speaking to my parents in my entire life. I'd been worrying about Dad's health off and on, but I'd reasoned with myself that his condition had been stable for a while. 'I've been concentrating on me, and what I might want for the future.'

'And what is it that you think you might want?' Della asked,

144

topping up her glass. 'Do you really think writing is the path for you?'

I tried to ignore the note of doubt in Della's tone. 'I definitely want to try writing down the new stories I've been telling the children, when I get the chance.' I smiled. 'Maybe I could show you those, if you haven't been able to get to the stories I gave you in London?' Della's eyes flicked towards the kitchen. I could see I was losing her attention already. 'And I think I've started to be able to imagine a future for myself as well – a family, a home, children. Having what you have.' Immediately, I could see I'd said the wrong thing. I didn't mean for it to come out that way. Della frowned. She sat back in her chair.

'Kate, the work we're doing together isn't about you wanting to become more like *me*,' she said slowly. 'It's about becoming the best version of *you*. Working out what it is that *you* want. I think you need to remember that children were never your priority. That was what first struck me about you. You seemed to know your own mind so well. You were certain about that one thing – something so many young women think they want because it's expected of them, by their families, their partners, society . . .'

'But I thought the point of this coaching was to find out who I really am. Don't people change as they grow?'

'Look, Kate, you may have spent a few weeks looking after my children, but that doesn't mean you know the reality of what it is to have children of your *own*,' Della said. 'I can see how this looks to you, to the outside world – and yes, we're lucky – but it takes a lot of hard work to set this all up. And not everyone can afford help, a nanny, all that. Some people have to do it all on their own. You've got to really want it; it's not just for show.'

'But I do want it,' I said, trying to get my head around the

idea that anyone might have children for show. 'Or I think I
do.' I remembered then how good Scarlett had always been
with our younger cousins. She was a natural with children
– fun, entertaining but not so keen that she scared them off.
Kids had flocked to her. Perhaps that's why I'd always thought
she'd be the mother of the two of us, not me.

'You think you do because we're here, and it looks easy.
Believe me, I know what it is to want a baby. To *really* want it,
more than anything. It's a biological thing, hormonal, it comes
over some women like an obsession, so that you would do
anything . . .' Her voice broke, and I thought she might cry. But
then she took a deep breath and carried on, her voice lowered.
'You're lucky not to have that. Jane, Eva . . . those others caught
in that insanity . . . They're the ones I feel sorry for.'

Della paused, looked up at the bedroom windows and then
back at me. 'You're good with the children. I can see that.
But don't fall into the trap all those articles want you to –
with their ticking clocks and their scare stories. Some women
are born to be mothers and others aren't. You don't have the
mothering instinct . . . the baby *hunger*. You should be glad
about that.'

I woke the next morning feeling uneasy, and the sensation
lingered throughout breakfast on the terrace. Della was being
particularly attentive to the children. Jasper, as usual, was the
one to sit on her knee. He was Della's baby, her 'little cherub'
she called him when she was in a good mood. Her relationship
with Tabitha was more complex; her affection waxed and waned.
Yet the more Della pulled away, the fiercer the competition for
her attention, and the more Tabitha strove to please. Now
Tabitha positioned herself at Della's arm, buttering toast and
passing it to her adoringly, while Della heaped on the praise.

After breakfast, Della suggested a swim, and the children

splashed excitedly after her into the pool, while I stood and watched, fully dressed, forgotten. I picked up the clothes that had been discarded and folded them neatly on the loungers while the children threw a ball around Della's head as she tried to swim lengths.

Della tired of the games quickly, and emerged, wrapping her lean, tanned body in a robe and retreating under an umbrella to catch up on her emails.

'Are you coming in, Kate?' asked Tabitha, splashing happily.

'Kate, Kate!' cried Jasper, his armbands waving as he gestured to me.

'No, you play. I'm going to watch.' The disappointment was clear on their faces, and I felt a pang of guilt. It was the first time I'd refused to join in with them. I knew I shouldn't punish them for enjoying their mother's company, but I couldn't help feeling pushed aside.

I was about to relent when both children came clambering out, ready for some new amusement.

'Mummy, will you play with us?' asked Tabitha.

'Yes, Mummy, what you doin'?' Jasper joined in, standing next to Della as she lay on a lounger by the pool, laptop on her knees. As he leaned over her, he took off his armbands, the trapped water splashing all over Della and her MacBook.

'Jasper!' Della shouted. 'What are you doing?' Jasper recoiled, startled, tipping backwards into the pool. He had no armbands on now, and his arms were thrashing about, his mouth open in panic. I watched, in horror, as for a few heart-stopping seconds he sank below the water. Della, consumed with the task of drying off her computer, looked up moments later.

'Jasper!' she screamed, but before she'd even got up from her lounger, I had jumped into the pool fully dressed, water streaming into my mouth and nose as I shouted his name, my arms clamping around his small body. My feet found the bottom and I brought Jasper to the surface, spluttering water and gasping. I sat him gently by the side of the pool and clambered out myself, patting him on the back while he continued to cough and cry, struggling for breath.

'Are you OK, darling?' Della asked, as I scooped Jasper up in a towel. 'Poor little thing. You gave us a fright.' Della stroked his head. 'But you really must be more careful around my things.' She turned to her screen, which remained blank, Tabitha whimpering beside her, while I carried Jasper into the house, fuming.

No mothering instinct. That's what Della had said to me. The woman who sat and watched while I rescued her two-year-old, without even a thank you. Who had been too busy looking at her laptop even to notice what was happening. My heart was pounding, adrenaline pumped through my body. But it wasn't just anger, it was fear – the split-second moment of thinking Jasper might be lost forever. The terror only now subsiding.

Holding his little body, heaving with sobs, wrapped in an oversized towel, I felt an overwhelming surge of love. It almost took my breath away, this desire to protect him at any cost, even from his mother, who hadn't followed us inside but was still sitting by the pool, pressing the power button with increasing urgency.

What would happen if I just kept on walking? If I got out of there, with Jasper – if I took him somewhere he would be safe and loved, unconditionally? I looked out of the window at Della, who had logged back into her computer now, ignoring Tabitha, who was kicking a chair absent-mindedly. She didn't deserve this life, these children. She wouldn't know what she had until it had gone.

Chapter Eighteen

Sophia's arrival was announced as everything else had been that summer, just moments in advance. Della's friend, a gossip columnist, would be coming to visit for a few days, from where she was staying in Cannes.

Sophia was short, slight, with bleached hair and heavy make-up, large sunglasses resting on her nose. She greeted the children half-heartedly, throwing barely a glance in my direction before turning away, distracted by something more interesting. I was dispatched for drinks, returning with a sparkling water that was immediately discarded as she sank into a lounger, resting her wedge-heeled espadrilles on the spotless white fabric.

'Now, Della,' she said, turning her entire body away from where the children and I stood, 'tell me *all* about what happened when Jonathan was here.' They leaned in together, lowering their voices, and I led Tabitha and Jasper away, aware of my role by now when visitors were present.

It had been quiet on the entertainment front since Jonathan and Dee had left, with Mark staying on in London and a potential visit from Amisha having been apparently vetoed by

Suzanne. But now Sophia had arrived, and although she was known for her social connections and outspoken charm, in person she lacked even the basic social niceties. She rarely looked me in the eye when she spoke, preferring to ignore my presence altogether if possible. Even in conversation with Della, she seemed detached, as if watching over her shoulder for someone else, despite the fact that we were, in her words, 'in the middle of absolutely fucking nowhere'.

'I mean, honestly, Della. You didn't tell me how remote this place was,' Sophia complained over dinner on her second evening. 'Even the bloody bees are bored around here.' She pointed to one that had settled drowsily in her large wine glass.

'I *am* sorry, Sophia.' Della was putting on a brave face, but I could see the visit wasn't going well. 'It is stunning, though . . . don't you think?'

I was washing up in the kitchen, having eaten with the children earlier, and I could hear a note of desperation in Della's voice as it carried through the open patio doors. Sophia's approval clearly mattered, and it wasn't forthcoming.

'If you like that kind of thing. I think we should go to Cannes tomorrow. Victor's having a party – it'll be fabulous, no doubt . . . And *Orlando* will be there.' She said the name in a mock whisper. I looked out of the window in time to catch Della giving Sophia a sharp look.

'Sophia,' Della hissed. 'For God's sake. He's only a *boy*. Besides, you know Kate and Mark are as thick as thieves these days. She's bound to pass on anything she hears.'

Sophia cackled, several glasses of wine in. 'That *mouse*? She's not going to say anything.'

Left alone with the children while Della disappeared off to Cannes, my anger only grew. All summer I had been clinging on to the desire to please her, to be acknowledged by her, even if I had felt let down by how quickly she had cast me aside. Now it seemed as though she might be off betraying the whole family – chasing after young men without a thought for Mark and the kids. Leaving me on my own to look after the two children she couldn't be bothered with. Which one of us wasn't cut out to be a mother?

It wasn't just that I felt abandoned; I was disappointed. The woman I thought I knew in London had been replaced by someone entirely different – someone cold and thoughtless, only out for herself and her own amusement. I suppose that was the moment the curtain fell. I felt I'd seen Della for who she truly was. All that time I'd been making excuses for her, trying to see things from her point of view. But when did she ever do that for anyone else? I thought I'd seen her at her very worst, and I couldn't understand why Mark put up with it.

The Mark I had got to know was so thoughtful and genuine. I couldn't see how he could be with anyone so selfish, so caught up in appearances. But then, I had seen how devoted he was to the children. Who knew how far he'd go to keep his family together?

That evening, as I sat alone on the terrace looking out at the still, darkening trees, my thoughts turned to my own parents. I had been gone for over a month, and though I'd told them I might not be able to call, I could only imagine their distress. One daughter gone, another out of touch. Mum left alone to look after Dad – what if he'd got worse in the time I'd been away? What if they'd heard from Scarlett and I had no idea?

I had no reception on my phone, and Della had left instructions to use the landline only in case of emergencies, but I decided to ignore her rules for once.

'Hello?' Mum sounded older somehow. 'Oh Kate, thank goodness. How *are* you?' I could hear the strain and relief in her voice. 'John, John! Kate's on the phone.'

'Katy! Where on earth have you been?' Dad sounded so happy I had to bite my lip.

'I've been here, Dad. In France, looking after the children.' Tears were streaming down my face already. I took a deep breath. I didn't want to give myself away.

'How is it?' Mum wanted to know. 'Are the kids being good? Is the family nice to you? Are you getting enough to eat?'

'The food's amazing. And the views. It's spectacular. You'd love it here. We're surrounded by nature and trees. It reminds me a bit of Eype actually . . .' As soon as I said the words, I regretted them. It looked nothing like Eype. It was more the feeling of being away, the vivid green, the sense freedom that made me think of those summers. The silence only lasted a few moments.

'When do you think you'll be coming to see us?' Mum asked.

'When I get back. In less than a month. As soon as I have a free weekend, I'll come up to Cambridge. How are you both?' I knew better than to ask after Dad's health when he was on the line.

'We're fine. No change,' Mum said, which I knew meant Dad's condition was stable. No major deterioration. And they clearly hadn't had any news about Scarlett. 'I've put clean sheets in your bedroom. I'll make a lasagne when you come . . .'

I smiled. 'I've got to go now – I'm on the landline. But I'll try to call you soon.' I didn't tell them I was on my own with the kids. Or how lonely I felt. How confused.

After I put the phone down, I wept, softly, for a long time. I didn't know what I was crying for, really. For my parents in their quiet, everyday misery. For the life I'd lived with them for too long, and the one I'd left behind in London, before it had even really started. For the situation I found myself in, caring for two children whose lives I'd once envied, and from whom I would soon be separated. For the family whose strange dynamic I was only now starting to understand.

Chapter Nineteen

To begin with, Mark's return felt like an invasion. The children and I had only been alone together for a few days, but with every hour that passed with them in my sole care I felt more involved, more invested in their wellbeing. If they really were being forgotten, abandoned, wasn't it my responsibility to make sure they were OK – to rescue them?

The sight of Mark's car, unexpected and unannounced, reminded me that they did have at least one loving parent. One who was possibly being betrayed at this very moment. And it took me straight back to the intensity between us in the nights before he left. Maybe Mark had been trying to communicate something to me, something I needed to understand.

The children and I had gone feral in the absence of other adults, spending the entire time in pyjamas or swimming costumes, picnicking when we were hungry and staying up into the evening. I'd taken to going to bed at the same time as them, which was getting later by the day. As Mark's car crawled up the driveway, we were running around the lawn in our swimming gear, in the middle of a long game of pirates and princesses. I waved, embarrassed, aware that I was in a bikini while he was fully dressed in work clothes.

The children ran at the car, shrieking and clambering to be pulled up and hugged. By the time Mark had disengaged himself, I had thrown on a T-shirt and was hastily attempting to create some order among the mess that surrounded us. It had been days since Manon had come, and I'd let the place descend into chaos.

'Looks like you guys have been having fun.' Mark smiled, looking around him and then at me. He was newly shaved, in a sharp suit. It felt as though he'd been away for weeks, not days.

'You're looking well,' he said, as we carried in some of the glasses and plates that had been left lying around. 'I hear Della's off living it up.' He raised his eyebrows with a look I couldn't decipher and turned to put the plates in the sink. I didn't know what to say. Did he suspect anything? Should I tell him?

'We've missed you,' I said, 'we all have. It seems like you've been gone a long time.' I thought of everything that had happened since he'd left – Jasper's near-miss in the pool, Della's neglect, Sophia's unwanted intrusion, the younger man who might be on the scene. What would Mark make of it all? Somebody needed to tell him what Della was like when he wasn't around.

But now wasn't the time. The children pulled him onto a kitchen chair, clambered onto his lap and began stroking his newly-soft chin.

'I like you better with your holiday face, Daddy,' said Jasper.
'Me too,' said Tabitha. 'Grow your beard again, Daddy!'
Mark laughed. 'OK then. If Kate agrees?' I had started on the washing up, but I turned and nodded, smiling at the sight of Mark squashed under the children, and the pleasure of being consulted.

155

'I've missed you,' he said. He was cuddling the children, but he looked over their heads. 'All of you.'

Rather than calling a halt to our makeshift routine, Mark joined in. He was fully in favour of eschewing clothes, mealtimes and regular routines. Instead, the four of us splashed around in the pool and played hide and seek in the forest. Sometimes I'd even get the luxury of a lie-down in the sunshine for half an hour, watching as the children rode around the garden on Mark's back and fell off, collapsing in giggles. With Della away, Mark seemed more inclined to put his work to one side. He brought his old acoustic guitar down from the attic, playing Beatles hits while the kids and I sang along. And he joined in with our story times, listening as I recounted the tales I made up for the children, self-consciously now, aware of his eyes on me.

'You're really good at it, you know,' he said, on his second evening back, 'at telling those stories. You cast a spell on us all – even me, and I've read enough kids' books to last me a lifetime.'

We were having a glass of rosé on the terrace after dinner. That was the one change to the regime that Mark had insisted on: he wanted the children in bed on time. 'Otherwise we don't get an evening,' he said, and now that he was there, I was inclined to agree.

'It's what I've always wanted to do,' I said. 'Write children's stories, get them published. I even used to do little drawings to go with them, but they're not very good.'

'I bet they are.' Mark smiled. 'You're always selling yourself short. I don't think you realise how good you are at a lot of things – how good you are with the kids, to be around . . .'

'Oh, come on . . .' My pleasure was tinged with embarrassment. 'You're not so bad to be around yourself, you know.

And I'm sure you're good at whatever that thing is you do at the bank . . .'

'Oh yes, that boring job nobody's even remotely interested in.' Mark caught my eye and smiled.

The sun disappeared behind the trees and a breeze picked up, carrying the scent of the pines, and the citrus-tinged after-shave Mark must have put on after his early evening shower. Had it been for my benefit, or force of habit? I'd been aware of taking longer over my appearance that evening, putting on a yellow sundress that brought out my tan and adding a touch of make-up for the first time in days.

I considered whether to raise the subject of Della's abrupt departure, to mention the name Orlando and see if it regis-tered. But Mark was looking away, his face angular in the shadows cast by the candles on the table. 'I don't even know how I got into banking, really. I always thought I'd be a rock star.' He laughed, pushing his hands through his hair self-consciously. 'Well, I was in a band. I always hoped we might make it. The finance stuff was just something to fall back on. And then, well life, kids, you know . . .' He shrugged, smiling. He didn't need to say her name. 'I sold out. But you could really make something of those stories. Don't give up on them, on your creativity.'

'What kind of music did you play?' I asked, trying to imagine the Mark I knew rocking out on stage.

'Oh, it was student stuff, really. Chili Peppers, Pearl Jam – that kind of thing. We wrote our own songs too. We were called The Sharks. We were quite a hit in Guildford.' He smiled, embarrassed. 'It all sounds deeply uncool now.'

'No, it doesn't. I loved that song, "Under the Bridge". My sister's boyfriend used to play it . . .' I tailed off, not wanting to get sidetracked into those days. 'I'd really like to hear some of your songs.'

157

'Are you sure?' Mark asked, already half out of his seat. 'Della hates me making a racket.'

'I'd love it.' I smiled, watching him head off eagerly to get his guitar and start strumming, his face transformed instantly – eyes closed, worry lines smoothed from his forehead. His voice was clear and melodic, even on old songs he said he hadn't sung for decades. It was teenage stuff – heartbreak, unrequited love – but the lyrics were touching and his delivery raw. At the end of each song he looked up uncertainly, searching for my response – the smile I couldn't suppress, the eyes that couldn't leave his face. It must have been encouragement enough, because he played into the night, moving on to the old nineties hits I was able to sing along to – Scarlett had introduced me to all those songs that had been well before my time.

After he'd finished we were both shy. 'I honestly can't remember the last time I played like that,' Mark said as we finally packed away for the night, 'the last time I felt like that. Like a different person . . . or maybe just like myself again.'

'I can't either.' It was as though I'd been transported back to my youth; everything else had fallen away. 'I can't believe you wouldn't play if you had a talent like that.' I could see the elation in his face as we walked into the kitchen, our eyes adjusting to the brightness of the light. If you cared about someone, how could you ever want to stop them doing the thing they loved? It would be like someone saying I wasn't allowed to write.

'Life gets complicated as you get older.' Mark turned to look at me as we put our glasses in the kitchen sink. 'But you should hold on to that optimism. It's a gift.'

He bent down and kissed me on the cheek, and then he was gone.

Chapter Twenty

The next morning the weather broke. I woke to rain drumming on the roof, and thought instantly of the towels and costumes hanging out to dry. By the time I got downstairs, Mark was already in the garden, dragging cushions off the sun loungers. We ran back and forth, our pyjamas dripping and bare feet slipping on the patio slabs, breathless, laughing at the ferocity of the rain, until finally everything was inside. Mark bolted the door behind us with a flourish and we turned to face the children, who were watching with amusement as pools of water formed on the kitchen floor.

'Have you been swimming . . . in your *pyjamas*?' asked Jasper, clearly worried he had missed out on all the fun.

'No, silly,' said Tabitha, always keen to fill Jasper in, 'Kate must have fallen in, and Daddy *rescued* her.'

'Kids, it's pouring with rain,' said Mark. 'Look outside. Look at us!'

We looked at each other and started laughing, the children joining in. Jasper jumped on his dad in the hope of getting wet himself, and we both found ourselves pushed onto the soaking cushions we had brought in, crushed together under their combined weight.

Suddenly Tabitha sat up. She looked first at me and then at Mark, with confusion in her eyes.

'Daddy, when's Mummy coming back?' she asked.

'Soon, little one,' Mark replied, getting up quickly and giving her a kiss on the forehead. 'Right, I'm going to get out of these wet pyjamas. And then . . . who wants pancakes for breakfast?'

'Me, me, me!' The children clambered after their father. 'Daddy, can I flip the first one?'

I walked up to my room alone. As I did, I had a realisation that felt at once urgent and overwhelming.

I had to go back to London.

Tabitha had picked up on something that had unsettled her, an atmosphere between Mark and me that I hadn't wanted to admit, even to myself. I couldn't stay here and play happy families any longer. It wasn't fair on anyone.

Later that afternoon, I borrowed Mark's laptop and hid away in my room, making arrangements for my return. First I emailed Layla and told her I might be in London sooner than I thought. I'd sensed from her messages that there could be a relationship with Pete on the cards, and I joked that I didn't want to play gooseberry, but perhaps we could both work at the café – it would be just like our first bar job together in Cambridge.

Next I opened up a long account from my parents of the neighbours' cat's untimely death, and a shorter one from Liam, who was struggling to cope with Layla's untidiness. He ended it with another anagram: *Eight letters: echo memo.* I smiled, scribbling it down on a piece of paper to work out later. I'd started to look forward to Liam's secret code.

As I looked at the screen, a message popped up. It was a

notification of an email, sent to Mark's account, which must have been running in the background. It was from Della, and it was so short, I'd read the whole thing before I'd even realised what I was doing.

Have you done it yet? Back on Monday. Let me know. Dx

It was so business-like and brief, it almost read like an order from a boss. It could have been about anything, really – something to do with the kids, a job Mark had promised to do around the farmhouse, some work he'd left unfinished.

It was probably nothing. I shut down the laptop and returned to the anagram. This one was easy. I worked it out in moments. And when I did, it seemed like a sign that the decision I'd made was the right one.

Come home.

It was nearly dark, and Mark was still poking at the barbecue expectantly. We had almost run out of charcoal, but he'd been sure there was enough for one last fire. Only now it wasn't hot enough to cook the cuts of lamb we'd bought. We had already drunk an entire bottle of wine waiting for the fire to catch and, with the optimism of one down, had begun on a second.

'It's no good,' Mark announced. 'They're still raw.'

'We could just eat the salad?' I suggested. 'There's a bit of bread and cheese, too.' I went inside to forage for food. Since Della's extravagant shopping expeditions had come to an abrupt end, supplies had run dangerously low.

As I stooped to rummage in the fridge, I tipped to one side, suddenly light-headed. I had drunk more than I was used to, and on an empty stomach. It was partly nerves. I had to tell Mark that I would be leaving at the weekend. I knew he would try to persuade me not to, not least because I would be leaving them without childcare. But I also knew it was the right thing to do.

I couldn't deny my feelings for Mark any longer. My fantasies about him had grown more elaborate with each day that passed. That he would realise it was me he had the real connection with, not Della. That he would decide he couldn't live without our conversations; the sense of freedom and connection. That our future could be filled with music and books and laughter – all things that seemed to be missing from his life with Della.

But Tabitha's expression that morning had reminded me of the real victims in all this: the children. I didn't know what Della was off doing. I couldn't tell Mark about Orlando, I realised that now. I had nothing to go on, really. That Sophia had mentioned his name to Della, and they had both left the next day. It was hardly evidence of an affair. And I didn't know what I was getting into myself, either. But I could see no good would come of any of it, least of all for Tabitha and Jasper. If I left now, I could go home, visit my parents, get my old job back. Della might still even pass on my stories to Alan. I didn't want to leave, but it had to be done.

But now I was drunk. And walking outside with arms full of cheese, bread and fruit, I could see that Mark was too.

'I've got to go,' I said as I put the food down on the table.

'To bed? But you haven't eaten anything. And it's not even nine o clock.'

'No, I've got to go back to London.' I sat down, not hungry at all now.

'What? But we're here another three weeks. What about the children? Why?' Mark looked utterly confused, and who could blame him? Now that I came to explain it, my certainty melted away. What could I say? That I was infatuated. And I'd convinced myself it would be better for everyone if I left – if I gave up the rest of my salary and reneged on the commitment I'd made to stay all summer and look after the children.

'It's . . . my parents,' I began, unsure where I was going with this.

'What, has something happened to them?' Mark looked concerned, as if preparing for bad news, and I felt a catch in my throat.

'No, they're fine. Well, as fine as they ever are.' Looking at his open face, the concern in his eyes, I knew it was time to tell him everything. That last family holiday, the disappearance, the search, Dad's illness, the whole story – a shorter version than I had given Della, but the essentials. I even told him about the day Della had come into the café, and my relief that finally, someone was interested in me, and not just in my mysterious sister.

'Oh Kate, I had no idea.' Mark put his hand on mine over the table, and then withdrew it quickly as our eyes met. 'I mean, I didn't realise you had all this going on. But . . . I don't understand. What's changed? Why do you need to leave now?'

I looked at him. I had lost my thread. 'I don't know. I worry about them, especially Dad. He might get worse. And I've got no way of contacting them . . .'

'But you used my laptop this afternoon. You can borrow it any time, you know that. And there's the phone . . .'

'I thought I wasn't allowed to use the phone.'

'Of course you can. Did Della . . . ?' He shook his head and looked away. 'Look, she doesn't mean to be, you know, difficult. She doesn't think sometimes. But you can't leave. We need you. We all do.' He held my eye, for longer this time, and for some reason I recalled the email I'd read that afternoon.

What was Mark supposed to have done? And why hadn't he told me that Della was coming back on Monday? Emboldened by the wine, I was about to ask him, but I noticed he was looking away, his eyes fixed on a point in the distance.

'I was married before, you know,' he said, quietly.

163

I looked at him, surprised, but he was concentrating on opening a third bottle of wine. I'd been determined to refuse another glass, but I watched as it was filled again, waiting for Mark to continue.

'Isabel was eight months pregnant when she died. It was an accident. A car. She was driving. I was at work.' It looked as if it was almost painful for him, to say the words, and I found myself silencing him with a hand on his arm.

'Mark, I . . . I'm so sorry.' He looked up and smiled. Grimaced really.

'It's OK. I don't mind talking about it. I never get to talk about her these days. Isabel. She was lovely. Gentle. She would have been a great—' He broke off. I found we were touching now, both of my hands on both of his, but I didn't move this time.

'And then I met Della. So different. Full of life. And so driven . . . There's nothing Della wants that she doesn't get. And she wanted me.' He shrugged helplessly.

'And the baby?' I asked, understanding as I did.

'Tabitha. She's Isabel's child . . . our child. The doctors managed to save her.' He looked at me sternly. 'You must never tell her that you know,' he slurred. 'Never tell anyone.' I nodded, piecing it together. So that was how Adele Walker, single magazine journalist, had so swiftly become Della Hunter, successful working mother.

'And so Adele,' I began, 'I mean Della—' Mark looked at me sharply.

'How did you know?'

'I found a book, on your shelves in London. It was written before you were together, I think?'

'Yes, that's right. When we met, she went by Adele professionally, though everyone called her Della. So when we married she changed her first name too – a new beginning, she said

. . . Della took us both on, me and Tabitha. She so desperately wanted a family and . . .' He paused. 'She does love them, you know.' He was looking up at the bedroom window. 'I know she gets impatient. But she wanted them *so* much. Sometimes I wonder if it was too much. No child . . . *no one* could be good enough to live up to those expectations . . .'

I felt suddenly angry, listening to Mark making excuses for his wife, trying to explain why she couldn't show him or their children the affection they needed. This woman who had steamrollered him in his grief, had brought up these children who could never be good enough and now had disappeared with her rude friend and her young lover. I was drunk and defiant, and I felt a rush of love towards Mark, in his loyalty.

'Of course you're good enough.' I squeezed his hand. 'You're *too* good.'

He held my hand against his cheek, and then he kissed it, pulling me forward. And then we were both kissing, Mark's hands on my face, his fingers pushing through my hair, running up my back. I barely remember getting upstairs, but we were in my room, pulling off our clothes in silence, hardly able to look at one another, as though by avoiding eye contact we could escape what we were doing. And then we were on my single bed, focused only on sensation, lost in another world, feeling waves of tenderness, closeness, the release of tension that had been building up for so many weeks.

And then I was alone.

Dawn light was creeping around the edges of the shutters as I finally drifted towards sleep, unsure of what would come the next day. There would be anxiety and guilt – there already was. But there was also, at that moment, a strength of feeling unfamiliar to me then. A sense I couldn't escape, of being undeniably, vividly, excitingly alive.

Chapter Twenty-One

I woke to find the children standing at the end of my bed, staring at me.

'My God! You frightened me.' I laughed, pulling the sheets up to my chin and realising I was entirely naked underneath them. Mark had visited my room again – it was the third night we'd spent together, and I hadn't moved an inch after he'd left for his own bed, so as not to break the spell. The fantasy in which he left Della, or she never came back, and we could stay together.

'You've missed breakfast,' Tabitha informed me. 'You've been sleeping for hours.'

'Daddy's gone!' Jasper announced, eager to impart the most important news.

'He told us not to wake you,' Tabitha added. 'He said you needed the rest. He's gone to London because he's got to go to work tomorrow.' She looked as if she was holding back tears, and I felt like I might cry, too. He hadn't said anything. Again.

This time it was even more of a betrayal, after everything that had happened between us. Each day we had spent together

I'd woken up resolved that nothing more would happen, that I would leave before the kids caught on. I'd passed through the day with the children, aware at every moment of Mark's proximity, his attention, his expression, and by the evening, the expectation, the tension, the longing had become too much to bear, at least for me. I had never felt so consumed by thoughts, fantasies, so ready to shut the rest of the world away.

But now, watching a tear roll down Tabitha's cheek, I knew I had to pull myself together.

'If Daddy's got to work then we'll have to make the best of it, won't we? Did you know he was leaving this morning?' I asked, lightly, sitting up and gathering the sheet.

'Well it is Sunday,' Tabitha reasoned. 'And he normally has to work on a Monday.'

'That's true,' I agreed, trying to square it in my own mind. Perhaps Mark had mentioned it at some point and I'd forgotten.

'But Mummy's coming tomorrow!' Jasper said, jumping up and down on the spot.

'Of course.' I forced a smile, feeling suddenly sick with guilt, and dread.

Over the past few days, when I had allowed my mind to stray to thoughts of Della's return, I'd imagined Mark would be here, too. That we would face up to her together. That it would somehow make it easier. We hadn't even discussed yet how we were going to handle it all. What we would tell her, if anything. There hadn't been time to talk about any of it.

Now I was faced with the prospect of seeing Della alone, with no way of knowing whether Mark had already confessed. And no way of contacting him to ask how to manage the situation. What if Della guessed immediately? Perhaps she already had her suspicions. I longed to be the one to escape to London, but Mark had persuaded me to stay, and now he'd gone without a word and left me with the children. There was no way I could leave too, at least not before Della returned.

'Did *you* know Mummy was coming?' It was Tabitha's turn to ask. Even a six-year-old could see this was an odd state of affairs, parents coming and going, unannounced and unexpected.

'I did,' I said, and that's when I remembered the email. *Back on Monday. Have you done it yet?*

Della arrived early the next morning, throwing open the kitchen door and hugging the children, who threw themselves on her.

'How are you, my darlings?' she cried, her deep voice echoing around the quiet house. 'I've missed you!'

'We made you cards,' Jasper said, running off to find his, featuring a blue wobbly potato head with two eyes, a mouth and nose underneath. 'It's you, Mummy!'

'That's wonderful.' Della laughed, catching my eye. 'It looks just like me, doesn't it?' I attempted a smile and didn't resist the hug she gave me.

'How's it been?' Della asked. 'Sorry I disappeared for so long. Sophia wouldn't let me out of her clutches, and then Jonathan turned up and, well . . . it's a long story. One for later on.' She raised her eyebrows with a smile.

Whatever resentments had been building up over the weeks before Della's departure had clearly evaporated, from her mind at least. It was a different Della who returned – friendlier, kinder. More like the woman I'd known in London, who had set aside so many evenings for me and my problems.

As the day wore on, all four of us decamping to the pool, and then to the lunch table, I started to wonder whether it had in fact been *my* behaviour – mine and Mark's – that had prompted the tension that had built up between us. I had no evidence that Della was cheating on Mark after all. Perhaps she'd gone away because she'd felt shut out. Maybe she'd suspected something all along. After all those long talks, the free sessions, the money she'd paid me, I had betrayed her at the first opportunity.

And for what? All the previous day I'd waited for Mark to call on the landline – to explain himself, to reassure me, to tell me what we should do. But no call had come, and I was completely in the dark. Had he told Della? Should I? Should I leave for London right away?

Della didn't seem to have any suspicions. She had brought gifts for us all – chocolate and animal soaps for the children, a printed scarf for me, bright yellow and dotted with small blackbirds.

'I thought it would suit you,' she said. 'I remembered that lovely bluebird scarf you had, that I haven't seen for a while. I wondered if you'd lost it.'

I held the scarf to my face, the coolness of the silk against my cheek waking me from whatever dream I'd been in, in which my actions didn't have consequences, and nobody would get hurt. I turned my head away and felt it grow damp with the hot tears that escaped. When I turned back, Della was helping Jasper open his chocolate, and I quickly dried my eyes.

'It's perfect,' I said. 'Thank you.'

Evening came around, and I still hadn't told Della how soon I was planning to leave. It was nearly the end of August, and there was a chill in the night air. We sat inside, in the warmly lit kitchen, eating pasta and drinking sparkling water. Della was taking it easier for the rest of the holiday, she said, and had cleared out the half-opened bottles of wine from the fridge, noting all the empties Mark and I had left.

'Looks like you two had a good time.' She smiled, and I felt the guilt sink a little lower into the pit of my stomach. 'Well, we've all been enjoying ourselves a bit too much. But now I really want to get down to my writing – we both should.'

I agreed, quickly. I'd barely even thought about my stories in the past days, and Della hadn't mentioned them for weeks. But embarking on a joint enterprise seemed like a good way to re-establish our bond, and I had making up to do.

That evening Della talked more openly than she had in a long time – about Cannes, the parties, the trouble with Sophia. 'The thing is, she doesn't understand that my life's different now. We used to work together, years ago, on a magazine . . .' I thought of Adele Walker, the transformation. 'We were always out drinking, cocktail bars, launches – every night. We could manage that in those days. Well, Sophia still can, but I can't . . . And she makes no bones of the fact that she can't *stand* the children.'

'Hmm, she wasn't exactly Mother Teresa,' I said, and Della laughed.

'Quite. I know she wasn't very nice to you, Kate, and I'm sorry about that. She's always a bit tetchy around me now. She's never forgiven me for marrying Mark, having the kids, all that. She was the one who introduced us, you know?'

'Really?' I'd assumed Sophia was part of Della's world, not Mark's.

'Yes, they dated for a while. She introduced him to his *first* wife.' She looked at me to measure the impact of this revelation. I feigned surprise at the news of Mark's previous marriage. My surprise at the fact that he had gone out with someone like Sophia was genuine.

'Yes, he was married before me. Not for long, though. It was a dreadful business, really. She was killed in an awful car crash.

170

He was like a wounded bird when I met him. So sad – broken, really. We met at one of Sophia's parties, and I couldn't bear to see anyone give up on life like that. So I took him on as one of my first clients . . . and it all went from there.'

I sat back, struggling with the effort of mentally reframing everything I had believed to be true. Mark had been part of this social world before he'd met Della. Kind, gentle Isabel had been friends with Sophia. And Della? She had simply been trying to help Mark. The romance had come after. Della had taken him on, she'd brought up his daughter as her own. I felt sick.

'Are you OK?' Della asked as she cleared away the dishes. 'You look a bit pale.'

'I'm fine,' I said. Despite my guilt, I didn't want the conversation to end. 'Is Sophia jealous of you, then?'

Della considered this for a moment. 'I don't think she wants what I have. But she doesn't want *me* to have it either. When we were in our twenties, we always talked about how awful it would be to settle down. Marriage, kids – it was like *death*. But when I turned thirty, all I could see everywhere I looked were babies, happy couples. Then I met Mark and . . . well, it all fell into place.' She shrugged, almost apologetically. 'But that never happened for Sophia.' I wondered whether the sympathy on Della's face extended to me, too. Would everything fall into place for me? Or would I become one of these Sophia figures, haunting the lives of my happier friends?

'Maybe I'll have one of those moments, when I turn thirty?'

'I don't think so, Kate. Not everyone does. Sophia didn't. And I think it's usually sort of there already, bubbling under the surface. No . . . I think you're destined for other things. *Wonderful* things. But not these things.' She gestured towards the children's cups and plates, the cards they'd drawn, their damp swimming costumes hanging on the rack.

171

I felt the irritation rise up. I was the one who'd supervised the drawing, taken the children swimming, looked after them for weeks on end. And I'd read Della's book jacket. She had been in her mid-thirties and still single when she wrote it. She'd planned every step of that transformation meticulously, just as she laid out in her chapters. So why paint it as a matter of fate, rather than something she had worked hard to achieve?

I felt tired, though. And guilty. I didn't have the energy to voice all that frustration, so I simply said, 'People change,' and left it at that.

'They do,' Della agreed, lost in her own thoughts for the moment. Then she looked up, her face holding that expressionless look I found so unsettling.

'Did you have a good time with Mark, while I was gone?'

Chapter Twenty-Two

The realisation came suddenly. It was a feeling. An almost imperceptible change in my body, a metallic taste on my tongue. It was early morning, and I lay still, trying to reason with myself. But the certainty flooded through me as quickly as the dread. How had I let this happen?

I listened for voices. The house was silent, empty. Della must have taken the children outside to the pool. She'd said the evening before that I could have a lie-in, since I was feeling so tired. I counted the days since my last period with mounting panic. I remembered there had been a day when it had been so heavy, I hadn't been able to get in the pool. I'd explained to Della and she'd asked Mark to watch the children. That had been before Sophia arrived, even before Jonathan and Dee. Which meant that on the Friday before Mark left, I would have been ovulating. And we hadn't used contraception.

I hadn't thought to bring any with me, and Mark didn't have any condoms, but he'd withdrawn every time, he said. There was no need to worry. At the time I'd been more concerned about covering our tracks. About what Della might find out. I couldn't believe I'd been so stupid, so caught up in the moment. What had I been thinking?

I tried to calm my breathing. I was probably being paranoid. In a few days, my period would arrive, and I would look back on this moment as one of those near-misses that almost sends your life on a very different track. Perhaps I would even laugh about it. For now, I felt like crying.

On Wednesday morning Della, the children and I drove home from the market with a fully stocked car. It was nearly September, and the days were getting cooler, a whisper of autumn spreading through the woods around us.

The fatigue and headaches had improved slightly over the previous days, and I had convinced myself that it was just my time of the month. I was certainly feeling moody enough. All I needed now was to take the pregnancy test I'd slipped off to buy in town, and I could put the whole thing behind me, ride out the next couple of weeks and return to normal life.

'How are you feeling today?' Della asked as we laid out bread and cheese for lunch. It was beginning to rain and so we were setting the table in the kitchen.

'Oh I'm fine, really. I'm getting my period, so that probably explains why I've been feeling so tired.'

'Are you?' Della asked, her back to me as she sliced the baguette. Putting the knife down with a clatter, she called the children down for lunch.

After a subdued meal I tried to sneak away, but Della wanted to lie down, so I had to be the one to take the children to the pool and watch impatiently as they splashed and played and sang annoying songs, ignoring the obvious chill in the air. It wasn't until after dinner that I finally got a moment alone. By then I was utterly convinced the whole thing was an overreaction. I almost smiled to myself as I sat on the toilet and tore off the wrapping around the thin plastic stick. So tiny, this thing that could change a person's future in a moment – but not mine. I was confident of that.

I read the instructions and peed carefully on the end of the stick. Then I looked away, humming a tune lightly to myself, one of the kids' silly rhymes from that afternoon.

When I looked at the stick there was one dark line. And there, next to it, extremely faintly, was a second.

I read and re-read the instructions. What did it mean if the second line was barely there? Could it be a mistake? I scoured the leaflet, with its instructions printed in both French and English.

If there were two lines, however faint, a pregnancy was confirmed.

There were two lines. One, and then another. There was no question, and as I realised it, I felt sick to my stomach. I bent over the toilet bowl, but nothing came. I stayed there for a long time, hunched on the floor, my head spinning, the cold dread settling inside me.

I was pregnant. With Mark's baby.

Chapter Twenty-Three

'I'm leaving for London tomorrow.' Della's announcement the next morning came entirely without warning, disrupting the breakfast table in an instant.

'But, Mummy! I thought you were going to take us to the beach?' Jasper's mouth turned down as he prepared for his tears to come bursting forth.

'Oh darling. You know I'd love to, but Mummy's got to work. Kate will take you to the beach.'

'But she doesn't have a car,' Tabitha said.

'Oh, yes. Well, I'm not going until tomorrow. I can take you to the beach today if you like. And then Daddy will be coming to help pack everything up, so cheer up.'

In my sleep-deprived state, it took a few moments to process what Della had said. She would be leaving. Mark was coming back. The situation was getting worse by the hour.

I'd spent the entire night planning my escape. I couldn't simply announce I was leaving – Della would never sit back and watch as I left her alone with the children. And I couldn't tell her the truth. So that left two options: disappear, or wait out the next eight days, until we were all due to return to

London, at which point I'd still be well within the window for an early abortion.

That morning, I had decided on the latter as the least disruptive to the children. But news of Mark's return changed everything. I may have been longing to see him before, but there was no way I could spend even a few hours alone with him now, let alone days – not knowing the secret I'd decided to keep from him, from Della, even from my parents. He'd see that something was wrong straight away. I had to leave as soon as possible.

'Would it be all right if I stay behind today?' I asked, as lightly as I could. 'I'm still not feeling great. I could do with the rest.' With the three of them out of the house for the day, I could pack my things and be gone before they got back. I could hitch a ride into town and catch a bus to the train station.

'Sorry, Kate, I need you today,' Della said. 'You can rest on the beach, can't you?'

'Of course,' I muttered. 'No problem. I'll go and get my stuff.'

I sat on my bed feeling trapped. How could I get away? Tomorrow, Della would leave me with the children and I would be stuck, at least until Mark arrived. I had less than twenty-four hours to make my escape.

We set off in the car for Sète, the children singing along happily to the Beach Boys while Della drove too fast down the motorway, my instincts heightened to a sense of imminent danger. Once there, it became apparent why Della had agreed to come so readily, and why she was so insistent that I join them. As we walked past the bars and cafés that lined the waterfront, Della looked around her, waving at a man in the distance. It was Jonathan, tanned, in a white shirt and Panama hat and, standing next to him, a younger man, dark-featured, with an even deeper tan and crisper white shirt.

'Della, darling, how are you?' Jonathan stood up from the waterside table where he and the man were drinking coffee and wrapped Della in a hug. 'And Kate, too. A pleasure as always.' He kissed me lightly on the cheek, before ruffling the children's heads affectionately. 'I didn't know you were *all* coming.'

Della looked at me and the children. 'No, Kate's going to find some entertainment for the kids. And I didn't know *you* would be here already.' She and the man shared a smile, before Della turned to me.

'So – off you go then.' She pressed some notes into my hand as I looked on in disbelief. 'Buy the kids lunch, ice creams, whatever. We'll meet back here at three p.m.'

'But . . . where's the beach?' I asked, taking each of the children by the hand.

'Yes, Mummy, we want to build sandcastles.' Jasper was waving his bucket and spade.

'Oh, this is the port,' Jonathan said, motioning to the rows upon rows of boats that surrounded us, 'the nearest beach is a drive away.'

'Well, it's the sea, isn't it? Same thing!' She smiled brightly at the children.

'But, Mummy, I thought you were taking us to the beeeach.' Jasper was beginning to whine.

'Who wants an ice cream?' I asked, leading them away in search of the nearest suitable café, and throwing another glance over my shoulder as we left. Was that Orlando? What was Della doing?

The children were fractious all day. There was nothing to entertain them in Sète, which catered to smart tourists and locals, not little kids. Eventually we found a playground, much to my relief, and I was able to sit on a bench while they ran giddily about.

I watched them, taking turns to slip down the slide, spinning too fast on the roundabout, giggling wildly, and I thought about the child beginning to form inside my body. Mark's baby. A secret to be kept even from its brother and sister. I had already decided I was going to leave that night. I would sneak out while everyone was asleep. I would go home, end the pregnancy and distance myself from the family. It was the only answer.

I felt tearful at the thought of leaving the children. They wouldn't understand – I'd be yet another one of the adults who came and went from their lives. And I'd be leaving them alone with Della, who I knew would take out her frustration on them.

If only I could take them with me. Mark and I could run away and set up home somewhere else with them and our own little baby. That's how it would be if this was an Enchanted Elsie story. Except that the usual roles would be reversed: Della the wicked mother, and me the kind stepmother. I would never be the sort of mum who promised to take my children to the beach only to abandon them. A mother who would rather spend the last afternoon she had with her family in the company of a younger man.

I felt a tug of love as Tabitha pushed Jasper on the swing, both of them laughing over some shared joke. Della didn't deserve these children. But it was me who had to leave.

Chapter Twenty-Four

After dinner, I packed my bag, opening and closing drawers as quietly as I could. I had lingered over the children's bedtime stories, giving them extra hugs and kisses as I said goodnight, tears streaming down my face as I pulled the door to and walked down the corridor for the last time.

I was in no state to go downstairs and excuse myself for the evening, but relations with Della had broken down to such an extent that afternoon, it didn't seem necessary. Della had been nearly an hour late to meet us in Sète. By the time she had turned up, the children were beside themselves and Della had no patience for them. For once, I had been unable, or unwilling, to smooth things over, and we had sat in the car in silence, as one and then both of the children fell asleep.

Now they weren't tired, and were making a fuss in their bedroom, shouting first to me and then to Della. I decided to ignore them. I had too much to prepare, and in fact the noise was useful, masking the sounds as I put my clothes and wash bag into my rucksack, discarding the books I had brought as too heavy for the journey.

I would have to walk at least an hour in the dark to the

nearest village – I had little hope of coming across a car in these parts in the middle of the night. If I left at four in the morning, it would be getting light by the time I got there, and I could pick up the first bus to Montpellier. From there, it would be a train to Paris and another to London.

I got into my rickety bed in the old farmhouse for the last time, setting the alarm on my phone to vibrate, under my pillow, so it would wake me and nobody else. Then I lay my head down, willing sleep to overcome me at this early hour of the evening, so that I'd have the energy for the journey ahead.

I listened as the children quietened, and eventually heard the sounds of Della locking up and climbing the stairs. I pictured the key, hanging to the right-hand side of the kitchen door. I would creep down, quietly lift it off the hook, open the door . . . and within a few days, I'd be able to put this whole mess behind me. I tried not to think about the children, who I would surely never see again, about Mark, even Della – who had seemed to offer my one chance at making a go of writing, of London, of another kind of life.

No, I'd just have to return to Cambridge. I'd been kidding myself that I ever really belonged in this world, with its designer furniture, the months abroad, the well-paid careers. Dan was right – I belonged to another, smaller kind of life. Mum had said they might even take me back at the library, though the prospect made my whole body heavy.

My thoughts lingered for a moment on the foetus, barely a dot, inside me now, and the baby they would never even know I carried. But I pushed that from my mind. This wasn't the right time, or situation. I had plenty of years ahead of me, if I decided I did want to have a child. For now, I was making the decision that was best for everyone. For me, for Mark, for Tabitha and Jasper, who would otherwise have a

181

half-sibling they knew nothing about, a family skeleton, a stain on Della's perfect brood.

As I closed my eyes, I pictured the photo on Della's mantelpiece in London, the one with the family, laughing, by what I now knew was the pool outside The Pines. In my mind, I was back in the living room, staring at the picture, and noticing a shadow in the corner. As I approached the mantelpiece to look more closely, I saw that the shadowy figure was me, standing in the background, watching sullenly – and to my side, a little blond child, my child, was holding my hand, head thrown back, crying and crying and crying . . .

The vibrations woke me with a start. It took a moment to register that it was my alarm. My heart rate picked up and I felt a surge of adrenaline. It was time to go.

I got up and dressed quietly, pulling on jeans and my heaviest jumper, slinging my rucksack onto my back and creeping down, avoiding the third stair that creaked terribly. Once in the kitchen, I closed the door behind me, to mask the sound of the patio doors being unlocked. Then I grabbed some apples and bread rolls, stuffing them quickly into my rucksack and jumping in fright as one dropped to the floor with a loud thud and rolled into the corner, under the table.

I stood, holding my breath, waiting to hear whether the noise had woken anyone. But the house was silent except for the dripping of the kitchen tap and the ticking of the old clock. I turned towards the door, leaving the apple and abandoning the possibility of any more foraging. I had the money Della and Mark had been paying me saved in my account. Once I got to a cashpoint, I would be able to withdraw some of it and pay for more food and a train ticket home.

I took one last look around the darkened kitchen, taking a mental picture of the room that had come to feel so familiar:

the abundant fruit bowl, the oversized clock, the creepy painting that could be a still life or a twisted face, depending which angle you looked at it. Then I turned to the doors and ran my hand up the side to the hook behind the curtain, where the key was kept. But my fingers couldn't find it. I tugged at the heavy curtain that covered the glass-panelled doors. The hook was empty. The key must have fallen on the floor.

I put down my rucksack and got on my hands and knees, scrabbling around in the half-darkness, my anxiety growing. I got my face level with the floor and looked under the dresser that held all the plates and cups, painted in gaudy reds and yellows. The key wasn't there. It wasn't behind the curtain, or under the mat; it hadn't slipped under the table or any of the chairs.

My eyes scanned the shelves, the windowsills, above the sink. In my desperation, I tried forcing the door handle, but it was locked. I had heard Della turn the key earlier.

I looked again at the hook, as though perhaps the key might have magically appeared. But it was still empty.

It didn't make sense. The key was always there. Every morning, when I'd come down early with the children, it had been hanging in its usual place. I knew it had, because sometimes we used it to let ourselves out, before anyone else woke up. Also, when I'd arrived, Mark had made a point of showing me where it was kept, in case of fire. It was true that I hadn't been getting up so early these past couple of weeks, since I'd been feeling so exhausted. I had stopped even noticing the key, because the doors were usually flung open by the time I came downstairs. But I had made a point of checking before taking the kids to bed that evening, and the key had been hanging on the hook, where it always was.

Now I gave in to my panic. I was trapped in this house,

and in a few hours, the children would be up. Then Della would leave and there would be no way out of this situation.

There must be some other door or window I could get out of. I paced around the living room, trying all the windows, then back to the kitchen windows, and finally the patio doors again. All locked. I rattled the door handle, tears forming as I banged my hands against the window in anger. Where had Della put the key? What was she playing at? What if there really was a fire?

And that's when the fear truly overcame me. Had Della taken the key for a reason? Was I being kept here – locked in this house against my will?

Thoughts circled faster and faster, the spinning, manic feeling I got sometimes, when pieces started to fit together. Della wanted to keep me here. She knew I was planning my escape and she'd made it impossible to leave. Well, I wasn't going to give in that easily. I slammed the heel of my hand against the glass, harder this time. I felt a crack. The top panel of glass gave way and then shattered, the shards jangling to the floor as my arm flew through the door frame.

I looked down. My hand was bloody and there was a slow trickle from the side of my wrist. But that didn't matter now. All that mattered was getting away. Breathless, feeling a jolt of pain in my arm, I felt for the handle on the other side. But it still wouldn't give. In desperation, I threw my rucksack through the hole I'd made in the glass, clearing out as much of the windowpane as I could. I was steeling myself to climb through the opening, framed with jagged glass, when I heard the click of the kitchen door.

'Kate, what on earth is going on?'

Instinctively, I reached for a shard of glass with my good hand. I turned and thrust it out in front of me, panting, my blood pooling on the floor.

184

'Let me out!' I hissed. 'Now!'

'What's this about Kate?' Della asked, edging towards me as if cornering a wounded animal. I backed against the doors, still brandishing the glass.

'Why is it locked?' I demanded. 'Where's the key?'

'It's always locked at night. You know that.'

'But where's the key? What if there was a fire? How would we get out?'

'It's here.' Della lifted the key from her dressing gown pocket. 'Is there a fire? Did you need to get out?'

'I'm going back to London,' I said, lowering my arm and letting the glass clatter to the ground as Della held out the key. 'Just open the door and I'll be gone. You can forget all about me.'

'What do you mean, you're going to London?'

'I'm leaving. Now.'

'But, Kate, *I'm* leaving later this morning. You know that. Why would *you* be leaving if you know *I'm* leaving? Who's going to look after the children?'

'Why would you hide the key?' I asked. 'Why are you trying to keep me here?'

'It's not hidden. It's right here. Go on then, open the door.' Della gave me the key and watched as I fumbled with the lock, throwing the door open to reveal pitch blackness, even the moon and stars obscured by cloudy skies. 'Now what?' Della asked. 'Are you planning to walk back to London? Honestly, Kate, what *is* this about?'

Something softer in Della's voice broke through my panic. The mist in my head cleared a little and I sank against the frame of the open door, aware suddenly how ridiculous this looked. I was shaking, crying, my hand and arm throbbing. I didn't protest when Della led me into the kitchen, bringing the rucksack in with us. I watched in silence as she closed the door behind me, kicking as much of the broken glass to one side as she could.

'Now, sit down,' Della said, pulling out a chair. 'I'll make us both a drink and you can tell me what's going on.'

I slumped over the table, my head resting on the smooth wood. All the stress of the past few weeks had caught up with me. I felt empty, defeated. I couldn't move my fingers. There was a sharp pain in my arm. All I wanted to do was sleep.

I didn't have the strength to resist as Della began cleaning and bandaging my arm, handing me a mug of tea, stroking my hair, feeling my forehead, talking me down as though I was an in-patient who'd tried to stage an escape.

'Kate, whatever it is that's going on, you need to talk about it. You've twisted things around in your head. I'm on your side.'

I turned to look at Della. Perhaps she already knew the truth and wanted me to put it into words. Maybe Mark had confessed, and Della had been waiting all this time for me to as well.

'Did something happen while I was away?' Della asked slowly, as if speaking to one of the children.

I nodded, looking down at my bandaged arm. Spots of blood were beginning to soak through the white. I dug my nails into the palm of my good hand.

'Between you and Mark?'

I looked up. 'I didn't mean for it to happen,' I said, tears starting to form straight away. 'I'm so sorry. We were here on our own and I thought you were off with a younger man like Sophia said—'

'What are you talking about?'

'Orlando.' I looked up at her, face blurred.

'Orlando? That's Jonathan's nephew. He's staying with him.

186

Sophia's been having some sort of flirtation but, honestly . . . he's far too young.'

'I thought you were having an affair with him. Yesterday, in Sète, the way you smiled at him.'

'I was saying hello, that was all. He's a young man visiting his uncle. Really, Kate, you did seem agitated yesterday. It was very hot. Maybe the sun had got to you. And whatever's been going on here. What happened between you and Mark?'

'It was only a few days, a few times.' I put my head in my hands, overwhelmed by shame.

'And then?' Della's voice was hard, but not furious. I looked up, trying to work out what she already knew.

'And then he left, without saying anything.'

'And?'

'And then you came back, and I felt terrible. So guilty, I could barely look at you. And you were so kind. You gave me that beautiful scarf. I thought about confessing, but I couldn't bring myself to tell you.'

'Do you have feelings for him now?'

I shook my head. I did, of course, but not ones I wanted to express. Especially now I realised Della had been innocent all along. It had been Sophia who was chasing Orlando. I had twisted everything in my mind. I'd thought the worst of Della, when she was the wronged party.

'You've been so kind, so generous, all of you. And the children. I care about them so much. I couldn't believe I'd done anything so stupid. I was drunk, and then . . . well, there's no excuse.'

'But you used protection?' The question was so unexpected, I didn't have time to think about how to respond. I thought Della would snap, or shout. I wasn't expecting this presence of mind. I felt like I was going to be sick. I put my hand to my mouth. Della looked me in the eye.

187

'Kate, what are you saying? Are you pregnant?' I was sobbing, barely able to see for tears. I nodded, helpless.

'But I'm going to take care of everything. That's why I'm leaving. I'm going to Cambridge. You'll never have to see me again. We can all forget about it. Forget this ever happened.'

Della's chair scraped on the floor, the noise making me jump. She stood up and walked towards the window, her back to me, looking out to the garden where the sky was beginning to lighten now, the birds starting up their chorus, the trees swaying gently. I tried to quieten my sobs, aware that it was Della who'd been hurt. She was the one who had to take all this in.

We were both silent for a long time. I waited, numb, for Della to respond, thinking that I would need to get moving before long if I was going to leave before the children woke up. I didn't want them to see me like this.

But before she even turned around, her body silhouetted by the rising daylight, her face in the shadows, I already knew that I wouldn't be leaving, not now. Della would have an answer. She would make everything all right. She was the only person who could help me now.

PART THREE

France, September

Chapter Twenty-Five

'What do you mean you're not coming back?' Mum was not taking this well, her voice high and shrill.

'She's only staying a few more weeks, aren't you, Kate?' Dad joined in, trying to calm things down.

'Well, no. A few months, probably. Quite a few.' I had waited until Della and the children had left before calling my parents. I didn't want to be overheard. I couldn't bear to have witnesses to my deception. I had never lied outright to them before. There had been plenty of times I hadn't told them the whole truth, but this felt different. Scheming. And the conversation was turning out even worse than I'd imagined.

'Look, Kate, we agreed to you moving to London for a few months,' Mum said. 'A few more weeks in France didn't seem such a stretch, but not this . . . Not disappearing abroad for God knows how long. The doctors said we should keep an eye on you. Make sure there aren't any relapses.'

'I'm an adult, Mum. I need to make my own life.' My guilt was making it almost impossible to speak without tears coming.

'And what about your dad? He's not getting any better, you know.'

'I'm fine, love,' Dad said. 'A few months isn't going to make any difference. And it's true that Kate needs to make her own way. You will call us, though, won't you?' Dad's faltering request triggered a fresh wave of remorse.

'Of course I will. And I'm going to be paid while I'm here. I'm saving up. I know you don't want to take my money, but it will be there, if we need it . . .'

'But why is she paying you, if you're on a writing retreat?' Mum wanted to know.

'It's a bit of both, really. I'm doing some work for Della, looking after things here, and she's given me this amazing opportunity to really make a go of my writing. I've got a fantastic house to stay in, no bills to pay, total solitude. I'm going to write a book, and then Della's going to show it to her friend, this literary agent. He knows a publisher who's in the market for exactly the kind of writing I'm doing. And I'll be home in no time – I'll need to be if I've got a publishing deal, won't I?'

'It's only because we worry about you,' Dad said. 'And we miss you. It does sound like a good opportunity, though. Perhaps we can come and visit?'

'No,' I said quickly, before my voice broke. 'I need some time alone. It's been so long since I did anything that was just for me. And I'll call all the time – we can talk, email. I need a few months, that's all. And then I'll be back.'

After I hung up, I got into bed, logging onto my email on my new laptop. To Layla I said that she'd been right all along – I'd met someone and was going to stay in France a bit longer.

He's lovely. And gorgeous – you'd really like him, I wrote, both hating myself and wishing it was true. *Could you let Pete know? And tell him I'm really sorry. Miss you! Kxx*

As I typed the words, I felt a pang. I did miss Layla. I

missed the company of people my own age. I felt an over-whelming desire to giggle and drink and stay up late chatting and smoking. By the time I got back to London, who knew where Layla would be?

Next, I emailed Liam to apologise. *Could you tell the land-lady I'm moving out? I know I'll lose my deposit, but I don't know how long I'll be, so there's no way I can hang on to the room. My parents will come and pick up my things. Sorry this is all so sudden and that I haven't been able to say goodbye. But I'll make it up to you when I'm back in London.* 'Gotten formed'. Love Kate x

It was the first time I'd responded to the game Liam had been playing over the summer. But I knew he'd hear from Layla about this mystery boyfriend and be discouraged. And it was true, in a sense: there had been another man. But not the one he would hear about. Not one who was available to me. And all this time, Liam had been there, keeping me in mind, sending me sweet, coded messages. 'Don't forget me.' I meant it.

I closed down the computer feeling nauseous. How had I got here? I lay on one side, listening as the wind battered the pines and rattled the windowpanes, trying to remember in all the conversations, huddled in corners while the children were distracted by the laptop, late at night after they had gone to bed, the exact moment when I had said yes. Perhaps there hadn't been one moment, just lots of little moments.

There had been plenty of tears. Especially on that first evening when, in a low voice, Della had described to me the struggle she and Mark had been going through to have a third child. How the doctors had told her it was unlikely to happen at this stage of life, the desperation that had overtaken her and, she now realised, had driven Mark away, towards me.

'I'm no saint, I understand those impulses,' she'd said, and I had thought of the day in Sète, the conclusions I'd jumped to – the wrong ones. Only then was it dawning on me how hypocritical I'd been. Della was only doing her best, like we all were. She hadn't taken on mythic qualities when she'd become a mother – superhuman selflessness, limitless patience. All she'd done was go away for a few days to have some fun, leaving her children with a paid nanny, and I'd judged her so harshly for it. I had bought into the cult of motherhood without even realising it.

And even if something had been going on between Della and a younger man, it didn't give me any right to do what I'd done with Mark, what we'd been building up to all summer, right in front of her, all while I was taking her money, staying as her guest. The guilt I felt was like a desperate hangover. Every time I thought it had receded a fresh wave would wash over me.

Della told me that night about her earlier struggle to conceive, to have children at all. The obsession that had consumed her, taken over everything. 'When you're used to being in control of your life, when you've always been able to make things happen, to come across something that doesn't work like that, it's . . . well, it's crushing. The one thing, the *one thing* you want most in the world, and you can't have it . . . Can you imagine that?' I thought about my search for Scarlett. I'd never felt that way about having a baby, but I recognised the longing Della described. The emptiness, the way your thoughts could become fixated on that sense of lack.

'But now there is a baby.' Della looked at me. It was the first time I had seen her crying and I was so caught up in sympathy, and remorse, it took me a few moments to catch up with what she was saying.

'You mean?'

'You would always be involved,' Della said softly. 'You'd always have a place in the family, as much or as little as you'd like.'

'You want me to have the baby?' Of all the scenarios I'd run through in my mind, this had never even occurred to me. The idea was too enormous to take in. I didn't know how to respond.

'Please, think about it,' Della had said, as we locked up that night. 'Take your time to consider all the options. There's no rush.'

Over the next few days, she returned to the idea over and over, building up a vision of the future in which, in return for a few months of my life, I'd be giving the family the greatest gift anyone could ever give. I could repay my debt to Della, absolve the guilt that had dominated my thoughts and dreams. And I'd have a part in Tabitha and Jasper's lives, in the life of this baby, who was already gaining strength inside me.

She talked about Alan then, too. Della had sent him my new stories a few weeks earlier. She hadn't wanted to tell me until she heard from him, but he liked them, she said. He thought I showed promise. There was a lot he wanted me to change. I needed to start anew, essentially – build them into a collection, with clear themes and connecting characters, but he wanted to read them when I'd finished.

'I don't want you to feel discouraged. It took me a long time to get to where you are with my writing. With an agent who's keen, who's got such good contacts. But there's a lot of work to do.'

I felt anything but discouraged, I'd told her. I couldn't believe anyone was taking my work seriously. And she laughed, reminding me how quick I always was to sell myself short.

We'd looked at his agency online, the illustrious clients he'd found deals for – ones whose names I'd seen in the library, even some I'd read myself.

It came to seem almost fated. I had become so close to the children, to Mark, to Della. I had struggled so hard to imagine a scenario in which I'd never see Tabitha and Jasper, never even lay eyes on Mark again, never be part of Della's world. Where I'd have to pack up my bags and go back to Cambridge, begging for my old job, proving Mum right, and Dan, and all those sour-faced colleagues. Now there was a chance I wouldn't have to. I could stay in France a few months longer as Della's guest, write, give birth to a longed-for child, and return to London with a manuscript. Perhaps the next time they saw my name would be on the spine of a book.

'We'd continue to pay you,' Della had said, taking me by surprise. 'To cover your loss of earnings, since you wouldn't be able to go back to your job. AIM is a registered business, I can put you on the payroll. You'd only be expected to carry out a few administrative tasks, remotely, to balance the books – but it would mean you'd be able to save up for months. Really establish yourself when you get back to London.'

I did a mental calculation: nine months of my current salary, with no rent or bills to pay. I'd be able to save enough to pay for help at home for Dad, for when he needed it. I'd never have another opportunity to make that kind of a lump sum – we wouldn't have to worry about him going into a care home for years to come. I knew my parents might struggle to accept the money from me, but they couldn't afford to turn it down. And then I'd be able to carry on my own life in London, without the guilt of leaving Mum alone to look after Dad.

At that point I hadn't even begun to try to imagine what it might be like to carry a baby, Mark's baby. To have a child for someone else. I was still so preoccupied by the obsessive thoughts that had seeded themselves in my head and would engulf me every time I lay down at night: that I had been right all along. I wasn't a good person. I couldn't be kind, couldn't do the right thing. I had been brought in to care for a family and I had betrayed them all.

Della seemed able to sense my mental state. Every conversation we had circled back to my anguish that night she'd found me trying to escape, how unhinged I'd been when I threatened her. What she'd seen must have frightened her, and eventually I confessed that things had been worse than I'd let on. My stay in hospital had been longer, and some days I still felt as though I was in recovery.

'All the more reason for you to stay here and rest,' she told me. 'Get over everything you've been through, rather than launching yourself into life in London, looking for an office job, in that horrible house. That's the last place you should be if you're feeling fragile.'

I had to admit I had been dreading the thought of returning to those dark rooms, the strip lighting.

'And no wonder you haven't been able to find work, really. They sense these things, employers. They enquire into any history of mental health problems. Any permanent job is going to ask for references, from that library where you worked, from me.'

I looked at Della, struggling to catch up. She wouldn't have to betray my confidence as a coaching client, would she? But then, if I stayed in France, I wouldn't even have to think about any of that.

'But how would I explain it to everyone?' I asked, one evening right at the beginning of September, days before the family was due to leave for England, the reality of what she was asking me starting to dawn.

'You wouldn't need to. None of your friends, your family, would need to know.' Della made it sound so simple. But could I really have a baby without telling my parents, Layla, Liam? 'Of course we'd visit, as much as we can. And Manon will be around. We wouldn't just leave you here on your own.'

'But do you really think we can . . .' I stopped. I could hardly put all my questions into words. 'Don't you think it will be hard, to bring up a baby I've carried? Especially if I'm still around . . . And won't Mark . . .' I couldn't continue that sentence. 'I mean, it would be so weird . . . Why are you being so nice about all this? How can you forgive me so easily?'

'We're all adults,' Della had said evenly. 'People make mistakes, and good can come of them, too, sometimes. Most families aren't nearly so conventional as you think, and people muddle along just fine.' I thought then of my own family, both deeply conventional and haunted by absence. Perhaps Della had a point. 'I care about you, we all do. I want to help you, like I always have, ever since I met you that day in the café. You seemed so . . . lost. You still do. And you remind me of myself at your age, somehow. Missing something. Unsure of the future. I want to help you achieve all you're capable of.'

That night Della told me a little about her own childhood, in a run-down village in Somerset, the distant parents, the two younger sisters who were the golden children. 'They were the ones who were wanted,' she said bitterly. 'I didn't fit into their plans, never measured up, never good enough . . .'

It sounded so familiar. Perhaps we were more alike than I'd ever realised. I thought of that cherished copy of *The Little Prince* on her shelf in London, the book that had guided Scarlett through a difficult childhood, and Della too, it seemed. The necklace she had given me. The scarf. All the encouragement and support. We seemed bound together then, in a way that was impossible to pick apart. Whatever happened now,

I was carrying Mark's child. One he and Della wanted to bring into the world. How could I say no?

By the time Della came back from Montpellier with a laptop for me and a stack of books – *Writing for Children, A Novel in a Year* – it seemed it was all decided. That evening, once the children were in bed, Della and I read through my stories. She had marked them up – sections she thought were working, ones Alan had concerns about, areas she thought I could improve. I became so caught up in excitement for this new project, I couldn't wait to get started. But first, Della said, she had something to show me.

I followed her up to their bedroom, entering it for the first time. Like the rest of the farmhouse, it bore no resemblance to the minimalism of their London home: polished wooden floors, a pine four-poster bed, large floor-to-ceiling wardrobes which could have been hewn from the very trees standing outside the windows. The only similarity being vast expanses of mirror, this time inside the wardrobe doors.

Della and I stood next to one another as she held up a series of maternity dresses – floral, striped, checked – all enormous, each with plenty of room to grow.

'Try this one,' she said, holding out a seventies-style floor-length floral number. 'You're due in May, so this will be perfect when it starts getting warm. Think how big you'll be by then!'

I forced a smile. It was impossible, and alarming, to imagine filling a dress that size.

'Oh, it looks gorgeous on you.' Della had pulled the dress over my vest and leggings, and was holding my hair up behind my head in the style she always wore. 'You'll be blooming by then, just you wait and see.' She twirled me around in front of the mirror as I eyed the loose fabric hanging around my middle in horror.

'It's . . . really nice. Thanks, Della.'

'I know it's a bit daunting, but I'm only giving you these now so that you'll have them when you're ready. I'll be back way before then.' She looked at me in the mirror and grinned. 'Come on now, smile! Oh look at you . . . Don't you think we look alike?' Della seemed giddy, almost girlish. 'We could be sisters, couldn't we? The baby will look like both of us, don't you think?'

I looked in the mirror. Della had pressed her head to mine, our fair hair mingling together, an arm around my shoulder, as if posing for a photo. It was true there was a resemblance – the hair, the blue eyes, though my nose was longer and my skin didn't glow in that expensive way Della's did. I could be her younger, less glamorous sister. But the similarity put me on edge. I already had a sister, one I looked less like – but who I should have been searching for.

As I wriggled free, I thought of the last time I had tried clothes on in Della's presence, in her room in London. That evening had been full of hope and excitement, as I remembered it now. A world away from the situation I found myself in today. Could I ever have imagined how much my life would change in the space of a few months? I folded the clothes Della had given me and retreated to my room, suddenly feeling the full weight of what I had agreed to do.

The real panic didn't take hold until after they had gone, though – the reality hitting as I watched Della's car receding down the driveway. Away from her certainty, alone and in silence, fears began to crowd my mind almost immediately. Did I really have the strength to carry a baby for someone else? How would Mark and I handle the arrival of a child we had conceived together? What would it feel like to watch him and Della holding the baby I had given birth to?

As darkness fell, I circled the house, making sure every last door and window was locked, trying to make out the shapes outside that seemed to shift before my eyes. But it wasn't until I was lying in bed, willing sleep to come, straining to hear every creak and bang, that my nagging anxiety took solid form. I thought about the clothes Della had made me try on. They couldn't have been more different to her London wardrobe. There, every item was designer, unmistakably expensive and chic. The piles of maternity dresses she had left for me were gaudy and cheap, a ragbag of mismatched styles and fashions. I couldn't picture Della wearing a single one.

It was a small detail for my mind to catch on, but it added to my growing unease – about the future, the next day, even closing my eyes. Where had those clothes come from? When would I see Tabitha and Jasper? Would Mark and I ever feel close to one another again? How could Della forgive us?

All variations, really, on the same question – one that circled endlessly, even as I clamped a pillow over my ears in an attempt to shut out the noise.

What was I doing here? What had I done?

Chapter Twenty-Six

I woke with a jolt to the sound of banging on my bedroom door. Sunlight warmed the thin curtains, making everything familiar again.

'Kate, Kate!' The accent was French. Manon.

'Yes?' I said, pulling the sheets around me. '*Oui?*'

'Town?' came the voice through the door. '*Voiture.*'

'Ah, yes.' I jumped up and pulled on my dressing gown, opening the door. There stood Manon, in a baggy purple dress, sleeves rolled up, greying hair pulled back from her face.

'*Désolée,*' she said, looking at the floor. '*Mais . . .* town?'

'*Oui,*' I nodded. 'Ten minutes.' I held up my fingers and Manon retreated downstairs.

Della had arranged for Manon to visit more regularly, taking me into town for anything I might need. It was only now, as I quickly dressed and went downstairs, that I realised how little attention I had paid to the housekeeper over the summer. She didn't speak a word of English, and I couldn't speak any French, but she had been an occasional presence – usually at times of the day when the children and I were out in the pool, or playing in the woods. Sometimes we would smile at one another in the kitchen, as she went about scrubbing or sweeping or mopping at lightning speed. She had come with the house, Della told me. It had been Manon's parents' place and she had sold it on when the upkeep got too much. 'A bit of an old hippy,' had been Della's description. 'She's a hard worker, though – she does wonders with that garden.'

As I sat beside Manon in her old yellow Citroën, rattling along the narrow wooded roads, I was able to observe her at closer range. The skin across her high cheekbones was deeply tanned and creased, her hair streaked silvery grey and her fingers that waxy yellow that came from years of smoking. She turned, aware of my gaze, and we both looked quickly ahead. It was uniquely awkward, being at such close range with not a word in common.

Manon dropped me in the centre of town, by the market square, and held up two fingers.

'*Deux heures?*' she suggested, gesturing to the café on the square, where I could find her when I was ready. I nodded, wandering off, unsure what to do with myself. It was market day, but the town had emptied since the end of tourist season, and now, in the chilly sunshine of early autumn, I found myself one of the few outsiders browsing around the stalls. I watched as people embraced and chatted, catching up on local news while I examined honey and olive soaps, acutely aware of my loneliness.

I didn't need to buy anything. Della had put in a weekly order with the nearest grocers, and the first delivery had arrived the day before, containing everything I might need but couldn't possibly imagine eating with the nausea that plagued me day and night. But I enjoyed the comfort of being surrounded by people, and moved through the stalls as inconspicuously as I could, remembering the times I'd visited with Della, Mark and the children. I pictured his smile, his ready laugh, his easy confidence. I imagined the children running between the stalls, Jasper fearless while Tabitha held herself back, watchful. What were they doing in London now? Were they thinking of me? Did Mark ever wonder how things might have turned out between us, playing out scenarios in his mind as I did, in the darkness of the night?

I found myself back at the café long before the agreed meeting time, and sat down awkwardly near Manon, who was deep in conversation with two men of around her age, late fifties perhaps or early sixties, long hair, one with round spectacles and all three smoking furiously. As soon as she spotted me, Manon noisily drew up a chair and made a big show of insisting, in French, that I join them and, at the same time, that they all put out their rolled-up cigarettes.

'No, no,' I said, sitting down. 'It's no problem.' But they all stubbed out their butts nonetheless.

'No good for *you*,' one man said, exposing his blackened teeth as he smiled widely at me, eyeing my stomach. Had Della told Manon I was pregnant? Surely she didn't know the full story. I shifted uncomfortably, wondering what Della had said.

'You, guest? Big house,' the man said with a grin, pointing up into the hills that loomed on the horizon. 'Long way,' he added, only increasing my anxiety. So they all knew I was up there alone. How far had word spread?

It soon became apparent that none of my companions had enough English to make conversation, and since my arrival had killed theirs, everyone drained their coffee cups and began to take their leave.

'I'm sorry,' I said to Manon as they stood up to go. 'I didn't mean to . . .'

'Pfff!' Manon smiled and chuckled to herself. 'Old man. Old woman.' She shook her head, laughing, and I laughed too, feeling a new warmth towards this small market town and the locals I'd hardly noticed during my summer in Della's bubble. How I'd love to make myself part of this community, if only for a few months. To befriend Manon and see another side of life so removed from my own. If only I could speak a few words of French. And if I wasn't marooned out in the hills, so far from anyone.

Manon dropped me at the empty house and I watched as her bright yellow car chugged away, leaving exhaust fumes hanging in the air. Looking out at the now-empty road, I felt a pang and then a cold dread engulf me.

'Do you still have the nausea?' Della looked concerned when she Skyped me that evening. 'It's a good sign, you know – it shows the pregnancy's progressing well.'

'Oh yes.' I grimaced. 'Still feeling sick all day every day, thanks.' And Della laughed, the relief clear on her face.

Della's nightly Skype calls were the only time I heard my own voice some days, and they had quickly become the main focus of my day. A rare moment of human contact, if an unsettling one. Della had insisted before she left that I made myself available at the same time every evening, so she could check I was OK. And she had made it clear that I wasn't to Skype anyone else. She didn't want me to have any visitors either, so apart from Manon, she was the only person I had contact with. She only called when Mark and the children were elsewhere, though I couldn't help hoping one of them might appear in the background. Sometimes I fantasised about calling at an unexpected time of day, in the hope that Mark might pick up. I just wanted to hear his voice. Catch a glimpse of him, see if that connection was still there. But I was too scared of Della's reaction to risk it. I was desperate to see the children, too. I still heard their voices in my head; phantom cries from other parts of the house taking me back instantly to that closeness, the sense of being needed. I missed the physical contact – with them, and with Mark. Now I was alone, I played the memories over and over, the closest I got to living, really.

Della barely mentioned the family. Her main line of questioning, aside from my wellbeing and that of the baby, was who I had spoken to and what I had said. She didn't want anyone to know I was pregnant, she said it would only complicate things. But she didn't need to worry – it was the last thing I was going to try to explain. I had mostly been avoiding calls and emails, unable to maintain the deception, though Della was keen that I shouldn't cut off contact altogether, in case anyone became concerned.

I tried to remind myself that Della was paying me for this time – money my family desperately needed. None of the administrative work she'd mentioned had materialised yet, so as far as I could tell, I was earning my salary by keeping her baby safe and well and being available to reassure her. Mostly, our conversations were limited to my health, and that of the baby. 'The most important thing is to keep you both rested,' Della said at the end of every conversation, ready to return to the warm glow of her kitchen, to the children, to Mark. 'And keep on with your writing, of course,' she sometimes added, when she remembered.

By now, writing was the last thing on my mind. The early enthusiasm I'd had for the new stories had melted away. Whenever I sat in front of the laptop, all I could think about were the questions and worries that swirled around my head day and night. When I did write, it was my obsessive thoughts that filled the page – about the baby, Mark, our alternative future together.

I wrote down the memories, too, which had begun to accost me in my solitude, day and night. It was as though my mind was compensating for the loneliness, recreating the voices and faces from my past. I seemed to be recovering whole scenes from my childhood that had lain buried for years. Inconsequential, mostly: afternoons spent lying on the grass with Scarlett in the garden, discussing friends and boys and the Spice Girls; a fight we once had about a red dress I had supposedly stretched out of shape. I remembered arguments, too, between Scarlett and my parents. Screaming matches during which I would lie in bed, my pillow over my head yet straining to hear, as accusations were thrown about – late nights, missed exams, too little love.

One particular scene came back to me in a rush one October evening, as I sat in the chilly living room, a blanket wrapped around me and my laptop on my knees. It was a night shortly after Scarlett had gone missing, when I had been lingering on the stairs, as I often did in those months, trying to pick up bits of information here and there. I could hear the TV on low in the background, *EastEnders*, or something equally shouty, and I could see through a crack in the door that Mum was crying quietly.

After a while, prompted by something on the screen, she had turned to Dad, sitting next to her on the sofa, and said the words that must have stayed with me, subconsciously, for so long: 'I could have been a grandma . . . And now that's not going to happen.'

I could still see her bent double with grief, Dad's soothing tone, his consoling hand on her shoulder. I had scuttled up the stairs, not wanting to see any more. Afterwards I lay on my bed, making sense of it all. I had probably said I didn't want to have children myself, but what did I know, really, at that age? Could she really have been so sure that, in losing

Scarlett, she had lost her only chance of grandchildren, of an extended family?

'No.' I said it out loud, and the sound of my voice shocked me. But then I shook my head, saying it louder. 'No!' Mum had been wrong. Who was she to map out my life for me, at such a young age?

I put my laptop to one side, pacing the room, going over all the little remarks, the pressures, all the decisions she'd made for me over the years. I'd always been controlled by her, trapped. And now here I was, trapped again.

I caught my reflection in the darkened window. I was talking to myself, muttering, dark circles under my eyes, my hair unbrushed and wild. I was shocked, angry, afraid. 'What?' I turned and shouted. 'What do you want from me?'

I woke up on the floor in the early hours, my eyes raw from crying. Exhausted, I crawled to the sofa for the blanket before allowing sleep to transport me away from the desperation of my waking hours once more.

That was the night things really started to unravel. When I began talking to myself, stopped taking care of my appearance, allowing my hair to become matted and surrendering myself to the mismatched maternity clothes Della had left me. Most days I spent pacing the house, as though looking for something, though I was never sure what – intruders, distractions, information?

One afternoon, I found myself searching through the attic, though I'd avoided it all summer, declaring it too spooky to enter during endless games of hide and seek with Tabitha and Jasper. I imagined them here with me now, laughing, daring me to go up and explore. The room was dark and low-ceilinged, a single naked lightbulb illuminating layers of dust and cobwebs running the full width of the rafters. I had only meant to poke my head up there, balancing on the ladder that had been folded in the hallway, but just out of reach I could see a single box, and I became desperate to know what was inside. Leaning across, I managed to hook it with a finger, and dragged it towards the hatch. Finally I heaved it down, landing on the floor alongside it with a thud.

I opened the lid. The box was full of books. Classics, thrillers, some Agatha Christies I hadn't read. I piled them up in my arms, so thrilled I almost missed another layer in the box, hidden below. Digging deeper, I found a pile of puzzle books and women's magazines, all well-read and ragged, the crosswords filled out, barely a page untouched. Unlike the novels, these weren't in English. The writing looked Eastern European, the fashions unfamiliar.

I stared at them for a while, before leaving them on the landing, picking up the books and retreating downstairs. But long into that afternoon and evening an uneasy feeling remained. I didn't know why, but the magazines seemed like a clue. A secret message left behind by some unknown visitor. I tried to think what Scarlett would have done in my position. Called Della to ask her, outright, where they had come from, probably. But I wasn't Scarlett. And I couldn't risk upsetting the delicate balance of our arrangement.

Instead I pushed them to the back of my mind, for now. I had the feeling I sometimes got doing crosswords with Dad. I knew there was an answer, hovering at the periphery of my vision, but I couldn't quite reach for it. Not yet, anyway.

Chapter Twenty-Seven

When the first kick came, I was lying on the sofa under a blanket, reading one of the Agatha Christies. I'd reached a tense moment when I felt a flutter in my stomach, unlike any sensation I'd experienced before. It felt almost alien, like a small creature was burrowing inside me; but rather than revulsion, I felt a rush of excitement, euphoria even. I lay perfectly still, waiting for it to come again. When it did, I laughed out loud with the shock and unexpected joy of it.

My baby was moving inside me. I wanted to tell someone, and Mark's face immediately appeared before me, the happiness he might have shared with me, in another life. Instead, the only person I could tell was Della, and I felt an instinctive desire to withhold this news from her. The baby was kicking; it was alive and well. It was *mine*. I felt it instantly and overwhelmingly. This was a moment for the two of us. I couldn't bear to think of Della's vicarious excitement; the pleasure she would claim as all her own.

When we spoke that evening, I said nothing. 'Any news?' Della prompted. She had been asking for a week or two whether I had felt anything, whether there were any outward signs of the pregnancy.

'Nothing yet,' I said. 'I'm sure it's fine, though. I've been getting plenty of rest.' I'd have to tell her eventually, but for the time being I wanted to keep this knowledge to myself.

'Have you? You look very tired. Strung out really,' Della said, looking with concern from the light and safety of her family kitchen.

'I'm OK, honestly. It's probably the hormones.' I smiled and smoothed down my hair, trying not to think about the hours of darkness ahead of me. Another night alone. My conversations with Della, and visits from Manon, were the only times now that I was able to hold it together, provide some semblance of sanity. Once darkness fell, my thoughts began to spiral, all the questions and fears coming at me faster than I could handle.

I considered asking Della about the magazines, and who they belonged to. But I didn't want her to think I'd been snooping around. Besides, she was already talking about an ultrasound that was booked for me at the hospital in Montpellier. 'I so wanted to come with you, but I can't get away, so Manon will drive you there. I hope you don't mind.'

If anything, I was relieved. Not just that Manon would be taking me, but that I would be going to a properly equipped hospital. Given how concerned Della was with the progress of the pregnancy, it had surprised me how wary she had been of any medical intervention so far. She hadn't wanted me to visit the local clinic, hiring a private midwife in Montpellier, who visited fortnightly.

'Now, I know it won't be the normal time, but I want you to call me as soon as you get back from the hospital. I want to know everything they say, OK?'

211

I agreed, and tried to change the subject, asking about Della's work, and how the group was going. But as usual, she shut down those conversations instantly. When I had asked how she had explained my absence, Della had shrugged. 'I said you'd decided to move on.' I thought of Jasmine and her sudden disappearance. Where was she now? Were the Janes speculating about what had happened to me? They couldn't possibly imagine the truth.

As we wrapped up, Della went through the arrangements for the scan. Manon didn't know any details about my pregnancy, she reminded me, only that the father wasn't around. 'And I've asked her to wait outside, OK?'

I nodded. 'She offered to come in with you, but I said that won't be necessary.' Della raised her eyebrows with a smile. 'I mean, she's quite strange, don't you think? I'm sure you don't want her hanging around.'

It was a frosty November morning by the time Manon arrived to drive me to the scan, and I had worked myself into a frenzy of anxiety. What if something was wrong with the baby? And why wasn't Della coming with me – surely she wanted to see the child she longed to bring up, growing inside my body?

Manon parked in front of a large, concrete bunker of a building and led me in, the high-ceilinged white echoing spaces seeming too bright and loud after my enforced solitude. There were people everywhere: talking, shouting, queueing. I resisted the urge to burrow into her arm as we sat on plastic chairs in the waiting room.

By the time I was called into the scanning room, there was no question of Manon waiting outside. She escorted me in, watching as my stomach was prepared with icy gel. Within moments we were both looking at a pulsing heartbeat on a screen.

My baby. There it was. Or there *he* was, as the sonographer told me, in limited English.

'A healthy boy. Good size.' She gave me a guided tour. 'His feet, his hands. The nose and the eyes. Look, he sucks his fingers!' She smiled and Manon and I both gasped, to see this foetus, so childlike in his gestures. I laughed, which in turn made him startle and kick his legs around a little, and I laughed again. He was so small, this little creature. So helpless and dependent on me.

It was only afterwards that I cried. In the car, silently, with my head bent forward so that my hair covered my face and the tears pooled on my lap. If Manon noticed, she didn't say anything. I pretended to sleep the rest of the way home and, after Manon left, I curled up in bed on my side.

When I woke, it was dark. Past nine. I opened my laptop and saw that I had missed twelve calls from Della. I was meant to have called her as soon as I got back from the hospital. She must be frantic.

Without taking even a moment to compose myself, I clicked to return the call. I caught sight of my face briefly in the video monitor as I listened to the dialling tone, and was wiping my eyes as Mark's face filled the screen. He looked older, paler, more tired than I remembered.

'Kate! Is everything OK?'

I nodded, taken aback, but Mark continued, breathlessly: 'Thank God. Della's going out of her mind. She convinced herself there's something wrong with our internet connection, so she's gone round to use Amisha's Wi-Fi.' He paused, as if noticing my expression for the first time. 'Are you all right? Is the baby OK?'

I nodded again. It shocked me, to hear Mark say those words 'the baby'. Somehow, I realised now, I'd convinced myself he was still in the dark about the extent of Della's plans, or

213

was trying to keep out of it, in denial. Instead he seemed fully involved, invested in the health of our child – the baby he and I had never even discussed, but were bringing into the world.

'He's fine,' I said quietly, searching Mark's face for signs of guilt, or regret.

'It's a boy! Oh Kate, that's wonderful news. And healthy? Everything where it should be?'

'Yes, very healthy, and active.' I was reeling. I had prepared myself for Della's pure excitement, its contrast to my own conflicting emotions. But not for Mark's.

He must have picked up on my discomfort because his tone softened, he dropped his voice.

'I'm sorry I didn't contact you after . . . well, you know. I shouldn't have left like that. But I didn't know what to say. Or what to do about it all. And then this happened, and Della seemed to have it all under control . . . I thought it would be better if I kept out of it.' He ran his hands through his hair, looking anxious. 'I'm so sorry, Kate. I do care about you. And the baby.'

'*Our* baby.' I could feel tears forming at the corners of my eyes. 'I thought when we were together, that it meant some-thing to you . . .'

'It did. You did. Look, in another world—' Mark looked away, distracted by a beep. 'Oh shit, Della's trying to get through. Look I've got to let her speak to you. She's going frantic. I'll call you later, Kate, OK? We can talk about every-thing. But I'm going to hang up now. Bye.'

And just like that, Mark's face was gone. The concerned eyes, furrowed brows, hollowed cheeks. All it took was those few words – *in another world* – and I was plunged into an alternative universe. One where he might turn up at any moment and take me and our baby away from this cold house, this uncertain future.

214

When Della's call came I was barely coherent, but I managed to distract her with details from the scan, the finger-sucking, the kicking I was now feeling hourly. I made no mention of my conversation with Mark. Of the hope he had reignited in me. Or of the dread that was growing inside me daily, as real and as energy-sapping as the baby it grew alongside.

Chapter Twenty-Eight

As the weather closed in around us and the days grew shorter, Manon took to visiting with home-baked cakes, cassoulets and flans. There was no mention any more of 'town'; instead she would find me shivering in one of the large, poorly heated rooms and tuck blankets around me, shaking her head and tutting. She had brought me a French–English phrase book, so I was able to look up some of the more frequent words I heard her using. '*Froid*' was one that came up a lot, as did '*incroyable*' and '*terrible*' – one I didn't need to look up.

Over and over, Manon insisted that she drive me '*chez moi*', where it was warm and accessible to the town. But tempting though it sounded, I knew I had to be here to receive Della's calls, and to be visited by the midwife. Any change to the plans would cause alarm.

More than anything now, I needed the money Della was paying me. Mum had made it clear in recent calls that Dad was deteriorating faster than either of them had expected. She even spoke to me alone once, late at night. She wanted to let me know that anything I could contribute would 'come in handy'. That was how she put it. Because she didn't want to admit what we had both known for a long time: that her salary wouldn't be able to make up the difference between the NHS treatment and the support they would need as he got worse. Straight away, I had transferred enough to cover a few months of extra care at home. In a couple of months' time, I'd be able to send more.

In between the calls from my parents and Della, and Manon's visits, I found myself pacing around the house, talking to myself and increasingly to the baby. Teddy, I called him. I hadn't intended to name him, but there it was. He was Teddy. He was my only company, after all, and the more he moved around inside me, the more attached I became.

He accompanied me as I circled the grounds outside in the daylight hours, checking for strangers, intruders – peering inside the pool, empty and full of leaves, and walking the length of the gardens, once vibrant with flowers and now as deserted and abandoned as I felt. He was there when I searched through the house, too – opening cupboards and checking behind doors. Rummaging through drawers, even through Della and Mark's wardrobes one afternoon, in my increasingly manic anger. Why shouldn't I explore every inch of my territory, after all? I'd been left here, alone. Abandoned, without a single visit for months now.

Standing on a chair, I got up to the top shelves, where I could see piles of brightly coloured fabrics. Silk scarves that Della must keep here for the summer months. Balanced up there, on tiptoes, a pattern caught my eye. It was a bluebird, like the ones on the scarf I'd lost. I tugged at it, nearly falling backwards as it slipped easily from under a pile of clothes.

I held the fabric to my face, sniffed the familiar scent. It was my scarf, I was sure. But why was it hidden away here at the top of Della's wardrobe? Perhaps it had got caught up in her things, packed away by accident at the end of the summer. But wouldn't Della have spotted it? She said herself that she'd noticed I'd lost it. She bought me a replacement. Just as she had given me a necklace to replace the one Scarlett had left.

Thinking about that necklace, my stomach sank. I hadn't seen it in weeks. I hadn't been wearing much jewellery over the summer and I couldn't think now when I'd last had it. I went up to my room to check, but it wasn't in any of the obvious places.

I walked slowly back to Della's room, turning it over in my mind. Had that ended up amongst Della's things as well – would I find it in her jewellery box? I almost didn't want to look. Why would Della be collecting my belongings? But it wasn't there either. I sifted through rings and bracelets, chains and costume pieces, but there was no sign of the lotus pendant.

In a small box to the side were a couple of watches, clearly Mark's, and a small, plain ring. I'd never seen Mark wear any jewellery except his wedding band, and I picked it up, turning it over in my hand, feeling the smooth weight in my palm. Inside it was printed a date – 9.7.05. It had to be the wedding ring from his marriage to Isabel; the timing was right. I slipped it onto my finger, and turned to Mark's side of the wardrobe, pulling out jumpers and shirts, burying my face in them and inhaling his citrus scent, one that took me instantly back to the summer.

Lying on the bed, I turned my face into Mark's pillow, his ring on my finger, my hand cradling my bump. I remembered the feeling of sitting up with him, as darkness crept around us, talking freely, the warm evening air seeming to hold us perfectly still in that moment. The connection between us, the attraction, all the possibilities the future seemed to hold then . . . It was the slam of a car door that made me sit up, confused, unsure how long I had been lying there. Had I fallen asleep? Had Manon forgotten something when she left that morning?

I got up and peered out of the window, but I couldn't see anything. The car must have pulled around the front of the house. Manon always parked at the back. So did Della – and surely she would have told me if she was planning to visit after all this time. What if it was Mark, arriving alone, just as I'd imagined? I threw his clothes into his wardrobe and closed the lid on Della's jewellery box with shaking hands. Then I reached for my phone and walked slowly down the stairs. Whoever it was still hadn't let themselves in, or knocked at the door. I started to panic. It must be a stranger circling the house. Seeing if anyone was home.

I could hear footsteps crunching on the gravel as I edged into the kitchen, my phone in one hand and in the other, a heavy rolling pin I kept near the door. My heart was pounding. This wasn't the kind of place you visited by accident. There could easily be two people, maybe more. How could I possibly protect myself and Teddy?

Slowly, I moved towards the kitchen window. If I could look out without being seen, then I might be able to see what kind of vehicle it was. A car, a van maybe? Standing on tiptoes, I could just make out the corner of a battered blue car. Not one I recognised. I leaned against the edge of the worktop, trying to get a better look, and as I did, I felt Teddy kick – pushing back against the pressure.

That kick brought me to my senses. What the hell was I doing, up here in this house, pregnant and defenceless? What was Della thinking – taking a risk like this with her future child, with me? If we got out of this unharmed, I would talk to Della and persuade her to let me stay with Manon for the rest of the pregnancy. I couldn't spend any more time up here alone.

I sank to the floor, my fingers shaking so much I could hardly enter the passcode on my phone. Should I call Manon, or the police? Who would get there first? Who would understand me better? Manon. She knew where I was. I wasn't even sure how I'd describe my exact location to the police.

I could hear the footsteps moving around the side of the building now. It was too late to make a break for the stairs. I crouched behind the kitchen island and fumbled with my phone, eventually finding Manon's name. It was ringing and ringing. I could feel my breathing go erratic. How was I going to protect Teddy?

And that's when I heard the voice. 'Kate? Kate!'

Oh my God. It was Layla. I rested my head against the wood of the cupboard door, feeling like I might faint. Gradually my breathing slowed. I pulled myself up and went to unlock the kitchen door.

'Shit, Kate!' Layla was staring at my stomach and then my face: my hair wild, my cheeks red with tears.

'Layla! What the hell are you doing here? Why are you creeping around the house?' Layla pushed past me, dumping an enormous rucksack in the middle of the kitchen floor.

'Shouldn't I be the one asking *you* questions here? What the fuck? When did this happen? When are you due?'

'How did you get here? How did you know the address?'

'OK, I'll tell you first. But then I want to know what's going on here.'

As I made tea, I listened to tales of Layla's epic journey, from London – where she had split up with Pete and quit the café, 'such a downer that place, I don't know how you could stand it' – to visit her mum at a commune in the Dordogne, then through the south of France with some guy, Thierry, who she'd met there. He'd lent her his car.

'And that's when I thought of coming to see you.' She smiled triumphantly. 'You sent us an email with your forwarding address, remember? And I thought, wouldn't it be funny to turn up, surprise you and lover boy. Maybe go on a little adventure together—' she stopped abruptly, looking at my stomach. 'Anyway, *that's* obviously not going to happen. So come on then, what's the story?'

The whole time Layla had been speaking, I had been thinking about what I could say. Not the truth, obviously, but what?

'I'm due in May,' I began, sitting down with two mugs and cupping mine in both hands to warm up. 'It's his, the guy I was seeing . . . Jacques. He's gone now. He doesn't know.' I looked down. 'It's better that way.'

'Things must have got pretty serious if he gave you that ring.' Layla nodded towards my hand, and I covered it quickly, ashamed by the impulse I'd had to slip it on, to feel closer to Mark.

'It's complicated.'

'Oh, Kate.' Layla put an arm around me. 'Bloody hell, you're freezing. This place is like an icebox. Why are you staying here if he's shoved off? Why don't you come back to London?'

I shook my head. 'I can't. I couldn't face my parents.'

'Oh come on, you're a big girl now. Twenty-five. This isn't some teen pregnancy.'

'No, I know, but . . . I'm not keeping it.' I avoided Layla's eye.

'Look, Kate, people do all sorts of things. They have abortions, they have babies adopted, they end up keeping them . . .'

I was desperately trying to hold in my tears. If only I could tell her the truth. 'I know. I know all that,' I said, shaking my head.

'So why don't you wait and see how you feel once you've had the baby?' Layla said softly, her arms around me as I let

221

it all go. 'Don't stress yourself out about it, love. The baby's coming now.'

I nodded. No point in contradicting her. There was no way I could explain that it was all arranged. That every last detail had been taken care of.

'It's a boy,' I said, wiping my eyes. 'Teddy.' I smiled.

'That's a lovely name.' Layla hugged me and bent down to address the bump. 'Pleased to meet you, Teddy. Hope you're nice and comfy in there.' And we both laughed at the strangeness of the situation.

Layla demanded a grand tour, exclaiming loudly at each new room we entered. 'This is enormous,' she said, as we finally ended up in my room. 'And you're here all on your own?'

'Just me.' I sat on my bed, exhausted from trudging up the stairs.

'Do you think I could stay for a bit?' Layla asked, uncharacteristically shy.

'Of course you can.' I pictured Della, and immediately pushed the thought from my mind. I'd been going to ask if I could stay with Manon, but being here with Layla – with a friend I could actually speak to – would be even better. Surely it was best for all of us if I didn't lose my mind?

Layla had been around a lot of pregnant women in her years on the commune, and she dealt with my needs and fears capably. She cooked stews and pies, fish and pasta, so that I was no longer surviving solely on Manon's kindness, and she was able to take me into town whenever we needed. In fact, she was determined that I continue to get out and about.

'You need to wrap up warm,' she admonished, when I complained of the cold. 'You're pregnant, not ill, for God's sake.' She took me out daily to walk around the woods,

222

collecting logs for the fire, and pine cones, interesting sticks and anything else she could find that might turn into a piece of art.

Layla's latest medium was natural sculpture and mosaic. It was the first time I'd seen her in work mode and I was impressed. I told her, with shame, about my failed writing retreat, and she insisted we both write down a plan of action: how many hours a day we were going to dedicate to our art. The only aspect of my new life that Layla found fault with was Manon.

I'd been excited to introduce them. With Layla's French, I thought she'd finally be able to tell me what Manon had been talking about all this time. But Layla wasn't impressed. 'God what a drag,' she said, rolling her eyes as Manon left the kitchen to find her cleaning products. 'She wanted to know all about what you're eating, how much sleep you're getting. It's as though it's her baby or something.'

I was disappointed, but also anxious. 'Did you at least tell her not to mention to Della that you're here?'

'Yes, yes. I said it very clearly. She said, "Of course not, Madame would not like it."' Layla spoke with an exaggerated French accent.

'Did she say why?'

'No. Only that Madame had left strict instructions to keep an eye on you. I got the impression that Manon wasn't very happy about me being here either.'

'No, I suppose not,' I agreed. 'But try to get on with her, for my sake Layla. She's my only ally around here.'

Layla looked at me strangely for a moment, and then she carried on chopping. Whatever she was thinking, she left it unsaid.

Chapter Twenty-Nine

The first warning came just before Christmas. Della and I were making our nightly call, with Layla banished upstairs, as usual.

'I've had all the papers drawn up now, so we can get those signed when I get back,' Della was saying.

'The papers? Oh, yes.' I had been putting off thinking about the formal side of it all, the adoption.

'I'll bring them with me when I come over,' Della said. 'You don't need to worry about them until then. So . . . you must be getting big by now. Stand up, let me look at you!' I obliged with a little turn, while Della cooed and fawned over my bump. Then her tone abruptly changed.

'Kate, what's that by the fireplace?'

I turned, panicked. Layla had left a piece of her art standing in the middle of the room. A figure of a woman, her belly rounded, made from sticks, pine cones and other objects she'd found around the farmhouse. It was a good omen, she'd said. To herald a healthy pregnancy.

'Oh, that.' I felt my heart thud. 'That's . . . something I picked up in town.' I moved to block it from Della's view.

'Really? You bought that?' Della looked unconvinced.

'Yes, it took my fancy.' I smiled, sitting down with the laptop once more.

'You're not refurnishing the house, are you?' Della was trying to make light of it, but I could see she was rattled. 'I hope you're not making work for Manon. I'd better check in with her. Make sure everything's as it should be.'

Afterwards, I took my anxiety out on Layla. 'What were you thinking, leaving that there?' Layla, naturally, couldn't see what the problem was. 'Does it matter that much if she knows I'm here?'

A few days later, Layla took the even riskier step of coming downstairs halfway through my Skype call. She was taking pains to be quiet, but my eyes must have flicked towards the door because Della picked up on it immediately.

'Who's there, Kate? Is someone with you?'

'No,' I said, quickly. 'Just a door banging in the wind.'

I felt instantly exposed. Had Layla heard anything Della had said, about the papers, or arrangements for the baby? And why was Della so suspicious? Maybe Manon had said something to give me away. Or I was acting differently. Either way, this time Della really was spooked. The following evening she announced she would be returning to the house in January. Layla and I had a matter of weeks left together.

Later that night as we watched the fire, my desperation rising, I gave voice to a question I'd been working hard to ignore.

'What if, when it came down to it, I decided I couldn't give the baby away?' I asked Layla.

'Oh Kate, I think you'd be a brilliant mum, I really do. And you can still do everything you want to . . . If that's what you decide.'

'No, but I mean, what if I'd already committed to having him adopted, and then I pulled out. What then?'

'What do you mean? Have you?'

'No, not exactly . . . I don't know. I'm being silly, really.'

'Look, the main thing is, he's your baby. And if you do decide to keep him, if you think that's what you want, I'll help you. I know I can be a bit unreliable, but I am handy.' Layla grinned. 'I'm sure Liam would be only too happy to help, too.' She gave an exaggerated wink. Liam was one of the subjects Layla liked to tease me about. Especially since she'd read an email from him over my shoulder the week before, with one of his anagrams and another plea to come home. But I didn't want to talk about Liam. Not now.

'You've been amazing,' I said to Layla. 'I don't know what I would have done if you hadn't turned up when you did.'

'I was worried about you when I got here, to be honest. You were a bit . . . unhinged. You seem a lot better now.'

Layla's eyes rested on my hand. I was still wearing Mark's ring. Looking at it now I smiled, imagining what Layla would make of Mark if he were to saunter into the living room and join us by the fire. Put another log on, cuddle up to me, stroke the bump. She'd like him, I knew. They'd make each other laugh, singing songs from the old days.

'He's not coming back, you know,' Layla said gently, watching me, locked in my private fantasy. But she meant Jacques – the unreliable French barman I'd invented. She didn't know anything about the married man I'd fallen for, the wife I'd made a promise to, the money they were paying me, that my parents were relying on. There were no words I could use to explain it all. There was no way to make Layla understand.

The days leading up to Layla's departure were fraught with tensions on both our parts. I combed the house, clearing away

226

every trace of her, replacing Mark's ring, even returning my scarf to Della's wardrobe to avoid arousing her suspicion. I was also eager for Layla to have a final conversation with Manon, in which they agreed a vow of silence. Layla was reluctant, both to speak to Manon, and to leave me on my own.

She was heading off to the commune in the Dordogne and had plenty of reasons for me to join her. 'It's much more creative there, and you'll have loads of people to help you once the baby comes. Plus you won't be getting in this Della's hair, messing up her rustic little show home, will you?' As usual, I didn't know how to respond. How could I possibly tell her the truth?

On the morning of Layla's departure, Manon arrived to clean. It was a cold day, and she unwrapped layer upon layer, while I handed her a cup of tea and left the kitchen, throwing a meaningful look in Layla's direction. This was Layla's chance: it was time to convey the importance of total secrecy.

I could hear the rise and fall of their voices from the living room. The language sounded melodic, harmonious. Then there was a short silence and Manon spoke more sharply, scraping her chair on the flagstones. I heard footsteps, a final barked sentence, and then Manon marched into the room, cleaning materials in hand. As she saw me, she lowered her head, carrying a bucket silently upstairs.

I joined Layla in the kitchen, where she was washing up.

'How did it go?'

'Fine,' Layla said, looking down as she rinsed the dishes. 'She's not going to say anything . . .'

'But?' I asked.

'But . . . she thinks there's something weird going on here.' Layla turned around to look at me. I did my best to smooth the worry from my face.

'What do you mean weird?'

227

'She didn't really say much more than that. She kept saying "*C'est pas normal.*" And I know what she means. It's not normal, is it Kate? Why *has* this woman had you here all this time as a sort of permanent house guest? Why are you having your baby here, in France? And why's she paying your hospital bills and stuff?'

'What?'

'Oh, come on, Kate. I'm not stupid. I know you don't get home visits from midwives without paying for them. And the hospital you're getting those letters from, it's a fancy one in Montpellier, isn't it? I don't need Manon to tell me Della's paying. But why – what's in it for her?'

'Don't people help each other sometimes? Does there always have to be an agenda? Why are *you* here? What are you getting out of it?'

'I'm here because I care about you. And I thought we were friends,' Layla said quietly, wiping her hands and turning to leave the kitchen. 'But friends tell each other things.' She stopped in the doorway a moment. 'There's something else she said . . . about other guests.'

'What did she mean? Other people who have stayed here before?'

'Yes, other young women, doing what you're doing.'

'What, being a nanny?'

'Not exactly.'

'You mean staying here on their own, like I have been?'

'Well, yes. One last year, who came with the family. But another one, before that, who was pregnant, like you. Staying here on her own. Just like you are.'

'What?' I held on to the back of a chair. 'Who? When was this?'

'I don't know. She didn't say any more than that, and then she stormed off.'

228

I went blank for a moment. And then, for some reason, a memory surfaced, of Jasmine's warning – the one she was never able to give. And Claire's, too. The invitation. My mind slowed, struggling to make connections, but the strands of thought were too far apart, too deep below the surface.

I watched Layla leave the room, slamming the door behind her in frustration. She was right. None of it made any sense.

Chapter Thirty

The snow was melting by the time Della blew in through the door, icy clumps attached to her boots. She was so preoccupied with the bump, stroking it, talking to it, she barely seemed to notice how wild-eyed and strung out I was. By then, I'd been snowed into the farmhouse for forty-eight hours, the first flakes settling just hours after Layla's departure. I'd hardly slept a moment since.

Della was upon me instantly, hands all over me, full of questions about the baby, his health, his movements. I flinched as she stroked my bump, unable to hide my instinctive recoil.

'Oh, sorry, darling. But I've been longing to feel him moving. How are you doing in there little one? Have you come to say hello to Mummy?'

The words stung and I shifted out of reach.

'Sorry . . .' Della said, looking hurt. 'Perhaps another time?'

'Yes, another time. I'm sorry. I've got a lot on my mind. In fact, can I ask you something?'

'Of course, what is it?' But Della was already picking up her bags, ready to go upstairs. It wasn't the right moment.

'Oh, don't worry. Get settled in. We can talk later.'

'Absolutely. I'm going to have a little rest. But afterwards I want to hear *everything*. Every kick, twinge, feeling . . . If anything happens, you tell me. OK?'

I nodded slowly, wondering whether there was any part of my body I could still call my own.

That afternoon, as Della slept, I put on my boots to go out and check on the bulbs Layla and I had planted in the garden. I had woken from my lunchtime nap with the idea that they might be struggling to breathe, buried beneath all that snow, and I was gripped by a need to uncover them, to nurture them and coax them into growth. I had crunched halfway across the frosted lawn when Della came out.

'Kate! What are you doing?' she shouted. 'You shouldn't be out here in this cold, in your condition. Come indoors, right now!' She spoke sternly, as though I was more patient than friend, and I bristled, determined to complete my task. I was barely six months pregnant. I didn't need bed rest.

'Kate! Come inside!' I picked up a spade and started scraping the snow aside to reveal tiny green shoots poking through the hard earth. My babies, I thought, satisfied, as Della reached me and pulled me sharply by the arm.

'I don't know what's been going on here, but things are going to change. You need to rest, eat and take care of the baby. You look like a madwoman out here, in your pyjamas and boots, gardening in the snow. What's got into you?' She was dragging me into the house, while I struggled against the pressure of her grip, trying to retain a little dignity.

'I've been fine, thank you. And the baby's fine. That's all you care about, isn't it?'

'No, it isn't,' Della said, as we entered the kitchen. My wrist throbbed as she let go of it. 'I'm worried about you. You look tired and too thin for your stage of pregnancy. I know the

231

bump is growing, but your face looks drawn. You need fattening up, like me.'

Della grabbed a small roll of fat from around her stomach and I realised in that moment what it was I'd been trying to put my finger on. Something about her was different. She still had that deep tan, even in mid-winter, and if anything her eyes and hair were even shinier than before, but something had changed. Now I saw that her face was fuller, she was thicker around her middle. She had allowed herself to gain weight.

'How else do you think I'm going to convince everyone it's me having the baby?' she asked with a smile.

I stared, taking a few moments to catch up. 'Do you mean . . .?' It hadn't even occurred to me that Della might try to pass the baby off as hers.

'Why do you think you've been our guest out here all this time?' Della asked.

'I thought we just didn't want anyone to know he was *my* baby. I didn't realise we were going to pretend he was *yours*.'

'Well, what did you think we were going to say?'

'That he was adopted,' I said, struggling to take it all in. 'I thought I'd be the only person who knew the truth.'

'And it will be a bit like that. No one will know you were our surrogate. They'll think I went away to France for the end of my pregnancy – I've told everyone I need bed rest, and time to finish my new book – and when I come back, I'll have a baby.'

My mind snagged on that word: 'surrogate'. It was the first time Della had used it. It made the whole arrangement sound much more official.

'But . . . how can you stay here until May? What about work? What about Tabitha and Jasper?'

'Oh, they'll be fine. It's only a few months, and they're with

Mark, and Chloe, the new nanny. They'll come and visit in the school holidays. And work, the group – that can all be put on hold. I'm on maternity leave, aren't I?'

I looked at her, hugging her arms around her expanded waist, barely able to understand what I was hearing. Della was really going to drop everything so she could pretend to the world that this was her baby. It meant that much – to be seen to be the real mother. The woman who had everything.

But how would she pull it off? And wasn't she worried about her children – about Mark? Della had spoken so casually about him and the new nanny, alone together in London. Had she already forgotten what had happened six months earlier – his infidelity? Who was to say it wouldn't happen again?

Della told me that Mark and the children would be visiting, with Chloe too, but they would all stay in Sète, where Jonathan had offered them the use of his house.

'But . . . it's been so long,' I pleaded, 'I've been looking forward to seeing them.'

'Oh Kate, don't be silly. They might be young, but they're not stupid. They'll see you're pregnant and they'll put two and two together straight away – especially Tabitha. And you know what kids are like. They'll tell everyone. Far better for me to meet them elsewhere, and for you to stay well out of the way until the baby's born.'

I looked Della up and down, wanting to be certain I was understanding all this. 'But surely they'll see you're *not* pregnant.'

'Honestly, don't worry.' Della laughed. 'I've been wearing baggy clothes. I'll tell them not to climb on me. They'll never know the difference. As long as they don't see you.'

I sank into a kitchen chair, struggling to process it all.

'Now, I'm going into town for a bit,' Della continued,

moving towards the door. 'I'll bring you something delicious and fattening for dinner!' Her laugh as she was leaving had a note of hysteria, and a memory emerged from nowhere of a beautifully illustrated Grimms' fairy-tale book I had as a child.

There was one story I had read over and over, both fascinated and appalled. It was Hansel and Gretel, and there was a picture I remembered clearly now – colourful and garish in style – of the children, wide-eyed and imprisoned in a cage in the witch's house. I thought of their faces, the horror when they realised what had happened. That they had been lured there and locked up against their will. Fattened up to await their fate.

We were halfway through dinner that evening before I gathered courage to broach the subject that had been on my mind for days now.

'Della, can I talk to you about something Manon said?'

'Of course. What was it?' Della paused, a spoonful of gooey chocolate hovering mid-air.

'Well, she didn't exactly say it to me. She was talking to herself, but she kept mentioning other guests. Other women who stayed here.'

'Yes?' Della looked at me, putting the spoon down. 'Friends of ours?'

'I don't know . . .' Della must surely be able to hear my heart pounding. 'Another woman who stayed here, last year. And another one before that, who was pregnant, like me . . .'

Della looked at me for a moment. 'I thought you couldn't understand French?'

'I can't, really. But I put the few words I knew together and, well, that's what I came up with. The others, pregnant, staying here.'

'Oh.' Della laughed, the muscles in her face visibly relaxing. 'Oh . . . I see what she meant. She must have been talking about Rebecca, my friend who stayed with us one summer, when she was pregnant.'

'No, it was definitely someone who was here, alone, and pregnant. Someone in the same situation as me.'

'Well, come to think of it, there was one nanny who was pregnant while she was here. Perhaps that's who she's thinking of. But . . . why would she even mention it? I'm sure we've all forgotten entirely by now, it was years ago. And really, what were we meant to do – sack her, when she was having a baby? Why on earth would Manon think you'd be interested in that?'

'I don't know,' I said, unsure myself now. 'I think it was something about this house not really being suitable for a pregnant woman, all the way out in the hills, all alone.'

'That's why I asked her to drive you around. And anyway, you wanted the chance to get back to yourself after the pressure you've been under, mentally. And to save money, to write . . . How is that going by the way?'

I felt shame, at the reminder of my outburst at Della, and the mention of my salary, the residual guilt I felt at receiving money for a job that didn't really exist. I found myself babbling – unprepared for the sudden interest in my creative progress, and eager to say the right thing.

'I had a few false starts, and it took me a little while to get going, but I'm really pleased with the way they're coming along now. I'll definitely have a finished collection to show Alan soon.'

Della reassured me that there was no rush. 'Now, there's nothing else you're anxious about is there? I can see you've got yourself into a bit of a tizz, up here all alone.'

'I suppose I have been a bit sad about not seeing the chil-

dren,' I confessed. And Mark, I thought, though I didn't
mention that. 'I feel more distant from them than ever.'

'They ask about you all the time. I've told them you've got
a new job for a little while, but you'll be back. You'll be part
of their lives again, as soon as you've had the baby. In fact,'
she said, standing up and fetching an expensive-looking leather
bag, 'why don't we get those papers signed while we think of
it, so the arrangements are all agreed.'

She handed me a sheaf of papers, covered in small print.
Scanning them, words jumped out, phrases that meant nothing
to me: 'surrogacy agreement', 'intended parents', 'parental
order'.

'So that's what this is,' I asked, 'a surrogacy?' I had spent
plenty of time googling adoption, familiarising myself with
my rights, the adoptive parents' rights. But I knew nothing
about all this.

'To all intents and purposes. Though in this case it will be
different because you'll still be involved. You don't need to
worry about reading it all. These are only preliminary papers,
setting out how it all works, the real documents come after
the birth.'

'So these are—'

'A formality,' Della finished off my sentence, brightly.

'Couldn't I have a few days to read through it all, make
sure I know what I'm signing up to?' I tried to smile.

'What's the matter, Kate? Have you changed your mind?'
Della's face drained of colour instantly. I could see her hands
shaking. I knew how much this meant to her. And what else
was I going to do, really?

'No, it's just, I'd like a bit of time – to understand how it
all works.'

'There's nothing in here I haven't already explained to you,'
Della said. 'And I need to get them sent off to the lawyers,

we've wasted a lot of time waiting until I was here in person. I don't want to slow the process down any more than we already have.' She handed me a pen.

'But, don't we need a witness?' I looked at the bottom of the page, where there was space for a third signature.

'Oh, don't worry about that, Manon can do it when she comes tomorrow,' Della said with a smile. 'It will be wonderful to be able to tell Mark it's all tied up. He's been so anxious about it all, so worried about you.' She looked at me and I felt my heart skip, along with a rumble of shame deep within me. 'Once you've signed them, I'll Skype him and we can find out what they've all been up to.'

I thought about the children in London, waiting for news of their new baby sibling. I pictured Mark's face, the concern in his eyes the last time we'd spoken. Della was finally going to let me speak to them again. How I longed to see them, even on a screen, to connect with them, to feel part of their world.

Besides, it wasn't as if I had any other options, isolated out here, after the promise I'd made to Della. Even if I took more time, I'd still end up making the same decision. I was in too deep.

And so I signed the papers, without reading another word.

I should have known that Della would disappear straight after, taking her laptop upstairs. She hadn't meant for us to Skype them together, of course not. Only that she would pass on their news once she had spoken to them. It was one more misunderstanding – another example of me hearing what I wanted to hear. Or perhaps, looking at it now, it was another deception. One of the many small lies and half-truths that had led me to this moment, to signing an agreement about my future with such far-reaching consequences, I couldn't even begin to understand them.

*   *   *

237

After she left me, I picked up my laptop, looking over all the work I'd done since Layla arrived. The stories were taking shape, developing into a series, with one central tale. It was one I remembered Scarlett telling me when I was younger, only altered, embellished.

One day, as Elsie walked through some dark woods, far from her sunlit meadow, she discovered a tiny fairy baby, abandoned and all alone. Taking pity, she took the small, sobbing bundle home and bathed her, clothed her, fed her on warm milk and soft bread. Elsie and the baby grew to love each other dearly, and she turned into a small, blonde fairy girl – sweet-natured and curious. When she had been with Elsie for a few years, the fairy child wandered into the woods where she had been found and stumbled across a family living in a tree trunk. They recognised their lost daughter instantly, even after all the years that had passed. But the little girl insisted on going home to Elsie, the only mother she had ever known. Having followed the child on her long journey to the meadow, the real mother confronted Elsie and begged to take her daughter home. Elsie wept and wept, but eventually she agreed to let her little fairy leave: she knew that the child belonged with the family who had lost her all those years ago.

Writing the end of that tale, I wept, too. But reading them all back, I could see it was the strongest story I'd written. It was the one that felt most true to life. The one I could never bring myself to read again.

Chapter Thirty-One

'It's happening.' I was standing in the doorway of Della's bedroom in the darkness, doubled over, pain radiating through my body like jolts of electricity. I stopped speaking to squeeze the door frame and pant, as I had read in the books. 'Della, the baby's coming.'

'What?' Della sat up in bed, sounding panicked. 'It's too early. We're not due in the hospital for days.'

'Honestly Della, they're really strong now.' I gasped and then began to moan, softly and then louder, thrusting my head down, chin against my chest, resting my head against the wall while the pain of the contraction overcame me. At least the sensation drowned out the fear, if only for a few moments at a time.

'How often? Are you sure it's not just those practice ones you've been having?'

'Yes, I'm sure,' I said, more urgently now, exhausted, between contractions. 'Can we go to the hospital please?'

'Of course,' Della said, pulling on clothes. 'Sorry, I'm half-asleep. Yes, we need to go, right now. Do you have your bag?'

'Yes, it's here,' I said, feeling another contraction building gradually at the base of my spine. 'I'm going to wait in the car.' I needed to sit. Needed to get there before the next one took hold. I staggered down the stairs and doubled over in the kitchen, sinking to all fours, my forehead resting on the cold stone. Della found me there moments later and half dragged, half carried me to the car.

'I don't understand it,' Della was saying as she sped along the empty motorway, an eerie light rising around us, silhouetting the trees and lone houses. 'That midwife said the head hadn't even engaged yet. And that was yesterday. How can this all be happening so quickly?'

I gripped the underside of my seat with both hands, my head bowed, groaning as the pain seemed to splinter my body.

'Just breathe, Kate, breathe,' Della shouted. 'Think about the lapping waves of the sea coming to carry the baby.'

Nothing about this was the way I had imagined, but particularly not Della's reaction. In the weeks leading up to my due date, she had gone over and over what a beautiful, spiritual experience the birth would be. How a relaxed mother delivered a relaxed baby. What she didn't want to talk about were the details. She didn't tell me a single story from her experience of having Jasper, and whenever I asked for specific information, she changed the subject. I assumed she was waiting for the celebrated doula to arrive and talk me through everything. The doula she was flying over to Montpellier. The one who was still in London.

'Is it OK if we don't talk?' I panted, preparing myself for another wave. In my mind, I pictured not the sea, but my family. There I was, on the brown sofa at my parents' house, surrounded by my mother, Layla, Scarlett, as she had been, smiling, stroking my forehead, as she had sometimes done

240

when I was upset. I imagined them encouraging me, holding my hands while I grunted through every tightening of my stomach, each one more painful than the last.

'You can do this,' they whispered. 'Do this for us.'

I can do this. I can do this. I can do this for you, I repeated over and over in my mind. But I was shrieking in agony by the time we pulled into the hospital car park. And Della, having entirely lost her composure, pushed me out of the car, driving away to find a parking space while I stumbled through the hospital entrance, shielding my eyes against the bright lights. I felt my legs go from under me. I watched the room rotate. I heard but didn't feel the thud.

When I woke, I was surrounded by masks. I became aware of an urgent beeping sound that seemed to have been echoing around my head for a long time, my thoughts pulsing in time to the beat. Where was I? Who were these people? There were eyes everywhere, some watching me intently, others directed away, busy in the lower regions of my body. Where were the eyes I recognised? Where was Della?

I could feel a pain throbbing in my right shoulder. I remembered the fall. Then I became aware of the urgency of the voices around me. I tried to raise my head, to look around – for Della, for anyone. But I couldn't move. I could feel nothing below my waist.

I was exhausted. I let my head fall back, my eyelids drop. I pictured my mother's face, Scarlett's, Layla's . . .

The next time I woke, all was dark. Silent. The room was empty. Only a dim glow from the hall outside lit one corner of a bare-walled, featureless room. A regular, calmer, beeping sound, told me I was still alive.

But where were my legs? I couldn't feel them. Confused, I looked down.

The baby. I remembered then. Where was the baby? My stomach was still large, but deflated, like a day-old balloon. I ran my hands down my body.

It was empty.

For the first time in nine months, I was entirely on my own.

Chapter Thirty-Two

I drifted in and out of consciousness, the lights above my head swimming into view and then receding as I gave in to the tug and allowed my eyes to roll back.

Each time I woke, I had the same thought process: Where am I? Followed by the panic as my eyes scanned the contours of the white room, trying to place it in my memory. Then I would remember. The hospital. And the next realisation would drop like a stone.

I heard my voice, croaky and unrecognisable, forming the same word over and over: 'Baby. Baby?'

At one point, I woke to find I was being changed by a nurse, sheets stained crimson with blood bundled into a basket and new ones laid around me in their place. She avoided looking at my face and I didn't have the strength to sit up. I tried to speak, but I couldn't find any words aside from that same one: 'Baby?'

The next time I woke, a different nurse was taking my temperature, leaving pills and a glass of water by the side of my bed, speaking in French and then walking away, flustered, when she realised I could understand nothing.

The pain I felt was general and hard to pin down. I could tell I'd had a Caesarean. I could feel the scar. But that wasn't the only source of discomfort. Throbbing, sharp stabs, dull aches. I couldn't be exactly sure what hurt and how. All I knew was that I had no strength in my body. I didn't have the energy to sit up. I could barely keep my eyes open for longer than a few moments. I felt like it couldn't be long before I would die, if I hadn't already. I didn't feel particularly scared. I was too tired for that. My only wish, the one thought that swam to the front of my confused mind every time I awoke, was that I wanted to see my son, my boy, before I gave in, and closed my eyes for good.

And then, he was there. I had no idea if it was night or day, or how much time had passed, but I woke to a snuffling noise. An unmistakable weight on my chest. My baby. My little boy.

He was tiny, warm, his body seeming to pulsate with every beat of his heart. My arms folded involuntarily around him, holding him to me. I felt light-headed with relief.

A nurse unfastened my nightshirt and helped the baby's mouth latch on to my nipple. I was aware of a light, tingling, fluttering feeling as he sucked and sucked, burrowing with his hands at my breast like a mole. I drank him in, too: his dark hair and pink skin, his eyelids closed with an intensity that first made me smile, and then brought tears to the corners of my eyes. I watched as he lost his way, his mouth straining to find me again, a little moan escaping. It seemed so natural, this animal instinct. So right that we should be together like this. So unimaginable that he might be taken away.

I forgot all about my exhaustion, my surrender. Instead, I was overcome by a love that felt fierce and raw. It was as if there was no skin between us. As if he breathed my breath. His smell was my smell. I felt in that moment that if anyone

244

tried to remove him from my body, I would tear at their skin, and scream with every ounce of energy I had left.

But then my mind began to drift. I couldn't focus, couldn't resist the drooping of my eyelids any longer. I felt my hands curl around his tiny back as I let my eyes close, clinging him towards me as I lost consciousness.

The next time I opened my eyes, I was alone. My hands were empty, my body cold. His dark, snuffling warmth had evaporated.

I was gripped by a panic so intense I thought I might scream. And then, a split second later, I remembered, as if learning the truth for the first time, but even more painful now that I had seen him, held him, fed him with my own body. He wasn't my baby. He would be with Della. Perhaps Mark had arrived by now.

I felt hollow. Tears ran down my cheeks and onto my pillow, creating a damp patch around my face. I could barely breathe. Barely see. Perhaps if I closed my eyes, they would stay closed. All this would be over soon.

When I woke, a nurse was reading my charts. I felt a little more strength had returned. Enough to lift up my head and ask the question once again: 'Baby?' The nurse looked at me, startled.

'Do you know where my baby is?' The nurse, dark-eyed, tired-looking, regarded me warily, as though I might be deranged. She shrugged and disappeared, returning with a doctor.

'How are you feeling?' she asked, in fluent English. 'I'm Doctor Joubert.'

'I'm OK.' It came out as a croak. I was struggling to open my eyes fully. 'How's the baby? Where is he?'

'He's still on the ward.' She checked my temperature and

blood pressure. 'Much better.' She nodded, taking notes. 'You had an emergency Caesarean. You lost a lot of blood. You and the baby both contracted an infection. He's OK now, but for you it became sepsis. You've been lucky, but you need to rest.' She carried on scribbling.

'But when can I see him? Can I visit him on the ward?' I tried to sit up.

'You won't be going anywhere fast. I'll ask if we can get him brought up to see you here.'

I nodded, and let my head fall back on the pillow. I wasn't sure how much these doctors and nurses knew about my situation, and I didn't want to get into details. I just wanted to see my baby. Della's baby. And to talk to Della.

She and Mark must be preoccupied, I reasoned with myself. Especially as the baby had been so sick. He was their first priority. So tiny. But still, I couldn't help feeling forgotten. Shut out.

After the doctor left, I closed my eyes. Violent visions assailed me – knives, syringes, blood. I watched a scene play out, only half-aware that it was a dream: doctors pulling the baby from my body with a rope, tugging at his arms and legs as he lay lifeless like a rag doll. A midwife handed him to Della, and Della walked away without a backward glance – leaving me lying there, paralysed, unable even to scream.

It was so hot. That was my first thought. And then that the sheets were soaking. I must have had an accident. I tried to lift myself high enough to pull the handle for some attention, but I couldn't.

It was the doctor who woke me, shaking me, trying to rouse me from a deep sleep I was reluctant to leave.

'What?' I said, with anger. 'What do you want? Della?'

I drifted in and out, unable to tell how much time was

passing. Everywhere I looked, I saw her face. Della holding the baby. With Mark, or Tabitha and Jasper. But they were nowhere. Where *were* they?

'Your infection is worse,' a voice said. 'We're putting in a drip.'

'Della?' I could hear myself asking. 'Is that you?'

I woke in the darkness this time, and immediately sensed a presence at the foot of my bed. Outside, the bustle of the ward continued, but in my room was the sound of someone breathing.

My instinctive response was fear. Who was lurking in the darkness? But as my eyes adjusted, I saw it really was Della this time, sitting in the visitor's chair that had remained empty since I had taken up residence in this room, watching me, her face in shadow.

'Della!' I lifted my head with difficulty. 'There you are. I was worried. How's the baby? How's he doing?'

'He's fine.' Della sounded calm, but I felt my stomach tense in panic. Something was wrong. Something no one had told me.

'Is everything OK?'

'I told you, he's fine.'

'How long have I been here? Where have you been? I thought you'd come and see me.' It was disconcerting, not being able to see her face. I had no idea how much time had passed. There was no clock in the room and the battery had long since run out on my phone.

'We have, Kate. Mark and I have been in and out, but you're always asleep. You've been here nearly three weeks. They say you've turned a corner now.'

'Three weeks?' I couldn't believe it had been so long, it felt like days. 'And the baby, how is he?'

'He's been given the all-clear. That's why I was waiting until you woke up. We're leaving with him, tomorrow.'

'To go where? To the farmhouse? Can I come with you?' I tried to sit up, to show how much better I was.

'Kate, you've been really ill. You need to stay here until you're totally recovered.'

'But . . . when will that be? When can I get out of here?' Why wouldn't she come near me – hold my hand, reassure me?

'Give it a few more weeks.' Della glanced at my medical sheet, my drip. 'I'll be back in three weeks' time, so you can sign the papers for the parental order. By then, we should have Ferdie's passport – and hopefully we can all travel to London.'

'Ferdie.' I tried out the name. It felt unfamiliar on my lips. 'Is it short for Ferdinand? Can I see him, before you go?' I thought of the tiny red fingers, the milky smell of his scalp.

Della shook her head. 'It's not worth the risk, Kate. You're both still so weak.'

'But . . . I'm not contagious, am I? You don't think . . . *I* infected him, do you?'

'He's fine, Kate. We're going to have some bonding time, me, him and Mark, up in the house.'

'Where are Tabitha and Jasper?' I was struggling to take it all in.

'They're with Chloe. Look, really, you don't need to worry yourself with all this. You get yourself better, and we'll be back in a few weeks with the paperwork. OK?'

She gave me a little smile, and I watched the door close behind her.

Chapter Thirty-Three

In the endless days that followed, Teddy was my first thought on waking. As I drifted off to sleep, I'd close my eyes and try to recreate the weight of him on my chest. The warmth. The rhythmic breathing. On and off, throughout the day, I'd imagine what he was doing – where his cot was placed, which window he looked out of, which birds he could hear.

He would always be Teddy to me. A little rebellion. I had never really thought about the act of naming before. Taking ownership of something, or someone. Teddy had grown inside my body. He had my genes, my cells. If anyone could claim the right to name him, it was surely me. And so I did, in my own head at least. It gave me some small sense of power, when really I had none.

Alone in my room, the days took on a monotonous routine: the mealtimes, the checks, the expeditions to the toilet and, gradually, downstairs. There were never any visitors, nothing to read that was in English, just one shared TV on the communal ward, always tuned to a series of soap operas I had to follow from hand gestures and facial expressions.

Apart from the odd nurse and doctor who could speak a

little English, I had no contact with anyone. On more than one occasion, I started to wonder if I was really there, whether anyone could actually see me. Some nights I woke in a sweat, having dreamt that I had died giving birth, that only the baby had survived.

In fact, I can see now, a part of me *had* died. I was empty – the child I had held within my body was no longer available for me to hold. I mourned the loss of life inside me, without a new life to welcome on the outside. And so I waited. Lingered on for the day when, finally, one of the doctors would tell me I was ready to leave. Or when Della and Mark would return to sweep me back to London.

'Can I go soon?' I would ask, every time a doctor appeared at the end of my bed. I always hoped it would be Dr Joubert, with the good English and the reassuring smile, but she never seemed to be on duty, and I was always met with the same resistance. I was still too weak, I needed rest.

I bought a phone charger from the hospital shop and got as far as dialling my parents' number, so desperate was I to hear a familiar voice. But as soon as Mum answered, I hung up. I'd be found out immediately. She'd be able to tell I was in hospital, that all wasn't well. That night I lay awake plagued by the cruelty of it – of prank calling a woman who had now lost both her daughters, who must be waiting at every moment to hear from one or the other of us.

I regularly rang the farmhouse, hoping to get through to Mark or Della before the credit ran out on my phone. But no one ever answered. I began to wonder whether they were really coming back for me. I knew it was an important time for them to bond, but didn't I matter at all?

I also bought a notebook and pen, so at least I could pass the hours writing. But the stories I'd worked on while I was pregnant, the ones I hadn't been able to finish before I went into labour, seemed so distant now it was as though someone else had written them. I had nothing left to say that could be put into words. All I could bring myself to write were letters, to the son I had only laid eyes on once, so briefly. And that was what I was doing, sitting up in my bed, scribbling furiously, when I became aware of shadows cast across the frosted glass in my door.

I could see two distinct figures, having what looked like an agitated conversation. As the door opened, I realised it was in English.

'Kate, darling!' Della swooped in and squeezed my hand, while Mark stood uncertainly in the doorway. He looked tired, clean-shaven, thinner than when I'd last seen him, so many months ago.

'Hello.' He smiled, and held up a hand in salute.

'Hello,' I managed, assailed by waves of gratitude and relief. Any resentment I'd built up over the weeks melted away with the appearance of faces I knew, and the possibility of finally getting out of there. With the sight of Mark, for the first time in nearly a year.

'How *are* you?' Della asked as she settled herself down, taking off her coat and hanging it carefully on the back of a plastic chair. She looked even more polished in this grim setting, her hair blow-dried and carrying a fresh, floral scent.

'I'm much better, thanks.' I sat up and tried to tidy my hair. 'Definitely ready to leave.' I grimaced. 'You've got to break me out of here!'

'Oh, we will.' Della opened a large handbag at her feet. 'First, though, we need you to sign this form. Mark,' she looked over at him, still lingering in the doorway, 'will you find a doctor to witness?'

'But . . . shouldn't I read it first?' I asked as Mark quietly let himself out of the room. I looked at the form blankly, row after row of typed words that meant nothing. What I really wanted was news of the baby.

'How's Te— . . . Ferdie? How's he settling in?'

'Oh, he's lovely.' Della smiled to herself. 'Doesn't sleep much, but he's a very calm little boy.'

'Really? He didn't seem that calm when he was inside me.' I tried to laugh, but Della seemed to wince. She rummaged around in her bag and handed me a pen.

'It's really just a final formality, after the papers you signed earlier in the year. All you need to do is sign here, and here.' Della pointed to sections marked out with a large cross. 'Once this is done, we can all get back to London and get settled in together.' She smiled, and I tried to respond. The thought of finally being able to hold my baby was almost too much to bear.

I attempted, as I had before, to skim the paperwork. The intended parents must be married or living together as partners. The surrogate must freely consent after six weeks. The conception must have taken place artificially.

I stopped and re-read that section. I looked up at Della.

'It says here we should have conceived artificially. But we didn't. Surely I can't . . .'

'Come on, Kate. Do you want all that to come out in court? That you slept with my husband?'

'In court? What do you mean?' I hadn't spoken to anyone for so long, I was finding it hard to follow any form of conversation. But this seemed to be leaping ahead at an alarming pace.

'It all has to go through the courts,' Della said, slowly. 'Like we discussed before? They'll look at our circumstances, the paperwork we signed in France, this proof that you have willingly handed over the baby, and then they'll make us his legal parents. It's very straightforward. You don't need to be there. It should all be over in a matter of weeks.'

'So you want me to sign it anyway?' I felt suddenly very tired. I couldn't remember ever discussing court, but then there was a lot I couldn't remember now. Perhaps we had talked it all through. I couldn't be sure any more. I felt at such a disadvantage, not being able to move, really. Surrounded by people I couldn't speak to. Cut off from everyone I knew. I was starting to doubt my own memory, my own mind.

It was true that I had known this day would come. And that I had been waiting for Della and Mark to come and get me. To take me to London. I was desperate to leave.

Now here they were. And as Mark walked into the room with a doctor in tow, the smile he gave me seemed so familiar, so intimate, it took me immediately back to our weeks together over the summer. It's all going to be OK, it seemed to say, we're in this together.

'Doctor Baudin said he'll witness the signature, if that's OK with you, Kate?' He spoke gently, putting a hand on my arm as he joined Della at my bedside. I saw Della tense and felt a surge of the old guilt, even here. I had betrayed Della. I owed this to her. To both of them. The money they had paid me over the past year would make my parents' lives bearable, and now I had it in my power to improve Della and Mark's future, too.

I picked up the pen and signed. The doctor signed too, then he left.

'We've got Ferdie's passport now, so we're going back to London in a couple of days,' Della told me.

'Hopefully I'll be able to get myself discharged and come with you,' I said, pulling my dressing gown around me. There was no way I was sticking around here if they were leaving the country.

'Let's see.' Della looked around her. 'You can always follow on. We're staying in Montpellier tonight. We're going to go and scan this and send it off to our lawyer now.'

And with a brief squeeze of my shoulder, they left me alone again.

'I'm going to be leaving tomorrow,' I announced when the doctor did her rounds that evening. 'I'm flying to London on Wednesday.'

It was Dr Joubert, finally back on the wards, and I was determined to be forceful this time. Enough waiting around. I was sick of being cooped up. I felt sure the hospital was making me worse, not better.

Dr Joubert looked confused. 'That's fine, if you want to leave. But you have this room for another two weeks. It was all paid for in advance.'

'But . . . the other doctors have been telling me I'm not allowed to go, that I'm not well enough.'

Dr Joubert shrugged. 'You can walk around, no? You're eating, your infection is clear. We thought you were staying here because your friends were paying for you to have your private room. To relax and, how do you say, recuperate?'

'To relax!' I looked around at the bare greying walls. Did she really think I'd be here if I didn't have to be? 'So, what – I'm free to go?'

'Of course, any time you like.' She smiled. 'I hope you got the rest you needed.'

After she left the room, I sat back, reeling. Had I been imagining it? I was sure I'd never been given the impression that I was free to walk out whenever I felt well enough. Then again, I could barely communicate with most of the doctors and nurses.

I thought of the money. Della and Mark had paid for a

room for eight weeks after the birth. It struck me as odd, but perhaps they'd done it once it was clear I was really very ill. In any case, it was motivated by kindness. And the good news was, I'd be able to leave with them in two days' time.

I'd speak to Della as soon as she arrived the next day, and we could go online to see if there were any tickets left on their flight. I fell asleep that night picturing the reunion – with Tabitha and Jasper, Mark, but most importantly with Teddy. My baby. I knew I'd have to stop thinking of him as mine; have to accept the name he had been given. Perhaps it would get easier as he got bigger, once he didn't seem like such a small, defenceless animal. I knew it would be painful, but I could hardly wait to smell his little head, to hold those curling fingers, to feel his weight in my arms. The perfect boy I had carried for nine months, and had barely yet begun to know.

By the time Della arrived late the following afternoon, I had showered, packed my bags, signed my discharge papers and dressed myself for the outside world. I'd allowed myself to imagine the room I'd book at Della and Mark's hotel, perhaps with an en suite shower, or even a bath. I'd order room service and eat food with a flavour for the first time in weeks. I'd see my little boy. I felt breathless with excitement as Della walked in, closing the door behind her with a tug.

'The paperwork has gone through,' Della announced, by way of greeting. 'The lawyer's happy with it. So we're all clear.'

'That's good.' I smiled. 'And the doctor says I'm free to go. I'm all packed and ready. But we'll need to see whether we can book another seat on the . . .' I fell silent as soon as I saw Della's face.

'What is it? Is there something wrong?'

Della's mouth was set; her eyes fixed on a point past the door.

255

'I think – *we* think – it's best if you don't come with us,' she said slowly.

'But we discussed it yesterday . . . I'll come and stay at the hotel, and see if I can get a seat on the flight. I was wondering what to do about my things though, they're still at the farmhouse . . .' I trailed off at the sight of Della's flinching jaw.

'Kate, you're not listening.' Della sounded as though she was struggling to keep her patience.

'But, I . . . what else am I going to do? I'm not staying here, in France, on my own, am I?'

'I don't know.' Della shrugged. 'That's not really my concern.'

'What do you mean? You're weren't going to leave me here . . .' I felt as if I was going to throw up. 'But . . . but I've just had a baby, for you. I'm alone here, because of you. And . . . I want to see him. I *need* to see him.'

Della moved towards where I stood, by my hospital bed. 'Listen, Mark and I have been talking, and since we've had Ferdie with us, we've realised it's not going to be possible to have you around. It's not helpful to the family, while we're bonding. I'm sure you'll understand. We've paid your final salary instalment. You've got all that money saved. I'm sure you'll be able to make other arrangements.' She said it so formally, as though I was an employee being dismissed. Some childminder who'd done a few shifts. Not a family friend, a long-term guest, the woman who'd carried her baby.

'But we talked it all through, all those months. You said I'd have a part in the—'

'You slept with my husband, Kate. Did you really think I was going to get over it just like that?'

'No, I . . . Like I kept saying, I couldn't believe how forgiving you were, how kind—'

'Yes, well, I feel differently now. Mark and I have had a

really intense time, bonding with Ferdie. We've talked it all over, we've come back together as a couple, and we don't want you coming between us.'

'But I . . . I thought we had an agreement.' My brain had frozen on that single point. I could hardly get my words out. 'I'd write my book, you'd send it to Alan, I'd come and live nearby . . .'

Della came right up to me now, close enough that I could smell coffee on her breath, her face inches from mine. 'Did you really think you could just slip into *my* family, with *my* husband and *my* children, and there would be no consequences? Did you think I'd sit back and watch you flirting with my husband, indulging my children, playing happy families, and do *nothing*? That I'd smile and shrug and send your pathetic book to a serious literary agent?' She was shaking with fury.

'But I thought I was part of the family . . . that I'd given you a gift.' I could hear the pleading tone in my voice. 'I thought I'd have a part in his life. I thought you wanted to help me.'

'Part of the family? You wanted to take *over* my family,' Della spat. 'Did you really think Mark was going to leave you for me? Can't you see he was just bored, a bit frustrated? It's over now, Kate. You had your fun.'

'Fun?' It was my turn to get angry now. 'I've been locked away, carrying your baby, for nine months. I've had him snatched away from me, I've barely seen him since he was born. I've been seriously ill. None of this has been *fun* for me.'

Della turned to leave, and I tried to calm myself. 'Listen, I know Mark and I betrayed you,' I said. 'I understand why you're angry. But what about the baby? Even if I don't see you or Mark again, you've got to let me see him, like you promised. I carried him for all that time. He's part of me.'

'Oh for God's sake, Kate. It's only the hormones talking. In a few months you'll have forgotten all about him. You never even wanted a baby, that's what you said.' She glared at me. 'Just keep away from us, OK?'

As she moved towards the door, I threw myself towards her, hanging on to her arm, frantic in my grief.

'You can't! You can't take him away forever! We agreed you'd let me see him. I'd never have gone through all this otherwise. I know I said I didn't want a baby, but once I carried him, once I held him, it was different. It *felt* different.'

'Read the paperwork you signed.' Della's hand was on the doorknob. 'You've given away every right you had to that baby. He's mine and Mark's.'

'You can't do this.' I was almost growling now, my body physically barring the exit. I had found a new strength, from somewhere, in the face of what I was about to lose. 'You can't do this to me. I want to see him sometimes, to be in his life. To see that he's OK, that he's growing up, that he's happy.'

'It's not really about what *you* want any more.' Della wouldn't even look at me now. 'It's all signed and agreed. We're going home to London. Keep away from us, OK?'

As she went to push past me, she turned once more, her voice lowered in warning.

'If I hear you've come back to North London, that you've taken up your old job, or you're living nearby, I'll take out a restraining order. Do you understand? I've got evidence – people will be willing to testify to how unstable you are, how you've stalked me, how you've tried to take over my life, my home, my family—'

'What? Who would say that?' I could hardly take it in. I couldn't even go back to London now? What was Della talking about?

258

'Sophia, Jonathan, Amisha . . . they've all seen how you are around me. How you want to *be* me. Hanging around outside my house. Trying to turn my children against me. You've even dressed up in my clothes, for Christ's sake. You stole my necklace. You wore my perfume. *You seduced my husband.*' Della lowered her voice to little more than a whisper. 'You don't want to test me on this, OK? Stay away. Don't even *think* about coming near my son.'

I couldn't hold back my tears, my body slack, my mind struggling to process this twisted version of events. All I could think of was my baby. My boy. In those moments when I had held him to my chest, before I had fallen asleep and surrendered him once more.

'But you let me see him. You let me feed him. You let me bond with him. I thought we'd have all the time in the world to get to know one another . . . And now you're taking him away? I'll never see him again?'

'Oh that? That was a misunderstanding. I wanted you to express some breastmilk, but they brought him to you instead. And you couldn't even do that, could you? You were too *weak*.' She looked me up and down. 'You think, just because you got pregnant without even trying, that you know the first thing about bringing up a child, about being a mother?'

I could barely stand up. I propped myself against the wall and turned to Della. 'I was more of a mother to those children last summer than you were. At least I paid them attention, took an interest in them. Why do you even want another child? You can't be bothered with the ones you've got.'

'Don't you *ever* judge me,' Della said, shaking in her anger. 'You don't know anything about me. You don't know what my own mother did, what I've gone through. You'll never know . . . You think there's tragedy in your life, with your

259

runaway sister and your ridiculous search? You're nothing. You're nobody. And you have *no place* in my family.'

'You won't get away with this,' I said wildly, as Della made it to the door. 'I'll go to the papers, I'll tell them what you've done.' At this, she turned to me, her face pale with rage.

'And who do you think they'll believe? A successful businesswoman and mother, or a pathetic loser with a history of mental health problems?' I froze. 'Oh yes, I know all the details. If you go public with this, I don't think you're going to come out of it well, do you?'

She looked at me, the challenge clear in her eyes, and then she slammed the door. I slumped to the floor as though reeling from a punch, my back resting against the wall, head lolling forward. All I felt inside was desperation, terror, physical pain. Reaching up with my hands, I clawed at my hair, my face, my eyes. My howls joined those of the women in the wards around me, their bodies torn apart, their babies ripped from inside them.

Chapter Thirty-Four

I struggled to open my eyes, but the night's tears had glued them shut. My throat was hoarse, my mind a blank. Everything was gone, taken from me.

The loss felt physical, violent. Though somehow I had always known it would be this way, or it seemed like that now. Della had taken it all too easily from the start. No one could be so forgiving after a betrayal like that, not straight away. I had torn her life apart, and now she had torn mine apart in return.

But how could I live, without his heartbeat inside me? Without the little flutters I had come to think of as his secret code? I felt them even now, my abdomen juddering and contracting cruelly, my breasts leaking milk, as though my body was playing tricks; reminding me of what I had lost. Whenever I closed my eyes, I saw his face as he rooted at my chest. I felt weak with the longing, and the grief.

I had crawled to the bed at some point in the night, and now I lay, fully dressed for my departure, staring at the small patch of sky I could see from my hospital bed, just a triangle at the top of the window, framed by grey hospital buildings. It wasn't so different from the view I'd had in the last hospital

I'd spent weeks in, in those dark months after I moved back to Cambridge. When the fine thread that had been holding my life together through university had unravelled. When I'd lost my grip on reality once before.

I watched as a fly batted at the glass, desperately searching for a way out of this airless room. Perhaps I could lie here and wait until some unsuspecting nurse left the window open and then we would both be free – the fly would escape upwards, my release would come as I fell.

I felt paralysed. Out of options. I thought of Della, Mark, the children, my baby. They would be flying home later today. Laughing, chatting, cooing – not a thought for me. It wasn't just the baby I had lost, it was all of them. Would Della even tell Mark about our confrontation? After all, I was out of the way. A problem solved.

What if I turned up at the court, though? They weren't counting on that. What if I appeared in person to contradict the agreement I had signed – surely that would make a difference?

Then I remembered the doctor who'd witnessed it. The formal language. I pictured myself, wild-eyed and desperate; Della cool and poised. I knew which way it would go. I had lied. I had signed a document to say I had been artificially inseminated. And I had signed papers before the birth, promising to hand over the baby as soon as he was born. Why would they believe me now? Especially once Della brought my past into it, my mental breakdown, how long it had taken to recover.

There was no getting away from it: I'd agreed to have the baby for Della and Mark. I had cheated and lied, and this was my punishment.

But how could I escape? How would I get home? Lunch came and was taken away. I looked in my purse. There were only a few coins. I picked up my phone, nearly out of credit. And then I scrolled down to the one person I knew I could call.

'*Oui?*'

'Manon, it's me.' My voice was croaky, but Manon recognised it immediately.

'Kate! *Comment ça va? Et le bébé? Comment allez vous?*'

'Hospital,' I said. 'Please come.'

Manon didn't hesitate. '*J'arrive,*' she said, and the line went dead.

An hour later, I walked out of the hospital without a word to anyone. Nobody stopped me, nobody said goodbye. Outside I found Manon, waiting in her beaten-up car. After we had embraced, she reached forward to take the bags.

I could tell from her face that my appearance was shocking. I'd seen as much in the toilet mirrors. Pale washed-out skin, puffy eyes, mouth red from howling. Manon helped me into the car, tucking a blanket around me that she produced from the boot.

As we juddered down the motorway, she muttered under her breath, sentences incomprehensible to me, though their meaning was clear. She was furious – she seemed aware that I had been abandoned. She wanted to take me to her house. '*Chez moi,*' she kept saying, '*pour manger.*' But I shook my head. I had to go to the farmhouse first. I knew where the spare key was hidden. I needed to collect my bags, the laptop with all my stories on it, everything I had left behind in the panicky early moments of my labour all those weeks before.

'Baggage,' I tried to explain. Manon nodded.

It was evening as we drove up into the darkening hills, and it seemed as though I saw the woods for the first time: menacing, dangerous, with twisted towering trees and blackness between. The approach to the house looked no different. The tiled rooftop, the familiar gateposts, the crunch of the gravel. But I was a different person now. My hands shook. Memories assailing me of the stupid, naive girl I had been. All those promises. Lies upon lies upon lies.

I was so lost in my thoughts, it took me a moment to register that there were lights on in the farmhouse. Not just in one or two windows, but shining through the patio doors and in the upstairs windows. Then I saw the car. The silver four-by-four, parked by the kitchen door, pale in the darkness. I froze. Della was here.

Manon's car came to a stop. For a few moments I didn't move. I could feel her eyes on me, but my brain had slowed down. Had someone heard us? Would Della come running out? Was she inside calling the police?

Then I remembered Ferdie. He must be here too. And at that realisation, the hum in my head grew deafening, everything else became background noise. I had to see my son one last time. To say goodbye. It was madness, after everything Della had said, but I couldn't help myself. I had to go in.

I climbed out of the car and Manon got out too. I turned to her and shook my head. I had been planning to ask her to wait for me, to go back to her house once I'd got my things, but I didn't want her to witness whatever was about to unfold. I took my overnight bag and walked forward on my own, motioning to Manon to drive away.

Reluctantly, without a word, Manon left. I watched her car roll slowly down the drive, and then I turned to face the house, eerily still and silent in the moonlight. I had to go in alone.

I let myself quietly into the kitchen. There was a row of suitcases lined up, ready to go, but no one to be seen. In one of the open bags I identified my laptop. In a bin bag to one side, I could make out the titles of the pregnancy books Della had bought me. But I could hear no voices, no cries. Could I sneak up to a bedroom and find Ferdie? Would there be time for one last cuddle?

I heard shifting upstairs, the scraping of drawers, and froze. Should I hide? There was no point. I'd have to make myself known eventually. Familiar footsteps progressed along the hall, falling heavily down the stairs. Before he even stepped out of the shadows, I knew it was Mark.

'Oh my God!' Mark dropped the bag he was carrying, and I sprang back in shock too, even though I had been the one waiting for his arrival.

'Shhh.' I held my finger to my lips.

'Kate, what the hell are you doing here?' Mark hissed. And then, 'Why are we being quiet?'

'I don't want Della to know I'm here,' I whispered, and Mark immediately dropped his shoulders, running his hands through his hair.

'She's not here,' he said, at a normal volume. 'But why are you here? I thought you were meant to be staying in hospital at least another week. That's what Della said.'

'Where is Della? Where's the baby?'

'In Montpellier with the kids, waiting for me, and the bags. We're leaving for London this evening. I'm just packing up the last of our things.'

'I've come to get my stuff, too. I didn't know where else to go. Not after what Della said yesterday . . .' I sat down, feeling weak. The relief at finding only Mark, not Della, the disappointment that my baby wasn't here, the sudden release of tension – it was all too much. I began sobbing.

Della and the baby were still in the country. If only I could pull myself together, I could talk sense into Mark. After everything we'd been through, surely he'd take pity on me. He'd see that Della couldn't cut me out of the baby's life entirely.

Mark sat down next to me, putting a hand on my arm. 'Come on.' He rubbed my shoulder. 'It's going to be OK.'

I looked up at him, his concerned face blurry through my tears. 'Will it? You should have heard what Della said. How angry she was. You know she's said I can never see the baby again?'

Mark nodded. 'What did you expect, though, really?'

'What she told me! That I'd be able to spend time with him, that I'd see you and the kids, that I'd drop in every now and then.'

'And you really thought that was going to work out?'

'Yes,' I cried. 'Yes, I did. I also didn't expect, after spending nine months carrying her longed-for child, to be told how weak I was. How pathetic. She was so cruel, Mark. You should have heard her.'

'Come on now. I know you're angry, but that's Della you're talking about. And she's been really hurt. By both of us. It's not going to help you to get vindictive.' He looked at me for a moment. 'Nothing more is going to happen between us – you do know that, don't you?'

I could hardly believe now, after everything I'd been through, that I ever thought it would. 'This isn't about *you*, Mark. This is about *my* baby. You've stolen him. You and Della. I want to be part of his life.'

'Kate, come on. You sound like a madwoman. He was never your baby. You can't try and turn this around now, just because you think you've changed your mind. Do you know how much Della wanted this? Do you know how much this means to—'

'Oh for Christ's sake. If I have to listen one more time to

how much Della wants *this*, and how much Della wants *that*. You of all people know what she's like. You said as much that night . . . "What Della wants, she gets." I remember it clearly. She wanted you. And she wanted this baby. And now she's got what she wanted. As usual.' I slumped in my chair.

'Look, I can see why you're jealous. I understand. You want Della's life. Or you want things to carry on between us. But that can't happen . . . so you're clinging on to the only thing that ties you to us.'

I let out a bitter laugh. 'You two really don't get it, do you? Yes, I *did* have feelings for you. And I suppose I wanted Della's attention, too. I wanted to be close to her. I envied you, all of you. I wanted to be part of this.' I looked around at the Aga, the farmhouse sink, the framed photos on the wall. 'But I've grown up, Mark. Carrying a baby, *having* a baby . . . it changes you. He's the important one now. All I want is to be part of his life, like you promised.'

'And there we were, thinking you didn't want children.' Mark looked at me strangely.

'What do you mean?' I tried to read his expression, but it had gone blank. He'd shut down.

'Oh nothing. It doesn't matter.' Mark looked at the clock. 'Listen, you don't need to worry about Ferdie. He's fine. Lovely. Healthy. We'll look after him as though he's our own. He *is* our own.'

'Ferdie.' I snorted.

'I know.' Mark smiled. 'Della's choice. It was the least I could do.' He scraped his chair back. 'Look, I've got to go. Della's going to be wondering where I am.' He stood up.

'You can't go.' I looked around wildly, trying to think of a way to stop him. 'You've got to see this from my perspective!'

'Come on, Kate.' Mark looked frustrated now. 'You didn't

want a child. You just wanted a bit of flirtation, a holiday romance. We had fun together, didn't we? And you were good with the kids. One day, I'm sure you will make a good mum. But this isn't your time, Kate, this is *our* time. Mine and Della's. This is our family. Go off, make a life of your own, find your own family.'

'I'm meant to make a life of my own, now that I've been ripped apart? You've packed up my life, my laptop, all my work – my *child* – and now you're going to leave, without another word. You really thought I'd just shrug off the past year and carry on as though nothing happened?'

'That's *exactly* what we thought,' Mark said, his voice raised. 'Clearly we were wrong about you.'

'Wrong about me? What do you mean?' A cold feeling spread through me – sickness, dread, something else . . . recognition. The pieces clicking together. 'Was this . . . Did you plan all this?' I thought of the Janes, the strange similarities, all women of a certain age. Was that why Della had brought the group together? Had she been grooming us, looking for the perfect candidate?

'What on earth are you talking about?' Mark glanced at the clock. He picked up his phone. 'Look, I haven't got time for this—'

'No, I mean it.' I stood up now, feeling a new strength surge through me. I thought of the other pregnant nanny, the strange maternity clothes. 'Della can't have children, can she? So Tabby was yours, and Ferdie is mine, but what about Jasper? Who gave birth to Jasper?'

'Listen, if you know what's good for you, you'll leave this alone, Kate.' Mark's fist was clenched around his phone, he made a move towards the bags.

'Shall I just ask Della?' I asked, trying to sound casual. 'I mean, maybe there's another woman out there who's been

pushed around, and lied to – who's had *her* baby snatched
from her, all so that you and Della can make the perfect
family. It shouldn't be too hard to track her down—'

Mark looked at me, the panic clear in his eyes. 'It's not like
that. And you can't speak to Della about that, ever . . . That
was a moment of weakness. You promised you'd never let on
to Della that I told you about Tabby, about anything—'

'We all break our promises, Mark.' He looked at me then,
caught my eye properly. Then he came back to the table,
reluctantly, pulling out a chair.

'Della has a condition,' he said, his tone flat. 'Endometriosis.
In the end, the doctors said there was no chance she'd conceive,
not at her age.'

I sat down. My legs were shaking. 'Couldn't you adopt?'

Mark pressed his fingers to his temples. 'You clearly don't
know Della as well as you think. She has to be in control.
Everything has to be perfect. You really think she'd take in
someone else's kids? You think she wants the whole world to
know she can't have her own?'

'So, what? She used a donor egg?'

Mark shook his head. 'Look, we tried. My God, we tried.
As soon as we got together, when Tabitha was tiny . . . Della
was so determined to have a baby. But a year went past, then
two. The whole thing was so hard on us both, I . . . She
pushed me away. And we had this nanny, she was there when
Della wasn't, and . . .'

'And you got her pregnant?'

Mark nodded, his eyes cast down. 'That's when Della had
the idea: she could have our baby. It would still be mine, and
she was blonde, like Della, so nobody would guess. She went
away . . .'

'Here?'

'Yes – and she had Jasper. And then she signed him over

269

to us and went back to Poland.' I thought of the magazines in the loft. 'It all worked out very well, for everyone . . .'

'So well, that Della decided to do it again,' I said slowly. I thought I might be sick. 'Why not just pay someone, a woman who *wants* to do it?'

'You can't do that. It's against the law – you have to go abroad. It gets complicated. And expensive – we don't have as much money as it looks, you know. But we covered her expenses, like we did yours. Paulina agreed to it. She was fine. We've never heard from her since.'

'Then how do you know she was fine?' I banged the table with my fist, my anger surprising us both. 'And what about me? Is that all I ever was to you – a surrogate? Was this whole thing set up from the start?' My mind was racing, pieces falling into place. 'Get together a group of young women and pick out the most vulnerable, someone who would make that sacrifice for your family, because they cared about you . . .' I heard my voice break.

'Come on, you know it wasn't like that. Della's committed to the group, it's her career. She invited you to come away with us because you clicked with the kids, with me. And then we got carried away, things happened, you got pregnant and . . . it seemed like the best outcome all round.'

'The best outcome?' I spat the words. 'To persuade me to have a baby under false pretences. And it's just a coincidence that I'm blonde, like Della? That all those women were?' I thought of the row of sunflowers. Jasmine, Claire, the warning.

'This is sounding totally mad now, Kate. You've been under a lot of stress, all that time in the hospital. Once you get back to your family, get some rest, you'll see that it's all worked out for the best.' He got to his feet, clearly desperate to leave. 'Look, take the laptop, your stories. I'm sure you'll find a publisher.' He handed me the computer, as though that would put everything right.

'Things might have worked out for the best for you and Della,' I said bitterly. 'No one thought for a minute about me.' It was then that I remembered telling Della about my period, her well-timed trip away. She had every angle covered. Or was Mark right – was I being paranoid? I was so confused I couldn't tell any more.

Mark shook his head. 'Believe what you want to. I was attracted to you. I did something stupid, but I did care about you. I *do* care. I can see that you're struggling, mentally – you've got issues. But you're going to be fine. In a year's time, this will be a distant memory.' Mark put his hand on my shoulder. 'The most important thing, Kate, is that you *have* to stay away. You can't come anywhere near us, near Della, especially knowing what you do.'

'So this is what you do, is it? Get a girl pregnant and then abandon her, leave her alone in the middle of nowhere, put your precious family first.'

'Della's my wife, Kate, we've got kids. They have to be my priority. But you'll be fine, you'll see. You'll meet someone, make a new life, move on.' He put his hand in his pocket, pulled out his wallet, put a bundle of notes on the table. 'Take this, for your flight home.' He picked up the bags. 'I've really got to go. It's all going to be OK. Take care of yourself.'

'Take care?' I shouted, balling my hands into tight fists. 'You think it's going to be that easy?'

Mark was walking towards the car, his head bowed.

'I've got rights,' I shouted, following Mark. 'That's *my* baby!' He threw the bags into the boot. 'MY BABY!' He slammed the door and revved the engine.

Watching him pull away, I screamed into the black night.

'You *did* get me wrong! You did! You picked the wrong girl to do this to!'

I screamed for a long time after Mark had gone and then, when my voice grew faint, I sank to the ground and sobbed – for myself, my baby, for the other woman who had suffered in this way, for the cruelty I hadn't known existed in the world. This couple with their money and their connections, who thought they could just use young women and throw them away.

When I came to, I was curled on the driveway outside the house, my hair damp with dew, shivering, but strangely calm. I knew what I had to do. The question was, how?

PART FOUR

Cambridge, 2017

Chapter Thirty-Five

So here I am, in another white room. Another small box designed to contain me. Like the French hospital, this one has high windows. Here, too, the walls are bare, greying. But the bed is less comfortable, changed less frequently. The noises in the distance more distressing.

If I'd known when I first met Della that this is where I'd end up, what would I have done differently? It's a game I like to play, to pass the time. When I'm not sifting through the memories, that is.

When was it that Della decided it would be me? Our encounter in the café, the day we met? But no, that was too early. The group meeting when I set myself apart from the others, when I announced I didn't want children? Perhaps. Our coaching sessions, when she'd sounded out my few friendships, my dysfunctional family, using her influence over me to encourage even greater distance, to cut me off yet further? Or maybe the dinner party, when I showed how easily I could be won over – flattered with a cheap necklace and a few compliments?

Then there's Mark, all the small gestures and remarks, the lingering eye contact and confidences. Had they all been part of the plan? Had he been building up to his moment all along? I think of the days we spent alone, with the children. The closeness I felt to him then. Our nights together. The attraction that felt genuine and mutual. That's when I doubt myself all over again – I'm being paranoid, finding clues where they don't exist, piecing things together where there's no connection.

It's enough to drive a person mad, this questioning. That's what everyone here thinks: that I'm insane. But I'm not, really. I'm angry.

Even if I had suspected – if I'd been able to join together the dots that would lead me here, to this room on the psychiatric ward – would I have done things differently? Would I want a version of the world without my little boy in it?

My parents don't know about him, of course. Neither does Liam. No one does, except Layla – and she's far away enough that I don't need to worry. She thinks he was adopted. And she's too busy to care much, on the commune in Totnes, with Thierry and their baby Anais, in all their breast-feeding, co-sleeping, sling-wearing contentedness. I can't read the emails any more. I delete them as soon as they arrive. It's too painful – these little updates on the kind of life I should be making for myself. If I hadn't lost three years, more, to Della and Mark.

Mum and Dad had known as soon as I got home to Cambridge that things weren't right. That I'd taken another turn for the worse, as Mum put it. They wanted me to stay with them while I got myself back on my feet. They didn't realise then how much worse things would get.

It was gradual, for the first few months. A phantom cry in another room. A plump baby in a supermarket, round kneed and chubby fingered – and I'd be set off, shaking, crying. The ache inside would become a stabbing pain, the palpitations would start, my breathing would go. The pounding in my ears. It would overcome me and I'd collapse, panting. The inhaler prescribed by the doctor didn't even touch the sides.

Panic attacks, he'd said. Unprocessed trauma, was the therapist's theory. But there's nothing we can do unless she'll talk to us, she told my mum, over my head, as if I was too far gone to understand.

I understood all right. I knew exactly what was going on. It suited me to play along.

Abandoned as a child by her adored older sister, my mum explained as the psychiatrist made notes, and I sat silently looking out of the window. What else was I going to tell them? The truth?

I knew by then that no one would believe the way Della and Mark had tricked me. Not my parents, not the doctors, the newspapers, the courts. If I could find the other mother, Paulina, it might be different. If there were two of us, perhaps then they'd listen. But just me? No way. Della had been too clever for that.

She'd thought of everything. I could see that now. Any way you looked at it, at every stage, I had agreed to her plan. I had no solid proof of her manipulation, her lies. No witnesses who weren't on her side. The police would think I was mad, or lying. If I went to the papers, Della would manage to twist it. I was a jealous nanny, a surrogate gone rogue. She was only trying to keep her family safe from an obsessive stalker. She wouldn't think twice about bringing up the mental health problems in my past.

And I had signed the papers, agreeing to give up my baby. Dragging the whole thing through the press would achieve nothing. Why would any court of law agree to reverse the decision that had already been made? Della had everything I lacked: money, reputation, powers of persuasion. I would be painted as a delusional loser.

For months, I'd been spending every evening on the laptop she'd given me. Not writing – I'd given up on that entirely now – but searching online for any tiny bit of information that might help my cause. The more I researched the legalities of it all, the more I realised how thorough she had been. Full days in the library, hours online in the evening, reading up on surrogacy cases, lawsuits, loopholes in the law, and still I came up with nothing. There were plenty of anomalies and test cases. The disputes and unhappy outcomes had stacked up over the years. But one thing was clear: if you had money, and wanted to buy a baby, you could. The further you were willing to travel, the more money you had, the easier it would be, the fewer rights the women had.

Only Della hadn't wanted to travel. And she hadn't wanted to use a donor who would volunteer to have her baby, as many women did willingly. No, Della wanted to do it her way, on her terms. And my life, my feelings? Collateral damage.

Other times, after a few hours of sleep, when the sun rose, I'd wonder if it really had all been an accident as Mark claimed. Just a coincidence that he and Della had turned to their own advantage. Whatever the truth, they had used me and tossed me aside, without a second thought.

As the year went on, I became more furious, not less. With myself, as well as with them. I had no copies of the paperwork I'd signed. I hadn't even asked for them. And so I had no proof of what I had agreed to. And no legal claim to my son.

My only hope, the one I became fixated on, was to find the other surrogate. If I could track her down then, perhaps, I would find she had been through the same thing. Maybe together we could build a case. Surely a judge wouldn't be able to dismiss two women with such similar stories? Then there was Claire. And Jasmine. How much did they know? If I could find them, and build a team of witnesses, perhaps I'd stand a chance. But there was only so much I could do on my own, from Cambridge. And that was where Liam came in.

He'd been taken aback, the first time he saw me. That much was clear from the way he pulled away as he greeted me – a double-take that betrayed his shock. I had barely eaten in the months since I'd given birth and my hair was dyed black, cut off in a jagged crop. It had been pure impulse: the desire to erase the past, to make myself look as different as possible from the girl I'd been – back when my sameness had made me stand out.

But Liam looked different, too. It had been nearly two years – he was broader, more substantial, his longer hair softening his angular face. I felt my shoulders relax at the sight of him, breathing in his scent as he hugged my bony frame awkwardly; I hadn't even registered the woody tang of his aftershave all that time ago, but now it returned me instantly to the house off Green Lanes, to my first and only taste of independence.

Liam perched next to me on the leather sofa, accepted a tea and a ginger nut, stealing glances as if to make sure I was really here, back in England, in this poky bungalow.

He was still living in the house-share, and still single, it seemed, or single again – who knew what had happened since we'd lost contact? He didn't question why I was living at home with my parents, or why I was being treated like this fragile child, barely let out of their sight. He didn't ask much at all that first visit. He seemed content just to sit near me, to submit himself to my parents' barrage of questions.

Eventually, Mum and Dad left us alone.

'I've missed you, Kate,' he'd said, in a low voice. 'You stopped answering my emails. I didn't know where you'd gone.'

I looked away, but he took my hand and I let him. It was good to see him. I felt the stirrings of something I hadn't felt

279

since those summer months with Mark: attraction, the sense of possibility. But I wasn't the girl he'd known in London. I was bitter, furious, consumed by one mission. And I needed to stay focused. Liam could help me: he was based in London, his knowledge of the web went beyond anything I could even imagine. I couldn't get sidetracked by emotions – I needed to get my son back.

I couldn't go into everything that had happened that summer, and so instead I told Liam about Scarlett, her disappearance, my search. I needed to find her, I said, and as part of that I needed to find a Polish nanny, Paulina, who had once worked for Della and Mark Hunter. And two women who had lived in Crouch End: Claire and Jasmine.

That was all we had to go on. And after months of extensive research, Liam had yet to come up with anything. There were thousands of Paulinas; locating the right one was as unlikely as finding a Claire in London. Meanwhile I grew weaker and more desperate by the day – emptier, more distracted, my grip on reality slowly diminishing.

I wasn't being sectioned, Mum said. I could leave any time I liked. But she couldn't cope any more, not when she was already so busy looking after Dad. The nurse I'd paid for only came a couple of hours a day, and Mum couldn't manage with us both. I needed help, she said, the kind she couldn't give me.

'Just another short visit,' she'd reassured me after she'd made the call. 'To make sure things don't get as bad as they did last time.'

That was two months ago, though it's hard to keep track of time in here. The days blur together – mealtime, bathtime, bedtime, mealtime. During my weekly therapist sessions, and in the group meetings, I say as little as possible – not so different from in Della's group sessions, really. Only now, instead of an airy designer lounge, we meet in a featureless common room, decked out with plastic chairs and scuffed tables. And rather than exploring what we want from life, our hopes, dreams and ambitions, we talk about what went wrong, the mistakes we made, how we ended up in here.

A New Life in Twelve Months, that's what Della's latest book promises. I saw it in a shop window, not long before I was admitted to hospital. There were billboards, too, a new morning TV slot having increased her fame. Everywhere I turned, there she was: that smooth, blank face, pale eyes hard like marble. I can still hear her voice echoing around my head, night and day, dripping with fake concern.

A new life is certainly what Della's given me. A life unrecognisable from the one I had when she sized me up in that café. A life filled with anger and loss, bitterness and humiliation.

Back in an airless cell. Back in a hospital. Back where I started.

Chapter Thirty-Six

Mum's coming to see me today, without Dad. I'm not sure what's prompted this rare parting of the ways, except that his carer will be there to help him with the kettle, but I'm dreading a full hour of interrogation, without Dad to mediate.

I'm sitting on a bench by the small patch of lawn when she arrives. Someone once tried to make these hospital gardens inviting, and there are remnants of rose bushes and straggling ivy growing up the columns that run along the edge of the ward. But the cuts have taken their toll, and no one's paid attention to the outside of this building for years. It's all crumbling brickwork, weeds blooming from every flower bed, plant pots littered with fag ends.

Mum looks neat and prim in contrast to her surroundings, picking her way around the edge of the grass, avoiding the skinny woman – even thinner than me – who's slumped on the next bench along, staring at her toes as she smokes cigarette after cigarette.

'Hello, Kate,' she says, in her brightest voice, 'how are you doing today?'

'I'm OK.' I try to smile.

'Listen, we need to talk,' she begins, resting her handbag carefully next to her leg, as though one of the inpatients might make a grab for it. 'This is no place for a young woman like you, and I won't watch while you do this to yourself again . . .' She pauses while we both remember. It had been a shorter stay last time, but probably no less painful for Mum. Only I know how much more complicated things are this time around.

'I know you think Dad and I don't understand anything about your life. You think we're old, out of touch, that we haven't got a clue what's going on around us . . .' It sounds rehearsed, this speech, and I slump down further in my seat. But then Mum drops her voice, forcing me to lean in.

'But I know,' she says, almost in a whisper. 'What happened to you.'

My mind goes blank. I hold my breath. How could she?

'At first I wasn't sure. I thought if it was true then surely you'd tell me, eventually. But the more I've thought about it, the more it seems like the only explanation . . . You were pregnant, weren't you?'

She looks at me, but I turn away, thinking fast – trying to work out how much she already knows. 'I've seen how you've been around babies. How you've reacted, even at the mention of someone else's child,' Mum carries on. I consider how good it would feel to collapse on her. To tell her everything. To have someone on my side at last. But I can't. I know how the story would come out. I've rehearsed it enough times. I know how mad it would sound, even to my own mother.

'It's OK, Mum. I've just been having a hard time . . .'

'Come on, Kate. I've been waiting all this time for you to talk to me, I thought perhaps it was something that happened with that family you went away with, or maybe it was about Scarlett. But it's been nearly two years, and you've been getting worse, not better. Then Layla had her baby and that seemed

283

to be the final straw . . . What happened? Did you lose a child?'

I feel the tears stinging behind my eyes. She doesn't know how close she's come to the truth.

'Look, Mum . . .' I stop short of lying to her face. I can't bring myself to do it. 'It's not what you think.' I grip the wood of the bench either side of my legs, willing myself to hold it together until she leaves.

'Kate, if it is that, then I know how you feel.' She pauses. 'I know . . . because I lost a baby, too.' Her eyes are welling with tears. She's making this so hard.

'Mum, come on. Scarlett wasn't a baby. She was practically an adult.'

'I'm not talking about Scarlett.'

She says it so quietly, at first I think I must have misheard. 'What did you say?'

'I lost a baby. Before Scarlett. Before you.'

'Did you have a miscarriage?' I ask, inching closer along the bench. My hands are shaking. I feel like I already know the answer.

'No,' she says, looking away. 'I gave a baby up for adoption. Before I met Dad. I was still a child myself, really.' She's clutching her fingers together, looking down at them, her tears falling onto her hands. I put my arm around her, instinctively. I can't remember the last time I did that. The last time I saw her cry. 'I was sixteen. They put me in a home . . . to have the baby.' Her voice breaks. 'They took her away. I wasn't even allowed to hold her.'

At this, I can't hold in my tears any longer. I hug Mum and we both cry, long enough that the woman on the next bench shrinks away, and then leaves. I have so many questions, but I'm afraid to speak. I'm worried I'll say too much. I think of the moment I woke up and found Teddy gone, my chest cold.

Of Mum having her own child taken from her. How can she have been through all of that and never said anything? Why didn't she tell me?

'Your dad knows,' Mum says, once her breathing has calmed, a tissue pressed to her eyes. 'I'd put myself on the adoption contact register, in case she ever wanted to get in touch. But by the time she did, you girls were at a difficult stage. She'd been adopted by a family near Bristol, she wanted to make contact. Dad and I talked it over, but we didn't think you'd cope with it – not when Scarlett was going through her teenage rebellion. Of course, then Scarlett found a letter from the adoption agency anyway . . .'

'Is that why she left?' I ask the question in a whisper, afraid to hear the answer – shivering at the idea that Mum might have known all along the reason for Scarlett's disappearance. But Mum shakes her head.

'No. She didn't take it well, as you can imagine . . . but I don't think it was that.'

It's the first time we've spoken this openly about Scarlett in years and I'm desperate for more, but I can sense Mum closing the conversation down, folding it away with her tissue, a neat square tucked into her pocket. She breathes deeply, clutching her bag to her side once more.

'You were always the sensible one, the thoughtful one.' She squeezes my hand. 'That's why it's so hard to see you in here.' She looks around at the courtyard, empty now as the smell of stewed meat comes wafting on the air.

'I always thought you were disappointed in me.' I say it quietly, the honesty between us opening something inside of me. 'That you were sorry it was me left behind, and not Scarlett. That I'd never be good enough for you.'

'Oh Kate, how can you say that?' Mum's eyes are filling. 'We've always been proud of you. You've needed looking after, but then you seemed to be doing so much better. You've helped us out so much since Dad's got worse. And now—' She breaks off. 'Look, I know something serious has happened to you. Maybe it's not a baby, maybe it's something else. But it's *something*. You don't just disappear off for a year and come back in the state you were in. I know you've had it tough over the years. But this woman you met, this family. What happened?' She's got both her hands around mine now, she won't let me look away. She seems ready to shake the information out of me. But her earlier words are still with me.

I'm the sensible one. The one who has to keep them going – especially after everything they've been through. I can't burden them with my problems, too.

I think of Mum as she must have been at sixteen. I can't seem to fit this version of her onto the woman I've known for so long. This girl, irresponsible enough to get pregnant so young. To have unprotected sex, like I did. To watch someone take her baby away against her will. To be haunted for years, perhaps forever. We have more in common than I realised, Mum and I.

But I know then that I am different, too. That I'm not going to give up and bury my pain like Mum did.

I look towards the door, aware that it's dinner time, and I'll be called any minute. My body has become attuned to the timings in here. Institutionalised.

'I'm going to come again, alone,' Mum says, 'and next time, I want you to tell me what's been going on. OK?'

I nod, still trying to picture the desperate young girl she once was, but instead seeing only an image of my own anguished face. The haunting eyes that look back from the mirror these days.

I already know, as I say goodbye, giving Mum an extra-long hug, that there won't be a next time.

Chapter Thirty-Seven

It's him. It has to be. My heart pounds as I take in the fair, wispy hair. The small mouth, open in protest. The eyes, tilted down at the edges, just like mine.

He falls on his bottom in a flower bed, picking up soil with a chubby hand and shoving it in his mouth. The nanny's too busy chattering with her friends to notice and it's all I can do to stop myself running over and scooping him up. Wiping his hands clean, showering him with kisses and walking away with him in my arms.

I watch, stomach churning, as he joins the other fat-legged children, waddling off behind bushes and through the carelessly opened gate. He hesitates, considering whether to make an escape, while Chloe and her friends gather around the hipster with the guitar, paid to sing songs to toddlers and their exhausted mums.

At least, I'm assuming it's Chloe: blonde, pretty, late twenties. She certainly looks the part. She could easily be another one of the Janes, except that Della seems to have wound that up now. In the three weeks I've been in London, in all the time I've been watching the house, I've seen no groups of women arriving or leaving.

It had been easier than I thought to walk out of the hospital. I'd admitted myself voluntarily, so I could discharge myself at any time – I didn't even have to tell my parents. And so I didn't. I simply packed my bag, got a bus to the station, and the first train to London.

I felt terrible about leaving them, but how could I explain? Liam had insisted on calling them as soon as I turned up on his doorstep. Just so they don't worry, he said. And he was right. Mum was frantic – insistent on coming straight down to London to collect me. It was Dad who talked her round in the end. I was an adult, he reasoned with Mum. I needed time to get myself together. They could trust Liam to keep an eye on me.

And he is doing his best. Watching my every move, serving up meals on a tray, sitting with me on the sofa every evening, laptop on his knee, as we scroll through his latest research. The students he rents with are away for the summer, scattered around Europe, so I'm back in my old room. But he can't watch me while he's at work. And it's in those hours that I've been making my little trips out: baby steps at first, to the end of the road, around the local park, and then further, up the steeper roads, along the brow of the hill, until eventually I reach my target.

That first day, I stayed outside Della's house for hours. I arrived too late to see the children return from school, but from across the road, crouched down beside a car, I watched as first Mark got home, and then Della. From a distance, they looked the same as they had always done – both tanned, smartly dressed, Della's hair shorter now. There was no outward sign of the damage they had wreaked.

It grew dark and I knew Liam would be worrying about me, but still I stood in the shadows, edging nearer, watching as the lights came on room by room, illuminating the tranquil lives inside. Della was bent over a laptop at the kitchen island while Mark cooked, glass of wine in hand, the shutters wide open for all to see. It made my stomach turn, but I couldn't tear myself away. Upstairs, an orange glow escaped from around the blind in the children's room – Teddy's room too now, perhaps. Or perhaps the guest room had been turned into his nursery and he was in there. Sleeping, like his brother and sister, unaware of the violence with which he had been ripped from my life.

Della's next book will be about family, becoming a mother in later life, how to juggle children and a career. *Your Family, Your Way.* When I'd seen it trailed on TV, I thought I was going to be sick. Now I could feel my nails leaving welts in my palms. Who did they think they were? Collecting other people's children like so many accessories, to be displayed on mantelpieces and avoided unless it suited them. I wanted to scream. That would not be my son's fate. I would not sit by as he was raised with disinterest, without the love he deserved.

It had taken a few more days to work up the courage to trail Chloe and Teddy to the park. But now here I am. A few feet away from the baby who was snatched from me, from my little boy. I can barely breathe for the longing welling inside me. And the fear.

Chloe's never met me. Even if she had, I look like a different person. If Della herself walked along now, chances are she wouldn't recognise me, not at first. But the prospect makes me shiver. I'm the only one who knows what a risk I'm taking by coming back to London. If Mum had any idea, she'd whisk me off to Cambridge in an instant.

But it's the thought of Mum that roots me to the spot. Ever since that day in the hospital, I've felt a new determination. I'm not going to spend my life regretting – wondering what my child looks like, what kind of a boy he's become.

289

I follow at a distance as he toddles towards the playground, Chloe walking behind with two other nannies. I watch, mesmerised, as he climbs into the sandpit, steals another child's spade, smashes a sandcastle, crying in frustration as Chloe finally notices and lifts him away.

Chloe doesn't love him like a mother would. She doesn't have the patience, the devotion of someone who has carried him for nine months. Instead she tugs his arm, dragging him to the bench where she sits down again. She shoves a dummy in his mouth and resumes her conversation, while he screams and tries to wriggle off her knee.

Watching him, I feel an absence, an ache, in my arms. I can almost weigh the space where he should be, where I held him, just that once, when he was so much smaller. He's two now, and I'm sure I can already see the signs of unhappiness, of neglect. If only I could run over, wrestle him from Chloe's arms and run away. But what would I do next? Where would we go? I gave almost all the money Della and Mark paid me to Mum and Dad, leaving only a small amount for myself, and I haven't worked since. The little I've got left would only see us through a few months at most. And then what?

For now, all I can do is watch and wait. And so I watch as Chloe finally bundles Ferdie into his pushchair and home for lunch. And I wait to be noticed, as I haunt them all the way home, daring to follow silently at a distance. And I keep waiting as I walk back to Green Lanes alone, for some kind of sign, a catalyst – a moment when my next step will become clear.

That evening Liam is extra attentive and it's all the harder to pin him down about the search.

'D'you want anything else?' he asks as he tidies up from the Thai green curry he knocked up after work. 'I bought tiramisu . . .' He thinks he's being subtle with his attempts

290

to restore me to a healthy weight, and I'm touched. But I still don't feel like eating, especially not tonight.

'I'm fine, really, Liam. Can we have another look through what you've found?' I take a bottle of cheap white out of the fridge. 'Do you want a glass?'

He shakes his head. 'Don't you think you've had enough?'

'God, you're as bad as my parents. You don't need to worry, I can look after myself.'

I leave him in the kitchen and settle myself down on the tatty sofa with my laptop, ready to circle through the usual websites – missing persons, Polish nanny listings. I am finding it harder to focus my eyes, but I haven't drunk that much, and in any case my tolerance is better now. My body's become used to the nightly medication.

Liam crashes around in the kitchen for a while and then joins me, wiping his hands on his jeans and ruffling his hair as he flops down next to me. He's grown it even longer since I said I liked it.

'Actually, Kate, I wanted to talk to you about something . . .'

'OK, but me first. I want to have a catch-up about all of this.' I wave my hand in the direction of the laptop. 'I feel like you've given up since I've moved in. You're not even trying to find Paulina any more.'

'What?' Liam sits forward, agitated. 'It's all I ever do. Every evening, all evening, I sit here looking up these names while you knock back glass after glass of wine. Who *are* these women? Why are you looking for them? What makes you think *I* can find them?' His cheeks are flushed. It takes a lot to get Liam angry, but I've managed it.

'Look, I'm sorry. I know it's weird. And frustrating. And honestly I will tell you everything one day, but for now I need us to really focus. Forget about everything else for a while.'

291

'There is nothing else, not for you. Sometimes I think you're only here because you think I'm somehow going to magically solve this weird mystery you've got going on with your sister.'

I don't say anything. Liam waits for a while – I know he wants me to contradict him, but I can't. Eventually he sinks back on the sofa with a sigh.

'That's what I wanted to talk about,' he says, fiddling with his shirt sleeve. 'Us. What's going on. If anything is . . .'

Looking at Liam, his head in his hands now, I think of the girl I was. Who had come to London so sure she was going to find her sister and establish a new life – who had been too preoccupied with family dramas to take any notice of Liam, of anyone really. I feel the sting of regret. How naive I was, to have put my life on hold for a sister who was off some-where, getting on with her own life. To have thought that was the worst thing that could happen.

Liam takes my hand and, not sensing any resistance, he kisses me gently. I kiss him back, for a moment. But I can't will my body into movement. It's too heavy with sadness, for what could have been and everything I've lost since then. For the person I've become – someone who would only bring unhappiness into Liam's life.

I pull away. I know now that there's something even worse than losing a sister, who wanted to be lost. And I know that it's already too late for me and Liam.

'I need to be on my own for a bit,' I say, getting up.

'Kate, don't leave now.' Liam pulls me towards him, but I resist.

'I'm sorry, I just . . .' I walk to the door.

Liam sits up. 'You just what? What is it? There's always something . . .'

I shrug. It's true. There is always something. And there always will be.

It is only then that I allow myself to accept for the first time the truth I've known ever since I arrived in London: Liam isn't going to find Paulina, or Scarlett. Staying with him while he continues his pointless search is only prolonging his misery.

'I'm sorry,' I say. 'So much has happened. I can't do this.' And I leave the room, as much for Liam's benefit as for my own.

The next morning, I wake at dawn, letting myself out of the house before Liam gets up. I'm feeling defeated, powerless again, as I walk along the ladder of streets leading up to Finsbury Park. It's shaping up to be a hot September day, the sun already high in the sky doing nothing to lift my spirits.

I don't know what I'm doing; where I'm walking to. Except that I do, really. Gradually the streets fill with children, speeding on scooters, or running precariously along pavements, followed by parents laden down with discarded coats and bags. I find myself drawn along with them towards the building at the top of the hill: Tabitha and Jasper's school. I want to catch a glimpse of them; perhaps even Teddy – or Ferdie, as I must remember to think of him now – if Chloe takes him along on the school run.

I position myself behind a tree a short distance from the school building and wait, scanning the little faces, hair tied back or tucked under sun hats, boys with caps pulled forward to shield them from the sun's glare. It's Tabitha I see first; such a big girl now, with her white socks pulled high and her pigtails neat, hanging either side of her long, anxious face. They're late and she's running around the corner towards the gates, followed closely by Jasper, almost unrecognisable as a boy of five, smart in his uniform, his curls cut short. Would they even remember me now, I wonder, inching further behind the tree just in case.

Next comes Ferdie, trotting along on his own, and my

stomach lurches with the frantic urge to step in and stop him getting too near the road. And then, moments later, reaching out to grab his arm, comes Della – her hair cut into a glossy bob, trailing bags and jumpers.

A gasp escapes me and I hide my face behind the tree trunk in panic. I assumed it would be Chloe who dropped the children off at school. Not Della. Here, in broad daylight. A few feet from where I'm standing. I'm frozen to the spot, my whole body trembling as I watch her push the two older children through the closing gates and into school.

What if Della sees me and goes to the police, like she threatened? A restraining order, a return to Cambridge in disgrace, it's the last thing I can handle at the moment. Especially now that I've seen my little boy, come so close to him, almost reached out and touched him.

But I can't run. I'll draw attention to myself. I know I have to stay where I am, behind a tree trunk that barely conceals me, until Della walks past on the other side of the road.

I stand still, facing the other way with my phone to my ear as if having a conversation, not daring to peep out from behind the branches. I'm furious with myself for taking such an obvious risk. Hanging around North London is too dangerous. It's only a matter of time before I get caught. And after last night, I can see that living with Liam isn't an option any more, either. I'll only hurt him more than I already have.

But how can I leave now that I've seen my baby? How can I leave my son?

A sharp cry jolts me back into the moment, and I crane my head to see what's happening. I can see Jasper sobbing, being dragged inside by a teacher, but it isn't him who is shouting, it's Ferdie. He's lying on the floor, kicking his little legs as all the classroom doors close for the beginning of the school day. Instead of picking him up and giving him a cuddle, Della is bent over, scolding him. Parents drift through the school gates, some catching Della's eye with a sympathetic smile, but others looking on with concern as Della continues to shout, pulling Ferdie's arm and dragging him, legs trailing, across the playground.

I'm frozen in horror, and not just because Della is headed towards me. It's the harshness of her voice. It takes me right back to that hospital room. The contempt on her face as she shouts at my son, it's the same look she gave me that day. I've tried so hard to bury the memory of that final confrontation, but it resurfaces now – the fury, the humiliation, the paralysis I felt. It's as though it's happening all over again, but this time I'm watching the missiles of hatred directed at my own son, his hand red from where Della has grabbed his wrist, his legs grazed from scuffing along the cement.

As I watch Della drag Ferdie off down the other side of the road, I try to remember a time I've seen her speaking to her other two children in that way. But I can't. I've seen her angry, frustrated, she's shouted at times. But this is different: this is a tone I have only ever heard her use with one person until now, and that's me.

Once they turn the corner, I stand there for a while longer, gathering my thoughts. But I know I've seen enough. There is no way I am leaving Ferdie to go through what I went through. The knot of anger in my chest twists a little tighter and I hold on to the tree, feeling I could rip it out of the ground and hurl it in my fury.

By the time I get back to the house, Liam has left for work, and I pace around, unsure what to do with myself. I can't think, I can't process, I can't focus on anything. There is one thought that circles around my head, over and over, drowning out all others. I have to rescue my son.

Chapter Thirty-Eight

By mid-morning the sun is beating down. Children are paddling in the pool and one indulged toddler is already having a pre-lunch ice cream, a spectacle that is causing trouble all around. I watch from the bushes as Chloe tries to drag Ferdie past the child, past the ice cream van and through the park to the café, picking him up and whispering into his ear, promises or threats, I can't tell.

I stand at a distance, observing the singing group in the park café from the outside, all those faces contorted in song. The wild-eyed new mothers in Breton tops; the veterans, chatting and breast-feeding between tambourine shakes; the mostly reluctant kids, crying or hitting each other with brightly painted shakers.

Ferdie stands apart, pulling on his denim dungarees, gazing out of the window in my direction, oblivious to the chaos around him. We've made a connection, I can feel it. It's as though he knows who I am. And he knows, somehow, that he belongs with me – not in there, in all that chaos.

When I'd left the house, I knew I would come to the park.

296

I didn't know if he would be here, but it was a good bet. And if he was, I didn't know what I would do.

But here he is. Calmer than outside the school this morning, but still subdued. Unhappy. I have to rescue him. There's no question in my mind. But how?

The session winds up and people begin to straggle out, a huddle forming outside the café as it had the day before, groupies waiting to catch a glimpse of their star. Chloe has caught the instructor's eye. They chat and laugh, oblivious to the annoyance of the other nannies and mums around them, each waiting for their turn to get feedback on their child's rhythm or way with a maraca.

I watch as Ferdie toddles towards the gate, a few feet from where I'm standing, on the other side of the hedge. It's open a crack, and he looks up at the only adult watching him: me. My breath catches and a smile takes over my face. I feel the thrill of being near him, close enough to touch him. Encouraged, Ferdie pushes the gate with his chubby arms, wobbles towards me. I glance up. Chloe still has her back turned. She couldn't care less. Nobody has noticed his escape.

Without even thinking, I lean forward and scoop him up. The relief at holding him, feeling his small solid body in my arms. It's almost too much. I close my eyes, breathe in the sticky sweetness of him. The heat of his scalp against my cheek. His feathery tufts of hair tickling my nose.

And in that moment, I know what to do. It's instinct that takes over as I turn and start to walk towards the park gates. All I can hear is throbbing, everything around us blurs. I can hardly believe I'm going to do it, but there is no stopping the forward motion once we've begun. I've got my back to the café, holding Ferdie low against my body so he isn't visible over my shoulder, talking to him in a quiet, soothing voice. Reassuring him. Stroking his leg as we stride away.

'Hello there. I'm a friend of your mummy's. I'm going to take you on a nice trip now. Would you like to get a biscuit on the way?'

I can see him looking up at me, but he doesn't struggle, and I don't want to turn my head, even a little. 'Clo-ee?' he says, quietly at first.

'We'll see Chloe later. We're just going out for a while.'

I'm nearly at the gates, and I still don't dare turn around. But I don't run either. Surely if anyone had spotted me I'd hear some commotion behind me. I can hardly breathe. In a few moments, we'll be out of the park.

'Clo-ee!' Ferdie says, a bit louder this time.

'Don't worry sweetie. We'll see Chloe soon.'

I'm gasping now, the adrenaline propelling me forward. But I have a strange presence of mind, my steps following a path, even though I haven't planned this. Through the gates I turn left, in the direction of the tube station, daring to glance over my shoulder as I do. That's when I hear a shout, the panic cutting through and almost stopping me still.

'Ferdie! Ferdie! Where are you? FERDIE!'

I feel my stomach flip over. I'm going to be sick. Chloe is shouting, running across the park. I'm about to drop him and run when I realise that she hasn't even seen me. She stops, scans the park, and then heads in the other direction, towards the swings, still calling 'Ferdie', 'Ferdie', over and over.

Ferdie has heard her and his body is tensed. He's starting to cry. As I duck behind the high hedges that surround the park, my arms still gripping him tight, I see a group of parents fanning out from the café, their heads turning this way and that. People start running in different directions, and I break into a run too, my feet pounding the pavement, away from the park.

Ferdie is screaming now, and as we round the corner towards the tube I turn my head to see whether we're being followed. Surely someone has heard him and come after us. Someone must have spotted us as we left the park.

But the street is empty, and in my terror I keep running, only slowing when we get to the station steps. We're attracting attention, with Ferdie roaring and me heaving him down the stairs, but no one stops us. No one says anything.

I fumble in my pocket for my Oyster card, bundle Ferdie through the gates and carry him down the escalator. The sign reads one minute until the next tube. Gasping for breath, I turn my head this way and that, scoping out the length of the platform, waiting until, any minute, someone grabs us from behind and wrestles Ferdie from me. But no one's paying us any attention, everyone locked in their own little bubble. We're entirely unnoticed, pushing further and further away from the entrance, into the crowd.

It's not until we reach the end of the platform, when the tube doors open and then close behind us, that I realise we've actually made it. And then, as I sit down with Ferdie on my lap and we head into the darkness of the tunnel, I realise what I've done.

People turn away from us in the tube carriage – the hysterical toddler and the panting, panicking woman. An older woman catches my eye and tries to smile, but looks away as soon as she sees my expression. All other heads are turned, headphones in, eyes down. I scan the stations on the map overhead, unable to think or even hear for the noise in my head.

What have I done? Where can we go?

I don't have anything with me. Just my handbag: wallet, keys, mobile. Should I go home? Grab some things?

But it's too risky. We need to get away from London. Me and my son. We need to get far away.

He's calming down now, his head drooping forward with the sway of the carriage. I watch us, reflected in the darkness: the fear in my eyes; his half closed. I could be his mother, I think. And then, I *am* his mother.

The thought strengthens me. I didn't plan this, didn't think it through. But I'd known deep down what I had to do. I'd followed my instincts. And now I need to find somewhere safe for us to stay, for the time being at least.

How long will it be before people start looking for us? Before the police are called? The tube pulls into Charing Cross. I hear the word 'overground' and stand up, get off, swept along in a tide of people heading for their train. Ferdie's fallen asleep and so I carry him over my shoulder, up the escalators, through the barriers, into the ticket hall. Eyes lowered, too terrified to look around me, I walk straight for the board, scanning it for the next departing train. Hastings. I buy a ticket from the machine with one hand, the other clamped across Ferdie. As I stride to the platform I dare to scan around me. I see two policemen, one mouthing into a walkie talkie. But no one stops me. No one says anything. And within a few minutes, I'm sitting on a train, watching London retreat into the distance, my son's warm body across my lap.

As I watch the houses dwindle and the fields speed past, I think of my mum. How many years has she spent wishing she had the chance to hold *her* baby? The other daughter I didn't even know had been missing all that time, along with Scarlett. Well that's not going to happen to me. Whatever I've done, whatever I've gotten myself into, I've got my son back. Now I need to work out my next move.

Chapter Thirty-Nine

We're watching the news. It's all we do now, on a loop. The twenty-four-hour news channel rolling around and around. Waiting, as though on a big wheel, until it's your turn to drop.

I say we. Really, I mean me. I only turn it on once Ferdie's asleep, or Teddy as I call him now. Then I sit up watching into the early hours, with him slumped across my knees. I don't want to risk having it on while he's awake, in case he catches sight of Della and Mark on screen and gets upset. More traumatised than he already is.

'. . . snatched from a London park'. There it goes and I turn up the volume. My stomach flips while I wait to hear whether there are any more developments. Whether they're any closer to finding us. Time to plummet to the ground again.

On the screen, is a picture of Della, Mark and their three children. It's similar to the one on their mantelpiece in London, except more recent, posed in a studio. There are Tabitha and Jasper, their faces lengthened, more composed. Mark, clean-shaven and groomed; Della even more glossy, with her whitened-for-TV teeth and her new power bob. In her arms, trying to escape but pinned to the spot, is Teddy. The boy now sleeping on my lap.

The picture can only have been taken a month or so ago I guess, looking down at his sleeping face. The same podgy cheeks, the long eyelashes. '. . . taken from the arms of his loving family,' the newsreader is saying. 'The police are appealing for information at this time.'

My head goes foggy, I feel dizzy as I wait to hear my name. But that's it. No mention of suspects, no indication of his possible whereabouts.

I stay glued to the screen for hours, the flicker illuminating Teddy's peaceful face in the darkness. The TV is the only bright spot in the room. The only furniture, really, in our faded, damp studio, on the top floor of this tall, seaside boarding house.

We needed no references, only a minimal deposit, and we can stay here as long as we like, the landlord said. At least until the money runs out. The walls are water-stained, with peeling paper and damp spots on the carpet, but there's a bed, a TV and a fridge. And at least we're safe, for now.

The only way the outside world can reach us is through the screen, which I've muted now as the news cycle rotates – terrorist threat, economic downturn, extreme weather. My pulse picks up every time the kidnapping comes around. That's what they're calling it: kidnap. They don't know the truth.

Each time, it's the same montage: the family photo, followed by a clip of Della smiling brightly on the sofa of a morning TV show, and then Della and Mark, their faces drawn, eyes lowered, walking hurriedly from their front door to a waiting car, Mark's arm protectively around Della's shoulders, shielding her from photographers and reporters.

The House Guest

Watching their faces, I feel sick. I recognise that bereavement, the crazed grief. I've felt it, too – at their hands. The sense that all it takes is a slight tear in the fabric of your life and suddenly the whole thing unravels. Overnight, you can go from one of us to one of them. Tainted.

I know how they will continue to suffer for weeks and months ahead, because I have suffered in that way. But not any more. I have my boy. I feel him sigh in my lap and I stroke his soft head gently. It feels right, him lying across me. I may have caused pain, but I have brought my own suffering to an end. Mine and Teddy's. Della and Mark brought it on themselves. Teddy and I will be better off this way.

While he sleeps, while the darkness cradles us, I can believe this story: that everything that has happened over the past three years has been leading up to this point. That this was the only option left to me. That I did what any mother would. But as dawn breaks, and the light of a new day begins to show through the thin curtains, my panic gradually rises.

Where will we go? What will we do? Della must know I've got him. Will she tell the police? Somehow I doubt it. Too risky. Even having lost her little boy, I can't imagine Della wanting to shine a light beneath the surface of her perfect family life.

Perhaps she'll tell them a story about an obsessive nanny: a strange woman who wouldn't leave her children alone. Maybe she'll allow the police to pursue their own investigations, and she will come after me herself. It's that thought that terrifies me most. As the room takes on its daytime shabbiness, as the light illuminates rotting wallpaper and creeping mould, it's the image of Della bursting through the door – Della, not the police – that haunts me.

And then Teddy opens his eyes, and there's no time to think any more. It's been the same ever since we arrived in Hastings.

303

The crying – incessant, deafening, drowning out all rational thought. When he cries, it's impossible to concentrate. It's like being possessed. I can't rest until he's calm. And so I search around in my bag for the only thing I've found that soothes him, my hand alighting on a small plastic shape.

I resented the sight of a dummy being thrust into my son's mouth by Chloe, silencing him, denying a voice to his emotions. Now I seize upon it with gratitude, and Teddy immediately sucks himself to silence. But the terror is still there in his eyes, every time he looks at me – this stranger. His birth mother.

How long will it last? How long before he gets used to me, trusts me, learns to see me for who I am to him? For now, his shock and confusion are evident in everything he does. His jerky movements as he stumbles around the flat; his wide-eyed bewildered gaze as he watches me circle the room, muting and un-muting the TV, pouring bowls of cereal, adding milk.

Mostly, his trauma is evident in his silence. He hasn't spoken a single word since we left London.

Over breakfast I chatter away, trying to reassure him, to coax a smile. I talk to him about my parents, his granny and grandpa, my sister who we're going to find one day. The ice creams and fairground rides we can enjoy once we're all settled, once we've got a place of our own.

Hastings pier is just visible from our top-floor window, and Teddy looks out wistfully from time to time, but there's no way we can risk making the trip, with his face all over the TV and newspapers. The furthest we've been is the corner shop, to buy supplies, a small clothes shop, and a chemist for hair dye.

Later, once I've cleaned up our breakfast, I take Teddy into the bathroom and wash the dye into his hair. The result is a brown a few shades lighter than my own. I clip his curls and then hold him up to the mirror, but he looks even more terrified, turning to me with his saucer eyes – his mouth tugging at the corners, building towards a howl.

I put him on the sofa, fumble around for a dummy, turn on the TV and find the channel with back-to-back cartoons, sinking next to him in defeat. This couldn't be further from the image of motherhood I've held in my head all the months we've been apart. But then, what can I expect? Teddy has been snatched from the family he knows, from the life he knows, full of luxuries and light and people. And now he's marooned here with me, on the top floor of a dingy building, no contact with the outside world, the hours ticking past slowly as we watch people going about their lives on the streets below.

Our room takes on different scents throughout the day and night – frying food replaced by the stench of weed and then, as darkness falls, the smell of cooking once more. The noises, too, are strange and unpredictable. A booming bassline rattles through our small room like a train, into the night, so loud I have to put on the subtitles for the news channel once Teddy has fallen asleep.

How long can we wait here? We can't travel abroad, without passports, documents, any kind of income. The money I have in the bank will only last us a couple of months at this rate. I can't even make contact with my parents, find out how Dad is. Who can we possibly go to for help?

On the fourth day, we venture out. We're running out of food, and I'm increasingly worried about Teddy, who won't even look me in the eye. He takes no interest in food, games, books, songs. His only preoccupation is the TV, but I think that's beginning to affect his behaviour, too.

I decide to risk a visit to the small playground down the road. We both look so different now, and it seems like the only way I'll be able to raise a smile from him, break out of the cycle of crying and silence. But though he doesn't object when I lift him into the swing, forcing his legs clumsily between the bars like the novice I am, he doesn't respond either. No laugh, not even the twitch of a smile as I push him higher and higher, until I feel like giving in, running away, leaving him to be found by some passer-by and handed in to the nearest police station. It's a scenario I play out repeatedly in my head. How I can get him to safety without implicating myself. How I can give him up without resigning myself to life in a prison cell.

I notice another mum staring at me as I push the swing, my child and me both in silence. I realise how I must look: distracted, depressed, both. Or maybe she's recognised me. There could be an e-fit or a picture doing the rounds by now. She might have spotted Teddy from the pictures – despite his darker hair, and the circles under his eyes.

I snap to, pull him from the swing, bundle him into my arms and stride away. In the shop on the corner of our road, I grab a basket in one hand, Teddy's wrist in the other, feeling exposed. There's a row of papers by the door and I scan them for headlines, but there are no pictures. No mentions of my son. I rush around the shop grabbing milk, butter, bread while his whines get louder. I'm muttering to him under my breath. Why does he insist on drawing attention to us?

I avoid eye contact with the other shoppers. Older people, mostly. A shabbily dressed man with a desperate look in his eyes, one that I recognise. He queues behind us with his cans and tries to get a smile out of Teddy, but gives up when confronted with his escalating wails. By the time we reach the counter, Teddy's head is thrown back and he's screaming, while I'm fumbling in my purse for the right money so we can get out quickly. The woman behind the counter has kind eyes, buried in soft folds of skin.

'Someone's ready for his tea,' she says, but her smile dies as she catches my eye. Something in my face must communicate that I'm not coping, that this is more serious than she realised. She can see the fear. Or maybe she's seen the pictures, too, and she secretly pressing an emergency button underneath the counter, calling the police to arrive and confront me.

By the time I've paid and gathered my bags, I'm ready to drop the whole act, to confess to this complete stranger. As we leave the shop, my eyes dart around, waiting for a team of police to swoop in, to grab Teddy, to restrain me. But the street's almost empty. Just a few shoppers, barely registering Teddy's screams. As we turn the corner and then close the front door behind us, I feel like sinking to my knees and joining Teddy in his howls. How long can we carry on like this?

I unpack the shopping, while Teddy stands as far from me as possible on the other side of the room, fingers in his mouth, looking at me with a horror that chills my blood. This is my own son. How long will it be until his fear begins to subside?

'How about a biscuit?' I say. But he shakes his head. Looks away. Starts to whimper again and this time he opens his mouth.

'Mummy.' He says it quietly and my heart leaps. It's the first word he's spoken since we got here, and it's Mummy. Me. But of course, it's not. He begins to sob and I realise it's Della he's calling for. He wants the mummy who brought him up, who he's seen every day since he was born, who gave him the life he knew.

'Oh it's OK, little one,' I say, crouching down to put my arms around him. But he pushes me away, more forcefully than I'm expecting, and I roll back on my heels, collapsing backwards, shocked, as he begins to howl. 'Mummy, Daddy, Tabby, Tabby . . .'

It's too much for me, and I sit with my head in my hands,

crying along with him, thinking of the family he's left behind – not only Della, whose cruelty had pushed me over the edge, but Mark, who I know to be a loving father, and his brother and sister, who I've barely even considered. It isn't just that he longs to be back with them. What must they be going through? What have I done to Tabitha and Jasper?

We both cry for what feels like a long time, until Teddy gradually quietens down and I look up to see that he's falling asleep. I lift him to the sofa, sit with him on my lap, the only time I can get close enough to cuddle him. It's in these moments that I let myself imagine what it could be like if Teddy really was my son in more than just blood. If he truly believed I was his mother.

The smell of marijuana drifts up through the cracks in the floorboards. A better life. Is that really what I'm offering Teddy here? On the run. No money. No prospect of making any. I'd been so consumed by the idea that he was being mistreated, deprived of love, I hadn't even stopped to consider whether I'd have it in me to provide for him, care for him, make him love me.

During that long night, as I sit still, unable to sleep, unwilling to move Teddy, the reality sinks into me like cold, hard concrete, filling any crack of doubt: I have made the biggest mistake of my life. Teddy will never truly get used to being with me. He will always remember what he had before. I will always be the other mother.

Chapter Forty

We've made it to the park. We couldn't sit in that fetid room any longer, the walls coming in on us, the smells invading our senses. We've got to start our new life together. It's the only way.

So we've ventured beyond the small local playground to a bigger one, surrounded by trees and bushes, a large slide framed by a sandpit, children soaring around us like birds.

It must be the weekend, I realise. I've lost track of the days. I watch as Teddy heads straight for the sandpit, knocking into a small dark-haired child as he climbs in and looking on, impassive, as the child starts to howl.

Is this Teddy's true nature? Or a response to the trauma? As I watch him pushing his way around the sandpit, leaving a trail of crying toddlers behind him, I consider whether he has somehow been affected by the violence of his birth. Or perhaps it's behaviour he's learned through example, further evidence of Della's neglect.

But for once, I'm determined to push that woman from my mind and enjoy the glow of the autumn sun on my face. It's warmer than I was expecting and I look around for a café. Perhaps I could treat Teddy to an ice cream, get myself a coffee, try to pretend we're a normal family. I can see a kiosk in the distance, but it's hard to tell whether it's open, and on the other side of the park a small white building looks shut, the door bolted with a heavy padlock.

I look back at the sandpit, at the place where Teddy was last sitting, but he's gone.

I stand up, feeling my chest constrict in panic. He must have gone to the swings, the slide. My eyes dart around the playground. What was I thinking? Why did I look away?

I start to run towards the swings, and then change my mind and decide to try the slide at the other side, where a group of children are clustered, waiting. I'm looking this way and that, my eyes swimming with tears, and all the time I'm thinking of Della. She's found us. How simple it must have been for her to scoop up Teddy and walk away, just as I did. Only easier – he would have run to her willingly. His mother, at last. Why hadn't I thought of this? Why had I brought Teddy here and turned away, even for a moment?

I run to the middle of the playground, spinning this way and that, shouting out his name: 'Teddy!' I call, and then, in desperation: 'Ferdie!' It's the first time I've said the name out loud in public, wary of drawing any connection between us and the missing boy. But I know Teddy isn't used to his new name, and my only thought now is finding him, getting him back.

'Ferdie!' I shout, and then, louder still, 'Ferdie, where are you?' Everything is spinning around me, the terror making it impossible to focus my eyes. I'm panting. I feel like I might faint.

And then, through the gates of the playground, I catch a glimpse of red. Teddy's T-shirt. I pound towards the gate, seeing as I do that he's standing next to a bench. A blonde woman with a deep tan is sitting by him.

Oh God. It's . . . No, it isn't, I realise as I run towards

them. It isn't Della. This woman is much older, her hair more obviously dyed. But had Teddy thought it was his mother? Is that why he'd run off?

'Teddy! There you are.' I crouch next to him at the bench and pull him towards me in a hug. 'You mustn't run away like that, OK? I didn't know where you were.'

Teddy looks at me, his eyes wide, tears forming. 'Do you understand?' I say, holding his face in my hands. 'You must never walk away from Mummy, OK?'

Teddy doesn't say anything. Perhaps he can hear the alarm in my voice. I turn to the woman on the bench with a smile, as if to reassure her that this is a perfectly normal scene, but she looks at me coldly and then down at her phone, typing something into the screen. My heart starts to pound. She must have sensed that something is off. She's looking up images. She's recognised us.

She's heavily made up, in a neat skirt and jacket, too smart for the playground. She doesn't seem to be attached to a child. I pick up Teddy and walk away fast, looking over my shoulder as we go. The woman's eyes are on us now. She's sitting perfectly still. This time, she doesn't look away.

I turn to Teddy, mumbling into his neck. 'What were you doing, little one? You had me so worried.' Had the woman been trying to lure him away? Was she working for Della?

I'm desperate to get us back to the safety of our room. I speed up my pace, whispering to Teddy as we walk towards the gates of the park, and then I hear him say something, almost under his breath.

I stop.

'What did you say?' I ask, placing Teddy on his feet and crouching down so I'm at eye level.

'Ice ceem,' Teddy says quietly, his high-pitched voice so surprising I can't help but smile.

'Ice cream? Is that what you were looking for?' I pick him up and hold him close, my heart still struggling to resume its normal pace. 'Is that why you wandered off? You silly thing.'

'Ice ceem.' Teddy looks at me. 'Peeease . . .'

'OK then.' I smile. I'd give anything to hear that little voice again, to keep hearing it, over and over. We walk off in search of a café, the woman in the park forgotten for the moment.

Back at the flat, I switch the TV on. Teddy has passed out on the bed, exhausted after our trip, and I turn to see his face filling the screen.

'Several potential sightings . . .' the newsreader is saying, 'though none have yet proved conclusive.' I take a breath and hold it, waiting for more. 'Della and Mark Hunter held a press conference earlier today . . .'

And suddenly there she is. Della. In close-up – beamed into the room, her dazzling white blouse making the surrounding walls appear even grimier. She's so much more put together, more beautiful, than the woman in the park today, and for a moment I feel reassured. She hasn't found me. If she has anyone on the lookout, they haven't tracked us down yet.

She looks desperate, and I'm aware of a jolt of sympathy, guilt. Then I remind myself that it's all an act with her, everything is. She's talking directly to the camera, tears escaping from the corners of her eyes, her hand gripping Mark's.

'If anyone knows where our little boy has gone, please, *please* contact us. Our hearts are broken. We can't live without him.' Mark puts a hand on her shoulder while she dabs her eyes and takes a deep breath. 'Someone, somewhere knows where he is.' She looks at the camera. 'You know who you are.'

It's only then that I notice a glinting on her chest, in the V of her open shirt, pale against her tanned skin.

312

It can't be. But I look more closely, and there it is, tiny, catching the light. The necklace. The lotus she gave me. The one I lost in the house in France. Either she took it back, or found an identical version. And she is wearing it now, when it matters most.

It's then that I realise. She knows I'm watching. She knows I'll see the necklace. It's a hidden message. You know who you are. *We* know who you are.

Chapter Forty-One

It's morning again and I'm steeling myself to leave the house. I haven't heard any sirens for at least half an hour. We need to get out. I need to make contact with Liam.

In the night-time hours, caught between my waking and sleeping dread, that had been the solution that presented itself to me. I'd thrown away my phone on the way to Hastings, so I would need to find an internet café, or a library. Somewhere quiet without too many witnesses. Liam will know what to do. I have to trust him.

But as I walk briskly to the library, Teddy in my arms, doubt begins to creep in. Liam's loyal. He's proven that to me over and over. But I don't want to drag him into what I've done. And who's to say he'd take my side, even if I did?

The computer room at the library is busier than I'd thought it would be, but hushed, the only sound the steady tapping of keys and Teddy's incessant high whine.

'Please, give me a minute,' I whisper, sitting him on a chair next to me and handing him a bag of crisps to keep him busy. 'I won't be long.'

I sit rigid in my chair, face glued to the screen, not wanting to establish eye contact with any of the students or older people who sit in front of the other computers, just a click or two away from a picture of Teddy's face.

I navigate straight to my email account. I haven't been online for over a week, and there are dozens of messages, mostly from my parents and Liam, even some from Layla, who hasn't been in touch for months. I skim through the subject headings – *Worried, Please call* – not wanting to click through and see how much more pain I've caused.

And then I scroll past one from Liam with a heading printed in block capitals: *URGENT. READ NOW.*

I open it, scanning the short message. Della. Visit. Get away.

I force myself to slow down, to read it from beginning to end, my throat dry, blood pounding in my ears.

Kate, your friend Della came to visit. Or, I thought she was your friend. She knew all about Scarlett and I knew you'd been close, so I assumed it would be fine to chat. But then she got angry. She wouldn't say why, but she's looking for you. I'm looking for you. Where are you? What have you done? If I'd known you wanted to get away, I'd have come with you. Just let me know you're OK, as soon as you can.

I look at the email date. Four days ago. I look around, suddenly alert to every face, every movement. I clasp Teddy's hand to mine as I delete the email. There is another, sent a day later.

I've just seen Della on the news. I'd seen the story, but I didn't put it all together until now. Kate, what's going on? Please get in touch and let me know you're OK. Whatever has happened, I can help you. Tell me where you are.

I close the email. Liam knows. Or he will do soon. And Della is looking for me.

I have to get away.

What had I been thinking, staying in one place for so long, so close to London?

I'm about to shut down the computer and leave the library, when another email arrives in my inbox. It's from Liam. And this one has a different heading: *SCARLETT.*

> Kate, whatever has happened, I'm here for you. And I need to see you. I've got news, about Scarlett. I can only tell you in person. Trust me, you're going to want to hear this.

My brain goes foggy. I feel like I'm going to faint. Liam has found Scarlett. I can't take it in, after everything else. Can it really be true?

> Just email me the address of where you are. I can leave as soon as I get your email. I won't bring anyone.

For a split second, I pause. Is it a trap? But I have to be able to trust Liam. I have to trust someone. And I need to know what he's found out about Scarlett.

I type in the address of the flat and press send, before I have the chance to change my mind. I'll let Liam reach us, discover where Scarlett is and then take Teddy with me to find her. This must be the solution I was waiting for. Scarlett will know what to do. She'll help us.

It's only as I leave the library, clutching Teddy's hand, that the words come back to me. 'I won't bring anyone.' What did Liam mean? Who would he be thinking of bringing?

As Teddy and I walk down the street, the obsessive thoughts

start up again. Is this a set-up? Is Liam helping Della to find me? I quicken my pace, scanning left and right as I drag Teddy along. They won't be here yet, anyway. All we need to do is get to the flat, pack our few belongings, and get on the next train out of here. There's still time. We can leave Hastings, cover our tracks and keep on running. To where, asks a voice in my head, but I refuse to listen. It doesn't matter: we have to get away.

I dart through the busy narrow streets, pulling Teddy this way and that, as we weave in and out between dawdling shoppers. It's late morning now and the old town is filling up. Everywhere I look I see blond heads, a glint of a gold earring, a flash of red, which could be her jacket but turns out to be a teenager's hoodie.

As we leave the old town, I spot two policemen rounding the corner and I pick Teddy up in one motion, throwing him over my shoulder so his face is out of view and putting my head down, crossing to the other side.

Back in the flat, I throw our few clothes and toys into two plastic bags and bundle Teddy out of the door. I've paid for another week, but I'll have to forget about that money. I post the keys through the letter box and sweep him down the hall.

Opening the front door, I take a deep breath and step outside. No sign of Della. Or Liam. And then I stop, hovering on the doorstep, considering the news that Liam has to give to me.

If he really has found Scarlett, can I pass up the opportunity to go to her? To take Teddy, and start again, together? Perhaps, once enough time has passed, we could even make contact with my parents. I imagine the tearful reunion as they discover not one but both of their daughters. Scarlett must have chosen somewhere far enough away that we've never been able to find her, in all our years of searching. What if I join her there, stay beneath the radar too? Finally a plan, an answer.

317

I spot the run-down café on the corner. Teddy and I could wait in there, by the window. We could keep watch, to see if Liam arrives, to make sure he's alone. We'll give him an hour, and then we'll leave. Any longer and the risk just gets greater.

I cross the road, order a coffee for me and a chocolate croissant for Teddy, who is already getting fidgety, picking up on my agitation, his round eyes watching mine for clues.

The café is empty, a bored-looking waitress behind the counter reminding me of my old self, with her stringy coffee-steam hair and cocoa-smudged apron. Except that this café is nothing like the one in Crouch End; Formica tables, chairs fixed to the floor, a TV blaring in the corner, distracting Teddy with music videos while he smears chocolate across his face.

I chatter to him nervously as we wait to see whether Liam will arrive, keeping my eye on the clock. I catch eyes with the waitress, see myself as she must see me: another mum, with another sticky brat, whiling away time in another café. Or has she seen the news? Is she going out back to make a phone call? The police could be here at any moment.

But for now, the street is eerily quiet. Just the odd car and midday shopper. No sirens. No Liam. No Della.

Teddy is getting restless. He starts to whine, and the waitress looks up, switches the channel. Cartoons. I give her a grateful smile, but she looks at me with bored eyes and goes back to her phone. I turn to watch the street. How much longer can we risk waiting here?

I'm about to get the bill when I see Liam's blue Fiesta pull up across the street. He folds his long body out of the small car. Slams the door. Looks around. I hold my breath as I wait to see whether anyone else will get out.

But they don't. And Liam's ringing on the doorbell of our building, his forehead wrinkled, his hand shading his eyes as he squints up at the windows and then down the street, looking around him before trying again.

I smile, despite everything. He's here. He's alone. He'll know what to do. I tap the window and watch him turn, wave, run towards the café. I feel safe for the first time in days.

'Kate!' Liam comes through the door and approaches me cautiously, eyes on Teddy. Then he puts his arms around me and I bury my head in his shoulder, trying to control my emotions, feeling weak with relief. He puts his hands on my shoulders and sits me down. He has a serious look on his face as he sits opposite, taking in the scene: me, Teddy, our plastic bags, my jumpy, panicked state.

'What the hell's going on?' he hisses, sitting down and ordering a black coffee. 'Is this . . . *that* boy?' He jerks his head in Teddy's direction, looks around to make sure no one has heard. But the café is empty, the waitress busy out back.

'Della came to see me,' he carries on. 'She told me about . . .'

'Just tell me about Scarlett,' I beg. 'We can get to all that later. Somewhere safer. Have you found her? Where is she?'

'Well, no. Not exactly.'

'What do you mean, not exactly? Have you or haven't you?'

'I went to see your parents, to find out if they knew anything about where you'd disappeared to. They're sick with worry, you know. Layla is too. We've been calling each other.' I nod, looking at Teddy, who is still engrossed in the cartoons.

'And?' I ask, after Liam pauses for too long. 'What did my parents say? Was it them who found Scarlett?'

'No one's found her.' Liam sounds impatient. 'Your mum gave me a letter to give you. Apparently it will explain a lot. It's in the car. But that's not important right now. What's important is what on earth is going on here.'

'So you did . . . you tricked me.' I can hardly believe it.

319

I'm already standing up, gathering my bags. 'I was right. You were just trying to find me. You don't have any news, do you? Have you told anyone where I am?'

'No.' Liam lays a hand on my arm and I sit down again. 'Of course not. I didn't tell anyone I was coming. But I needed to see you. To hear your side of the story.'

'*Side of the story*? What are you talking about?' And then I realise. 'Della told you, didn't she?'

Liam nods. 'Yes, she came back. What the hell are you doing, Kate?'

'She told you I had a baby for her. That I promised I would give him to her, and then I changed my mind.'

'Yes, she did.' Liam is looking at me warily, as though I might grab Teddy and run at any minute. 'She's beside herself.' He looks at Teddy, glazed eyes fixed on the screen. 'But she's not angry. She's concerned for you. And she says she won't press charges. If you bring him home, she'll help you – get you help.'

'I bet she will.' My laugh is bitter, but my stomach is churning with disappointment. I can't believe Liam would think I'd be capable of something so cruel. 'You really think I'd have done this, I'd have *taken him*, if I didn't truly believe he should be with me.'

'But you did agree to have him for Della?' Liam asks slowly.

'Yes, but . . .'

'As a surrogate?'

'Well, not exactly, no.'

'Did you sleep with her husband?' Liam has lowered his voice even more, he's stirring a spoon around in his cup, avoiding my eyes.

'Yes.'

'And you got pregnant. You said they could keep the baby – because Della couldn't have one of her own?'

'Yes. But they said I could be part of his life. Part of the family. They tricked me. They stole him from me!' My voice keeps rising until Liam glares at me. We both look around, but the waitress is still in the kitchen, clattering cups.

'What part could you have possibly played in their family once you'd slept with her husband?' Liam asks, looking hurt himself. 'Really, Kate. Listen to yourself. You're a grown-up. You must have known what you were getting yourself into.'

I'm reeling. Everything I could say, every defence I could offer, has melted away. To hear it repeated back to me in this way, from the mouth of the person I trust the most in the world. How can I put it into words – the lies, the manipulation? How can I make him see?

'Kate, I know about what happened to you.' Liam puts a hand on mine. The room begins to spin. 'Your mum told me all of it – that breakdown, the hospital. And I understand. Honestly I do. You've been through so much, from such a young age. It's no wonder you weren't able to cope. Your mum's so worried about you. We all are.'

I can't speak. Tears are running down my cheeks. Teddy looks up and starts crying, too. Loud sobs fill the café, and I can't tell whether they're coming from me, or him, or both of us.

'Come on,' Liam says gently, his arm around my shoulders. 'Let's go home. Let's take Ferdie home. We'll get you the help you need. We'll get you better.' He pays the bill and guides me out of the café, crossing the road, gripping my arm as though I might take off at any moment. And he's got Teddy over his other shoulder, uncharacteristically quiet now, not whining, or crying. Perhaps he's relieved, too. That someone has come to save him. That all this is finally over.

Because I do feel relief. I can't deny it. As we approach Liam's familiar blue Fiesta, with the pine tree freshener and

321

the scrape down one side, I feel my legs shaking as though they might give way. The thought of sinking into a seat, being clipped up and driven away to whatever fate I might face at the other end. An end to this uncertainty; this impossible, unsustainable situation I've created.

I'm ready to submit. To sleep. To resign myself to whatever plays out at the end of our journey. It's only as we reach the car that a word from Teddy jolts me back to reality.

'Mummy.' He says it loudly and with a clarity that makes me catch my breath. I look up to where he's cradled, on Liam's shoulder. Finally he feels it. Perhaps it's not too late to hope that we could make a new start. We could take Liam with us. Go somewhere far away.

'Mummy!' He says it louder this time. 'Mummy!' But he's directing his shout over Liam's shoulder, and I freeze. The world turns on its axis. I realise it's not me he's calling for at all.

That's when I see her. Climbing out of a large black Range Rover I hadn't even noticed parked further down the road. The blond bob swinging as she spins around, a blur of white and gold and yellow as she pounds down the street towards us.

Terror glues me to the spot. I'm unable to move a single muscle in my body – like I have been so many times in my dreams. The powerlessness is even more overwhelming than the shock, the fear.

'Oh my God, it's her. You brought her with you!' I cry, the full force of Liam's betrayal hitting me deep in the gut.

'I didn't, I swear. I didn't know she was—' But there's no time for Liam's pleading, because Della reaches us and wrenches Teddy from Liam's arms, holding him close, burying her face in his hair and howling his name uncontrollably. I stare, speechless, at the wild, raw emotion I had no idea Della was capable of.

322

'Mummy, Mummy, Mummy!' Teddy is whimpering now, clinging to Della in the way I always hoped he would to me, as though he might never let go. Watching them together, I feel as though I've been stabbed; it's a body blow of grief that leaves me breathless.

'How could you?' Della looks up at me between her sobs and her eyes are frightened, mascara smeared down her cheeks. 'How could you take him from us?'

'How could *you*?' I spit back, feeling a surge of fury. I look around, waiting for the other cars, the sirens. I just want to have my say before they come for me. 'I only did to you what you did to me.'

'It's not the same,' Della cries. She's cradling Teddy like a baby, smoothing his hair. 'I know you were upset when we cut you out. But you must see why we had to do it. You were delusional, it seemed like you'd stop at nothing to be part of our family. It was out of control . . .' She turns to Liam, for the sympathy she knows she'll see reflected in his face. I can't even look at him now. He doesn't know what really happened.

'You know the truth,' I hiss at Della. 'You know what you did to me, how you used me, how you manipulated me – and that's going to stay with you for the rest of your life. You may have been able to shrug off that Polish nanny, but you won't be able to get rid of me so easily.'

Della stares at me, the shock evident on her face. I can see she still has no clue what Mark told me at the farmhouse, and I realise I'm one step ahead.

'I know about it all. I know about Tabitha; about Jasper. I know I wasn't the first.' I'm trying to keep my voice steady, but really I'm thinking fast. What can I do with this knowledge? How can I use it to my advantage? 'And by the time we're through with all of this,' I look around, gesturing down the road towards the police I know will be arriving any minute, 'everyone will know. You might have Ted— Ferdie back, but do you think he's going to thank you, when he's older, for what you've done? Do you think any of them will?'

Della's panicking now. I can see from the looks she's shooting towards the car that this isn't going the way she planned. Then I hear a door click and jerk my head to see Mark getting out. He stands by the car, looking taller, more imposing than I remember. He's nearly the same height as Liam, but much broader, his face hard and lined with worry. Liam's standing between Della and me, watching us both warily, waiting for the next move.

'Listen, Kate,' Della says, her voice quieter now, 'I don't know what you're talking about. But I can see you've been hurt. Much more than I realised. And I'm sorry about that, really I am. I thought you'd get over us, move on with your life, but I can see that hasn't happened.' She's looking to Liam now, playing to her witness.

'But why me? That was what the group was all about, wasn't it? Find some young women and single one of them out. I see you've stopped the meetings now. You got what you wanted.'

'Kate, you must be able to hear how deranged that sounds. I stopped the meetings because my writing and media work took over. But that doesn't diminish from what the group achieved, how important it was to me for the two years it ran.'

'The two years it took for you to find a surrogate. Why didn't you choose someone who *wanted* to have a baby for you?'

'I never *planned* for you to sleep with my husband, to get pregnant.' I can hear Della trying to contain her anger. 'But you agreed to give us the baby. You knew you would be giving him up. You had nine months to prepare yourself for that.

324

Whereas I . . . I brought Ferdie up for two years. I lived with him, I loved him, he's my son – he's part of our family,' she gestures to Mark, and Teddy turns his head, spotting him for the first time.

'Daddy,' he cries reaching out towards Mark, and Della walks a few paces towards the car, handing Teddy over, while I stand there, body flinching, unsure what to say next, how to make my case. 'Daddy!' Teddy flings his arms around Mark's neck and as I watch them both, hugging and crying, something inside me breaks. I can't keep this up any more. I don't know what's right or who's in the wrong. All I know is that I can see a family – a loving, bonded, family. And Teddy – Ferdie – hasn't taken a second look at me. I may have carried him, but he doesn't *know* me. He doesn't love me.

I'm crying too now, into Liam's shoulder as he holds me up, steeling himself against my collapsing body. Della has joined us and she's watching me, waiting for me to get control of myself.

'Kate, we're a family,' Della says, quietly. 'I know what it's like to be brought up by parents who haven't given birth to you. I was adopted. Raised by a couple who weren't my parents. And I know that, even when you find your birth mother, your birth family, things don't always work out the way you think they will.'

I look at Della, trying to process this information. 'We need to get Ferdie home,' she continues. 'We need to be together.' She's looking at me. Waiting for me to protest. But the fight has gone out of me now. I can see where his home is, and it's not with me. No matter how much I might wish it was. I'm just waiting for the next bit – will they escort me to the police station? Or are the police waiting until Ferdie has left the scene before they arrest me? I watch as Della instructs Mark to strap Ferdie into the car seat; as my son is taken away.

'I'm not going to press charges,' Della says. 'I told Liam I wouldn't, and I won't. It will be much simpler all round if we just find him, on a tip-off from the public. No names, no stories. OK?'

I look at her, amazed all over again by her presence of mind, her aptitude for smoothing over any problem.

'But . . . won't the police come looking for me?'

'Why would they? I've never mentioned you to them. They don't know anything about you. All you need to do is get yourself away from us – and stay away.' Her voice is hard-edged, those last words in warning, and I nod, quickly.

'I will. I'll stay away.' I watch Mark close the door on Ferdie, feeling the grief building inside me like a wave. I'll never see him again. I know that now. 'And I won't say anything about Jasper, Tabitha, any of that—'

'Good,' Della says, shutting down the conversation. 'As long as you don't, then you don't need to worry about being found. If you do, well . . . I'm sure a case like this, a high-profile kidnapping, could be reopened at any time.' She's trying to sound threatening, but her voice breaks in the final words and when she looks at me, there's a vulnerability in her eyes I've never seen before, genuine fear. She knows how much she has to lose. How much we both have.

'Let's just call it quits shall we?' she says, in a quiet voice, and I nod. I hold her eye, and for the briefest moment I get that feeling again – the connection, stirring something in the pit of my stomach. It's as though she's trying to communicate something, testing me almost.

And then Della turns, and goes back to the car. I watch it drive away, with my little boy inside, and I wait for the wave to break.

Chapter Forty-Two

The full force of the separation hits me once we're in Liam's car, leaving the pier and seaside apartments behind us. I'm so lost in grief, sadness, regret, I don't even hear him at first.

'. . . really think she must have followed me . . .' he's saying, but I'm looking out of the window at the birds circling the electricity masts, thinking about what I've lost, that animal connection, the sense of rightness. Though did it ever really feel right, once we were together? It didn't for Ferdie . . .

'Are you angry with me?' Liam asks.

'What? No, I'm not angry with you,' I say, feeling exhausted.

'Because, really, I didn't tell her where you were, or where I was going. I didn't tell anyone.'

'I know. I believe you. But Della's smart. She would have been watching you.' I look over at Liam, eyes fixed ahead, hands still shaking – nobody's idea of a failsafe accomplice.

'It didn't even occur to me . . .' Liam falls silent. 'What did you mean, when you said you weren't the first? What was all that about the group?'

'Oh, it doesn't matter now. I'll tell you all about it sometime, but I haven't got the energy.' I watch the cars fly past us in the other direction, speeding along to their own individual fates.

'I do believe that you really thought you were doing the right thing, you know. But I also think you need some help. Help I can't give you on my own. I'm taking you back to Cambridge,' he says, as though he expects me to protest, but I've no strength left. Anyway, I want to see my parents, make sure Dad's OK. And I can't go back to London, not now.

'I'll stay with you there, if you like?' Liam asks tentatively, and I nod, attempting a smile through my tears as he hands me a tissue. 'Whatever you need, I'm here. And I'm sure Layla will visit too. She's been so worried. We all have.' I can feel Liam's eyes on the side of my face. 'I went through everything, looking for you – your emails, browsing history, files.' He pauses. 'Those stories you've written are really good, you know. You shouldn't give up on them. You should send them to someone. Get them published.'

At this I do smile. I catch his eye and something passes between us. An understanding, an acceptance. Once I would have felt annoyed, my privacy invaded. But those barriers have fallen away between us now, after everything that's happened. And I'm touched, that he took the time to read them, to appreciate them.

'Do you want to read Scarlett's letter now? It's in the glove compartment. I said to your mum I'd give it to you.'

'Scarlett's letter?' I sit up, my chest tight. 'You didn't say it was a letter *from* Scarlett. I thought it was a letter from my mum, *about* Scarlett.'

'No, she told me it's the letter Scarlett left behind. When she ran away. She said she'd agonised for years about showing it to you, but you were too young, and then you had that breakdown. It never seemed like the right time. I haven't

328

looked at it, but I promised I'd give it to you, when I found you . . .'

I'm not even listening any more. I'm searching through the litter, bits of paper, receipts until my hand lands on an envelope. Fingers trembling, I open it, scared of what I'll find inside.

The handwriting is so familiar – the bubble-shaped o, the fat round m – that I can hardly breathe. Scarlett was so young when she left, I realise, looking at the writing. She seemed old to me at the time. Even now, I think of her as an adult, making grown-up decisions, when really she was just a child. I inhale deeply as I start reading, blocking out the noise of the road, the pitter-patter of rain on the windscreen, the click-click of Liam's indicator . . .

Mum,
By the time you read this, I'll have gone. We both know why I can't stay. I know you don't want me to make the mistakes you made – but I'm not you. I'm me. And I'm going to do what's right for my baby.

The word makes me stop. I feel the bile rising in my throat, but I have to read on.

I'm not having an abortion just because you messed up your life. I know you're desperate for me to get rid of this baby because you had to give away the baby you had at my age, and it 'ruined your life' (thanks for that, by the way – good to know the life you made with your two other daughters is so awful). But times have changed. Nobody thinks it's weird to have a baby at seventeen any more. I'll bring it up and do the best I can, and if I have to do that without your help, then I will.

329

Luke couldn't care less, but I've got a friend who's going to help – she's found somewhere for me to stay for a while, back where she's from, so you don't have to worry about me. And don't come looking for me, either. None of my other friends know where we're going.

Look after Kate. She's too young to get caught up in all this.

I wish you and Dad weren't so stuck in your ways, but we've been over this so many times and I'm not getting rid of my child – not for you, and not for anyone.
Scarlett

My head is spinning. I read it twice through before the tears start falling. I have to move the letter quickly so I don't blur the ink – as though it's an ancient artefact, which, in many ways, it is. So Mum knew all along why Scarlett had left. She was pregnant. She wanted to keep her baby, and Mum didn't want her to. But why didn't she tell me, that time in the hospital? Why did she keep the secret, even when I was old enough to understand?

I think back to that conversation I overheard all those years ago, between Mum and Dad. 'I could have been a grandma . . .' At the time, I had assumed she thought I'd never have kids, but I realise now that she was talking about Scarlett's child. All that time, she knew she had a grandchild out there in the world, who she might never know. I can barely imagine the guilt, the misery, the grief she must have been through – for the daughter *and* the grandchild she'd lost.

But if only she'd told me. If I'd known all this time that I was looking for Scarlett and her child, that might have helped. And at least I'd have had some answers – I'd have understood why she left.

I think about the friend Scarlett mentioned in the letter.

Who was it? Surely Mum could have found out, worked out where she came from and gone looking – brought Scarlett home before it was all too late. But they must have tried all that years ago. All those trips away at weekends when I was little. They must have been following leads all that time. And now it is too late. I'll never be able to find out who the friend was after all these years.

All the way home, I wrestle with my anger. How can Mum have kept this from me for so long? But there's one answer I keep coming back to, and it's shame. Shame that she drove her daughter away, rather than accepting her child. The same shame that stopped her from telling me about her own baby, who had been adopted all those years before. The shame that will prevent me from telling her about the baby I gave birth to, the baby who was snatched away.

I see it clearly, as we pull into the driveway of the bungalow, the smell of rain still lingering, the sky heavy with more. The three of us – Mum, Scarlett, me – locked in shame, through the generations. For the mistakes we've made, the children we've fought to hold on to, the ones we've lost and may never find. And it's this realisation, and the sadness and regret that come with it, that stops me from screaming at Mum when I walk in. From shaking her by the shoulders and asking her why, why, why?

Instead we embrace, Dad joining from the other side, and we hold on to one another for a long time, in the dark hallway, Liam standing in the doorway uncertainly. And then, without a word, I hand Scarlett's letter back to Mum. She looks at me, tears gathering in her eyes, but I nod. I understand. I don't ask her any questions, just as she doesn't ask any of me. I'm led to my old bedroom, laid down on clean sheets, and left to fall into a deep, dreamless sleep.

* * *

When I wake, I'm in utter confusion. I look around for Teddy, for the TV, for the door. But it's not there; he's not there. It's then that I remember where I am, and what has happened, and what I've lost. For a moment I feel I can never get up and face the world again. But then I hear talking from the other room, and smell toast and fresh coffee, which my parents never make. And I can tell from the pale light around the edge of the curtains that it's morning. I must have slept all afternoon and evening. It's the next day and Liam's still here. I need to get up and find out what he's told them.

The room falls silent as I walk in, pulling my old dressing gown around me. My parents are in their usual positions at either end of the dining table, eating toast and drinking tea. Liam is perched awkwardly between them, a cup of coffee in hand. A pile of sheets are in the corner, from where he's made a bed on the sofa. On the table, beside the toast rack, is my parents' newspaper and on the front, folded but still visible, a picture of Della and Mark, smiling, just the top of Ferdie's head between them. The headline reads FERDIE FOUND!

My eyes flick towards Liam. He shakes his head quickly. He hasn't said anything, and I can see that no one has even opened the paper yet. I sit down slowly next to it, wondering whether I can whip it away, hide the evidence. But I don't know who I'm trying to kid, really. They must have seen the news in the past week or so. They'll have seen all the stories about the missing boy. They must know it's the same Della Hunter, the one who took me away, who I worked for all that time in France.

Even so, nobody says anything beyond 'Morning Kate', and 'You slept a long time!' And so I rest my arm across the cover while I butter some toast.

As I pick up the mug of tea that Mum's poured me, something catches my eye. It's a small picture to the far side of the page and I can see Mum's looking at it, too. It's Adele Walker, that earlier version of Della, the same picture I saw in the book she had hidden in her house.

'Adele Walker, a journalist, before she was married,' the caption reads.

'I thought she looked familiar,' Mum says slowly, looking up at me. 'That's your Della, isn't it?'

'Yes,' I say. 'But you never met her, did you?'

'No,' Mum agrees. 'I saw her on that book that turned up, but I never met her. I knew Adele though.' She looks again at the picture. 'A nasty piece of work, she was. I always thought, if she hadn't come along, given Scarlett the push she needed, well, she might not have . . . Things might have been different.' Her voice has taken on a faraway quality, as though she's speaking from another room. I look around at Liam's blank face, Dad's concerned frown and then back at Mum, the horror only now sinking in.

I feel my stomach contract, the picture swims in and out of view. I think of the letter. *I've got a friend who's going to help.* 'You mean that friend from the letter. That's Adele?'

Mum shrugs. 'We always thought so. She disappeared from Cambridge around the same time. None of Scarlett's friends knew her, really. No one knew where she'd come from, or where she might have gone. But she'd been hanging around in the months before Scarlett left. She didn't go to the school. She was older. Lived on her own, no family to speak of. She just seemed to . . . arrive. She started knocking around with Scarlett, causing trouble. And then, when everything happened, she was suddenly everywhere – offering advice, going along to appointments, sticking her nose in where it wasn't wanted . . .' I've never heard Mum sound so bitter. 'If it wasn't for her, who knows . . . Scarlett might have stayed.'

The rain has started up again outside, drumming on the

conservatory roof, but other than that the room is silent as we take it all in.

'And then she turned up at the café where I worked, all those years later,' I say, trying to fit it all together. But I can't. It doesn't make sense. How would she have found me? How did she know where I'd be? We met by chance.

'Who was it who tipped you off about that job?' Dad asks, and for a moment my mind goes blank.

'It was a girl from school,' I say, struggling for her name in my confusion. 'Amy. I didn't remember her really, but she remembered me . . .'

'You never met her in the end, did you?' says Dad. It takes me a while to catch up. 'But she was the reason you moved to London in the first place. She told you the café needed people . . .'

I'd never seen her picture, never even spoken to her. How could I be sure it was really Amy at all? All that time I'd wondered why Della picked me out that day, but what if she'd set the whole thing up? How long had she been waiting for me to fall into her trap?

It's too much to take in. All I can think is that Della, all along, had known Scarlett, and she'd never let on. All those conversations, all my grief, and she'd never told me they'd been friends. Perhaps even that she'd helped her run away. Does she know where she is now? I think of the copy of *The Little Prince*, on Della's shelf, so familiar – could that have been Scarlett's copy?

'But . . . I don't remember Adele,' I say to Mum, though as I do, I think of the familiarity, the striking sense of having known Della before.

'I'm not sure you'd have seen her much,' Mum says. 'I didn't like her hanging around here, I made that pretty clear to Scarlett.'

'And that book you had of Della's,' I ask, 'it just turned up?'

'It arrived by post,' Mum says. 'I thought you must have sent it, but then you didn't say anything, so . . .' So it fell into the category of things we never spoke about, never mentioned.

'But what did she want from us?' I say, asking myself more than anyone else. Had it been power? Or amusement? Perhaps it was all a game to her. But why the interest in our family? It doesn't make any sense, and my mind drifts back to Scarlett, to where she might be now. Her child would be seventeen by now. We don't even know if it's a boy or a girl. Does Della know?

The rain has stopped now, and I walk into the conservatory, to where one of Mum's giant puzzles is laid out. It's a water-colour, Constable, and the pieces are collected into groups by colour, blue-grey sky, vivid green grass, browns and whites for the animals. I've watched her do them so many times, I can almost trace her movements – always starting with the corners, the edges, and then working in patches, towards the middle. She's got stuck on the sky, I can see that. She's missing a piece – sometimes that's all it takes. One little square, an unremarkable puff of cloud or a grey smudge, and she'll have the key that unlocks the rest of the scene, the puzzle fits itself together from that point onwards.

As I study the grey squares, an image comes to my mind of Della, watching our family from afar. Only it's not Della, it's Adele – she's younger, unsure of herself, on the outside, on her own. We're sitting in a restaurant – unusual for us. Mum's birthday, I think. I'm eight, or nine. It's a Chinese restaurant. I can picture it now, the red velvet banquettes and paper dragons hanging on the walls, and through the window, on the other side, I see Adele, that face, from over the street, watching us. Is it an image, or a memory? I can't tell any more.

I turn to look at my parents and Liam, still at the table. Mum and Dad are studying the newspaper story; Liam's watching me, uncertain where to put himself in this strange family scene. But I turn away from him. I need to think. And I want to find this puzzle piece.

I sort through them, turning the squares over one by one, searching the pile, all the while scanning my memories, trying to make a match.

I think of all the conversations we had in Della's bright white lounge, the leafy London garden, the French farmhouse kitchen. One night, late, we had talked for hours about what would happen if I had the baby. About how we'd make it work. What we'd do, together. That night, Della had confided for the first time about her two younger sisters, about how she'd never measured up, always felt like she was on the outside, when they were the wanted ones. That was the word she used: 'wanted'.

She hadn't told me then that she'd been adopted. I'd assumed she lived with those sisters. But what if . . . I turn over another square. Finally, the one I'm looking for. The wisp of cloud in just the right place. But I don't put it in the puzzle. Instead, I tuck it into my pocket and open the conservatory doors, walking out into the garden.

I breathe deeply and look around at the beech trees, the rockery, the flowers my parents have tended for so many years, making a life for us, putting love and care into our surroundings.

Yesterday Della said she had found her birth mother, but things didn't work out. Those words come back to me now, and I think of the baby Mum gave away, the older half-sister Scarlett and I never met. She would be in her forties by now.

Mum said she'd told the agency she wasn't ready to get in touch. But that didn't mean she hadn't come looking, watched us from afar, felt the sting of a second rejection – turned away after all those years by the mother who'd given her up as a baby. What better revenge than to split up a family – help a daughter run away, prey on the weakness of the one left behind?

'Don't we look like sisters?' That's what she'd said to me, when I was trying on those maternity clothes in her bedroom in France. The clothes I'd be wearing to have her baby. Who better to choose as a surrogate?

But even as the thoughts rush upon me, I banish them. They're too big, too overwhelming. Too much for any of us to take in.

And then I breathe in the fresh scent of wet grass and my brain makes another leap. Somerset. That's where Della grew up. Is that where she took Scarlett? Back home, far away from her mother – our mother. And what if Scarlett is still there? Maybe she's established a life for herself, with her child, far enough away that nobody ever came looking.

I turn to look at my parents, doubled in reflection through the window. As I trace the outline of the puzzle piece with my finger, in the pocket of my dressing gown, I feel a fierce protectiveness. They can never know. Whatever Della wanted, she's got it now. She'll leave us alone. I know too much. We've all got so much to lose.

But that doesn't mean I can't go looking for Scarlett. After all, I can't ignore this new information. Can't overlook what might be the clue we've been searching for all these years. I don't need to tell my parents that's what I'm doing.

I take the puzzle piece from my pocket, hold it in two fingers, and throw it as far as I can, into the bushes at the bottom of the garden – the bushes where Scarlett and I used

337

to play hide and seek; where she'd sneak a cigarette when my parents were in bed, me watching from our bedroom window.

I don't know why, but I feel better afterwards – the piece hidden in the garden, where no one will ever find it. And I walk towards the house. Towards my parents, and Liam, who has already whipped the paper away and is ushering them to the sofa, mugs of tea in his hands. He looks up and smiles at me, and I smile back, thinking as I do that perhaps Liam and I could take a holiday. A couple of weeks in the West Country. It wouldn't hurt, would it?

I go in through the conservatory, closing the doors behind me and joining Liam in the living room. I take hold of his hand, and as he looks at me, I realise that I am ready to start again. I may have lost, but I have also been found.

Acknowledgements

I want to thank my brilliant agent Sophie Lambert, who read this book at an early stage and has been unwavering in her encouragement, advice and support, and my editor Phoebe Morgan for her enthusiasm and insight, as well as all at C&W and HarperCollins.

Thank you to my early readers, Erin Kelly, Gemma Loughran and Becky Hunter, for their many invaluable suggestions, major and minor, as well as those friends who have been with me since the story's beginnings: Ruth Tanner, Lucy Wake, Georgie Lloyd, Jo Sargent, Gemma Taylor, Megan Hung, Helen Gateley, Marta Prytys, Davina Lambie, Hannah Borno, Charlotte Fall and all at Flag, Rosie Ifould, Clare Longrigg and my *Guardian* colleagues.

A special thanks to Sarah Maber and Rufus Purdy, who gave me the push I needed to take this novel seriously, and to all at Curtis Brown Creative, especially Anna Davies and my hugely supportive writing group: Ella Dove, Catherine Jarvie, Sarah Shannon, Sean Lusk, Victoria Halliday, Ben Walker, Jo Cunningham, Robert Holtom, Bill MacMillan, Ahsan Akbar, Lynsey Urquhart, Georgina Parfitt and Paris Christofferson.

Thank you to my parents, Ellie Chambers and Andy Northedge, to my sister Laura Northedge, Gregg Hutchings, Kit and Cassie, to Maureen Skeels and in memory of David Skeels, for all the help, support, love – and child care.

And to Nigel, Sammy and Matilda, who gave me the encouragement, confidence and, most importantly, time to write this book, all my love, always.